The

anu

the Prince

When Two Worlds Collide

KATHY WINSLOWER

DEDICATION

Dedicated to those who believe in the transformative power of love, and to the dreamers who find solace in the pages of a captivating love story.

May your hearts be forever touched by the enchantment of true love's embrace.

CONTENTS

CHAPTER 1:

A CHANCE ENCOUNTER

Olivia Grey, a famous actress known for her captivating performances on the silver screen, took a much-needed break from the glitz and glamour of Hollywood life. Seeking comfort and a change from the demanding life of a movie star, she embarked on a vacation to the picturesque kingdom of Creudor. She had never travelled to Europe before and was eager to learn about its history, culture, and cuisine.

Quietly, she strolled through the vibrant streets of the local market. She was overcome by the bright sights and noises as she wandered through the neighborhood market. The smell of fresh bread and pastries filled the air. And the locals were rushing around, carrying baskets of fruits and vegetables.

Olivia browsed the quaint shops as the sun cast a warm warmth over the cobblestone streets. The market was a riot of color, smelling of freshly picked vegetables, buzzing with conversation, and residents bartering over their items. Freshly prepared coffee and the sweet perfume of blossoming flowers blended in the air, and there was a vivacious chatter and laughter in the background.

Dressed in a casual yet effortlessly chic ensemble, Olivia's brunette locks cascaded down her shoulders, and her tan skin glowed under the warm Creudor sun.

Her striking black eyes scanned the scene, taking in the unique sights and sounds of the unfamiliar city. Her heart open to the possibility of a new adventure.

It was then that fate intervened, weaving its magic into the tapestry of their lives.

Olivia paused at a vendor's stall to buy some handmade souvenirs for her friends back home. She picked out a few of the items for her friends back home. She was just about to pay, when she heard a sudden deep voice behind her.

"That's a bit too overpriced, don't you think?"

Olivia turned around to see a tall man standing in front of her. His blazing red hair appeared to twirl in the sun's rays. He was wearing a casual shirt and pair of trousers, which she quickly noticed. As she met his piercing look, she had a chill down her spine. The moment their eyes locked, it was as if time had stopped.

"I'm sorry?" Olivia stuttered, surprised by his sudden appearance.

Nicolas, found himself captivated by Olivia's earthly beauty. His piercing blue eyes, filled with curiosity and warmth, locked onto Olivia's, creating an invisible connection that neither could ignore. As Olivia neared, she noticed a mischievous glint in Nicolas's eyes, a spark of adventure and spontaneity that mirrored her own spirit. He effortlessly commanded attention; his charm undeniable. With each step, Olivia's heart quickened, nervousness and anticipation coursing through her veins.

Nicolas stepped toward Olivia, a smile playing at the corners of his lips. "Well, aren't you a sight for sore eyes?" he remarked, his voice laced with a charming accent.

Olivia's heart skipped a beat as she returned his smile. "And here I thought the markets of Creudor were just for fresh produce. Little did I know they held such captivating treasures," she quipped, her tone playful yet sincere.

Nicolas chuckled, the sound sending a delightful shiver down Olivia's spine. "It seems we have stumbled upon a hidden treasure, indeed."

"I didn't catch your name?" Olivia said playfully.

"Nicolas," he replied with a charming smile. "And you are?"

"Olivia," she replied, returning the smile.

"You haven't been here before, have you?" he asked.

"What gave me away?" Olivia giggled.

"Well for once, you were going to pay way over the regular prices."

"Ah, I see." She shrugged. "Guilty as charged."

"So, Olivia, would you care to explore these streets together?" he asked, extending his arm with a gentle gesture of invitation. "I would love you keep you from over paying for the rest of the day."

"I would be delighted," she replied, placing her hand in the crook of his arm.

And so, amidst the lively market, the pair embarked on an impromptu adventure. They strolled hand in hand, as if their connection had been forged by destiny itself. They meandered through cobblestone streets, their laughter mingling with the melodic tunes of street musicians. The world around them seemed to fade into the background as they delved into spirited conversations, exploring each other's passions, dreams, and quirks.

Olivia's eyes sparkled with delight as she took in the vibrant displays of local artisans, their wares showcasing the rich culture and craftsmanship of Creudor. Nicolas could not help but be captivated by her infectious energy and genuine appreciation for the simple joys of life. With each step they took, their connection deepened, as if the world around them was a mere backdrop to their blossoming romance.

A mischievous grin played on Nicolas's lips as he spotted a quaint café nestled in a quiet corner of the market. "Shall we take a break and indulge in some fine pastries?" he suggested, his voice laced with warmth.

Olivia's eyes lit up with anticipation. "I can never resist

a delicious treat," she replied, her voice filled with playful enthusiasm.

Together, they ventured into the café. There were many customers, who sat at the outdoor area. The clink of cutlery and the gentle hum of conversation, filled the air.

Seated at a corner table, Olivia and Nicolas savored their freshly baked pastries, delighting in the delicate flavors that danced upon their tongues. The warmth of the café enveloped them, creating an intimate sanctuary within the bustling market.

As they savored their treats, their conversation flowed effortlessly, each word a brushstroke painting a vivid picture of their lives. Olivia shared anecdotes from her whirlwind life in Hollywood, her tales laced with humor and self-deprecating charm. Nicolas listened intently, hanging on her every word, his admiration for her flair and resilience growing with each passing moment.

They spent the afternoon weaving through the labyrinthine streets, their conversation flowing effortlessly. As they continued their stroll, the sky transformed into a vivid tapestry of purples and pinks, casting a romantic hue over the city.

Reluctantly, Olivia realized that their time together was drawing to a close. The impending separation tugged at her heartstrings, but she knew that their parting was only temporary. With a slight hint of reluctance, she made plans to meet Nicolas again the following day for

13

their eagerly anticipated first date. It would be a night filled with laughter, shared stories, and the thrill of discovering each other on a deeper level.

As they reached a quaint street corner bathed in the soft glow of street lamps, Olivia turned to face Nicolas, her eyes shimmering with a kaleidoscope of emotions. "I can't wait for our date tomorrow," she confessed, her voice laced with a hint of nervous excitement.

Nicolas smiled, his eyes reflecting the same anticipation. "Nor can I, Olivia. I've been counting down the minutes since the moment we met," he admitted, his voice filled with a mixture of sincerity and tenderness. He reached out and gently took her hand in his, his touch sending a jolt of electricity through her veins.

Olivia's heart fluttered as their fingers intertwined, their connection growing stronger with each passing second. The world around them seemed to fade into the background, leaving only the two of them in this moment of undeniable chemistry. Time stood still, and in that fleeting instant, Olivia knew that she had found something extraordinary.

With a promise of tomorrow lingering in the air, she bid him goodnight, her mind buzzing with anticipation for the magical evening that awaited them. As she walked away, her steps light and her heart brimming with newfound joy, she couldn't help but embrace the thrill of new love that coursed through her veins, knowing that her life was about to be forever changed by the enchanting romance she had stumbled upon.

***

Hours later, Olivia found herself in the opulent grandeur of a charity gala held in the heart of Creudor. The grand ballroom exuded an air of elegance and sophistication, its polished marble floors reflecting the flickering glow of countless candles adorning the opulent chandeliers above. The soft strains of a string quartet filled the air, lending an enchanting melody to the gathering.

Adorned in a stunning black gown that hugged her curves in all the right places, Olivia's presence commanded attention as she gracefully made her entrance. The rich fabric cascaded down her figure, accentuating her every move with an alluring grace. Her hair was styled in loose, cascading curls that tumbled effortlessly over her shoulders, and a touch of crimson adorned her lips, adding a hint of mystery to her already captivating allure.

Her heart quickened its pace as she surveyed the room, taking in the sea of elegantly dressed guests engaged in animated conversations and graceful waltzes. The atmosphere was alive with anticipation and excitement, and Olivia could feel the palpable energy that enveloped the space. Yet, amidst the crowd, her gaze was inevitably drawn to a figure standing at the center of the festivities.

There he was—Nicolas, dressed in a navy-blue tuxedo

which was tailored to perfection, highlighting his broad shoulders and lean physique. A white silk scarf draped loosely around his neck, adding a touch of effortless sophistication to his ensemble. He stood tall and confident, a magnetic aura emanating from him that drew the attention of all those around him.

Their eyes met across the room, locking in a gaze that transcended time and space. In that fleeting moment, the world seemed to fade away, leaving only the two of them in their private sphere of connection. Nicolas's eyes, filled with anticipation and longing, mirrored the emotions swirling within Olivia. A wave of recognition passed between them, as if their souls had met in some long-forgotten dream.

Olivia felt a magnetic pull, an invisible thread that drew her closer to this enigmatic stranger whom she had met earlier that day. Every step she took brought her nearer to him, her heart beating in harmony with the rhythmic music that echoed throughout the ballroom. The gazes of other guests, once fixed on the dazzling surroundings, now turned to witness the unfolding of an extraordinary encounter.

As Olivia made her way toward him, their surroundings blurred, and it felt as if the world existed solely for the two of them. The sound of laughter and music faded into the background as their eyes locked once more. The world around them seemed to fade into a blur, their connection becoming the focal point of their shared universe.

"Oh, hello you," he said with a smile that played at the corners of his lips, his eyes sparkling with an intoxicating combination of curiosity and desire.

"Oh, we meet again," Olivia said as she blushed, grateful for the dim lighting that hid her growing excitement.

"Olivia, you look absolutely stunning," Nicolas said, his voice filled with genuine admiration.

"Thank you, Nicolas. You don't look too bad yourself," she replied playfully, her eyes sparkling with delight.

With a gentleness that belied his regal stature, Nicolas brought Olivia's hand to his lips, leaving a lingering kiss upon her knuckles. "Thank you for gracing me with your presence, Olivia."

"I must admit, Nicolas, this enchanting evening has brought a sense of wonder to my heart," Olivia whispered, her voice filled with a hint of playful curiosity. "But I find myself yearning to know more about the man behind the captivating facade. What is it that brings you to this grand event?"

Nicolas's lips curved into a tender smile, his gaze never leaving Olivia's as they continued their graceful dance. "Ah, my dear Olivia, you have stumbled upon a secret of mine," he replied, his voice laced with a touch of mystery. "Though I have walked among these guests tonight, I bear a deeper purpose in attending this gala."

Olivia's brows furrowed slightly, a blend of anticipation

and intrigue growing within her. "And what might that purpose be?" she asked, her voice barely a whisper, as if afraid to break the delicate spell that had woven itself around them.

Nicolas paused for a moment, his eyes searching Olivia's face as if contemplating whether to reveal his truth. Finally, he took a breath and spoke, his voice filled with both pride and vulnerability. "I am not merely a guest here tonight, Olivia. I am the Prince of Creudor."

A gasp escaped Olivia's lips, her eyes widening in surprise. The revelation sent a rush of emotions cascading through her—astonishment, excitement, and a touch of apprehension. The magnitude of his position suddenly cast their blossoming connection in a different light, adding an unforeseen layer of complexity to their burgeoning romance.

"The Prince of Creudor?" Olivia repeated, her voice barely audible. "I... I had no idea, Nicolas."

Nicolas reached out, his hand gently cupping Olivia's cheek. "I understand if this revelation changes things, Olivia. But know that the man standing before you now, is the same person you met earlier today—the one who saw beyond the glamour and recognized the true essence of your spirit."

Olivia's gaze softened, her eyes searching Nicolas's face for any hint of deception. Yet, all she found was sincerity and a glimmer of vulnerability. "You're right,

Nicolas," she whispered, her voice filled with a newfound resolve. "Titles and positions may shape the world around us, but they do not define the connection we share. I choose to see the man before me, not the prince."

A sense of relief washed over Nicolas, his eyes shining with gratitude. "Olivia, you possess a rare quality—a genuine heart that sees beyond the surface. It is why I am drawn to you, why I find myself captivated by your presence."

Nicolas's voice, rich and velvety, washed over Olivia, sending shivers down her spine. Her cheeks flushed with a delicate pink hue as she said, "So, Prince Nicolas, huh? That's something you missed to tell me earlier."

A soft chuckle escaped Nicolas's lips, and he extended his arm toward her, a silent invitation to dance. With a graceful sweep of her hand, she accepted his invitation, placing her delicate fingers in his strong, confident grasp. Her heart pounding in her chest as their bodies came together in perfect harmony. The melody of a waltz filled the air, guiding their graceful movements across the polished ballroom floor.

"Well," Nicolas spoke in hushed tones. "I don't usually say that I am a Prince, to every beautiful woman I meet."

Olivia nodded. "So, did you know who I was?"

"Yes, I did." Nicolas admitted. "I believe that we have a

few mutual friends who have been trying to set us up for years."

"Really?" Olivia looked at him, surprised. "So how come that we never went on a date?"

"I have to apologize to you for that." He said in a low voice. "Had I known that you were so amazingly down to earth in real life, I would have jumped at the chance to be with you."

"Alright!" Olivia joked, "I forgive you."

As the night unfolded, Olivia and Nicolas danced, their bodies moving in perfect synchrony to the melodic strains of a live orchestra. Their laughter mingled with the sweet notes of the music, and the world around them faded into the background. It felt as if they were the only two people in the room, cocooned in their own.

As they swayed in each other's arms, Olivia could not help but be mesmerized by the way Nicolas's blue eyes twinkled with genuine interest and affection. The weight of their shared connection hung in the air, unspoken yet undeniable.

"Tell me, Olivia," Nicolas began, his voice tinged with curiosity, "What led you to Creudor? Such a beautiful place, but not where one might expect to find a Hollywood star."

Olivia's gaze softened, her smile turning wistful. "I needed a break from the chaos of my world. Creudor seemed like the perfect escape. A chance to recharge and rediscover myself away from the constant spotlight."

Nicolas nodded, his hand tightening ever so slightly around her waist. "I can understand that. Sometimes, the simplicity calls to us, even in the middle of our busy lives."

Their conversation ebbed and flowed, their words a symphony of shared experiences and dreams. The hours melted away, and Olivia lost herself in the enchanting spell Nicolas had cast over her. They laughed, they shared their passions, and they bared their souls, finding solace in the connection they had stumbled upon.

As the dance came to a graceful conclusion, Olivia found herself breathless and exhilarated. "You are an incredible dancer, Nicolas," she said, her voice filled with genuine admiration.

Nicolas smiled; his gaze fixed on Olivia's eyes. "Thank you, Olivia. But it was your grace and elegance that made the dance truly magical."

Olivia blushed, a rosy hue spreading across her cheeks. "I must admit, this evening has been beyond my wildest dreams. I never imagined finding myself here, in the company of a prince."

As the night drew to a close, Nicolas walked Olivia back to her hotel, their hands entwined. The knowledge that they would soon part ways weighed heavy on her heart, but she refused to let the melancholy overshadow the magical evening they had shared. They stood in front of her hotel room, their eyes locked in a heated gaze.

"Olivia, I know we've only just met, but there's something about you that makes me feel like we've known each other for years," Nicolas said softly, brushing a strand of hair away from her face.

"I feel the same way, Nicolas," Olivia replied, her heart pounding in her chest.

With a gentleness that belied his regal stature, Nicolas brought Olivia's hand to his lips, leaving a lingering kiss upon her knuckles. "Thank you for gracing me with your presence, Olivia. This evening has been nothing short of extraordinary."

A shiver coursed through Olivia's body at his touch, her breath catching in her throat. "The pleasure was all mine, Nicolas. I can't remember the last time I felt so alive and connected to someone."

Nicolas's gaze bore into hers, his voice a mere whisper. "Perhaps, Olivia, this is only the beginning of something truly remarkable."

Nicolas leaned in, and Olivia felt his lips brush against hers, sending shivers down her spine. She closed her eyes, savoring the moment, and felt herself being pulled into a passionate kiss.

As they parted, Nicolas looked into her eyes and whispered, "I can't wait to see you again tomorrow,

Olivia."

Their eyes held a silent promise, a glimpse into the vast possibilities that lay before them. With a final, longing look, they reluctantly parted ways, their hearts heavy with the weight of anticipation and uncertainty. Olivia smiled, feeling a wave of happiness wash over her. She watched as Nicolas walked away, feeling giddy and excited about their first date.

As she closed her hotel room door, Olivia could not help but wonder what the future held for her and Nicolas. She had never felt this way before, and she knew that this was just the beginning of a grand adventure.

As Olivia lay in bed that night, the echoes of their laughter and the warmth of Nicolas's touch lingered. She could not deny the spark that had ignited between them, nor the way her heart soared in his presence. The actress who had experienced love only through the lens of a camera found herself falling for a prince, and the thought both thrilled and terrified her.

Little did they know, their chance encounter was merely the beginning of a journey that would test their love and redefine their lives. As the moon cast its gentle glow upon the kingdom of Creudor, Olivia closed her eyes, her dreams filled with visions of a future entwined with a prince who had captured her heart.

***

CHAPTER 2:

WHISPERS OF THE HEART

As Olivia approached the courtyard of a charming coffee shop, she was greeted by the radiant sun, which made her heart race with thrill. She felt a sense of eagerness for the unexpected rendezvous that Nicolas had arranged for her, wondering what he had in mind. Settling comfortably at a snug table located beneath a tree that glowed with blossoming floral arrangements, she could not resist appreciating the graceful petals that created an enchanting leafy shade above her.

A few moments passed before Nicolas arrived, with a gleam of mischief in his eyes. He had a friendly smile as he welcomed Olivia, making her feel both secure and enthusiastic.

"Olivia, it's so wonderful to see you. I'm ready for an adventure. But the question is, are you?" he said.

Nicolas could not believe that he was able to set up a date with Olivia Grey, renowned for her beauty and talent across the world. He knew that she was accustomed to lavish wining and dining, but he wished to think outside the box.

Olivia tilted her head with interest as she answered, eagerly waiting for his plans. "Nicolas, I'm always down for an exhilarating adventure. What do you have in store?"

Nicolas desired to introduce Olivia to his beloved world, one that he felt strongly about. His efforts to get to know her better led him to plan a unique and inventive date. He hoped to create an environment where their bond could flourish without limitations.

Holding her hand, Nicolas sent waves of excitement through Olivia's body. "I want to reveal a world beyond the glitz and glamour, one where our souls can fly unrestrained." He whispered softly, giving Olivia goosebumps. "Today, we will discover the concealed gems of Creudor. We'll venture into the heart of the countryside, where we can bask in mother nature's beauty."

Olivia's heart skipped a beat, captivated by the mystery and romance of Nicolas's plans. She had always been drawn to the wonders of the natural world, and the prospect of uncovering its secrets alongside Nicolas filled her with anticipation.

Nicolas led Olivia on an adventurous journey to a splendid location nested amidst the mountain ranges enveloping Creudor. The sun radiant and the weather balmy, the picturesque landscape was simply awe-inspiring. Hand in hand, they strolled while conversing and sharing light-hearted moments with each other.

Upon reaching the mountain peak, Olivia was left breathless yet exuberant. It was her very first hiking expedition, and the thrill of it was exhilarating. They rested upon a rock, beholding the spectacular vista beneath them. Olivia snuggled up against Nicolas, tilting her head on his shoulder, feeling content and at peace.

"This is amazing," she said. "I've never experienced anything like this before."

"I'm glad you're enjoying it," Nicolas replied, smiling at her. "I wanted to show you something different, something that's important to me."

Olivia looked up at him, and for the first time, she saw a vulnerable side to the prince. She realized that despite his royal status, he was just a man, with hopes and dreams like everyone else.

"What is important to you?" she asked softly.

Nicolas took a deep breath. "Humanitarian work," he said. "Helping those in need, making a difference in the world. It's something I've always been passionate about."

Olivia was surprised. She knew that Nicolas was a prince, but she had never imagined him to be so altruistic. She was moved by his passion and sincerity.

"I feel the same way," she said, smiling at him. "I've been involved in various charitable organizations throughout my career. It's something that's important to me too."

Nicolas's eyes lit up. "Really? That's amazing."

Olivia felt a sense of excitement and possibility. She had never met anyone like Nicolas before, someone who shared her values and passion. She leaned over and kissed his cheek, feeling a deep connection between them. Feeling embarrassed, she picked herself up and stared up at the clouds.

Nicolas chuckled to himself; he was not expecting her to kiss him on his cheek of all places. He watched Olivia as she looked up at the sky. Sensing her embarrassment, he decided to change the scenery. But just as he was about to ask her something, she looked at him.

"You know, Nicolas," Olivia started softly, her voice tinged with a hint of melancholy, "I was married once before. It's something I don't often talk about, but I believe in complete honesty between us."

Nicolas listened attentively, "Olivia, whatever you share with me, it doesn't change how I feel about you. I want to know everything that has shaped the person you are today," he reassured her, his voice warm and reassuring.

A wistful smile played on Olivia's lips as she reflected on her past. "We were high school sweethearts, my ex-husband and I. It seemed like a magical romance, and everyone expected us to end up together. So, after college, we got married, almost as if it was the natural progression of things."

Nicolas nodded in understanding, as he offered his silent support and to let her share the story.

"But sometimes, life doesn't follow the script we had envisioned," Olivia continued, her gaze searching Nicolas' eyes. "After just a few months of marriage, we both realized that we were not the right fit for each other. We wanted different things, and staying together would have meant sacrificing our own happiness."

Nicolas nodded, his understanding and empathy shining through. "Olivia, I want you to know that your past doesn't define you in my eyes. What matters most is the person you are now. We all have our own journeys, and I am grateful that ours has brought us together."

Tears welled up in Olivia's eyes as she felt an immense sense of relief wash over her. "I understand if my past is a deal breaker for you, but I couldn't go on without being honest."

Nicolas touched her face gently, his thumb brushing away a stray tear. "Olivia, let me assure you that being divorced is not a deal breaker for me. I embrace every part of you, including your past. What matters the most is the future that we are building together."

In that moment, Olivia felt a weight lifted off her shoulders, knowing that she was accepted and loved unconditionally. They shared a tender embrace, their hearts entwined, as they celebrated the unbreakable bond they had forged.

"Why don't we go back down then?" he suggested to lighten the mood.

As they made their way down the mountain, they talked about their shared passion for humanitarian work and how they could make a difference. Nicolas had a vision of starting a foundation that would help the people of Creudor and beyond. Olivia was inspired by his idea and promised to help in any way she could.

Finally, they reached the bottom of the mountain. Nicolas turned to Olivia and took her hand in his.

"I know we come from different worlds," he said, looking into her eyes. "But I feel a real connection between us. I want to get to know you better, to explore what's possible between us."

Olivia felt her heart skip a beat. She had never met anyone like Nicolas before, someone who was so passionate, caring, and genuine. She knew that there were challenges ahead, but she was willing to take the risk.

"I feel the same way," she said, smiling at him. "Let's see where this takes us."

They hugged each other tightly, feeling the warmth and connection between them. Slowly, as they walked back to Nicolas's car, they knew that their lives had changed forever. They had found a shared passion, a connection that was rare and precious, and they were excited to explore where it would lead them.

Nicolas then drove Olivia to the outskirts of Creudor, where the rolling hills painted a breathtaking landscape. They arrived at a picturesque vineyard, nestled among rows of lush green vines heavy with plump grapes. The air carried the sweet scent of blooming flowers, and the warm breeze whispered through the leaves, creating a serene atmosphere.

As they strolled hand in hand through the vineyard, Nicolas could not help but admire Olivia's grace and charm. Her dark locks cascaded like a waterfall down her back. Her radiant smile brought a warmth to his heart. He was completely captivated by her presence, feeling as though the world had conspired to bring them together.

Olivia's eyes widened with delight as they approached a beautifully set soft blanket in the midst of the vineyard. A sumptuous picnic awaited them, with an array of delectable treats and a bottle of fine wine. Nicolas had gone the extra mile to ensure this date would be unforgettable.

"Nicolas, this is incredible," Olivia exclaimed.

Nicolas beamed at her, his blue eyes sparkling with delight. "I wanted to create a special day for us, Olivia. A chance for us to delve deeper into who we are beyond our public personas."

They settled onto the plush picnic blanket, savoring the delectable food and engaging in animated conversation. The hours slipped away as they shared stories of their childhoods, their dreams, and the trials they had faced along their individual paths. Despite their societal differences, they discovered an unexpected kinship, a shared understanding of the challenges that came with their respective roles.

Olivia spoke passionately about her love for acting, her desire to use her platform to make a difference in the world. Nicolas listened intently, his admiration for her growing with each word. He shared tales of his adventures and his humanitarian work, the fulfillment he found in helping those in need. Their shared passion for making a positive impact in the world forged an unbreakable bond between them.

As the sun dipped below the horizon, casting a warm golden glow across the vineyard, Nicolas gazed at Olivia, his voice laced with vulnerability. "Olivia, there's something about you that stirs my soul. I never expected to meet someone like you, someone who understands the weight of responsibility and yet manages to shine with such authenticity."

Olivia felt her heart skip a beat. She had never met anyone like Nicolas before, someone who was so passionate, caring, and genuine. She knew that there were challenges ahead, but she was willing to take the risk.

Olivia's heart fluttered at his words, her eyes shimmering with unspoken emotions. "Nicolas, I feel the same way. You have a way of bringing out the best in me, of making me believe in something greater than myself."

Their connection intensified, the invisible thread that bound them growing stronger with each passing moment. But doubts began to seep into Olivia's mind. She could not ignore the glaring differences in their backgrounds, the scrutiny they would face from society should they pursue their growing feelings. The weight of their realities loomed large, threatening to dim the flame that burned between them.

"I can't help but wonder, Nicolas," Olivia whispered, her voice tinged with uncertainty, "Are we simply caught up in a moment of escapism? Can an actress and a prince truly find lasting happiness together?"

Nicolas reached out, gently cupping Olivia's face in his hands, his gaze unwavering. "Olivia," he said, his voice filled with conviction, "love knows no boundaries, no societal expectations. Our connection is real, and it transcends the labels that society places on us. I believe that if we're willing to fight for it, we can find happiness together."

Olivia's heart swelled with both hope and apprehension. Nicolas's words resonated deeply within her, and she realized that their love had the power to defy conventions and overcome obstacles. But the weight of their public lives and the potential backlash loomed large in her mind.

"I want to believe that, Nicolas," she replied, her voice trembling slightly. "But the world we live in can be unforgiving. Can we truly navigate the challenges and still protect what we have?"

Nicolas's gaze softened, and he brought Olivia's hand to his lips, planting a tender kiss on her knuckles. "Olivia, love is a risk worth taking. Yes, there will be challenges, but we have each other. With love as our anchor, we can weather any storm that comes our way."

Olivia's heart swayed, torn between the fear of what could go wrong and the overwhelming desire to explore the depths of her connection with Nicolas. She took a deep breath, her eyes locked with his.

"You're right, Nicolas," she whispered, her voice filled with determination. "Love is a risk, but I'm willing to take that risk with you."

A smile tugged at the corners of Nicolas's lips as he pulled Olivia into an embrace, their bodies fitting perfectly together. In that moment, they made a silent promise to each other—a promise to defy the odds and let their hearts lead the way.

As the day unfolded, Olivia and Nicolas shared intimate stories, dreams, and fears. They discovered a shared passion for humanitarian work, a desire to make a positive impact in the world. Their conversation flowed effortlessly, each word strengthening the bond between them.

They walked together; their hands intertwined into each other's. Olivia could not help but be drawn to Nicolas's innate ability to find joy in the simplest of moments. She admired his compassion for others and the way he fearlessly pursued his dreams.

"Nicolas turned to Olivia, a soft smile gracing his lips. "Olivia, I've always believed that love has the power to transcend boundaries and change lives. Together, I know we can make a difference in the world."

Olivia's heart swelled with a mixture of admiration and affection for Nicolas. She had always been passionate about using her fame for good, but she had never met someone who shared her unwavering dedication to making a positive impact.

"Nicolas, your commitment to humanitarian work is inspiring," she said, her voice filled with sincerity. "I've always believed that we have a responsibility to use our influence to uplift others. Together, we can create change, not just in Creudor, but beyond its borders."

Nicolas nodded; his eyes gleaming with a sense of purpose. "Olivia, I have a proposition for you. What if we combine our talents and resources to launch a joint initiative? Together, we can create a foundation that focuses on empowering underprivileged communities, providing access to education and healthcare, and advocating for social justice."

Olivia's eyes widened in awe and excitement. The idea of joining forces with Nicolas to make a tangible impact ignited a fire within her soul. She reached out, clasping his hand, their fingers intertwining.

"Nicolas, I love that idea. Let's create something extraordinary together," she said, her voice filled with determination. "Let's use our positions to bring about real change, to give a voice to those who are unheard."

The setting sun bathed them in a warm embrace, casting a golden glow over the vineyard. They continued their walk, their conversation flowing effortlessly, fueled by the shared belief that love and compassion could transform lives.

In that moment, the world around them seemed to fade away, leaving only the two of them, united by a common purpose and an unbreakable bond. The winds whispered their secrets, carrying the promise of a future filled with love, adventure, and the pursuit of their dreams. Time seemed to stand still as they basked in the beauty of the moment, cherishing the connection they had forged against all odds.

***

As Nicolas parked the car outside Olivia's hotel, a sense of melancholy tinged the air. The evening had been a whirlwind of enchantment and connection, but the reality of their separate lives loomed before them.

Olivia turned to face Nicolas, her eyes reflecting a mixture of fondness and regret. "Nicolas, I can't express how much I've enjoyed tonight. You've shown me a side of Creudor that I never could have imagined. But tomorrow, I have to return to Los Angeles. My work commitments beckon, and it breaks my heart to leave."

Nicolas reached out, gently taking Olivia's hand in his, his touch a comforting reassurance. "Olivia, my dear, I understand the demands of your career. But know that distance will never diminish what we've found together. We will find a way."

Olivia's eyes shimmered with unshed tears, her voice struggled with the uncertainty. "Nicolas, I want to believe that. But our worlds are so different, and the challenges we'll face... they won't be easy. Can we truly make this work?"

Nicolas leaned closer; his breath warm against her cheek. "My darling Olivia, I can't promise that it will be easy. But what I can promise you is that I am willing to fight for our love, to defy the odds and prove that true love knows no boundaries. We will find a way, together."

A soft smile tugged at Olivia's lips, her heart swelling with affection for this extraordinary man who stood before her. She nodded, unable to speak for a moment as emotion threatened to overwhelm her. She wanted nothing more than to lose herself in Nicolas' embrace, to taste his lips once more, but she knew that they both needed time to digest all that had transpired.

"I wish I could stay, Nicolas. I wish that we didn't ever have to say goodbye. I..." Olivia's words caught in her throat as she thought of the magic she had experienced at his side, the ecstasy that had exploded within her. Her face flamed red with embarrassment.

Nicolas noticed her sudden discomfort. "Olivia, what is it?" he asked gently as he leaned towards her.

Olivia met his gaze, a pained expression on her face. "Nicolas, I don't know how to explain this. I've never felt anything like this feeling. I know that I will miss you terribly."

Nicolas squeezed her hand gently. "Olivia, I feel the same. There is so much that I want to share with you. You make me feel like I am walking on air."

As she looked at him, Olivia's lips formed a slight grin, yet she found it hard to respond. Her body hummed with desire, and a small whimper escaped from her throat as she tried to pull her hand free from Nicolas' grip.

Nicolas noticed her discomfort and leaned forward, brushing her lips lightly with his own. "Olivia, there's no rush. We can take our time. You only have to ask and I will be there."

Olivia nodded; her eyes bright with unshed tears. She pressed herself closer, leaning in to kiss Nicolas as she poured out her heart to him. The level of feeling that she experienced was something entirely new to her, and she sensed that she could not survive without it.

Nicolas responded eagerly, returning her kiss with passion. He pulled away briefly and brushed his lips against her forehead. "Let's go inside. You must be exhausted."

Olivia nodded in agreement and rose from the car. Nicolas escorted her to her hotel room, his arm draped protectively around her waist. She did not want him to leave, and she could feel that he felt the same.

As they reached the door of her hotel room, a veil of sadness came upon her. She turned to Nicolas and said goodbye; their eyes locked in an unspoken understanding of the challenges that lay ahead.

With reluctance, Nicolas released Olivia's hand, but not without a promise. "Until we meet again, my love," he whispered, his voice filled with longing.

Just as Olivia began to open the door, a gentle tug on her arm pulled her back. She turned, her heart racing, to find Nicolas standing before her, a look of longing etched upon his face. Without a word, he bridged the distance between them while his fingers caressed her soft skin with utmost gentleness.

In that moment, time seemed to stand still as their lips met in a passionate and lingering kiss. The world around them faded into insignificance as their love blazed like a wildfire, igniting every inch of their beings. Olivia's arms instinctively wrapped around Nicolas, drawing him closer, unwilling to let go.

Their kiss was a sweet surrender, a testament to the depth of their connection. It held a promise of the love that refused to be extinguished by the vast expanse that now separated them. As their lips parted, a trail of longing lingered in the air, an unspoken vow that their love would endure.

Olivia gazed into Nicolas's eyes; her voice soft yet filled with yearning. "Nicolas, this moment, this kiss... it only makes it harder to say goodbye. But I wouldn't trade this for anything else. You've awakened a love in me that I never thought possible."

Nicolas caressed her cheek, his voice filled with equal parts longing and determination. "Olivia, my love, this kiss is a promise—a promise that no matter the distance or the obstacles, my heart belongs to you."

Tears welled up in Olivia's eyes, emotions surging through her like a tidal wave. She brought her hand to her lips, still tingling from the touch of Nicolas's kiss. "I will hold onto that promise, Nicolas. And I will eagerly await the day when we meet again."

With one last lingering gaze, they reluctantly released each other. Olivia turned to open the door; her heart heavy with the weight of their parting.

She glanced back at Nicolas, "Until then, Nicolas. Take care of yourself."

Olivia stepped inside and she closed the door behind her. She found herself leaning against the door as she allowed herself a moment to collect her thoughts. The taste of Nicolas's kiss lingered upon her lips, a bittersweet reminder of the love they shared.

The knowledge of their impending separation was a painful weight that lay heavy on her chest, but the lingering effects of the kiss lingered on her lips. Olivia would cherish the memories of their time together until she saw him again. She prayed that he felt the same.

***

CHAPTER 3:

BACK TO REALITY

The plane journey back to Los Angeles felt like an eternity for Olivia. She sat in her seat, gazing out of the window, lost in her own thoughts. The memories of her time with Nicolas in Creudor played like a reel in her mind, each moment etching itself deeper into her heart.

As the plane touched down and the cabin doors opened, Olivia's excitement mixed with a tinge of sadness. She gathered her belongings and made her way to the airport exit. And just as Olivia stepped out of the airport, the familiar chaos of flashing cameras and shouting voices greeted her. A swarm of paparazzi had gathered, eager to capture every moment of her return.

The swarm of paparazzi had gathered, hungry for any glimpse of her. Anxiety clenched her chest, but as she scanned the crowd, her eyes found Justin waiting for her, a calm and composed figure amidst the chaos.

With practiced ease, Justin maneuvered his way through the crowd, shielding Olivia from the intrusive camera flashes and insistent questions. His tall frame seemed to provide a shield of protection as he expertly navigated the path to the waiting car.

"Stay close to me, Olivia," Justin murmured, his voice a soothing reassurance amidst the chaos. "I've got you."

Olivia's heart swelled with gratitude for Justin, her trusted confidant and friend for the past three years. They had formed a bond that transcended their professional relationship, and Olivia knew she could always rely on him, both as a dedicated assistant and a compassionate companion.

As they reached the waiting car, Justin held open the door, a gentlemanly gesture that mirrored his genuine care for Olivia's well-being. She slipped inside and sank into the soft leather seat, a sense of relief washing over her as the car door closed, muffling the noise and chaos outside. Justin followed suit, settling into the driver's seat. His expression softened, concern evident in his eyes. "Are you okay, Olivia?" he asked, his voice filled with genuine care.

Taking a deep breath, Olivia nodded. "I'm alright, Justin. Just a bit overwhelmed by all of this." She gestured towards the rearview mirror, where the paparazzi continued their relentless pursuit.

Justin reached over, placing a reassuring hand on Olivia's shoulder. "You're doing great, Olivia. Remember, they're here for the superstar that you are. Let's not let them steal your joy. We'll get you home safely, away from the prying eyes."

Olivia's tense shoulders relaxed under Justin's touch, a wave of gratitude washing over her. "Thank you, Justin. I don't know what I would do without you."

He smiled warmly, his eyes reflecting a deep sense of camaraderie. "You don't have to worry about that. I'll always be here for you, no matter what. We're a team."

Olivia nodded, a soft smile gracing her lips. "Indeed, we do. Three years together, and I couldn't ask for a better friend and a dedicated professional. Also, your fashion sense is impeccable."

Justin chuckled, his playful spirit shining through. "Well, you do inspire me to stay on top of the latest trends. It's all part of my job, after all."

As Olivia settled into the car, Justin glanced at his

phone, a hint of excitement in his eyes. "Olivia, you won't believe the buzz on social media," he exclaimed, unable to contain his enthusiasm.

Curiosity piqued, Olivia leaned closer, her interest piqued by Justin's tone. "What's going on, Justin? Did something happen while I was away?"

Justin grinned, holding up his phone to show Olivia a series of posts and articles. "It seems like the paparazzi didn't miss a beat at the airport. Your casual airport look has caused quite a stir. Everyone is raving about your impeccable style and effortless elegance."

Olivia's eyebrows furrowed in surprise as she scrolled through the images and comments. She hadn't expected such a reaction to what she had considered a simple, comfortable outfit for her travel. It seemed that every detail, from her perfectly tousled hair to her choice of accessories, had garnered attention and admiration from fashion enthusiasts and fans alike.

An assortment of astonishment and amusement washed over her. "Well, I guess I didn't realize my airport fashion choices would create such a buzz," she chuckled, shaking her head in disbelief. "I suppose even the most ordinary moments can turn into something extraordinary in the eyes of the public."

Justin nodded; his eyes gleaming with pride. "It just goes to show how effortlessly you carry yourself, Olivia. Your style has always been an inspiration, and people can't help but be captivated by your natural grace and charm."

Olivia's cheeks flushed with humility. She had always embraced fashion as a form of self-expression, never expecting it to become a focal point of public fascination. But in that moment, she couldn't deny the joy that sparked within her. It was a reminder of the impact she could have, not only through her work but also through her presence and personal style.

Soon, their car glided through the busy streets, gradually leaving the chaos of the paparazzi behind. Justin's presence provided a sense of security and stability amidst the whirlwind of fame that surrounded Olivia.

With every passing minute, Olivia's anxiety melted away as their conversation shifted to lighter topics. Justin recounted amusing anecdotes from his recent shopping adventures, eliciting genuine laughter from Olivia. Their bond transcended the professional realm, evolving into a deep friendship filled with trust, loyalty, and shared experiences.

The hum of traffic and the distant sounds of the city formed a backdrop to her thoughts, as memories of her time with Nicolas continued to dance through her mind.

She could not help but smile, the radiant energy of their moments together filling her heart with joy. Each stolen glance, every gentle touch, and the magnetic pull between them had left an indelible mark on her soul. Their connection was undeniable, a love that defied the boundaries of time and place.

Lost in her reverie, Olivia was startled as the car came

to a stop in front of her apartment building. She blinked, taking a moment to collect herself before stepping out onto the familiar pavement. She entered the building, the doorman offering a friendly nod of recognition. As the elevator carried them upward, Olivia's anticipation grew. She longed for the solitude of her apartment, a sanctuary where she could reflect on the whirlwind romance that had captured her heart.

Finally, the doors opened, revealing Olivia's cozy abode. Soft lighting illuminated the space, casting a warm and inviting ambiance. The walls were adorned with photographs, capturing cherished moments with friends, family, and, of course, Stella and Max. The living room boasted a plush, oversized couch, perfect for curling up with a good book or cuddling with her furry companions. Soft sunlight streamed through sheer curtains, casting a warm glow that enveloped the space. The scent of a freshly lit candle wafted through the air, creating an atmosphere of calm and tranquility.

"Home sweet home," Olivia said out loud, her voice filled with gratitude and a hint of longing.

Stella and Max greeted her with wagging tails and joyful barks, their excitement matching her own. She knelt down, embracing them tightly, finding solace in their unconditional love and comforting presence.

"Oh, my sweethearts, I missed you both so much," she whispered, peppering their furry heads with gentle kisses.

As Olivia settled into her familiar surroundings, her

heart still brimming with the echoes of Nicolas's presence. She could not help but daydream about him, his warm smile, and the way his touch ignited a fire within her. With a sigh, she sank into her favorite armchair, her loyal companions snuggling up beside her.

Settling into her familiar surroundings, Olivia couldn't help but let her mind wander to Nicolas. She sat on the couch, her fingers tapping idly on her phone, contemplating whether to reach out to him. A mixture of excitement and nervousness fluttered in her chest as she typed a message.

Just landed back in LA! Missing your smile already.'

Almost immediately, her phone chimed with a response, causing her heart to skip a beat.

'The feeling is mutual, my enchanting Olivia. I won't ever be the same without you.'

Soon, the hours slipped away and Olivia found herself immersed in a flurry of flirty text messages with Nicolas. They exchanged playful banter, their words carrying a hidden depth of longing and affection. Each message sent her heart aflutter, as if she were experiencing their connection all over again.

Unable to contain her emotions any longer, Olivia turned to Stella and Max, who were lounging nearby. With a soft chuckle, she confessed to her furry friends, "You won't believe it, my darlings," she confessed amidst a whirlpool of giddiness and wonder. "I think... I might have fallen in love with Nicolas."

Stella and Max tilted their heads, their eyes brimming with curiosity. Olivia chuckled, caressing their fur. "Yes, I know it sounds crazy, but there's something about him, something so extraordinary that has captured my heart. He's captured my heart in ways I can't even begin to explain."

Stella, her tail wagging in approval, nuzzled against Olivia's leg, as if to reassure her that love was worth pursuing. Max, ever the loyal companion, rested his head on Olivia's lap, as if silently offering his support. They were her silent confidants, offering comfort and understanding without judgment.

Olivia continued, her voice softening with tenderness. "I can't help but daydream about our time together, about the moments we've shared. The way he looks at me, as if I'm the only star in his sky. It's like we've known each other for a lifetime, even though our paths have only just crossed."

Lost in her thoughts, Olivia found solace in her canine companions. She whispered to them, her voice filled with both hope and uncertainty. "I don't know where this journey will lead, my dears, but I do know that love has a way of weaving its magic. And if Nicolas feels the same way, if he believes in this connection as strongly as I do, then perhaps, just perhaps, we might have found something truly extraordinary."

The dogs seemed to understand every word, their presence a comforting reminder of the unconditional love that accompanied Olivia on this journey. She buried her fingers in their soft fur, finding solace in their presence as she let her mind drift back to the memories they had shared.

As the day turned into evening, Olivia's apartment was bathed in a soft, warm glow. She curled up on the couch, Stella and Max snuggled beside her, their steady breaths creating a sense of calm. With her phone by her side, she eagerly awaited the next message from Nicolas, her heart dancing with anticipation.

In that quiet moment, Olivia allowed herself to fully embrace the love that had bloomed unexpectedly in her life. She knew that the road ahead would not be without its challenges. But she was determined to follow her heart, to embrace the possibilities that lay before her.

***

As the morning sun cast its gentle rays upon the grand halls of the royal palace, Prince Nicolas of Creudor, affectionately known as Nick, awoke to the rhythm of a kingdom in motion. With a sigh, he rose from his ornate canopy bed, the weight of his royal responsibilities settling upon his broad shoulders. As the third in line to the kingdom, Nicolas had been groomed from a young age to uphold the traditions and values of the royal family.

Stepping into his meticulously tailored attire, Nicolas fastened the golden buttons of his regal ensemble. The crisp navy coat and perfectly pleated trousers were adorned with the emblem of the royal family—a symbol of his lineage and duty. As he adjusted his cufflinks, Nicolas glanced at the portrait of his late mother, Queen Amelia, that hung on the wall. Her gentle smile served as a reminder of the love he had never known but had heard whispered in the tales of her grace and kindness.

In the sprawling palace, adorned with regal tapestries and priceless artifacts, Nicolas's footsteps echoed along the marble corridors. Descending the grand staircase, Nicolas was greeted by the sight of the opulent dining hall, adorned with glistening chandeliers and an extravagant spread of delicacies. The air was infused with an aura of formality and tradition, as servants moved with graceful efficiency, ensuring every detail of the meal was executed to perfection.

Taking his seat beside his father, King Edmund II, Nicolas felt the weight of his royal responsibilities settle upon him once more. His father's stern countenance softened slightly as he met his son's gaze, a mixture of pride and expectation reflected in his eyes. The king's presence commanded respect, a testament to his unwavering dedication to the kingdom.

"Good morning, Father," Nicolas greeted, his voice tinged with respect and warmth. "Good morning, Freddie."

"Good morning, my dear sons," King Edmund replied, his voice filled with a hint of paternal affection. "I trust you both had a restful night."

Prince Frederick nodded, his expression filled with playfulness for the day ahead. "Indeed, Father. Rested and ready for the tasks at hand."

The morning meal commenced, accompanied by the clinking of silverware and the occasional murmur of conversation. As they savored the carefully crafted dishes, the king-initiated discussions on matters of state affairs, addressing the challenges and opportunities that lay before them. Nicolas listened attentively, absorbing the weight of his father's wisdom, as he navigated the delicate balance between his desire for personal happiness and his duty to the kingdom.

Amidst the discussions, the topic of Prince Frederick's impending marriage to Princess Sophia of Kechaedor arose. It was an event of great significance, one that would solidify diplomatic ties and strengthen the alliances between their kingdoms. King Edmund's eyes gleamed with a glimmer of excitement as he spoke of the preparations.

"Frederick's wedding draws near, my sons," the king announced, his voice carrying a hint of pride. "The union between our kingdoms and the House of Kechaedor shall forge a bond that shall endure for generations to come. The ceremony will be a grand affair, a testament to the unity between our lands."

Prince Frederick, sitting across from Nicolas, leaned forward with a mischievous grin. "Indeed, Father. The preparations are well underway, and I can assure you, the celebration will be unforgettable. Sophia and I have been reviewing the arrangements together. She brings a radiance that surpasses even the grandest of festivities."

Nicolas smiled, genuinely happy for his brother. "Freddie, I am thrilled for you. Princess Sophia is a remarkable woman, and I have no doubt that your union will be a symbol of strength and unity."

King Edmund's gaze shifted between his two sons, pride and responsibility evident in his eyes. "Remember, my sons, that our duty extends beyond our personal desires. The choices we make have consequences that ripple through the kingdom. As Prince Frederick embraces his future as king consort, Nicolas, you must consider the impact of your own decisions."

Nicolas nodded, his mind briefly drifting to Olivia, whose presence had ignited a flame within him. He understood the weight of his father's words, the delicate balance between his heart's desires and the obligations that awaited him.

"I understand, Father," Nicolas replied. "I will bear the kingdom's welfare in my heart as I navigate the path before me. But, in matters of the heart, I ask for your understanding and support."

The king's expression softened, a glimmer of empathy shining through his eyes. "Nicolas, my son, your happiness matters to me. I ask only that you consider the implications of your choices and the impact they may have on the realm. Love is a powerful force, but it must be tempered with wisdom and responsibility."

Nicolas glanced at his father, a mixture of gratitude and resolve in his gaze. "Thank you, Father. Your wisdom guides me."

The meal continued, but Nicolas's thoughts wandered back to Olivia, the woman who had captured his heart against all odds. He pondered the advice his father had given, grappling with the realities of his position as a prince and the challenges that lay ahead. Love, he realized, would require courage and sacrifice, but he was determined to find a way to merge his heart's desires with his responsibilities as a future ruler.

With breakfast concluded, Nicolas proceeded to the royal study, a room filled with shelves of meticulously arranged books and historical artifacts. It was here that he delved into his daily duties, attending to matters of state, reviewing reports, and engaging in correspondence with dignitaries from neighboring states.

On this particular day, an air of excitement tingled in Nicolas's veins as he prepared for a grand royal event. The ballroom had been adorned with cascading flowers, and the chandeliers sparkled with a thousand crystals, casting a soft glow upon the opulent surroundings. As the guests arrived, elegantly dressed in their finest attire, Nicolas stood tall at the center of the festivities, welcoming each dignitary with a genuine smile.

Amidst the swirl of conversation and laughter, Nicolas's gaze sought out his elder brother, Prince Frederick, whom he trusted implicitly. Finding a moment of respite from the crowd, Nicolas approached his brother, the two of them finding solace in a quieter corner of the ballroom.

In the midst of their conversation, Nicolas found an opportunity to share his own secret. Leaning closer to his brother, Prince Frederick, he whispered, "Freddie, I must confide in you. I've met someone... someone who has captured my heart." His voice trembled under the mixture of excitement and vulnerability, knowing the weight of his brother's opinion in matters of the heart.

Prince Frederick's piercing blue eyes widened with intrigue as he listened attentively. "Tell me more, brother. Who is this enchantress that has bewitched your soul?"

Nicolas could not help but smile, his thoughts drifting to Olivia. "Her name is Olivia Grey. She's an actress—a woman of remarkable talent and beauty. Our paths crossed unexpectedly, and since then, she has occupied my every thought."

Prince Frederick arched an eyebrow, his expression shifting from amusement to concern. "An actress, you say? I must admit, I have seen her in a few of her movies. She possesses a captivating beauty, both inside and out. Her talent shines through the screen, and it's no wonder she has enchanted you, Nick."

Nicolas's eyes widened in surprise. "You've seen her movies? What did you think of her performances?"

Frederick leaned forward, a thoughtful expression on

his face. "I must confess, brother, I was truly captivated by her on-screen presence. She has a rare talent, one that leaves a lasting impression."

Nicolas's heart swelled with pride. To have his brother acknowledge Olivia's talent and beauty meant a great deal to him.

"I'm glad you appreciate her, Freddie," Nicolas replied, a note of relief in his voice. "She is so much more than just her on-screen persona. When I'm with her, there's a sense of warmth and authenticity that envelops us. She sees me for who I am, not just as a prince, but as Nicolas. It's a feeling I can't quite put into words."

Frederick's playful grin softened, replaced by a sincere expression of brotherly concern. "My dear Nicolas, you know the expectations that come with our position. The Royal code and our duty to the kingdom must always be our priority."

Nicolas nodded, understanding the weight of his brother's words. "I know, Freddie, but there's something about her, something special. We had a connection, a bond I can't explain. I can't get her out of my mind."

Prince Frederick sighed, placing a hand on Nicolas's shoulder. "Brother, I understand the allure of forbidden love, but we must consider the consequences. Our world is one of duty and obligation, and love does not always follow the path we desire. This commoner, this actress, may not fit within the constraints of our world. It would be unwise to pursue this further."

Nicolas's gaze faltered for a moment, torn between his heart's desire and the obligations that lay before him. "But what if she's the one, Freddie? What if she's the missing piece of my life?"

Frederick's eyes softened; his voice filled with brotherly affection. "Nico, I want nothing more than your happiness, but we must be realistic. Think of the responsibilities we carry, the duty we owe to our kingdom. Love can be a complicated matter, and sometimes sacrifices must be made."

Nicolas nodded, a mixture of sadness and determination evident in his eyes. "I hear your counsel, Freddie, and I value your wisdom. I will take your words to heart, but for now, I cannot deny the feelings that have stirred within me. I will tread carefully, but I cannot forget her."

Prince Frederick placed a hand on Nicolas's arm, offering silent support. "I understand, brother. Just remember, the choices we make shape our destiny. Whatever path you choose, know that I will stand by your side."

In that moment, amidst the grandeur of the royal event, Nicolas found solace in the touch of his pocket, where his phone discreetly rested. With practiced finesse, he exchanged subtle text messages with Olivia, their secret communication a testament to the strength of their connection. He knew that his world and hers existed in different realms, but the flicker of a forbidden romance had ignited a flame within him that couldn't be easily extinguished.

As the day unfolded, Nicolas gracefully fulfilled his princely duties, attending to matters of state and engaging in diplomatic exchanges with visiting dignitaries. Yet, his thoughts continually wandered to Olivia, the memory of her radiant smile and the sound of her laughter lingering in his mind. The weight of his responsibilities and the expectations placed upon him as a member of the royal family seemed to momentarily fade away whenever he thought of her.

In the quiet moments between royal engagements, Nicolas stole glances at his phone, eagerly anticipating Olivia's responses. Their conversations, though limited, provided a sanctuary where their worlds could merge, if only through words on a screen. The anticipation of their next encounter, the possibility of stolen moments amidst the constraints of their separate lives, fueled Nicolas' determination to pursue a love that defied the boundaries set before him.

With the weight of his brother's words lingering in his mind, Nicolas vowed to navigate the delicate balance between duty and desire. Little did he know that fate had already set in motion a series of events that would test the boundaries of love, challenge the traditions of the kingdom, and ultimately shape the course of his own destiny. In the depths of his soul, Nicolas knew that his heart had found its match in Olivia, and no matter the obstacles that lay ahead, he was willing to fight for a love that transcended kingdoms and defied the expectations of his title.

***

CHAPTER 4:

BOTTLE OF DESIRES

Nicolas's heart raced with anticipation as he packed a small bag, carefully selecting the essentials for his journey. It was a rare occurrence for him to have time off from his royal duties. His decision to slip out of the palace grounds without informing the staff about his destination was not driven by rebellion, but rather by a desire for a taste of freedom and spontaneity.

With each item carefully placed in his bag, he couldn't help but feel a sense of exhilaration. The weight of his royal responsibilities seemed to momentarily lift, replaced by a sense of liberation and a longing for adventure. It was a rare opportunity for him to step out of the confines of his role as Prince Nicolas and simply be himself.

As he made his way through the palace corridors, he moved with purpose and caution, avoiding the watchful eyes of the staff who would surely question his sudden departure. His heart pounded in his chest, a mixture of excitement and nervousness coursing through his veins.

Once outside the palace gates, Nicolas blended seamlessly into the busy streets of the city. Clad in casual attire and with a cap pulled low over his face, he walked with a purposeful stride, blending in with the throngs of people going about their daily lives. It was liberating to be just another face in the crowd, free from the expectations and scrutiny that came with his title. His disguise had successfully evaded the prying eyes of the paparazzi who constantly sought glimpses into his life.

Nicolas walked to a nearby street, the crisp morning air filling his lungs as he scanned the area for a taxi. Spotting one a short distance away, he raised his hand and hailed it with a sense of purpose. The yellow cab pulled up to the curb, its tires crunching on the gravel, and Nicolas climbed inside.

"Good morning," he greeted the driver with a warm smile.

"Morning, sir," the driver replied, glancing at Nicolas through the rearview mirror. "Where can I take you today?"

"To the airport, please," Nicolas answered, settling comfortably into the backseat. "I have a flight to catch."

The driver, oblivious to Nicolas's true identity, treated him like any other passenger, which allowed Nicolas to relish the anonymity and freedom for a little longer. As the taxi whisked him away from the palace, his thoughts turned to Olivia. He couldn't shake the image of her radiant smile from his mind, and the longing to be with her grew with each passing moment. The taxi merged into the flow of traffic, and Nicolas gazed out of the window, watching the cityscape pass by in a blur. The familiar sights and sounds of the city began to fade away as he mentally prepared himself for the journey ahead. He could not help but feel both excitement and nervousness at the same time. This impromptu trip was a leap of faith, a chance to pursue the yearnings of his heart.

Lost in his thoughts, Nicolas's phone buzzed with a message. It was Olivia, replying to his text from earlier. Her words danced across the screen, filling him with warmth and anticipation. He couldn't wait to surprise her in Los Angeles, to see her face light up with joy when she realized he had journeyed across continents just to be with her.

Arriving at the airport, Nicolas navigated through the bustling crowd, his mind focused on one thing: reaching Los Angeles, the city where his heart yearned to be. Shouldering his bag, Nicolas made his way towards the entrance of the airport, the sounds of rolling suitcases and chattering travelers filling the air. He took a deep breath, reminding himself of the purpose behind his journey – to surprise Olivia. With every step, he could feel the weight of his responsibilities lifting, replaced by a sense of liberation and adventure.

Walking through the sliding doors, Nicolas entered the bustling terminal, his heart beating with anticipation. He glanced at the departure boards, scanning for the flight that would take him to Los Angeles, where his beloved Olivia awaited. Approaching the airline counter, Nicolas requested the last available economy ticket to Los Angeles. The attendant, oblivious to his true identity, smiled warmly and handed him the boarding pass. It felt exhilarating to blend in with the other passengers, to be treated as just another traveler seeking a new experience.

As he joined the line at the check-in counter, Nicolas couldn't help but smile, his heart fluttering with excitement. He was on a quest for love, breaking free from the confines of his royal life to chase a dream that had ignited his soul.

Finally, it was his turn to pass through security. He took a deep breath, knowing that once he stepped onto that plane, he would be one step closer to Olivia. His pulse quickened as he handed his boarding pass to the attendant, maintaining his low profile and ensuring his true identity remained a secret.

As he made his way into the departure lounge, Nicolas's thoughts were consumed by Olivia. Images of her radiant smile and the magnetic connection they shared danced in his mind, fueling his determination to surprise her.

Nicolas found a seat in the bustling departure lounge, his eyes scanning the room for any sign of his boarding gate. The soft murmur of conversations filled the air, intermingling with the occasional sound of a departing announcement. His heart raced with anticipation as he checked his watch, realizing that the time to board was drawing near.

Surrounded by fellow travelers, Nicolas couldn't help but observe the diverse array of individuals occupying the lounge. Couples shared tender embraces, bidding each other farewell with promises of reunions, while families wrangled their excited children, preparing for their own journeys. The atmosphere was a tapestry of emotions, a testament to the power of human connections and the allure of adventure.

His eyes caught sight of an elderly couple seated across from him, their weathered hands intertwined. Their love for each other was evident in the way they shared stolen glances and exchanged gentle smiles. Nicolas couldn't help but feel a pang of longing, yearning for the day when he and Olivia would grow old together, their love standing the test of time.

Nicolas grabbed his phone from his pocket and subtly typed a message to Olivia. His fingers danced across the screen as he composed a casual message, asking her what she was up to.

'Hey, Olivia! What are you doing this evening?'

A few moments passed, and Nicolas felt a jolt of anticipation as Olivia's reply appeared on his screen. Her words sent a surge of warmth through his veins.

'Hey, Nicolas! I'm actually having my weekly dinner with my friends at a private bistro cafe in downtown Los Angeles. What are you doing?'

A smile tugged at the corners of Nicolas's lips. He had hoped for such an opportunity, a chance to surprise Olivia in the midst of her routine. The universe seemed to align in their favor, presenting him with the perfect moment to sweep her off her feet.

The café sounds amazing! May be the next time I'm in town, we could go together?'

As he awaited Olivia's response, Nicolas's mind buzzed with thoughts of their impending meeting. He envisioned the look of surprise and delight on Olivia's face when she realized he had traveled all this way to be with her.

After what felt like an eternity, Olivia's reply appeared on the screen, accompanied by a cascade of excited emojis.

'Nicolas, that would be incredible! It's Café L'amour. It's very private and has amazing ambience.'

Nicolas's heart skipped a beat as he read Olivia's response. Café L'amour—it sounded enchanting, the perfect backdrop for their reunion. As the minutes ticked by, his gaze shifted to the digital display above the gate, indicating that it was time to board. A wave of excitement coursed through him, his heart beating in rhythm with the anticipation of what lay ahead. He took out his boarding pass from his pocket, clutching it firmly as he proceeded toward the gate.

Engaged in his own thoughts, Nicolas was brought back to reality by the voice of a fellow traveler behind him. He turned, meeting the curious gaze of a young woman, her eyes filled with intrigue.

"Excuse me, but you seem familiar," she said tentatively,

a hint of recognition in her voice.

Nicolas's heart skipped a beat, momentarily taken aback. However, he maintained his composure and smiled warmly at her. "Perhaps you've seen me in the papers," he replied, subtly deflecting the conversation away from his true identity.

The woman nodded thoughtfully. "That must be it. Well, safe travels to you."

"Thank you," Nicolas responded with a nod, grateful that his secret remained intact. He returned his focus to the boarding process, stepping forward as the line moved steadily forward.

Finally, it was his turn to present his boarding pass. The gate attendant glanced at his ticket and returned a polite smile. "Enjoy your flight, sir," she said, gesturing for him to proceed.

Nicolas stepped onto the jet bridge, his heart swelling with excitement. He walked along the enclosed passageway, the sound of his footsteps echoing in his ears. With each step, he felt a renewed sense of purpose, a determination to seize this moment and pursue the love that had captured his heart.

As he crossed the threshold of the aircraft, Nicolas felt a surge of anticipation. The flight attendants greeted him with warm smiles, and he made his way down the narrow aisle to find his seat. Glancing out the window, he caught a glimpse of the tarmac, the planes lined up in orderly fashion, ready to take flight.

Taking a seat by the window, Nicolas glanced out at the runway, the anticipation building within him. The hum of the aircraft's engines provided a soothing backdrop, lulling him into a state of quiet reflection. He thought about the countless times he had traveled in luxury, shielded from the world by the opulence that came with his royal status. But this time, he embraced the simplicity of economy class, relishing in the anonymity it afforded him.

As he settled into his seat on the plane, Nicolas glanced at his fellow passengers, a diverse fusion of individuals from different walks of life. It was an entirely new experience for him, being surrounded by ordinary travelers who were oblivious to his royal status. With his hoodie pulled low and cap snugly in place, he blended seamlessly into the crowd.

Soon, the airplane taxied down the runway. But Nicolas could not help but steal a glance at the 7-year-old girl seated next to him. Her bright eyes sparkled with curiosity, and he couldn't resist striking up a conversation.

"Hello there," Nicolas greeted with a warm smile. "I'm Nicolas. What's your name?"

The little girl tilted her head slightly, studying him with intrigue. "I'm Emma," she replied cautiously. "Are you a prince?"

Nicolas chuckled softly, amused by her astuteness. "Well, Emma, I suppose you could say that. But right now, I'm just a regular person on a journey."

Emma's eyes widened with curiosity. "Where are you going, Mr. Nicolas?"

Nicolas leaned in conspiratorially, lowering his voice. "I'm going to surprise the love of my life in Los Angeles. It's going to be an adventure!"

Emma looked skeptical, crossing her arms over her chest. "I don't think girls like surprises. My mom says surprises can be scary."

Nicolas pondered her words for a moment, understanding the perspective of a young girl who was yet to fully comprehend the complexities of love and relationships. He decided to share a story with her, hoping to shed some light on the magic of surprises.

"Well, Emma, love is a bit like a fairy tale," he began, his voice filled with wonder. "Sometimes, surprises can make a person feel special and loved. It's like opening a treasure chest, not knowing what wonderful things await inside. Love is about creating beautiful moments and memories together, and surprises can be a part of that."

Emma's skeptical expression softened; her curiosity piqued. "Tell me more, Mr. Nicolas. What kind of surprise are you planning?"

Nicolas leaned back in his seat, a playful glimmer in his eyes. "Ah, that's a secret! But I can tell you this much. Love is about showing someone how much they mean to you. And sometimes, surprises can do just that. They can bring joy, excitement, and a touch of magic to a person's life."

Emma mulled over his words, her doubt slowly transforming into curiosity. "Maybe surprises aren't so bad after all. But what if the surprise goes wrong?"

Nicolas smiled reassuringly. "Well, Emma, sometimes surprises may not turn out exactly as planned, but that's okay. As long as it comes from the heart, even a small surprise can bring a smile to someone's face."

Emma's eyes lit up, a newfound sense of wonder shining through. "Maybe I'll surprise my mom someday too!"

Nicolas nodded, delighted by her enthusiasm. "I'm sure your mom would love that, Emma. It's the thought and effort that count the most."

As the flight continued, Nicolas and Emma shared stories, dreams, and laughter, forging a unique connection in the midst of their journey. Nicolas cherished the innocence and wisdom of a young girl who reminded him of the beauty and simplicity of love.

As the plane touched down in Los Angeles, Nicolas's heart beat with anticipation. He retrieved his bag from the overhead compartment, eager to embark on the next chapter of his adventure that would forever change the course of his love story.

***

Sitting comfortably amidst her giggling pals, Olivia found herself in their regular haunt - a private café. This cozy spot was a haven tucked away in a tranquil nook of the bustling city, where they could unwind and just be themselves, without the prying gaze of reporters. Having wrapped up a taxing day of filming, Olivia was grateful to be there, and a feeling of relief washed over her. The burden of work had been lifted, and she was determined to maximize her well-deserved leisure time.

As her friends filled the cozy ambiance with laughter and chatter, Olivia felt a sense of kinship. She was reminded that fame and money hadn't robbed her of the simple joys of friendship and companionship.

"Alright, so let's make this interesting," Olivia said, placing a coin on the table. "Whoever spins the bottle and lands on me has to buy all of us drinks."

Her friends burst into laughter, amused by the familiar tradition they had upheld since their first meeting. Samantha, a tiny dark-haired woman with striking green irises, styled her locks in an elevated ponytail. She was one of the few people who truly knew Olivia beyond her on-screen persona.

"Are you sure about that, Olivia?" Samantha asked, a mischievous glint in her eyes. "You know the odds are against us. But hey, I'm up for the challenge."

Olivia flashed a confident smile. "Absolutely sure," she replied, her tone brimming with eagerness. "We're celebrating our last day of filming, and I think we should have some fun while we can. Besides, who would dare spin the bottle on me?"

Her friends joined in the laughter, aware that Olivia's remark was more than just a playful challenge. They knew she was the least likely to be chosen, given her status as an accomplished actress and the rarity of finding someone willing to take such a risk. Only one person had ever spun the bottle on her—her high school sweetheart who was now her ex-husband.

As the café brimmed with laughter and anticipation, Olivia allowed herself to get lost in the carefree atmosphere. Her infectious laughter mingled with that of her friends, filling the air with joy and warmth. The bottle spun around the table, and excitement built up, casting a subtle electric energy over the room. Tonight, felt different from their usual lighthearted gatherings, whispering of untold possibilities.

"It landed on me!" Samantha exclaimed, pointing to the bottle. "I'm sorry, but I can't buy you all drinks. I don't want to break the rules."

Olivia placed a comforting hand on Samantha's. "Don't worry, Sam. You can afford it," she said, reassuring her friend. "Let's just enjoy the game."

Samantha looked at Olivia, her emerald eyes pleading for understanding. "I know, Liv. But I don't want to bend the rules just because it landed on me."

Olivia smiled, squeezing Samantha's shoulder gently. "Don't be silly. It's alright. I understand."

As the bottle continued its spin, Olivia believed the game was coming to an end. But amidst the merry commotion, her gaze inadvertently fell upon the entrance of the café. A young, handsome man, with fiery red hair and piercing blue eye, walked in.

As the bottle spun again, Olivia's gaze collided with Nicolas', and a jolt of warmth coursed through her veins. The moment seemed to stretch, holding them in a gentle embrace as the bottle gradually came to a stop. With a charming smile, Nicolas broke the spell by speaking up.

"Mind if I join?" he asked, his voice laced with a hint of playfulness.

"Nicolas!" Olivia exclaimed as she rushed to him, a mixture of delight and disbelief in her voice. "What are you doing here?"

Nicolas smiled; his eyes locked with hers. "I couldn't stay away any longer, Olivia. I had to see you," he confessed, his voice filled with sincerity.

Olivia's initial shock transformed into a radiant smile. She embraced him tightly, her heart overflowing with joy. "I can't believe you're here," she whispered, her voice laced with emotion.

Pulling back slightly, Nicolas held her gaze, his eyes filled with unwavering devotion. "I've come all this way to be with you, Olivia. Nothing can keep us apart," he declared, his voice brimming with determination.

Olivia's eyes shimmered with tears of happiness. "I've missed you, Nicolas," she admitted, her voice filled with longing. "I've been counting down the days until we could be together again."

Nicolas tenderly brushed a stray strand of hair from Olivia's face, his touch sending shivers down her spine. "No more counting days, my love," he whispered. "I'm here."

As they stood in there in the cafe, time seemed to stand still. Their lips met in a passionate kiss, sealing their reunion and igniting a flame that burned brighter than ever. The world around them faded into the background as their love enveloped them, cocooning them in a bubble of pure bliss.

Just as Olivia and Nicolas were lost in their passionate kiss, the sound of a throat being cleared abruptly interrupted their moment. They reluctantly pulled apart; their eyes still locked with desire. It was Olivia's friend, Samantha, a mischievous twinkle in her eyes.

"Ahem," Samantha cleared her throat, a playful smirk on her face. "Am I interrupting something, or can Nicolas join our little spin the bottle game?"

Olivia blushed; her cheeks tinged with a rosy hue. "Oh, Samantha, you always have impeccable timing," she said with a sheepish smile.

"Thank you," Nicolas chuckled, his eyes dancing with amusement. "I'd be delighted to join," he replied, his voice filled with charm.

He gracefully took a seat, his hands lightly resting on Olivia. The touch sent a rush of tingling sensations through Olivia's body, and she blushed, unable to recall a time when someone had thanked her so earnestly. Her gaze flickered to meet his eyes, which held a depth that captivated her, unknowingly beckoning her to venture into the depths of his heart.

Samantha leaned in, greeting him with a warm smile. "Hello, Nicolas," she said, giving him a quick wave. "It's nice to meet you."

Nicolas returned the gesture, his gaze shifting to Olivia. "Hello, everyone," he greeted, settling into his newfound place among the group.

The game continued, and Samantha selected Olivia as the next spinner. As the bottle spun on the table, Olivia's heart skipped a beat, a mixture of anticipation and curiosity coursing through her. She wondered whose gaze fate would direct toward her this time. The bottle came to a stop, its neck pointing directly at Nicolas.

Nicolas, his ocean eyes sparkling with intrigue, flashed a sheepish grin. "Well, looks like fate has chosen us," he said, breaking the momentary silence that had fallen upon the group.

Olivia looked at Nicolas, her face betraying her surprise. "You're kidding me right. This isn't your ordinary spin the bottle, is it?" she asked.

Nicolas laughed. "No, it's not. I'm sure you've realized

by now that there are rules."

"Rules?" Olivia asked, her brows furrowing.

"Yes, rules," Nicolas said, leaning in closer to her.

Nicolas flashed a sheepish grin. "Well, looks like fate has chosen us," he said, breaking the momentary silence that had fallen upon the group.

"Well, well, well, it seems fate has a plan," Samantha teased, her eyes glimmering with mischief. "Looks like it's time for our lovebirds to answer a question. Olivia, ask Nicolas something you've been dying to know."

Olivia's mind raced with possibilities; her curiosity piqued. She locked eyes with Nicolas, a shy smile playing on her lips. "Tell me, what's the most adventurous thing you've ever done in your life?" she asked.

Nicolas leaned back, a contemplative expression on his face. "Hmm, let me think," he pondered, his eyes fixed on Olivia. "Well, it has to be where I travelled so far in a whim, just so that I could be with you," he replied, his voice laced with sincerity.

Olivia's heart fluttered, her eyes sparkling with adoration. "You mean that?" she whispered; her voice filled with wonder.

Nicolas reached out, gently taking her hand in his. "Every word," he affirmed, his thumb tracing circles on her palm. "Right from the very moment I met you, I knew that I had to follow my heart. Even if it meant stepping into the unknown."

Olivia's mind raced with the implications of Nicolas's words; her thoughts clouded with emotion. "I can't believe that you would take such a leap of faith for me," she said, her voice thick with emotion. "But I have to admit that I feel the same way. I want to take this journey together, to love each other with no holds barred."

Nicolas's eyes shimmered with devotion, and he leaned in, his lips brushing softly against hers. The kiss was delicate, tender, and filled with unspoken words. Olivia lost herself in Nicolas's embrace, her heart pounding with longing and excitement. As their lips parted, she felt an energy course through her body, a sign that this was truly meant to be.

Olivia glanced at her friends, who sat beside her, observing the tender moment with unbridled affection.

"Now, that was worth interrupting," Samantha teased, her emerald eyes dancing with mischief. "What's next, Nicolas? What's your question for Olivia?"

Nicolas sat back; his eyes filled with wonder. "Alright, I have a question for you. What is the most delicious thing that you've ever eaten in your life?"

Olivia let out a laugh. "I'd have to go with the cheesecake here. The strawberries are amazingly rich, and the cheesecake is just heavenly," she said, her eyes shining with delight.

Nicolas nodded thoughtfully. "That's sounds great. Maybe I'll be able to have some with you?" he said, his tone filled with promise.

Olivia's cheeks turned a shade of red, and she gazed into his eyes. "Maybe you will, Nicolas. After all, it's definitely the most delicious thing in the world."

"I don't know," Nicolas whispered, his eyes filled with desire. "Because I can definitely think of something that might be even better."

Olivia bit her lip, unable to break away from the intensity of his gaze. She leaned in closer, her eyes fixed on his lips.

"Nicolas, are you flirting with me?" she asked playfully.

"I wouldn't dream of doing anything else," Nicolas replied, his eyes holding her in an unyielding embrace.

Olivia was captivated by the intensity of his gaze, her thoughts consumed by his lips. The electricity between them seemed to intensify with each passing moment. She could not remember a time when her heart had felt so full, her body overcome with desire.

Nicolas pulled back, a shy smile on his lips. "Olivia, I think we've created quite a stir in here," he whispered, glancing at her friends with a sheepish grin.

Olivia's eyes widened as she glanced at her friends, who sat beside her, watching the romantic moment unfold with unbridled affection. "Oh, my goodness! I'm sorry, everyone," she apologized, her cheeks flushed with a rosy hue. "We're both just really excited to be together again."

Samantha smiled knowingly. "Oh, don't worry about it, Olivia. We're all very happy for you. And besides, you two have our full support."

The group laughed, breaking the tension.

As the evening progressed, Nicolas and Olivia fell into an easy rhythm with the group. The conversation flowed easily, their voices filling the air with warmth and laughter. And soon they found themselves quietly stepping away from the table, leaving their friends behind in a haze of laughter and curious whispers. As they walked through the café's door, a rush of cool evening air greeted them, as if the universe itself was conspiring to set the stage for their encounter.

Hand in hand, Olivia and Nicolas stepped out into the starlit night. The world seemed to shimmer around them, as if the universe itself was celebrating their union. The stars shined brighter than ever, bathing the world in a soft light.

"It's beautiful here," Olivia said, her eyes gazing into the heavens.

Nicolas placed his arm around her shoulder, his body enveloping hers in a warm embrace. "It certainly is," he replied, his voice laced with a quiet confidence.

They stood together for a moment; their gazes locked in a deep, soulful gaze. Olivia's heart beat with anticipation, longing and desire coursing through her veins.

"Nicolas, can I ask you something?" she said hesitantly.

Nicolas smiled, his eyes holding her in an unwavering embrace. "You can ask me anything," he replied, his tone laced with sincerity.

Olivia paused for a moment, gathering her thoughts. "I don't want to be with you if there's any chance that our relationship could go wrong," she began. "And I don't want to drag you into something you might regret."

"Olivia," Nicolas whispered, his voice filled with unbridled passion. "I'm here in this moment with you, because I choose to. Because I do want to be with you. And I know that you are worth the risk."

Olivia bit her lip, her heart overflowing with a sense of adoration. "Nicolas, you've made me the happiest person in the world."

She leaned in, brushing her lips against his. As their kiss deepened, she felt his intensity coursing through her body. Thereby, igniting a fire within her that burned with such unquenchable desire.

The two lovers lost themselves in their passionate kiss, oblivious to the rest of the world. Their hearts raced, a chorus of desires and yearnings filling their souls. As the kiss deepened, a newfound passion ignited between them, drawing them closer together.

The world around them seemed to melt away, and their

gazes met with a silent, unspoken intensity. Olivia could not remember a time when she had been so consumed with desire, her thoughts clouded with emotion and longing. She was drawn to Nicolas's gaze, a magnetism that captivated her, beckoning her to venture into the depths of his heart.

Their lips met in a soft, tender kiss. The soft touch sent a shiver down Olivia's spine, igniting a newfound passion.

"You must be exhausted. Let me take you home." she whispered; her voice thick with longing.

Nicolas leaned in, pressing his lips against hers. The kiss was tender and passionate, a burning fire that ignited Olivia's desire. As their lips parted, Nicolas locked his gaze with hers.

"Olivia, there's no other place I'd rather be," he replied, his voice filled with adoration. "Lead the way."

Olivia took his hand in hers, leading him towards her apartment. Their fingers intertwined, the connection between them as strong as ever. She felt a newfound connection with Nicolas, one forged by the courage to follow one's heart.

As they reached her apartment, a surge of electricity coursed through Olivia's veins.

"Nicolas, I do want to be with you," she whispered, her voice thick with longing. "But I don't know if I can handle any unexpected surprises."

Nicolas nodded; his eyes filled with a deep understanding. "I don't want to pressure you into anything that you're not comfortable with. If you need time, I will wait. Just know that I'm here for you, always."

Olivia took a deep breath, her heart swelling with an unexpected emotion. She knew she could not rush into this, but the prospect of being with him stirred up feelings she had never experienced before.

"Thank you, Nicolas. I really appreciate that," she said, her voice thick with emotion.

They entered the apartment, sitting side by side on the sofa. The lights were dim, and the air was filled with the soft melody of jazz music.

Nicolas wrapped his arm around Olivia, pulling her in close. "Olivia, I would cross an ocean for you in a heartbeat. I just want you to make you happy," he said, his tone laced with sincerity. "I care about you more than you can imagine. And if this isn't what you want, then I don't mind waiting."

Olivia's heart melted, a range of emotions coursing through her veins. She knew that Nicolas had gone above and beyond to make sure her happiness came first.

"Nicolas, I really appreciate your generosity," she began, her voice thick with emotion. "But I need you to know that I'm willing to take this step. I want to be with you too, even if it's not easy. We can face whatever comes together, as long as we have each other."

Nicolas nodded, his gaze locking with hers. "I'm glad to hear that," he replied, his voice laced with passion. "I want to be with you, just you and me. No matter what happens."

Olivia leaned in, brushing her lips against his. The kiss was soft and tender, igniting a newfound passion in her heart. As the kiss deepened, a sense of desire consumed her, igniting a fire in her belly. She felt Nicolas's hands caressing her back, gently moving downwards. His touch sent shivers down her spine, and she pressed her body against his, yearning for the contact of his skin against hers.

She felt Nicolas's lips travel down her neck, sending a wave of pleasure through her. A moan escaped her lips as his tongue traced circles on her collarbone. She could not remember a time when she had been so consumed by desire, her body aching with an intense need to be touched.

As Nicolas's lips continued their journey downward, Olivia felt an unexpected heat building in her belly. She closed her eyes as she let out a moan of pleasure. Her mind raced with anticipation and desire, and she felt Nicolas's hand move downwards, brushing softly against her skin. His touch was gentle and tender, igniting a newfound passion in her.

A shiver ran down Olivia's spine as his fingers touched her thigh, brushing softly against her skin. Her heart raced, and she bit her lip, holding back her moans. As his fingers inched closer to her center, she felt a surge of excitement rush through her body, her mind consumed with longing and desire.

"Nicolas, don't stop," she whispered, her voice laced with need.

Olivia felt her heart pound against her chest, creating a sense of urgency coursing through her. She was lost in the moment of passion, completely consumed by a wave of pleasure that washed over her.

Nicolas gently pushed her back, easing her onto the sofa. His hands traced circles on her hips, drawing small circles on her thighs. A wave of excitement rushed through Olivia's body as he leaned in, pressing his lips against hers. Their kiss was tender and passionate, filled with unspoken emotions.

Olivia felt Nicolas's hands slowly move upward, gently caressing her skin. Her breath caught in her throat as his fingers moved closer to her core. His fingertips brushing softly against the fabric of her panties.

She held her breath as she felt Nicolas's hands slide into the waistband of her skirt, pushing them down her hips.

"Oh, Nicolas," she moaned, her body tingling with desire.

She felt his tongue gently brush against her neck, kissing the sensitive skin around her collarbone. Her pulse raced, and her mind was filled with longing and desire. As he eased himself off the sofa, she felt his tongue travel downwards, licking the sensitive flesh of her inner thigh.

A wave of pleasure rushed through Olivia's body as he licked her slit, gently flicking his tongue against the swollen bud. She cried out loud, arching her back as she felt the intense sensations. She was consumed by a wave of desire, her body aching for his touch. As his fingers traced shapes around her folds, she reached out and pulled him up. She wanted to feel the warmth of his skin against hers.

"Nicolas, please," she whispered, her voice filled with need. "I want you."

Nicolas smiled, leaning in to kiss her. Their lips met in a soft, tender kiss. She could taste herself on his tongue as she hungrily moaned into his mouth. But he pulled away and raised himself up. She watched as his clothes fell to the floor, revealing his toned chest. His body was muscular, but not bulky. She ran her fingers through his hair, her eyes lingering on the hard lines of his body.

His muscles rippled beneath her fingertips, lightly touching his chest. A moan escaped his lips, and she leaned forward. She wanted to take her time as she slowly brushed her lips against his skin. She loved being in control and him melting away under her touch. She licked his chest, trailing her tongue across his skin. He tasted like salt and sweat and she felt herself growing wetter and wetter with each passing second.

He groaned when she kissed again him as she heard the desperation in his voice. She held on to his muscular shoulders as she quickly turned over, switching their positions.

Now it was her turn to tease him. She knelt on the floor, touching his hardness. She heard him gasp in pleasure and smiled inwardly as she began to caress him down there. His groans of pleasure, brought a smile to her face. She moved her gaze to his face, that was filled with such raw passion. His eyes were filled with desire and she felt a rush of excitement course through her body. She wanted to make him beg for her touch.

"Nicolas, I want to taste you," she whispered as she continued to tease him. Slowly, she moved her tongue up and down the length of his manhood. He moaned and she could feel the tension building within him. But she pulled herself away and walked straight in to her bedroom, where she quickly undressed herself and lay on the bed waiting for him.

Nicolas followed her and they collapsed together in a tangled heap of arms and legs. His body felt warm and strong next to hers and she pulled him close. She felt safe and secure in his arms and knew that no matter what happened, she would always have him to turn to.

Together they lay on the bed with her arms wrapped around his shoulders and her legs secured around his hips. She felt his body press down hardly against hers. In an unexpected moment, he slowly entered her, sliding into her core. She let out a gasp in surprise as he began to move, filling her up.

Nicolas, lost in pure pleasure, began to thrust into her,

moving slowly at first. His pace increased as he felt her opening up for him. He leaned down, capturing her lips with his own. She moaned into his mouth as he pressed his tongue against hers.

Olivia arched her back, letting out a moan of pleasure. Nicolas began to move slowly, rocking his hips back and forth. She felt him enter deeper, stretching her walls, sending a wave of ecstasy through her body.

As his movements became more intense, she felt his hands wrapping around her, pulling her even closer to him. She arched her back, as she let him overpower all her defenses. A sense of urgency coursed through her body as he thrust into her. The feeling of him inside her was intense, sending her body over the edge. He slid in and out of her core, thrusting harder and harder until she could barely breath. She felt a familiar pressure building in her belly and knew she was close to climaxing.

She closed her eyes, feeling herself release, as she moaned out into the night. As she came, she cried out, waves of pleasure washing over her. Nicolas continued to move, thrusting deeper and deeper. She could feel him getting close to release, and she clutched onto him, pulling him into her.

"Oh God, Olivia," he cried, as his body shuddered.

His words sent a wave of pleasure through her body and she gasped, clutching him tightly. She felt him stiffen as he came, moaning her name loudly. He rode out the orgasm, still buried deep within her core. As the sensations began to subside, she held him close, relishing the feeling of being in his arms.

"You are amazing," he whispered into her ears. "I don't know how I could ever be without you again."

Olivia laughed. "I don't know how I could ever be without you either," she said, kissing him softly on the lips.

She wrapped her arms around him, pulling him close. He nuzzled into her, holding her in a gentle embrace. She had never felt so connected with anyone before like this. She realized that her life could never be the same again. Her heart was filled with an indescribable joy, and she knew that he was the one she wanted to spend the rest of her life with. Her mind reeled with the intensity of their encounter, and she felt herself drifting off to sleep. They fell asleep together, their hearts beating in unison, a song of love and passion.

***

CHAPTER 5:

TOP OF THE WORLD

The next morning, Olivia woke up to the sound of the ocean crashing against the shore. She sat up on her bed, her eyes still heavy from the night's sleep. As she stretched, her mind began to wander, a gentle smile playing across her lips. Blinking away the remnants of sleep, she found herself cocooned in a cozy bed, adorned with a soft blanket that whispered of warmth and protection. A soft smile graced her lips as she realized it was Nicolas's thoughtful gesture.

As she sat up, stretching her limbs, a sense of contentment washed over her. The events of the previous night played like a reel in her mind, each moment etching itself into her memory with profound significance. She couldn't help but be captivated by the effortless connection she shared with Nicolas, a bond that seemed to deepen with every passing second.

Glancing at the clock beside her bed, Olivia's eyes widened in surprise. It was already 9:30 in the morning. She hurriedly slipped out of bed and quickly dressed herself. She knew there was so much more to be explored, so many precious moments to be shared with the man who had captured her heart.

With hunger gnawing at her stomach, Olivia made her way to the kitchen, her anticipation growing with each step. And there he was, a vision of casual charm, clad in a simple t-shirt and track pants, his hands deftly maneuvering pans on the stove. The tantalizing aroma of breakfast filled the air, mingling with the intoxicating scent of freshly brewed coffee.

His concentration was interrupted by the enthusiastic presence of Olivia's beloved dogs, Stella and Max, who eagerly wagged their tails, circling around him with playful excitement. Nicolas had taken it upon himself to feed them their breakfast, his affectionate nature extending not only to Olivia but to her furry companions as well.

Olivia could not help but smile at the scene before her. Stella, a lively and energetic Labrador, nudged Nicolas's hand with her nose, urging him to go faster with her breakfast. Max, an affectionate and mischievous terrier, bounced around him, his eyes fixed on the sizzling aroma emanating from the stovetop.

"Looks like Stella and Max have found a new breakfast buddy," Olivia remarked, her voice laced with amusement as she approached Nicolas.

"Well, well, it seems I have won over the hearts of these two rascals," Nicolas remarked with a warm smile.

Olivia beamed with delight, watching as her dogs basked in the attention of Nicolas. "They don't warm up to just anyone so quickly. You must have a special charm, Nicolas."

Nicolas bent down, a grin lighting up his face as he reached out to scratch Stella behind the ear. "I think we've formed a mutual admiration society," he replied, his eyes sparkling with affection for the four-legged creatures that had found their way into Olivia's heart. "Perhaps they sense that I have a soft spot for them, just like their owner."

Then he turned, a warm smile spreading across his face as his gaze met Olivia's. The moment seemed suspended in time, the world around them fading into insignificance. There was an unspoken understanding between them, a shared acknowledgement of the intimacy they had discovered in each other's presence.

"Good morning, beautiful," Nicolas greeted, his voice laced with affection. "I hope you slept well."

Olivia's heart fluttered at the endearment, her smile growing wider. "I slept like a dream," she replied, her voice filled with genuine gratitude. "Thank you for taking care of me."

Nicolas's eyes sparkled with tenderness as he placed a plate of mouthwatering pancakes before her. "It's my pleasure, Olivia. I want to make every moment with you special."

As they settled down at the table, Stella and Max obediently took their positions nearby, their eyes eagerly fixed on the food before them. Olivia's eyes shimmered with appreciation as she took in the lovingly prepared breakfast.

"You've already made every moment special," she whispered, her voice filled with sincerity.

"Bon appétit," Nicolas said, his voice filled with warmth as he gestured for Olivia to dig in.

Olivia's taste buds were tantalized with each delectable bite, savoring the flavors that Nicolas had skillfully infused into the breakfast. Amidst bites of fluffy pancakes and sips of rich coffee, their conversation flowed effortlessly, their laughter and banter filling the air.

They sat at the table, their conversation flowing effortlessly as they savored each bite, their laughter mingling with the morning sunlight that streamed through the window. In that moment, the world outside ceased to exist, and it was just the two of them, bound by an unbreakable thread of affection and possibility.

As they finished their meal, Olivia reached across the table, her fingers gently entwining with Nicolas's. Their eyes met, and in that shared gaze, they found reassurance, comfort, and an unspoken promise of a future filled with love and adventure.

"Thank you for this beautiful morning," Olivia whispered, her voice barely audible. "I never want this feeling to end."

Nicolas squeezed her hand, his touch sending a surge of

warmth through her. "Neither do I, Olivia," he replied, his voice filled with conviction. "I'm here, and I'm not going anywhere. We have so much more to discover together."

Olivia felt a renewed sense of hope stir within her, as if the possibilities of their love were endless. After a delightful breakfast together, Nicolas could not help but notice the sparkle in Olivia's eyes as they lingered over their empty plates. He leaned back in his chair, a mischievous smile playing on his lips.

"You know, Olivia," Nicolas began, his voice filled with excitement, "I've been thinking. Is there something fun that we can do together while we're here in Los Angeles?"

Olivia's face lit up, her expression mirroring Nicolas's enthusiasm. "Actually, there's something I've always wanted to do but never had the chance," she admitted. "I've always dreamt of experiencing the thrill of the amusement parks here in Los Angeles."

Nicolas's eyes twinkled with delight. "That sounds absolutely fantastic! Let's make it happen," he exclaimed. "But I have an idea to make it even more adventurous. How about we go incognito? We can wear disguises and enjoy the fun in secret, away from the prying eyes of the paparazzi."

Olivia's eyes widened with intrigue. She had always craved a taste of anonymity, a chance to immerse herself in the joys of everyday life without the weight of public scrutiny. The thought of exploring the amusement parks with Nicolas, hidden behind disguises, ignited a sense of adventure within her.

"I love that idea!" Olivia replied, her voice filled with excitement. "To be able to experience the thrills and laughter of the amusement parks without the constant flash of cameras sounds like a dream come true."

Nicolas's grin widened as he leaned closer. "It's settled then," he whispered, his voice tinged with playfulness. "We shall be two ordinary individuals lost in the crowd, sharing laughter, exhilaration, and unforgettable moments."

As the plan took shape, Nicolas and Olivia brainstormed ideas for their disguises. Excitement filled the air as Nicolas and Olivia ventured into Olivia's closet, ready to embark on a transformation that would grant them the freedom to roam the streets of Los Angeles incognito. Rows of dresses, jackets, and accessories awaited them, each item holding the potential to mold their identities into unrecognizable forms. Their goal was to blend in seamlessly with the crowd, to immerse themselves fully in the spirit of fun and adventure.

Olivia's eyes sparkled with a mischievous glint as she rummaged through her wardrobe, pulling out various articles of clothing and holding them up to her body. "How about this?" she asked, displaying a vibrant, sequined jacket. "I could pair it with some oversized sunglasses and a hat. No one will suspect a thing!"

Nicolas chuckled, admiring her playful enthusiasm. "That's a fantastic choice, Olivia. It's the perfect combination of style and disguise. But what about me? I need an equally cunning disguise to join you on this adventure."

They continued their search, exploring the depths of the closet like treasure hunters seeking hidden gems. Nicolas tried on different hats, scarves, and coats, experimenting with different combinations until he found the ideal ensemble that would render him unrecognizable.

"Look at this," Nicolas exclaimed, holding up a vintage leather jacket. "With a scruffy beard, a pair of aviator sunglasses, and a hat pulled low, I'll be the epitome of undercover charm."

Olivia's eyes lit up with delight as she visualized the transformation. "Yes, Nicolas! You'll be the mysterious stranger, and I'll be the glamorous enigma. Together, we'll create a whirlwind of excitement and intrigue."

With their disguises meticulously planned, Nicolas and Olivia spent the afternoon trying on various combinations of clothes, accessories, and hairstyles. They laughed, twirled, and posed in front of the mirror, reveling in the thrill of their impending adventure.

As they admired their alter egos in the mirror, Nicolas couldn't help but feel a rush of gratitude for Olivia's infectious spirit and her willingness to embrace the spontaneity of the moment. The connection they shared was deepened by their shared love for adventure and the desire to explore life's wonders together.

"Now that we've transformed ourselves, Olivia, we can delve into the heart of Los Angeles, completely undetected," Nicolas said, a playful smile curving his lips. "We'll be like two stars hidden amidst a constellation, dancing in the night sky."

Olivia's eyes shimmered with anticipation as she took Nicolas's hand. "Let's make memories that will last a lifetime, Nicolas. Tonight, we'll be anonymous wanderers, creating our own story."

***

As Nicolas and Olivia approached the gates of the amusement park, the air buzzed with anticipation. The sight of the colorful rides towering against the clear blue sky filled them with a childlike wonder, igniting a spark of joy within their hearts. They exchanged excited glances, their eyes twinkling with the promise of adventure.

The sound of merry-go-round music filled the air as they made their way through the entrance, immersing themselves in the lively atmosphere. The scent of freshly popped popcorn and sugary treats wafted through the air, tempting their taste buds and adding to the sensory overload.

Nicolas and Olivia marveled at the sense of freedom that came with their incognito status. They held hands, their fingers entwined, as they ventured into the whimsical world of thrilling rides and whimsical attractions. Slowly, they navigated through the crowd, their disguises allowing them to blend seamlessly with the other park-goers. They observed families laughing together, couples stealing sweet kisses on the Ferris wheel, and friends challenging each other to daring rides. It was a world of carefree exhilaration, where worries were left at the gates, and the only currency that mattered was the currency of joy.

Olivia's eyes gleamed with excitement as she pointed towards a roller coaster, its tracks looping and twisting against the vibrant backdrop of the park. "Shall we, Nicolas?" she asked.

Nicolas could not resist her infectious enthusiasm. "Absolutely, my love," he replied, his voice mirroring her excitement. "Let's embrace the thrill and make unforgettable memories."

They joined the line for the roller coaster, the anticipation building with each step they took forward. As they waited, Nicolas stole glances at Olivia, marveling at the way her eyes sparkled with excitement and her laughter danced in the air. It was in these moments that he realized how lucky he was to have found someone who shared his zest for life and his desire to make every moment count.

Finally, it was their turn to board the roller coaster.

Nicolas and Olivia strapped themselves into the seats, their hearts pounding in sync with the rhythm of the ride. As the roller coaster roared to life, they held hands tightly, their fingers interlaced as they prepared to embark on a whirlwind journey through twists, turns, and exhilarating drops. The roller coasters carried them through loops and twists, their laughter mingling with the screams of joy around them.

As the ride soared through the air, laughter bubbled from their lips, carried away by the wind. They screamed with a mixture of fear and delight, their hearts pounding in unison. In that moment, it was as if time stood still, and there was only Nicolas, Olivia, and the electric pulse of their shared experience.

When the roller coaster came to a stop, Nicolas and Olivia stumbled out of their seats, their faces flushed and their bodies tingling with adrenaline. They exchanged exhilarated glances, their eyes reflecting the sheer euphoria of the moment.

"Wow, that was incredible!" Olivia exclaimed, her voice brimming with excitement.

Nicolas smiled, feeling a surge of exhilaration coursing through his veins. "It was indeed," he agreed. "But you know what's even more incredible?"

Olivia raised an eyebrow, curiosity lighting up her features. "What?"

Nicolas took a step closer, his eyes locked with hers.

"The way you light up with joy, Olivia. The way your laughter echoes in my heart. It's the most incredible thing I've ever experienced."

With flushed cheeks and adrenaline still coursing through their veins, Nicolas and Olivia wandered over to the row of colorful carnival games. The air was filled with cheerful music, the excited chatter of participants, and the clatter of prizes being won and displayed with pride.

Olivia's eyes sparkled with determination as she eyed a ring toss game. "I've always wanted to win one of those big stuffed animals," she admitted.

Nicolas grinned, captivated by her enthusiasm. "Well, today is the day we make that dream come true," he declared, his voice brimming with playful determination.

They approached the booth, where a friendly carnival worker greeted them. Nicolas handed over the tokens, and the worker explained the rules of the game. Olivia positioned herself, the rings clutched in her hand, ready to test her aim and precision.

With a flick of her wrist, Olivia sent the first ring soaring through the air. It twirled and spun before landing on one of the pegs, earning her a small prize. Her smile widened, fueling her determination to conquer the challenge.

Nicolas watched in awe as Olivia's determination grew with each throw. Her focus was unwavering, her eyes fixed on the target. The crowd around them seemed to fade into the background as she entered a zone of pure determination and focus.

As the final ring left her hand, time seemed to slow down. It soared through the air, its trajectory taking on a magical quality. The crowd held its breath, waiting in anticipation. And then, with a resounding clink, the ring found its mark, landing perfectly around the peg.

Cheers erupted from the crowd, mingling with Olivia's exclamation of joy. She turned to Nicolas, her eyes shining with triumph. "I did it!" she exclaimed.

Nicolas could not help but be swept up in her contagious joy. He embraced her tightly, spinning her around in a joyous twirl. "I knew you could do it," he whispered, his voice filled with admiration.

As the carnival worker handed Olivia a large, fluffy panda bear, Nicolas could not help but be filled with a sense of awe and gratitude. It was not just a stuffed animal; it was a symbol of their shared victory and the memories they were creating together.

Olivia held the panda bear close to her chest, a wide smile gracing her lips. "This will always remind me of this day," she said, her voice soft with emotion.

Nicolas leaned in, his lips brushing against Olivia's ear. "And it will remind me of you and the way you bring joy into my life," he whispered, his voice filled with love.

Their fingers intertwined as they continued their exploration of the amusement park, the oversized teddy bear acting as a witness to their laughter, stolen kisses, and whispered promises. With each step they took, their connection deepened, their love blossoming amidst the vibrant backdrop of the carnival.

As the sun began to set, casting a golden glow over the park, they found themselves on a Ferris wheel. The cool evening breeze tousled their hair as they shared a cozy gondola, their gazes locked as they ascended to new heights. The adrenaline-fueled rush had settled, leaving behind a sense of contentment and an unspoken understanding.

"Today has been magical," Olivia murmured, her voice barely above a whisper.

Nicolas gently brushed his thumb against her cheek, his eyes overflowing with tenderness. "And it's only the beginning," he whispered back, his voice carrying a promise of endless adventures and a future filled with love.

Olivia leaned her head against Nicolas's shoulder as he put his arm around her. "Thank you for making my dream come true," she said, her words filled with gratitude. "This day, this adventure, is something I'll cherish forever."

Nicolas tightened his grip around her, his heart overflowing with joy. "Olivia, every moment spent with you is an unforgettable memory for me," he confessed, his voice filled with sincerity.

As they sat there on top of the Ferris wheel, basking in the glow of the amusement park's lights, Nicolas and Olivia knew that their time in Los Angeles would be an unforgettable chapter in their love story. They gazed into each other's eyes with a sense of excitement and adventure that permeated the air. With their hearts intertwined and the world at their feet, the possibilities stretched out before them. A blank canvas waiting to be painted with their love and shared experiences.

***

CHAPTER 6:

A SECRET HABIT

As the sun began to set on their memorable weekend, Nicolas and Olivia found themselves standing at the entrance of Olivia's apartment building, their hands tightly clasped together. The bittersweet reality of their impending separation hung in the air, casting a shadow over their otherwise radiant smiles.

Olivia's eyes glistened with sadness as she looked up at Nicolas. "I don't want this weekend to end," she confessed, her voice laced with a tinge of longing.

Nicolas brought her hand to his lips, pressing a gentle kiss against her knuckles. "Neither do I, my love," he whispered, his voice filled with genuine regret. "But duty calls, and I must return to Creudor."

Olivia nodded; her gaze filled with understanding. She knew the weight of his responsibilities and the obligations that came with his royal status. Their love was a delicate dance, one that required them to navigate the realms of duty and passion.

"But we'll be together again soon," Nicolas reassured her, his voice filled with determination. "I promise."

Tears welled up in Olivia's eyes as she leaned in, resting her forehead against Nicolas's. "I'll hold you to that promise," she whispered, her voice barely above a breath.

Nicolas cupped her face in his hands, his eyes searching hers with unwavering sincerity. "You are my everything, Olivia," he declared, his voice filled with unwavering devotion. "No distance or time can dim the love I have for you."

They stood in a tender embrace, their hearts beating in sync, neither wanting to let go. Time seemed to stand still as they soaked in the precious moments they had left together. But as the last rays of sunlight disappeared behind the horizon, Nicolas knew he had to begin his journey back to Creudor.

Reluctantly, Nicolas pulled away, his hands lingering on Olivia's shoulders. "Until we meet again," he murmured, his voice filled with a mixture of love and sadness.

Olivia nodded; her voice filled with unspoken emotions. "Safe travels, my prince," she whispered softly.

With one final, lingering look, Nicolas turned and began to walk away, his heart heavy with the ache of separation. But with every step he took, he carried with him the memories of their time together, the warmth of Olivia's touch, and the promise of a future where they could be together without constraints.

As Nicolas settled back into his royal duties in Creudor, the weight of his responsibilities seemed to multiply. Days filled with endless engagements, meetings, and public appearances left him with little time to spare. Despite the demands of his position, his thoughts never strayed far from Olivia, their time together etched in his heart and mind.

During the rare moments of respite, Nicolas would steal away to a quiet corner of the palace, his phone clutched tightly in his hand. He longed to hear Olivia's voice, to see her radiant smile through the screen of his phone, but the demands of his position often rendered those desires unattainable.

However, as Nicolas tried to reach out to Olivia, he found himself met with silence. Each call went unanswered, and his messages lingered without response. Doubt began to creep into his mind, like a whispering shadow casting a pall over his once-optimistic heart.

Restless nights turned into days filled with unease. Nicolas questioned the distance that seemed to grow between them, his imagination conjuring up a multitude of scenarios. Was she losing interest? Had he done something wrong? The doubts gnawed at him, feeding his fears and leaving him feeling vulnerable and uncertain.

With a longing in his heart, he dialed her number and waited, the sound of the ringing echoing in the stillness of the night. Finally, Olivia's surprised voice came through the line.

"Nicolas! It's been so long since we've talked," she

exclaimed, her voice brimming with warmth.

Nicolas couldn't help but smile at the sound of her voice. "I've missed you, my love," he confessed, his voice tinged with longing. "The demands of my duties have consumed my days, leaving me with little time to even think."

Olivia's understanding voice soothed his weary soul. "I know, Nicolas. Your position carries great responsibilities, and I admire your dedication," she said, her words filled with unwavering support. "But I miss you too, and it's hard not having you by my side."

Nicolas's heart ached with the knowledge of how their separation affected Olivia. He longed to hold her, to assure her of his love, but distance stood as an unwelcome barrier.

"I promise, Olivia, that once this wave of engagements subsides, I will make every effort to be there for you," Nicolas vowed, his voice filled with determination. "Our love will endure this challenging time, and we will be stronger for it."

Olivia's voice carried a hint of sadness. "I believe in us, Nicolas," she said softly. "But it's difficult not having you here, not being able to share our lives together."

Nicolas's grip on the phone tightened. He could feel the weight of their separation pressing upon him, urging him to find a way to bridge the distance between them.

"I feel the same, Olivia," he whispered, his voice filled

with sincerity. "Please know that even though my days may be consumed by my duties, my heart belongs to you. You are my constant source of inspiration and strength."

Each passing day brought with it a deep longing to hear her voice and feel her presence, but their conversations became infrequent, reduced to fleeting texts exchanged between his packed schedule. Nicolas would anxiously check his phone, waiting for a reply that seemed to take longer and longer to arrive. Every unanswered message and delayed response stirred a storm of doubts in his mind, fueling his fears of growing apart from the woman who held his heart. Doubts began to creep into his mind, and a sense of unease settled within him.

One evening, as the weight of his responsibilities threatened to suffocate him, Nicolas sought solace in the company of his brother, Freddie. The two siblings had always shared a close bond, finding comfort in each other's presence during times of triumph and hardship.

Nicolas found Freddie in the grand library of the palace, perusing through old volumes of history. He approached his brother, his expression a mixture of frustration and longing. "Freddie," he called out, his voice tinged with a hint of desperation.

Freddie turned, his eyes meeting Nicolas's troubled gaze. "What's the matter, brother?" he asked, concern etched on his face.

Nicolas let out a heavy sigh, his shoulders slumping

with the weight of his emotions. "It's Olivia," he confessed. "We hardly have time to talk anymore, and when we do, her replies are delayed. I feel like we're drifting apart."

Freddie's brow furrowed, and he set aside the book he had been holding. He approached Nicolas, placing a comforting hand on his shoulder. "Nicolas, you have to understand that being a prince comes with its sacrifices," he began, his voice gentle yet firm. "Sometimes, the demands of our position force us to prioritize our duties over personal matters."

Nicolas's eyes filled with shades of disappointment and defiance. "But Freddie, she's the love of my life," he protested, his voice filled with a deep longing. "I can't just let her slip away."

Freddie regarded his brother with a mixture of sympathy and pragmatism. "Sometimes, love alone isn't enough," he replied, his voice tinged with a touch of sadness. "You have to consider if the sacrifices you're making are worth it, if the relationship can withstand the challenges that come with your position."

Nicolas's frustration turned to anger, his voice rising in protest. "I won't give up on her, Freddie," he declared, his eyes filled with determination. "She's worth every sacrifice, every challenge."

Freddie's gaze softened, and he took a step closer to Nicolas. "I understand your feelings, brother," he said, his voice laced with empathy. "But it's important to be realistic. Love alone can't always conquer all."

Nicolas's fists clenched at his sides, his emotions simmering beneath the surface. "I refuse to believe that," he muttered, his voice filled with defiance

With a heavy heart, Nicolas turned and walked away, leaving Freddie standing in the grand library. Nicolas retreated to his private chamber, his heart heavy with disappointment and confusion. He reached for his phone, hoping to connect with Olivia and find solace in their conversation, but a sinking feeling settled in his chest as he heard her tone on the other end of the line.

"Nicolas, it's been too long," Olivia's voice resonated with longing. "I've missed you."

A smile tugged at the corners of Nicolas's lips as he responded, his voice filled with sincerity. "I've missed you too, my love. I'm sorry for the distance that has grown between us, but I'm determined to change that."

Olivia let out a sigh, her tone distant. "That's sweet, Nicolas," she said, her voice lacking the usual affection.

Nicolas's heart sank at the sound of her voice, sensing the distance that had settled between them. "Olivia, it's been so long since we had a proper conversation," he began, his voice filled with genuine concern. "How have you been?"

There was a brief pause on the other end of the line, and when Olivia finally spoke, her words were tinged with a vague sense of distraction. "I've been busy,

Nicolas," she replied, her voice lacking its usual enthusiasm. "Work has been demanding, and I've been caught up with other commitments."

Nicolas could sense the strain in her words, the thinly veiled excuse that she used to justify their lack of communication. His heart ached, and he struggled to find the right words to express his emotions. "Olivia, I understand that life gets busy," he said, his voice laced with disappointment. "But we need to make time for each other. We can't let our connection slip away."

There was a long pause on the other end of the line, and Nicolas's heart raced with anticipation as he waited for Olivia's response. Finally, she let out a sigh, her voice distant. "Nicolas, I'm sorry. I really am," she murmured, her words heavy with uncertainty. "Listen, I have to go. There's this party I need to attend. We'll catch up later, okay?"

Nicolas felt a lump form in his throat, a wave of confusion and sadness welled up inside him. "Party?" he repeated, his voice barely above a whisper. "Olivia, what do you mean? Is something wrong?"

Olivia hesitated for a moment; her voice filled with a hint of regret. "I can't explain it right now," she replied evasively.

A wave of confusion washed over Nicolas, his mind racing to grasp the sudden change in Olivia's demeanor. "Sure, Olivia," he replied, his voice tinged with disappointment. "Take care and have fun at the party."

With that, Olivia bid a hasty goodbye, ending the phone call abruptly, leaving Nicolas with a whole lot of frustration and concern. He sat there, staring at his phone, feeling a sense of emptiness settle upon him. He could not help but wonder what had caused this sudden shift in their dynamic. Had he done something wrong? Was there something bothering her that she hadn't shared?

Nicolas paced back and forth in his chamber, his thoughts consumed by questions and doubts. He desperately wanted to reach out to Olivia, to understand what had changed between them, but he knew he had to give her space.

As the minutes turned into hours, Nicolas found himself lost in a sea of unanswered questions and unspoken fears. He could not shake the feeling that he had lost something precious. Days turned into weeks, and Nicolas found himself caught in a web of uncertainty. He longed for the deep connection he and Olivia once shared, but their conversations became shorter and more strained. The gap between them seemed to widen with each passing day, and Nicolas felt a sense of helplessness wash over him.

***

Back in her Los Angeles apartment, Olivia stood in front of her lavish dressing room mirror, carefully examining her reflection. Her eyes were bloodshot from another sleepless night. The bright lights that had once brought her joy now served as harsh reminders of her hidden struggle. Her once radiant smile now appeared forced, her eyes filled with uncertainty. The allure of her fame seemed to fade in comparison to the void she felt inside. She wondered if Nicolas would still love her if he saw the broken pieces she tried so desperately to hide.

Her hand trembled as she reached for a small vial tucked away in a drawer, her heart pounding with a mixture of anticipation and fear.

"Just one more," she whispered to herself, the voice of addiction urging her on. But deep down, she knew it was never just one. It was a slippery slope that threatened to consume her.

That night, Olivia attended a glamorous fashion show event. The flashbulbs blinded her as she stepped onto the red carpet, the cameras capturing her every move. She forced a smile, but deep down, the anxiety gnawed at her.

As the night progressed, Olivia found herself surrounded by a sea of familiar faces, each one a reminder of the relentless competition she faced. The weight of expectations became unbearable, and the allure of escape whispered in her ear. Feeling suffocated by the glamorous facade she had built, Olivia discreetly slipped away from the crowd. In a dimly lit corner, she found solace in the company of an old acquaintance, Vanessa, known for her wild party lifestyle.

"Olivia, darling, I haven't seen you in ages!" Vanessa exclaimed; her voice tinged with excitement. "You look like you could use a little fun. Let's live a little, shall we?"

Olivia hesitated for a moment, her mind waging a war between responsibility and desire. She yearned for a temporary reprieve, a momentary escape from the pressures that weighed her down. Giving in to the allure of the night, Olivia nodded and followed Vanessa into a world of decadence and indulgence.

Days turned into nights, and Olivia's indulgence in alcohol and drugs escalated. She sought solace in the temporary oblivion they provided, numbing her insecurities and fears. Days turned into nights, and Olivia found herself caught in a relentless cycle of addiction and self-doubt. The glitz and glamour of the red carpet masked the shadows that loomed over her. She would hide her struggles during the day, putting on a brave face for the world, and then retreat to the solitude of her private sanctuary, where the demons of her addiction awaited.

Her heart ached with the weight of her secret, the fear of losing everything she had worked so hard for. But as her relationship with Nicolas grew deeper, she found herself longing for his understanding and acceptance. She knew that keeping her struggles hidden was a barrier to true intimacy, and she yearned to break down those walls.

Nicolas was the one person who saw beyond the glamorous façade and reached into the depths of her soul. But would he still look at her with the same adoration if he knew the darkness that resided within?

Days turned into weeks, and Nicolas dedicated himself to his royal duties, focusing on the responsibilities that came with his position. But his thoughts and hopes remained intertwined with Olivia, a flame that flickered but refused to be extinguished.

Just when he had resigned himself to the idea that their love might have faded away, his phone rang, interrupting his train of thought. His heart skipped a beat as he read Olivia's name flashing across the screen. With trembling hands, he answered the call, his voice filled with a mixture of relief and anticipation.

"Olivia, it's you," Nicolas breathed, his voice betraying his emotions.

There was a moment of hesitation on the other end of the line, followed by a soft sigh. "Nicolas, I'm so sorry for my absence," Olivia spoke, her voice tinged with regret. "I miss you. I miss us."

Nicolas listened intently, his heart yearning for an explanation, for the reassurance that their love was still intact.

"But please know, my love, that my feelings for you have never wavered," Olivia continued, her voice filled with sincerity. "I have missed you more than words can express."

Relief washed over Nicolas, his doubts dissipating like morning mist. "Olivia, I've missed you too," he confessed, his voice filled with sincerity. "I've realized how much you mean to me. I want to give us another chance, to work through whatever challenges we face together."

Olivia's voice trembled slightly as she responded. "I've been reflecting on our relationship, Nicolas," she admitted. "And I've come to the same conclusion. I don't want to give up on us either."

A surge of excitement and determination coursed through Nicolas's veins. "Olivia, I want to come and visit you," he declared, his voice brimming with certainty. "I want to see you, to hold you in my arms again. We need to talk, to reconnect."

There was a brief pause on the line, and Nicolas held his breath, anxiously awaiting Olivia's response. Finally, her voice came through, "I would love that, Nicolas," she replied, her voice carrying a newfound hope. "I want to see you too. Let's find a way to make it work."

Nicolas's heart soared at her words. He quickly began to make arrangements, determined to bridge the physical distance between them. "Olivia, I'll make the necessary arrangements to come and visit you," he assured her, his voice filled with determination. "I want to make things right, to remind you of the love we share."

Olivia's tone softened; her voice now filled with genuine affection. "If you're willing to do that, then I'm willing to give us another chance. I believe in us, Nicolas."

Relief washed over Nicolas, a renewed sense of hope flooding his heart. "Thank you, Olivia. I promise you won't regret this decision. I will do everything in my power to make you feel loved and cherished."

As their conversation continued, the air between them lightened, the weight of their previous miscommunications dissipating. Nicolas shared his plans for his upcoming visit, eager to make every moment count. Olivia, in turn, expressed her excitement, her voice brimming with anticipation. She tries her best to keep her addiction under wraps, fearing that it would destroy the growing connection between her and Nicolas. But it becomes increasingly difficult to hide her struggles as she and Nicolas spend more time together.

***

The setting sun cast a warm, golden glow over the beach, painting the sky with hues of pink and orange. Nicolas and Olivia sat side by side, their fingers intertwined, as they watched the waves crash against the shore. The tranquility of the moment was punctuated by the sounds of seagulls calling overhead and the gentle rustle of the ocean breeze.

As the colors of the sky deepened, Nicolas could not help but notice the change in Olivia's demeanor. Her usually radiant smile had faded, replaced by a hint of sadness that lingered in her eyes. Concern etched his features as he turned towards her, his voice filled with gentle concern. "What's going on, Liv?" he asked softly, his hand reaching out to touch her cheek. "You seem distant lately."

Olivia's breath hitched, and for a moment, she hesitated, uncertain whether to reveal the turmoil that had been brewing within her. The weight of her thoughts and emotions had become too heavy to bear in silence. With a deep sigh, she looked into Nicolas's eyes, finding solace in his unwavering gaze. "I... I am good," she stammered, her voice barely above a whisper. "Just tired."

As Olivia watched the waves crashing along the shoreline, a battle waged within her mind. Thoughts of her addiction consumed her, gnawing at her conscience and urging her to reveal the truth to Nicolas. The weight of her secret pressed heavily on her chest, making it difficult to breathe. She longed to confide in him, to seek his understanding and support, but the fear of rejection held her back.

Her gaze shifted from the tumultuous ocean to the man beside her, Nicolas, who had become her anchor in this stormy sea of emotions. Memories of their laughter, their shared dreams, and the tender moments they had cherished together flooded her thoughts, intensifying the conflict within her. How could she risk losing the love they had cultivated, the bond they had forged?

A knot formed in Olivia's throat as she wrestled with her inner turmoil. The temptation to keep her addiction hidden, to maintain the façade of normalcy, grew stronger with each passing moment. She took a deep breath, trying to steady herself, but the words remained trapped within her, suffocating her with their weight.

In an attempt to numb the pain and quiet the racing thoughts, Olivia ordered one too many drinks during dinner. The alcohol slid down her throat, providing a temporary escape from the torment within. With each sip, her anxieties faded, replaced by a hazy numbness that clouded her judgment.

Nicolas observed Olivia's change in demeanor with growing concern. His brows furrowed, and he reached across the table, gently touching her hand, his voice filled with worry. "Olivia, are you okay? You've had enough to drink," he said, his tone tinged with both care and caution.

Olivia's eyes, glazed and distant, flickered with a tint of vulnerability. She withdrew her hand from his grasp, a flicker of frustration crossing her face. "I'm fine, Nicolas," she replied, her voice laced with bitterness. "Just let me enjoy myself."

Nicolas sighed, recognizing that pressing the issue further in that moment would only lead to resistance. He understood that Olivia needed space to confront her own demons, but he made a silent promise to himself to address the situation once they were away from the prying eyes of the restaurant.

As the night grew darker, the once idyllic beach

transformed into a hauntingly beautiful landscape. Olivia's steps faltered; her coordination impaired by the effects of alcohol. She stumbled over the sand, her attempts to regain her balance proving futile.

Concern etched across his face, Nicolas hurried to her side, wrapping his arms around her to steady her. "Olivia, let me help you. You're in no condition to walk," he insisted.

Olivia's resolve began to crumble as tears mingled with the salty breeze. She buried her face in Nicolas's chest, her sobs muffled. "I'm sorry, Nicolas," she sobbed, her words slurred. "I didn't want you to see me like this."

Nicolas held Olivia close, his heart aching at the sight of her pain. His love for her remained steadfast, unwavering despite the cracks that had begun to appear in their journey. He gently stroked her hair, his voice filled with understanding and compassion. "Olivia, it's okay," he whispered. "We all have our struggles. What's important is that we face them together."

With gentle determination, Nicolas guided Olivia to the waiting taxi, his hand securely wrapped around hers, providing both physical and emotional support. The car ride was filled with a heavy silence, punctuated only by the occasional sniffle from Olivia, her tears still streaming down her face.

As they arrived at Olivia's apartment building, Nicolas paid the driver and carefully helped Olivia out of the car, his touch gentle yet firm. They walked slowly towards the entrance, Olivia's steps unsteady and her body weighed down by the burden she carried. Each footfall seemed to echo with the weight of her struggles, while Nicolas stood beside her, unwavering in his support.

Once inside her apartment, Nicolas guided Olivia to the living room, a familiar space that had witnessed both their joy and their pain. They sank onto the couch, the cushions embracing them, and a comfortable silence settled around them. The room was bathed in the soft glow of a dimly lit lamp, casting a warm and intimate atmosphere.

Nicolas observed the subtle changes in Olivia, his gaze filled with empathy and concern. Her once vibrant spirit had dimmed, replaced by a hollowness that he could not ignore. He reached out and tenderly brushed a strand of hair away from her face, his touch a gesture of both comfort and understanding.

Olivia's eyes met his, the depths of her pain mirrored in their depths. She felt the weight of her secrets bearing down on her, the fear of rejection gnawing at her heart. She wanted to speak, to let the truth spill from her lips, but the fear held her captive, imprisoning her in a web of silence.

"Olivia, we need to talk," Nicolas said gently, his voice filled with concern as they sat on the couch, their surroundings bathed in the soft glow of the evening. "I've noticed a shift in you lately. You seem distant, lost. Is everything okay?"

Olivia's heart sank as she faced Nicolas, the guilt and shame etched on her face. She had never intended to hurt him, but she had unwittingly allowed her personal demons to infiltrate their once-idyllic love affair. She took a shaky breath, her voice tinged with sorrow. "Nicolas, I'm so sorry," Olivia whispered, tears welling in her eyes. "I've been struggling. The pressures of my career, the constant scrutiny—it's all become too much. I thought I could handle it, but I've let it consume me."

Nicolas reached out, his hand gently resting on Olivia's, a silent reassurance of his support. "Olivia, you don't have to carry this burden alone," he said, his voice filled with empathy. "I care about you deeply, and I want to be here for you. Let's face this together."

Olivia fidgeted with her hands; her gaze fixated on the floor. She knew the time had come to reveal her hidden struggles, to let Nicolas see the depths of her vulnerability. Taking a deep breath, she looked up, her eyes meeting Nicolas's. "There's something I need to tell you," she began, her voice quivering. "I... I have been battling with addiction, Nicolas. Drugs and alcohol have been my demons for far too long."

The weight of Olivia's confession hung in the air, a fragile moment of truth that could either fracture or fortify their connection. Nicolas's expression softened as he absorbed her words, his eyes reflecting a mixture of understanding and unwavering support. "Olivia, I won't pretend to understand what you're going through, but I want to be here for you," he said, his voice filled with empathy. "I care about you, and I don't want you to face this alone. Let me help you."

Olivia looked into Nicolas's eyes, her heart torn between gratitude and fear. The weight of her secret had consumed her for far too long, and the realization that Nicolas was offering a lifeline stirred a flicker of hope within her. Her tears fell freely now, her voice a raw plea. "Please, Nicolas. Help me."

The walls she had built around her heart began to crumble, revealing the raw vulnerability that lay within. As Olivia shared her deepest fears and insecurities, the weight that had burdened her for so long lifted ever so slightly, replaced by a newfound sense of relief.

"I've been afraid, Nicolas," she admitted, her voice barely above a whisper. "Afraid that if you knew the truth, you would turn away, that my flaws would overshadow everything we have together."

Nicolas, his eyes filled with tenderness, reached for her trembling hands. He squeezed them gently, his touch offering solace and reassurance. "Olivia, love isn't about perfection," he said, his voice filled with conviction. "It's about acceptance, understanding, and supporting each other through the darkest of times. You are more than your struggles, and I believe in you."

Olivia's heart swelled with relief. She had kept her addiction hidden for so long, fearing judgment and rejection. But in Nicolas's unwavering support, she found the courage to face her demons head-on. She allowed herself to be vulnerable in his presence, knowing that his love was a sanctuary she could rely on.

Nicolas held Olivia tightly, his arms providing a safe haven amidst the storm. "Olivia, I admire your courage in opening up to me," he whispered, his voice filled with compassion. "I want you to know that I'm here for you, every step of the way. We'll face this together."

Olivia's eyes welled up with tears, a mixture of gratitude and vulnerability. "Nicolas, I've been battling this alone for so long," she confessed, her voice laced with a hint of exhaustion. "The fear of being judged, of losing everything... it's been suffocating. But with you by my side, I feel there's still hope."

Nicolas gently stroked her hair, his touch soothing her troubled mind. "You don't have to face this alone anymore, Olivia," he reassured her. "We'll find the support you need. There are resources, professionals who can guide us through this journey. And I'll be right here, holding your hand through it all."

Olivia's heart swelled with gratitude as Nicolas's words washed over her like a soothing balm. She took a deep breath, allowing his reassurances to seep into her being, dispelling the lingering doubts that had haunted her for so long.

"You're right," she whispered. "I won't let my past define me. I will find the strength to heal and grow. I promise you that."

Nicolas leaned forward, capturing her gaze with his

steady, unwavering eyes. "I believe in you, Olivia. You are so much more than your past. You're resilient, courageous, and filled with endless potential. And I believe that our love is strong enough to withstand anything."

As their lips met in a tender, affirming kiss, Olivia felt a surge of hope and renewed purpose. The darkness that had shrouded her addiction was slowly dissipating, replaced by a newfound light that emanated from within.

***

CHAPTER 7:

MEMORIES OF LOVE

Overnight, Nicolas had made a secret arrangement, leveraging his influence and connections, to secure a stay at a secluded private rehab center for Olivia. He wanted her to have the best possible environment for her recovery, away from the prying eyes of the public and the pressures of her career. It was a gesture born out of love and a deep desire to protect her.

Olivia woke up in a daze, her mind struggling to grasp the reality of the situation. It took a moment for her to realize that Nicolas was gently washing her face, his touch tender and comforting. Her head spun with confusion and a lingering sense of disorientation.

"Nicolas?" she murmured; her voice barely audible.

He looked at her with a mixture of concern and determination. "It's time, Olivia," he said softly, his voice filled with compassion. "I've arranged everything. We need to get you to the rehab center."

Olivia blinked, trying to process his words. She saw the clothes he had laid out for her, neatly folded on the bed. She felt herself being vulnerable at his care and attention to every detail.

"I... I don't understand," she stammered, her voice still tinged with grogginess. "How... how did you...?"

Nicolas offered a small, reassuring smile as he helped her sit up. "I planned all of this, Olivia," he explained, his voice steady and soothing. "I wanted to give you the best chance at recovery, away from prying eyes and distractions. I've arranged for a car to take you to the rehab center. You'll be safe there."

Olivia's heart swelled with many emotions—gratitude, disbelief, and a flicker of fear. She looked at Nicolas, her eyes searching his face for answers. "But why, Nicolas? Why are you doing all of this for me?"

He reached out, taking her trembling hands in his. "Because I need you, Olivia," he said, his voice unwavering. "I want to see you heal, to support you through this journey. You deserve a chance to reclaim your life, and I want to be there for you every step of the way."

A tear rolled down Olivia's cheek as his words sank in. She felt overwhelmed by the depth of his love and the selflessness of his actions. It was in this moment that she realized just how much she meant to him, and she made a silent vow to herself to fight for her recovery— for him and for herself.

As the night wore on, Nicolas helped Olivia get dressed, carefully selecting comfortable clothes that would accompany her on this transformative journey. He packed a bag with essentials—a journal, a few cherished photographs, and meaningful mementos. His touch was gentle, his movements deliberate, as if he were handling something fragile yet precious.

The car arrived silently in the dead of the night, its headlights casting a soft glow in the darkness. Nicolas guided Olivia outside, holding her steady as she took her first steps towards her path to healing. The cool night air caressed her face, filling her lungs with a renewed sense of purpose.

As the car door closed behind her, Olivia glanced back at Nicolas, a mixture of gratitude and apprehension in her eyes. "Thank you, Nicolas," she whispered, her voice choked with emotion. "For everything."

He offered her a reassuring smile, his love shining through his gaze. "Take care, Olivia," he replied, his voice filled with tenderness. "I'll be here, waiting for you when you're ready to come back to me."

With that, the car pulled away, carrying Olivia into the unknown—a journey of self-discovery, healing, and hope. And as she looked out into the night, she clung to the belief that with Nicolas's unwavering love and support, she would emerge from the darkness, stronger and ready to reclaim her life.

As she stood outside the entrance of the rehab center, Olivia's heart raced with nervousness. She took a deep breath, mustering the strength to face the unknown. Once inside, Olivia was guided through the intake process, her emotions a whirlwind of anticipation, fear, and determination. The rehab center exuded a sense of tranquility, its walls adorned with calming artwork and the faint scent of lavender lingering in the air. She was led to her room, a cozy space with neutral tones and a comfortable bed, where she would begin her healing journey.

As she settled in, Olivia's phone buzzed with a text notification. It was from Nicolas, a simple message that warmed her heart amidst the uncertainty.

'You're stronger than you know. I believe in you, Liv. Take all the time you need. I'll be here waiting. Love, Nicolas.'

Tears welled up in Olivia's eyes as she read his words, a reminder of the love and support she had found in him.

She replied with a heartfelt message, expressing her gratitude and promising to give her all in her recovery.

She crafted a carefully worded message to her assistant, Justin.

'Hey, Justin. I wanted to let you know that I'll be taking a few personal days off. I need some time for myself, away from work and the spotlight. It's important for my well-being, and I hope you understand. I'll be in touch soon. Take care.'

As she hit send, Olivia could not help but feel a pang of guilt. She valued Justin's loyalty and support, and keeping him in the dark about her true situation weighed heavily on her. But she knew that she needed this time away, away from the demands of her career, to focus on her healing and rediscover herself.

***

The first day at the rehab center was a challenging experience for Olivia, as she grappled with the physical and emotional effects of withdrawal. As the morning sun filtered through her room's curtains, she rose from her bed, her body feeling heavy and fatigued.

Olivia, now known as Avila Consilio, dressed in the provided plain, comfortable clothing, her glamorous attire a distant memory. Her once lustrous hair hung loosely around her shoulders, devoid of the perfect curls and impeccable styling that had become her trademark. Without her usual makeup, her face bore the rawness and vulnerability of her journey towards recovery.

Stepping into the common area, Olivia joined the other residents, who were deep in their own battles, each with their own story to tell. The staff, unaware of her true identity, referred to her as Ms. Consilio, treating her with the same compassion and respect accorded to everyone else.

The day began with group therapy sessions, where Olivia found solace in sharing her struggles and listening to others' stories. The room echoed with pain, resilience, and hope, as they forged connections, forming a support network within the walls of the rehab center.

As Olivia settled into the group therapy session, she found herself surrounded by a diverse group of individuals, all united in their quest for recovery. The room was filled with a mix of emotions—tears, laughter, and raw vulnerability. It was a safe space where their stories could be shared without judgment or shame.

Sitting in a circle, each person took turns opening up about their experiences, their battles with addiction, and the hurdles they had faced along the way. Olivia listened attentively, her heart growing heavy with empathy as she heard their tales of pain, loss, and resilience.

One by one, the residents bared their souls, revealing the deep-rooted wounds that had led them down the path of addiction. Olivia felt a sense of connection, realizing that although their stories were different, they shared a common thread of pain and a shared desire for healing.

When it was Olivia's turn, she took a deep breath, her voice steady yet laced with vulnerability. "My name is Avila, and I've been battling addiction for far too long," she began, using her adopted name. "Drugs and alcohol became a way for me to escape, to numb the pain that was eating away at my soul."

As Olivia shared her struggles, she felt a weight lift off her shoulders. The honesty in her words reverberated throughout the room, resonating with those who had also experienced the grip of addiction. The residents nodded in understanding, their eyes filled with empathy and support.

Throughout the session, Olivia found solace in the shared experiences and the empathy she received from the group. She realized that they were all on a journey toward recovery, each at different stages but united in their determination to reclaim their lives.

As the day wore on, Olivia encountered the physical symptoms of withdrawal. Waves of nausea and intense cravings tested her resolve, threatening to derail her progress. But with the guidance of the medical team and the unwavering support of her fellow residents, she persevered.

In the afternoon, Olivia attended individual counseling sessions, delving into the deep-seated issues that had led her down the path of addiction. She confronted the traumas and insecurities that had haunted her, gradually unraveling the layers that masked her true self. With each session, she gained a clearer understanding of her triggers and developed strategies to overcome them.

Throughout the day, Olivia engaged in therapeutic activities such as art therapy and meditation. Through painting, she expressed her emotions, allowing the strokes of the brush to convey what words sometimes failed to articulate. In meditation, she found moments of tranquility, grounding herself in the present and nurturing her inner strength.

In the evening, Olivia retreated to her room, exhaustion seeping into her bones. She lay on her bed, staring at the ceiling, her mind swirling with thoughts. Doubts and fears crept in, but she reminded herself of the purpose that had brought her here, the desire for a life free from the clutches of addiction.

In the days that followed, Olivia remained committed to her recovery, attending therapy sessions, and leaning on her support network. Nicolas, true to his word, remained a pillar of strength and understanding. He encouraged her when she faltered, held her hand when the cravings threatened to overwhelm her. His love became the light that guided her through the darkest of nights.

As Olivia made progress in her recovery, she discovered a newfound sense of self-worth and resilience. She no longer defined herself solely by her addiction but by the strength she found within to overcome it. With each passing day, the withdrawal symptoms gradually subsided, replaced by a newfound clarity and resilience. She began to connect with her authentic self, stripped of the fame and the facades that had defined her public persona.

The staff and fellow residents saw Olivia, not as the famous actress Olivia Grey, but as Avila Consilio, a woman on a path to healing. They celebrated her small victories and offered support during her moments of weakness. Together, they navigated the complexities of recovery, reminding one another that they were more than their addictions.

Olivia's transformation became evident as she engaged in therapy and embraced the tools and coping mechanisms offered at the center. She discovered the strength within herself, untapped and waiting to be unleashed. With each passing day, she embraced the challenges, knowing that the road to recovery was a lifelong commitment.

As Olivia's time at the rehab center neared its end, she felt a bittersweet gratitude. The center had become her sanctuary, a cocoon where she had grown and found solace. But she also knew that the real test would begin once she stepped back into the outside world.

On her last day, Olivia stood among her fellow residents, a community forged in the crucible of recovery. They hugged and exchanged heartfelt goodbyes, promising to stay in touch and continue supporting each other beyond the confines of the rehab center.

With her bags packed and a renewed sense of purpose, Olivia walked out of the rehab center's doors, the sunlight warming her face. Nicolas stood waiting, a proud smile on his lips, unaware of the immense transformation that had taken place within her. With him were Olivia's loyal companions, Stella and Max, their tails wagging with excitement as they sensed their owner's return.

He had eagerly awaited the day when Olivia would complete her program, ready to embrace her as a stronger, transformed version of herself. And in the midst of it all, he made a silent promise to himself: to cherish and protect her, no matter what challenges lay ahead.

A smile spread across Nicolas's face as he took in the transformation that had taken place during her time in rehab. He noticed the subtle changes in her posture, the spark in her eyes, and the aura of resilience that surrounded her.

"Olivia!" Nicolas called out, his voice filled with warmth and love. Stella and Max tugged on their leashes, eager to greet their beloved owner.

Olivia's eyes lit up when she saw Nicolas standing there, his presence a soothing balm to her soul. She rushed forward, enveloping him in a tight embrace, tears of joy streaming down her face. "Nicolas, I missed you so much," she whispered, her voice filled with gratitude.

Nicolas held her close, his arms providing a safe haven amidst the tumult of emotions. "I missed you too, Olivia," he murmured, his voice filled with tenderness. "You've done incredible things, and I'm so proud of you."

As Stella and Max circled around them, their tails wagging uncontrollably, Olivia knelt down to greet her furry friends, showering them with affection. They barked with delight, their wagging tails a testament to their unconditional love for her.

As they made their way back to the car, Nicolas reached out to take Olivia's hand, their fingers entwined in a silent understanding. "Are you ready to go home?" he asked, his voice filled with love and support.

Olivia nodded, a sense of contentment washing over her. "Yes, I'm ready. I'm ready to embrace a new chapter in my life," she replied, her voice filled with determination.

With Stella and Max settled in the backseat, Olivia and Nicolas drove off, heading towards a future filled with hope and endless possibilities. As the wind tousled their hair, Olivia couldn't help but feel an overwhelming sense of gratitude for the unwavering love and support she had received from Nicolas and her furry companions.

They say that the journey of recovery is not one taken

alone, but with the support of loved ones. And as Olivia glanced at Nicolas, his hand on the steering wheel, she knew deep in her heart that their love was the anchor that would guide her through the challenges that lay ahead.

Together, they drove towards a sunset that painted the sky with hues of gold and pink, a symbol of the new beginnings that awaited Olivia and the infinite beauty that life had in store for her.

***

Nicolas could not contain his excitement as he drove Olivia, Stella, and Max to a private airfield. He had been planning this surprise for weeks, knowing how much Olivia deserved a celebration of her strength and resilience.

As they arrived at the airfield, Olivia's curiosity piqued. "Nicolas, what's going on? Where are we going?" she asked.

Nicolas smiled mischievously, his eyes sparkling with delight. "It's a surprise, Olivia. I've planned something special for you, something that will take your breath away," he replied, his voice filled with anticipation.

Olivia's heart raced with a combination of curiosity and wonder. She trusted Nicolas implicitly and knew that whatever he had in store for her would be incredible. She eagerly followed him as they boarded a luxurious private jet, the engines roaring to life as they prepared for takeoff.

As they soared through the skies, Olivia gazed out of the window, marveling at the breathtaking view below. The vast expanse of clouds stretched like cotton candy, and the sunlight danced on the plane's wings, painting a picture of freedom and possibility.

After a smooth and comfortable flight, the plane touched down on the runway of the island of Creudor, a hidden gem nestled in the azure waters of the Mediterranean. The island was known for its pristine beaches, charming villages, and breathtaking landscapes.

As Olivia stepped off the plane, a warm breeze enveloped her, carrying with it the scent of saltwater and adventure. Nicolas took her hand, leading her towards a waiting car that would take them to their private villa.

Driving through the picturesque streets, Olivia couldn't help but feel a sense of wonder and gratitude. She had come so far in her journey of recovery, and this trip was a testament to the love and support that surrounded her.

As they arrived at the private villa, Olivia's eyes widened in awe. The villa was a luxurious haven, overlooking the turquoise waters of the Mediterranean Sea. The lush gardens and sparkling pool beckoned, promising moments of tranquility and relaxation.

Nicolas opened the door, revealing the stunning view that awaited them. "Welcome to your sanctuary, Olivia," he said, his voice filled with tenderness. "This is your place to unwind, rejuvenate, and celebrate how far you've come."

Olivia's eyes welled up with tears as she took in the beauty that surrounded her. She turned to Nicolas; her voice filled with gratitude. "Thank you, Nicolas. This is beyond anything I could have imagined. I am so lucky to have you by my side."

Nicolas pulled her into a tight embrace, his love enveloping her like a warm embrace. "You deserve every bit of this, Olivia," he whispered, his voice filled with affection. "This trip is a celebration of your strength and a reminder that you are capable of anything."

As Olivia, Nicolas, Stella, and Max settled into the villa, they embarked on days filled with relaxation, exploration, and cherished moments. They spent their mornings strolling along the pristine beaches, their toes sinking into the soft sand, and their afternoons indulging in local cuisine, savoring the flavors of the island.

But just as Olivia blossomed in her newfound strength, Nicolas's own inner struggles became more apparent. The loss of his mother and the strained relationship with his family cast a shadow over his heart, one that he had concealed for far too long.

One evening, as they sat in the tranquil gardens of the royal estate, Olivia noticed the melancholy in Nicolas's eyes, the weight he carried upon his shoulders. She gently reached for his hand, intertwining her fingers with his.

"Nicolas," she began softly, "I can see that there's pain you're holding onto. You've been my rock throughout my journey, and now it's my turn to be there for you. Please, let me in. Share your burden with me."

Nicolas sighed; his gaze fixed on the horizon. "Olivia, my mother... she was taken from us too soon. Her absence has left an indelible mark on my soul. And the dynamics within my family... they are strained, to say the least. I've carried the weight of their expectations, the fear of disappointing them, for as long as I can remember."

Olivia squeezed his hand gently, her voice filled with empathy. "Nicolas, you don't have to face this alone. Just as you've stood by me, I'll stand by you. Together, we can create a space where you can heal and find peace."

Nicolas turned to her, gratitude and vulnerability etched upon his face. "Thank you, Olivia. It means the world to me to have your support. I've kept these emotions bottled up for far too long, afraid of burdening others. But with you, I feel safe."

Olivia smiled, her eyes filled with warmth and determination. "Nicolas, therapy has done wonders for me, and I truly believe it can do the same for you. It's not about burdening others; it's about allowing yourself the opportunity to heal and grow. You deserve that, my love."

Nicolas hesitated. "I've always been skeptical of therapy, Olivia," he admitted. "But seeing the transformation it has brought into your life, I'm willing to give it a try. I want to break free from these chains that have held me captive for so long."

Olivia's heart swelled with pride for Nicolas's willingness to embrace change. She knew that taking the first step could be daunting, but she also believed in his strength and resilience. "I'm here for you, every step of the way," she assured him.

With Olivia's unwavering support, Nicolas felt a glimmer of hope ignite within him. He knew that facing his inner demons would not be easy, but he also realized that the love they shared had the power to carry him through even the darkest of times.

Promising to embark on this new chapter together, Olivia and Nicolas held each other tightly, finding solace in the strength of their bond. They made a pact to prioritize their mental and emotional well-being, understanding that their personal growth would not only benefit themselves but also enrich their relationship.

On their last evening in Creudor, as they sat by the fireplace, the crackling embers casting a warm glow,

Olivia mustered the courage to voice her thoughts. "Nicolas, I love you."

Nicolas's eyes met hers, a gentle smile gracing his lips. "Olivia, I've loved you since the first day we've met. And I will love you forever."

As they sat there, lost in each other, the world outside faded away. For that moment in time, it was just the two of them, wrapped in the warmth of the fire and the comfort of their love.

Olivia reached out and took Nicolas's hand, her heart overflowing with love and gratitude. "Nicolas, being with you has shown me the many depths of love. You've been my rock, my guiding light, and I can't imagine my life without you."

Nicolas squeezed her hand, his eyes shimmering with emotion. "Olivia, you've taught me what it means to truly love and be loved. With you, I've discovered a depth of happiness I never thought possible. You are my everything."

In that intimate moment, time seemed to stand still. The crackling fire danced before them, its warmth mirroring the flicker of love that illuminated their souls. Their connection transcended words, as their hearts spoke volumes in the silent exchange of glances.

In the midst of the crackling flames, Olivia leaned in and gently kissed Nicolas's lips, the sweetness of their love lingering in the air. The touch of their lips ignited a fire within their souls, reminding them of the depth of their passion and the strength of their bond. As the night grew deeper, they remained nestled in each other's arms, relishing the serenity of the moment. The outside world could wait, for this night was theirs to savor—a celebration of their love and the infinite possibilities that lay ahead. They knew that tomorrow would bring new challenges, new adventures, but for now, they reveled in the beauty of the present—a moment etched in their hearts forever.

***

CHAPTER 8:

LOVE IS UNVEILED

Back in the bustling city of Los Angeles, Olivia delved back into the world of acting, finding solace and purpose in her craft. She threw herself into auditions, rehearsals, and long days on set, immersing herself in the lives of her characters. She threw herself into her acting work, determined to channel her emotions and experiences into her performances. With each script she delved into, she found solace and a sense of purpose, using her craft as a form of catharsis. The characters she portrayed became her vessels for expression, allowing her to explore the depths of human emotions and connect with her own inner journey.

However, amidst the glamour and excitement, Olivia could not help but carry a part of Creudor within her. Thoughts of Nicolas and their time together weighed on her mind, intertwining with her dedication to her work. She often found herself lost in moments of reflection, cherishing the memories of their shared laughter, intimate conversations, and the transformative love they had discovered in each other's arms.

Meanwhile, in the tranquil surroundings of Creudor, Nicolas embarked on a transformative journey of self-discovery through intensive therapy. In the safe and confidential space of his therapist's office, he unraveled the layers of his past, digging deep into the wounds that had shaped his life.

Nicolas sat across from his therapist, a small, cozy room providing a safe space for him to delve into the depths of his emotions. Dr. Jessica Oakley, a compassionate and attentive presence, listened intently, offering a supportive atmosphere for Nicolas to explore the wounds that had shaped his life. The air felt cold as he prepared to delve into one of the most significant wounds he carried—the death of his mother during childbirth. It was a pain that had shaped his entire life, but one he had rarely allowed himself to confront.

Dr. Oakley observed Nicolas with empathy, her gentle gaze encouraging him to open up. She knew the weight of this loss had always lingered within him, its impact far-reaching and profound.

Taking a deep breath, Nicolas began to speak, his voice trembling slightly with raw emotion. "Dr. Oakley, I've carried this deep sense of guilt and responsibility for my mother's passing. Growing up, I always felt like I was the reason she wasn't here with us. My family, they never directly blamed me, but I could sense it in their eyes, their distant treatment."

Dr. Oakley nodded, acknowledging the pain Nicolas had carried for so long. "It's common for individuals who experience the loss of a loved one at such a young age to internalize feelings of guilt, even when there is no rational basis for it. The mind tries to make sense of a tragedy, often seeking to assign blame or responsibility. But it's essential to remember that you were just a child,

Nicolas. You were not responsible for what happened."

Nicolas's shoulders relaxed slightly, his burden feeling a little lighter with each word spoken. "I've never really allowed myself to grieve properly, to confront the depth of my emotions surrounding my mother's death. I've spent my life trying to make up for her absence, trying to prove myself to my family. But it's exhausting, and it feels like I'm living a life that isn't truly mine."

Dr. Oakley offered a compassionate smile, her presence providing a safe space for Nicolas to open up. "Grief is a complex journey, Nicolas. It's natural to have a longing for what was lost and to want to honor your mother's memory. But it's also crucial to recognize that your own life deserves to be lived authentically. In order to find healing and happiness, we need to confront and process our emotions."

Nicolas nodded, the weight of his guilt and the burdensome expectations gradually loosening their grip on his heart. "I suppose I've been holding onto this pain and guilt for far too long. It's time for me to acknowledge that my mother's passing wasn't my fault and that I deserve to live a life that brings me joy and fulfillment."

Dr. Oakley leaned forward, her voice filled with warmth and encouragement. "Indeed, Nicolas. You have the right to forge your own path, independent of the past. By addressing these unresolved feelings, you can pave the way for healing, not just for yourself but also in your relationships with your loved ones."

Nicolas took a deep breath, a newfound determination shining in his eyes. "I want to break free from this cycle of guilt and self-doubt. I want to create a life that aligns with my true desires and values. I want to find peace within myself and foster healthier connections with my family."

Dr. Oakley smiled; pride evident in her expression. "That's a powerful declaration, Nicolas. It takes immense courage to confront our wounds and choose a different path. Through our work together, we will explore ways to support you in finding that peace and forging a life that reflects your authentic self."

In the intimate therapy sessions, Nicolas courageously confronted this painful truth, sharing the depths of his emotions with his therapist. He expressed the guilt that had gnawed at him, the belief that he was somehow to blame for his mother's tragic fate. The therapist listened attentively, providing a compassionate and nonjudgmental space for Nicolas to explore his feelings, fostering an environment where healing and self-acceptance could take root.

As the conversation deepened, Dr. Oakley gently guided Nicolas to explore the complexity of his family's dynamics, helping him unravel the layers of unspoken blame and resentment. Nicolas started to recognize the ways in which this underlying tension had affected his relationships, causing him to doubt his own self-worth and struggle to form authentic connections with others.

"Nicolas," Dr. Oakley began, her voice filled with

empathy, "it's understandable that the unexpressed blame within your family has had a profound impact on your sense of self. When we internalize the unspoken messages from our loved ones, it can be difficult to separate our own worth from the expectations placed upon us."

Nicolas nodded; his gaze thoughtful. "For so long, I've tried to conform to the image of what they wanted me to be, to live up to their expectations. But it's exhausting, and it has left me feeling empty and disconnected from my true self."

Dr. Oakley encouraged him to explore further, delving into the specific ways in which these dynamics had affected his relationships. "Tell me, Nicolas, how have these unexpressed feelings influenced your connections with your father and brother?"

Nicolas sighed. "With my father, it's always been this unspoken understanding that I have to live up to his legacy, to be the perfect prince. And my brother... well, he resents the public attention I receive, the privileges that come with my fame. It's created this constant tension between us, and I've always felt like I had to prove myself."

Dr. Oakley nodded, validating his experiences. "It sounds like the weight of expectations and unspoken resentment has strained your relationships, creating a barrier to genuine connection. But Nicolas, it's important to remember that you are not defined solely by your position or what others expect of you. Your true worth lies in your authenticity and the qualities that make you who you are."

Nicolas absorbed her words, a mixture of realization and relief washing over him. "You're right, Dr. Oakley. I need to find the courage to embrace my own truth, to let go of the need to constantly prove myself and seek validation from others."

Dr. Oakley smiled warmly, acknowledging his progress. "Indeed, Nicolas. It's a journey of self-discovery and acceptance. By understanding the impact of these dynamics and recognizing your own worth, you can begin to create healthier, more fulfilling connections with your family and beyond."

Nicolas leaned back in his chair, a newfound sense of liberation coursing through his veins. "I want to break free from this cycle, to forge a genuine bond with my family and live a life that brings me joy. It won't be easy, but I'm committed to doing the work."

Dr. Oakley's eyes sparkled with encouragement. "I believe in your resilience, Nicolas. Together, we will navigate this journey, uncovering the depths of your own self-worth and finding ways to foster meaningful connections that are based on authenticity and mutual respect."

As the session drew to a close, Nicolas felt a renewed sense of hope and determination. Through therapy, he began to understand the complexities of his family's dynamics, the impact of unexpressed blame, and the ways in which it had hindered his own growth. With each session, he grew closer to embracing his true self and building the foundations of healthier relationships, free from the weight of unspoken resentment.

The therapist guided Nicolas in reframing his perspective, helping him separate the misplaced guilt from the truth. He came to realize that his mother's death was a tragic accident, not a result of his own actions. It was a gradual process of self-forgiveness, as he learned to release the burden of responsibility he had carried for so long.

***

The soft glow of the computer screen illuminated Olivia's face as she sat in the makeup chair at the bustling filming studio in Los Angeles. It was early morning, and she was preparing for another day on set. As she waited for her makeup artist to apply the final touches, she eagerly connected with Nicolas through their weekly video call.

In the quiet confines of his bedroom in the Creudor Royal palace, Nicolas sat on the edge of his bed, the moonlight filtering through the curtains. It was nighttime there, and he was getting ready to retire for the evening. As he adjusted the laptop over his knees, he smiled at the familiar face of Olivia appearing on the screen.

"Nicolas, it's so good to see you," Olivia greeted, her eyes bright with anticipation. "How has therapy been going? I've been thinking about you."

Nicolas leaned back against the pillows, his voice filled with a mixture of excitement and relief. "Olivia, it's been transformative. Dr. Oakley has helped me navigate the depths of my family dynamics and the unspoken blame that has haunted me for so long. I've had some major breakthroughs."

Olivia's gaze filled with curiosity and warmth. "Tell me, Nicolas. What has been the most significant breakthrough for you?"

Nicolas took a deep breath, his eyes reflecting a sense of liberation. "It's understanding that I am not solely responsible for my mother's death. The burden of guilt and self-doubt I've carried all these years—it's not mine to bear alone. Dr. Oakley has helped me see that my family's unexpressed blame is a reflection of their own unresolved emotions."

Olivia nodded; her expression filled with empathy. "That's a powerful realization, Nicolas. It must have been such a relief to recognize that you're not alone in shouldering that burden. And it's not your fault."

A soft smile played on Nicolas's lips. "Exactly, Olivia. It's like a weight has been lifted off my shoulders. I can begin to heal and build healthier relationships with my family from a place of authenticity."

Olivia's eyes sparkled with pride and admiration. "I'm so proud of you, Nicolas. It takes strength and courage to confront those deep-rooted issues. I'm here for you every step of the way."

Nicolas reached out and touched the screen as if he could feel Olivia's presence. "And I'm here for you too, Olivia. We're each on our own journeys of growth, and I'm grateful to have you by my side."

As the conversation continued, they shared updates on their respective lives. Olivia spoke about the filming process, her passion for her craft, and the support she received from her cast and crew. Nicolas shared stories of his progress in therapy, his newfound clarity, and the steps he was taking to nurture his relationships with his family.

"Nicolas, I have something important to discuss with you," Olivia began, her voice filled with anticipation. "I would love for you to meet my parents. They've been asking about you, and I think it's time for them to get to know the amazing person you are."

Nicolas's eyes lit up with a mixture of surprise and delight. "Olivia, meeting your parents would be an honor. I've been wanting to take our relationship to that level, and this feels like the perfect opportunity."

A smile spread across Olivia's face as she continued, "They're really excited to meet you. They've seen how happy you make me, and they want to get to know you."

Nicolas nodded; his expression filled with warmth. "I would be delighted to meet them, Olivia. Let's plan a trip to New York. We can spend a few days there and make it a special occasion."

Olivia's heart skipped a beat at Nicolas' enthusiastic agreement. The prospect of introducing him to her parents filled her with excitement and nervous anticipation. The video call had brought them closer despite the distance, and now they were ready to take the next step in their relationship.

A smile spread across Olivia's face as she leaned closer to the screen. "That's wonderful, Nicolas! I can't wait for you to meet my parents. They've been eager to meet you ever since I told them about our relationship."

Nicolas returned her smile, his eyes filled with affection. "I'm honored and thrilled to meet them, Olivia. It means a lot to me that your parents are supportive of us."

Olivia's heart swelled with warmth at Nicolas' words. She knew how important family was to him, and she was grateful that her parents were open-minded and understanding. They had always supported her choices, even when they had not fully understood them.

"Nicolas, my parents are divorced, but they're still on speaking terms. They'll be delighted to meet you, I'm sure," Olivia explained, her voice filled with anticipation. "We can have dinner at their favorite restaurant in New York. It's the perfect setting for this special occasion."

Nicolas nodded, a glimmer of excitement in his eyes. "I trust your judgment, Olivia. Lead the way, and I'll follow. I want this to be a memorable evening for all of us."

Olivia's eyes sparkled with excitement. "That sounds perfect! I'll talk to my parents and arrange everything. We can explore the city together, show you some of my favorite spots, and, of course, have a memorable first meeting with my parents."

Nicolas reached out and gently touched Olivia's hand through the screen. "I want to make a good impression and show your parents how much I care about you."

Olivia leaned closer to the screen; her voice filled with affection. "Nicolas, I have no doubt that they will adore you, just as I do. You're kind, caring, and everything I've ever dreamed of. I can't wait for you to meet them and see the love and support that surrounds me."

As they continued to discuss the details of their trip and the excitement grew, Olivia could not help but feel a surge of happiness. She knew that introducing Nicolas to her parents was a significant step, a symbol of the depth of their connection and the potential for a future together.

In the midst of their conversation, the stark contrast of the Los Angeles morning and the Creudor nighttime served as a reminder of the vast distance between them.

Yet, their connection remained strong, bridging the physical gap with love and support.

"Have a fantastic morning, my love," Nicolas whispered, his voice carrying across the distance.

Olivia's heart swelled with love as she returned his sentiment. "Good night, Nicolas," she replied, her voice filled with warmth.

With a final exchange of "I love you's" and virtual kisses, they reluctantly ended their call. The screen faded to black, leaving them to their own worlds for the night and the day that awaited them.

As Olivia closed her eyes, she carried Nicolas's words of love and encouragement with her. In her dreams, she saw a future where they continued to support each other through their individual journeys, growing stronger together with each passing day.

In the quiet of his bedroom, Nicolas felt a sense of peace wash over him. The knowledge that Olivia was by his side, even from a distance, filled him with a renewed sense of purpose and determination. With her love and unwavering support, he knew he could face any challenge that lay ahead.

And so, as the night turned to day and the day turned to night, Olivia and Nicolas embarked on their individual paths of self-discovery and healing, knowing that their love would remain a constant source of strength and inspiration.

***

In the bustling streets of New York City, Olivia and Nicolas ventured out for a special dinner with Olivia's parents. The city lights illuminated their path as they walked arm in arm, Olivia's heart brimming with excitement to introduce Nicolas to her family.

Olivia's parents had always been her pillars of support, and their approval meant the world to her. Though divorced, they had managed to maintain a cordial relationship, putting their differences aside for the sake of their daughter.

Their destination was a charming Italian restaurant tucked away in a quaint corner of the city. Soft jazz music spilled out onto the street, creating an inviting atmosphere. The cozy restaurant exuded an intimate ambiance, the soft glow of candlelight casting a warm hue upon the faces of the diners. Olivia could hardly contain her excitement as they stepped inside, the warm ambiance embracing them.

She spotted her parents sitting at a corner table, exchanging smiles and engaged in lively conversation. With a deep breath, Olivia approached them, her eyes shining with nervous anticipation. Her mother looked up and caught sight of her, her face lighting up with joy.

"Olivia, darling! You look absolutely stunning," her mother exclaimed, rising from her seat and embracing her tightly.

Olivia returned the embrace, feeling a surge of love and gratitude for her parents. "Thank you, Mom. I'm so glad you're here."

Her father joined in the warm embrace, a proud smile on his face. "Olivia, my girl, it's always a pleasure to see you. And who is this handsome gentleman you've brought with you?"

Olivia turned to Nicolas, a radiant smile on her face. "Dad, Mom, this is Nicolas. He's the one I've been telling you about."

Nicolas extended his hand, a genuine smile adorning his face. "It's a pleasure to meet both of you. Olivia has spoken so highly of you, and I'm honored to be here."

Olivia's parents exchanged surprised glances; their curiosity piqued. They had expected Nicolas to be charming, but they had not anticipated his genuine warmth and humility.

As they settled into their seats, Olivia's parents, Richard and Evelyn, greeted them with much warmth. Richard was a small business owner, who loved his only daughter more than anything else. Evelyn worked as a piano teacher, exuded a quiet charm that instantly reminded Nicolas of his own mother's spirit.

Over the course of the evening, laughter and heartfelt conversations filled the air. Olivia's father, Richard, regaled Nicolas with stories of his customers at his boutique, while Evelyn shared funny moments she shared with her students. Olivia and Nicolas, themselves shared stories of their adventures, their eyes sparkling with shared joy. It was a magical night, filled with love, warmth, and a sense of belonging. The clinking of glasses and hearty laughter filled the air as they indulged in delectable Italian cuisine.

As the night progressed, Olivia's parents could not help but notice the undeniable connection between their daughter and Nicolas. Evelyn's eyes twinkled with motherly intuition, and she leaned toward Nicolas, her voice filled with genuine curiosity.

"So, Nicolas, tell us about how you and Olivia met?"

Nicolas's smile radiated warmth as he recounted the unexpected encounter in Creudor, the initial attraction that blossomed into a deep and profound love. He spoke of Olivia's resilience, her kindness, and the way she had inspired him to embrace his true self.

Richard listened attentively, his fatherly mind analyzing the nuances of Nicolas's character. He observed the unwavering commitment in his eyes and the way he made Olivia's happiness his top priority. It was clear that Nicolas cherished and respected his daughter.

As dessert arrived, Olivia's heart swelled with gratitude. Seeing her parents and Nicolas connecting, getting to know each other, brought her immeasurable joy. In that moment, she realized the significance of this meeting. It was not just about her and Nicolas; it was about weaving together the tapestry of their lives.

Olivia's heart overflowed with a sense of fulfillment. She looked at her parents, her voice filled with love and gratitude.

"Thank you both for accepting Nicolas into our family. Having you here, seeing you connect, means the world to me. I love you."

Her parents enveloped her in a warm embrace, their love and pride evident in their eyes. Richard spoke with a father's tenderness, his voice tinged with emotion.

"Olivia, my darling, seeing you happy is all we've ever wanted. Nicolas is a remarkable man, and we're grateful to have him as a part of our lives. You deserve every happiness."

Nicolas, standing beside Olivia, could not help but feel a surge of gratitude for the love and acceptance he had received from her parents. He clasped Olivia's hand, his voice filled with sincerity.

"Richard, Evelyn, thank you for welcoming me into your family. Olivia means the world to me, and I promise to cherish and protect her with all my heart."

As they bid farewell to her parents, and stepped out of the restaurant, the atmosphere shifted. A flash of cameras and the clamor of excited voices shattered the serenity of the moment. The paparazzi had descended upon them, their lenses hungry for a glimpse of the famous actress and her royal partner.

Olivia instinctively moved closer to Nicolas, seeking refuge in his protective presence. Her heart raced, and her hands tightened around his arm as they hurriedly made their way through the frenzied crowd. The paparazzi shouted questions, their flashes blinding and relentless.

Amidst the chaos, a few persistent photographers managed to capture images of Olivia and Nicolas together, their love immortalized in the pixels of gossip magazines and entertainment websites. It was a bittersweet moment, a reminder of the price they paid for their fame and the invasion of their privacy.

Inside a waiting car, Olivia took a deep breath, her eyes meeting Nicolas's in silent understanding. "I'm sorry you had to go through that," she murmured, her voice tinged with frustration. "This is not what I wanted for us."

Nicolas squeezed her hand gently, his voice filled with unwavering support. "Olivia, it's not your fault. We knew this would happen, but we'll navigate through it together. Our love is stronger than any headline or photograph."

They walked away from the chaotic scene, hand in hand. The paparazzi may have captured a moment in time, but they could never capture the essence of their love.

As the car drove away, Olivia's mind swirled with conflicting emotions. The intrusion of the paparazzi was a harsh reminder of the sacrifices she had to make for her career, the constant scrutiny that threatened to overshadow the happiness she found in her relationship.

She was determined to protect the sacredness of their connection, to shield it from the prying eyes and judgment of others. And as she rested her head against Nicolas's shoulder, she drew strength from the depth of their love, ready to face whatever challenges lay ahead, united in their journey.

***

As Olivia and Nicolas stepped inside the luxurious hotel room, a wave of relief washed over them. The room was adorned with elegant furnishings and floor-to-ceiling windows that offered breathtaking views of the iconic New York City skyline. The familiar comfort of privacy provided solace after the whirlwind encounter with the paparazzi. The door closed behind them, shutting out the chaos of the outside world.

Breathing a sigh of relief, Olivia moved toward the window, gazing out at the city lights that twinkled like distant stars. But their brief moment of solace was abruptly shattered as their phones erupted with incessant buzzing and ringing. She pulled out her phone that nestled in her handbag and saw a barrage of missed calls, text messages, and notifications flooding her screen.

Nicolas, equally intrigued by the commotion, reached for his phone, which sat on the nearby table. The screen lit up with a frenzy of notifications, causing his brows to furrow in surprise.

Olivia's voice trembled as she began scrolling through the news headlines on her phone. She could hardly believe her eyes. Their relationship was now plastered across every tabloid and gossip articles, making them the center of international attention.

"They wasted no time, did they?" Olivia remarked, her voice tinged with a mixture of amusement and disbelief. "It seems like the entire world knows about us now."

Olivia's hand trembled slightly as she scrolled through the overwhelming stream of news alerts and notifications on her phone. Her brows furrowed as she clicked on one of the articles, her eyes widening with disbelief. The headline screamed in bold letters, capturing their relationship in sensationalized phrases that distorted the truth.

"Olivia Grey and Prince Nicolas: A Love Fit for Royalty or a Scandal in the Making?"

Nicolas, seeing the distress on Olivia's face, took her hand in his, his voice filled with reassurance. "We knew this day would come, my love. Our love story has taken the spotlight, but we won't let the opinions of others define us. We'll get through this together."

Olivia nodded, taking a deep breath to steady herself.

She knew that fame came with its share of challenges, but this level of intrusion and misrepresentation still caught her off guard. She braced herself for the inevitable invasion of their privacy, the relentless scrutiny that would follow.

The room suddenly felt suffocating as the weight of the media storm pressed down on them. Olivia's voice trembled as she voiced her concerns.

"Nicolas, I never wanted our relationship to become tabloid fodder. It's painful to see our personal lives dissected and distorted."

Nicolas tightened his grip on her hand, his eyes filled with determination. "We can't control what the media says or how they twist our story," Nicolas said firmly. "But we can control how we respond to it.

Olivia found comfort in his words, feeling her resolve strengthen. She knew that Nicolas was right—they couldn't let the media dictate their happiness or tarnish their love. Together, they would face the challenges head-on, united in their commitment to each other.

"Nicolas, I won't let their words define us," Olivia declared, her voice filled with determination. "Our love is real, and that's all that matters."

As they put their phones aside, Olivia and Nicolas sought solace in each other's embrace. In the midst of the chaos, they found refuge in their love and the unwavering support they provided for one another. The world outside may have been buzzing with speculation and judgment, but in that moment, they remained steadfast in their commitment to each other.

With the city's skyline as their backdrop, they made a silent vow to navigate the storm with grace and resilience. They would not allow the intrusive gaze of the media to dampen the authenticity and depth of their love.

And as the city outside continued to buzz with the news of their relationship, Olivia and Nicolas found solace in the knowledge that their love was real, unbreakable, and resilient enough to weather any storm that came their way.

***

CHAPTER 9:

OUT OF THE WOODS

As the sun began to peek through the curtains of their New York hotel room, Nicolas slowly stirred from his sleep. He opened his eyes, his gaze falling upon the peaceful face of Olivia, who lay beside him, her hair tousled, and a gentle smile gracing her lips. For the first time in his life, Nicolas felt like he was truly home.

Unable to resist the overwhelming surge of love that filled his heart, Nicolas leaned in closer, his lips softly brushing against Olivia's. The gentle kiss was meant to remind her of the depth of his affection, to convey the unspoken words that resided within him.

Olivia stirred, her eyes fluttering open, and she met Nicolas' gaze with warmth and tenderness. The kiss had awakened her senses, bringing a sense of contentment and joy to her being.

"Good morning, sweetheart." Nicolas's voice was soft, and he couldn't help but smile when a small blush spread across Olivia's cheeks.

"Good morning," she murmured, reaching up and pulling him down for a long, slow kiss.

"I hope you slept well," Nicolas whispered, his voice filled with love.

Olivia smiled, her fingers tracing gentle patterns on his cheek. "I did, especially with you by my side. There's something magical about waking up next to you. But did you sleep well, my love?"

Nicolas's heart swelled at her words, his love for her radiating through his entire being. He brushed a strand of hair away from her face, his eyes filled with adoration.

"I don't think I slept at all," he whispered, running his fingers through her hair. "I think I spent the whole night watching you sleep."

Olivia smiled, leaning up and pressing a tender kiss to his cheek.

"It was very sweet of you," she whispered, snuggling closer to him.

"How could I not watch you? You are the most beautiful woman in the world, my Olivia. I have never been so lucky, nor so grateful for anything in my entire life," Nicolas said softly, gazing into her eyes. "I love you so much."

Olivia's eyes glistened, and she sniffled slightly. "I love you, too, sweetheart."

Nicolas's heart melted as he held her close, kissing the top of her head and resting his cheek against her soft hair.

"Olivia, being with you feels like a dream come true. Every moment spent with you is a precious gift for me."

Their gaze lingered, communicating a depth of emotions that words alone could not express. In that silent exchange, they reaffirmed the bond they shared— a love that transcended distance, time zones, and the challenges they had faced together.

Olivia nestled closer to Nicolas, feeling his warmth enveloping her. Their embrace spoke volumes, filled with a sense of comfort and security that only true love could provide. As they lay intertwined, their hearts beating in unison, the outside world faded into insignificance. In that hotel room, their love was the only thing that mattered, shielding them from the pressures and expectations of the outside world.

With a gentle touch, Nicolas caressed Olivia's cheek, his voice a mere whisper against her skin. "Olivia, I want you to know that my love for you knows no bounds."

Olivia's eyes shimmered with unshed tears, overwhelmed by the intensity of the emotions that flowed between them. "Nicolas, with you, I feel complete."

Their lips met again, a tender and passionate kiss that sealed their love in that moment. Olivia smiled as she gently pushed him away, sitting up. "I have to use the bathroom," she said, giving him a mock apologetic look.

Nicolas laughed and shook his head, flopping back on the bed. "I swear, women never let a man sleep in."

"It's what makes us so great," Olivia replied with a wink, disappearing into the bathroom.

Nicolas heard the door shut behind her and sighed happily, staring up at the ceiling. He could hear her humming softly in the bathroom and smiled. This was what he'd been hoping for ever since he met Olivia. It was not perfect by any stretch, but it was his. He could live with that.

As Nicolas reached for his phone from the bedside table, his hand trembled slightly with anticipation. The soft glow of the screen illuminated his face as he unlocked the device, revealing a flurry of messages from his personal secretary, Jack Smith. His heart quickened as he read the urgent subject line that dominated the screen.

"URGENT: Royal Summons from the King"

Nicolas's brows furrowed with concern as he began to read the content of the messages. Each word weighed heavily on his mind, stirring a sense of both duty and uncertainty.

"The King requests your immediate presence at the royal palace in Creudor. It is of utmost importance that you and Olivia attend the meeting. His Majesty wishes to discuss a matter of great significance."

Nicolas's heart raced as he absorbed the gravity of the situation. His father's summons was not to be taken lightly, and he knew it signified a matter of utmost importance within the kingdom. He glanced at the closed bathroom door, where Olivia was still getting ready, and contemplated how this sudden turn of events would impact their lives.

As Olivia emerged from the bathroom, a towel wrapped around her damp hair, she noticed the apprehensive look on Nicolas's face. Concern etched across her features as she approached him, her voice filled with gentle inquiry.

"Nicolas, is everything alright? You seem worried."

Nicolas sighed, his eyes meeting hers, filled with a mix of emotions. "Olivia, I just received a message from Jack. My father, the King, has summoned us to the royal palace in Creudor. He wishes to discuss something of great significance."

Olivia's eyes widened in surprise, her mind racing with possibilities. "What could it be? Why would your father summon us?"

Nicolas shook his head, his voice tinged with uncertainty. "I'm not sure, Olivia. But when my father calls for a meeting like this, it usually indicates an important matter that requires our attention. We must be prepared for anything."

Olivia moved closer to Nicolas, her hand reaching for his, seeking to offer him comfort and support. "Whatever it is, Nicolas, we'll face it together."

A flicker of gratitude glimmered in Nicolas's eyes as he squeezed Olivia's hand, finding solace in her unwavering presence. "Thank you, Olivia."

With renewed determination, Nicolas set his phone aside, his focus shifting to the love they shared and the strength they drew from each other. While uncertainty loomed in the air, their unwavering bond would be their guiding light.

"We'll be alright, Olivia," he assured her, his voice filled with conviction. "No matter what awaits us at the royal palace."

Olivia met Nicolas's gaze, her eyes brimming with unwavering determination. "Yes, we will."

With a shared resolve, they began packing their belongings, their minds abuzz with thoughts of the upcoming meeting with the King. As they gathered their essentials and made arrangements for their journey to Creudor, their bond strengthened, fueled by the knowledge that they could face any obstacle as long as they were together.

In the midst of their preparations, Olivia's mind wandered to the significance of this meeting. She couldn't help but wonder about the implications it held for their future. Little did she know that their lives were about to take another unexpected turn, one that would test their love, loyalty, and commitment like never before.

With their bags packed and their hearts prepared, Olivia and Nicolas left their hotel room, embarking on a journey that would lead them back to the land of royalty and tradition. They carried with them a sense of anticipation and a shared determination to face whatever awaited them in the royal palace. As they stepped into the bustling streets of New York, their hands intertwined, they were ready to embrace their destiny, uncertain of what lay ahead but steadfast in their love and devotion to each other.

***

As the private jet touched down on the Creudor runway, Nicolas and Olivia exchanged a glance, their eyes filled with a mixture of anticipation and apprehension. The door of the aircraft swung open, revealing the familiar face of Jack Smith, Nicolas's trusted personal secretary.

The soft breeze of Creudor welcomed them as they descended the steps onto the tarmac. Two sleek black sedans stood waiting nearby, chauffeurs standing at attention. Jack Smith approached them, a respectful bow preceding his words.

"Your Highness, Miss Grey," he began, his tone formal yet warm. "The King has requested that you travel separately to the royal palace. Prince Nicolas, if you would please accompany me in the first vehicle, and Miss Grey, the second vehicle will transport you safely."

Nicolas and Olivia exchanged a quick glance, a mixture of surprise and curiosity flickering in their eyes. The request for separate travel arrangements was unexpected, yet they knew better than to question the King's wishes.

"Thank you, Jack," Nicolas replied, his voice betraying a hint of curiosity. "We will follow your instructions."

Olivia nodded in agreement, a sense of anticipation tingling in her veins. She trusted Nicolas and knew that their love could withstand any distance, even if it meant a temporary separation during this important visit to the royal palace.

As Nicolas and Jack entered the first sedan, Olivia watched them depart with a mixture of longing and determination. She climbed into the second vehicle; her heart resolute as she prepared for the journey to the royal palace.

As the sedan rolled forward, Olivia gazed out the window, taking in the sights of Creudor. The lush green landscapes and majestic architecture reminded her of the rich history and traditions that surrounded the royal family.

Inside the vehicle, Olivia's mind wandered, contemplating the reason behind the separate travel arrangements. She wondered if this was a customary practice or if it held a deeper significance. Perhaps the King had specific matters to discuss with Nicolas, requiring privacy and confidentiality.

Lost in her thoughts, Olivia's eyes settled on the passing scenery, her mind playing through various scenarios and possibilities. She knew that the upcoming meeting with the King would likely shape their future, and a blend of nerves and excitement coursed through her veins.

As the sedan navigated the winding roads toward the royal palace, Olivia couldn't help but reflect on the strength of their love. She was reminded of the countless challenges they had already faced together and the unwavering bond that held them tightly. No matter the physical distance that momentarily separated them, their hearts remained intertwined.

Arriving at the grand entrance of the royal palace, Olivia stepped out of the vehicle, her eyes fixed on the towering structure before her. It was a testament to the history and power of the royal family, and she couldn't help but feel a surge of awe and reverence.

With each step toward the entrance, Olivia's anticipation grew. She knew that within those palace walls, their lives would be forever changed. The meeting with the King would shape their destinies, both individually and as a couple.

As Olivia entered the grand foyer, she felt exhilarated. She steeled herself, ready to face whatever lay ahead, knowing that Nicolas would soon join her, and together they would navigate the uncertain path that awaited them.

Olivia was shown into an elegant waiting room adorned with opulent furniture and tasteful artwork. As she entered, a palace attendant greeted her with a respectful bow.

"Miss Grey, please make yourself comfortable," the attendant said, gesturing toward a plush armchair. "You will be informed of the next steps shortly."

Olivia took a seat, her eyes scanning the room, absorbing the rich details and the sense of history that seemed to permeate the very air. Despite her surroundings, her mind wandered to the imminent meeting with the King and the unknown purpose it held.

The minutes stretched into what felt like hours as Olivia anxiously awaited further instructions. She tried to occupy her mind by observing the intricate details of the room, but her thoughts kept drifting to the upcoming meeting with the King.

Just as Olivia began to wonder if she had been forgotten, the door swung open and a servant in the palace livery appeared before her with a polite bow. "Miss Grey, the King is ready to receive you now," the servant announced.

Olivia's heart skipped a beat as she rose from her seat, a mixture of nerves and excitement coursing through her. She followed the servant through ornate corridors, the sound of her footsteps echoing in the vastness of the palace.

They reached a set of grand double doors guarded by towering statues, and the servant opened them with a flourish, revealing a lavish chamber where the King awaited.

King Edmund, a distinguished figure with silver hair and a regal demeanor, sat in a high-backed chair at the head of a long, polished table. Sunlight streamed through the large windows, casting a warm glow upon the room.

"Welcome, Miss Grey," the King greeted, his voice commanding yet tinged with warmth. "Please, join me for afternoon tea."

Olivia curtsied respectfully, her heart pounding in her

chest as she approached the table. She took her seat opposite the King, a delicate porcelain teacup and saucer placed before her.

As they sipped their tea, the King's piercing blue eyes studied Olivia with a mixture of curiosity and scrutiny. Olivia felt the weight of his gaze, but she remained composed, her demeanor respectful and poised.

"Miss Grey, I have heard much about you," the King began, his tone measured. "You have captured the heart of my son, Prince Nicolas, and that is not a feat achieved easily. Our conversation today will help me understand the depth of your intentions and your suitability for our royal family."

Olivia took a moment to gather her thoughts, her voice steady as she responded. "Your Majesty, I am deeply committed to Prince Nicolas. Our love has grown stronger through the challenges we have faced together. I understand the responsibilities and expectations that come with being a part of the royal family, and I am prepared to embrace them."

The King nodded; his expression serious yet thoughtful. "It is commendable that you acknowledge the weight of the role you may assume. But let me make one thing clear, Miss Grey. Our royal lineage demands loyalty, discretion, and unwavering commitment. There will be expectations placed upon you, and you must understand the importance of upholding our traditions and values."

Olivia listened attentively, her heart swelling with a mixture of determination and genuine respect for the

King's words. She recognized the gravity of her position, the impact her actions could have on the kingdom and its people.

"Your Majesty, I assure you that I will honor the traditions and values of the royal family," Olivia replied with unwavering resolve. "I am committed to supporting Prince Nicolas and contributing to the betterment of Creudor in any way I can."

The King's stern expression softened, a hint of approval glinting in his eyes. "Your words are promising, Miss Grey. But actions speak louder than words. Time will reveal the truth of your commitment."

Within seconds, he rose from his seat, extending a hand toward Olivia. "Well, Miss Grey, it has been a pleasure to meet you," the King said warmly.

Olivia's heart swelled with gratitude and relief as she shook the King's hand. The weight of the moment settled upon her shoulders, but she stood tall, ready to embark on a new chapter of her life—a chapter that would test her in ways she could never have imagined.

***

As the King made his way to the official royal briefing room, his footsteps echoing through the ornate corridors of the palace, he felt a mixture of anticipation and concern. The presence of his trusted royal aide,

Marcus, known affectionately as Marco, provided a sense of comfort in this pivotal moment. They entered the room where Prince Frederick and Prince Nicolas were engaged in a serious discussion with Jack, their personal secretary. The room was adorned with rich tapestries and antique furniture, reflecting the regal heritage of the monarchy.

"Your Majesty, we've been waiting for you," Prince Frederick said, his tone carrying a hint of impatience.

The King nodded, acknowledging his eldest son, before taking his seat at the head of the table. Marco stood at his side, his expression reflecting a mix of concern and disapproval. The atmosphere in the room became palpably tense, signaling the gravity of the impending conversation.

"Let us proceed," the King said, his voice commanding the attention of everyone in the room.

Jack, with a stack of newspapers and magazines in hand, stepped forward and began his briefing. He carefully handed over the stack of newspapers and magazines, their headlines screaming scandal and intrigue.

Silence enveloped the room as the King, Prince Frederick, and Prince Nicolas absorbed the weight of the revelations about Olivia's past. Marco's stern gaze lingered on the headlines; his disapproval evident in his furrowed brows. The room fell into a tense silence as the weight of this information settled upon them.

Jack took a deep breath, his voice filled his sense of

duty. "Your Majesty, Prince Frederick, Prince Nicolas, I regret to inform you that the tabloids have unearthed information about Olivia's previous marriage and subsequent divorce. The media is portraying her as a divorced actress seducing a Prince."

A heavy silence settled upon the room, the gravity of the situation sinking in. The King's expression remained stoic, while Prince Frederick's features hardened with concern. Prince Nicolas, his heart torn between love and duty, felt a pang of anxiety coursing through him.

Marco, his voice laced with disapproval, broke the silence. "Your Majesty, this revelation casts a shadow on our esteemed monarchy. We must consider the potential consequences of Prince Nicolas pursuing a relationship with an actress who has a questionable past."

The King's eyes shifted from the headlines to his sons as he spoke, "Gentlemen, we find ourselves facing a delicate situation. The reputation of our monarchy is at stake, and we must tread carefully."

Prince Frederick's brows creased in disapproval; his voice filled with concern. "Father, these revelations about Olivia's past could tarnish our family's reputation. We must take this matter seriously."

The room fell into a momentary silence as the King contemplated the conflicting perspectives of his sons and Marco's disapproval. He understood the weight of duty, tradition, and the need to protect the monarchy's reputation.

Prince Nicolas, his heart heavy with conflicting emotions, spoke with determination. "Father, I understand the concerns, but Olivia is more than the tabloid headlines. She has brought joy and love into my life. I believe in our connection, and I am willing to face the challenges that lie ahead."

After a pause, the King spoke, his voice filled with empathy. "My sons, I appreciate your differing opinions. We must consider the impact on our family, our people, and our monarchy. Let us not rush into judgment, but rather navigate these uncharted waters with wisdom and compassion."

Marco, though reluctant, nodded in acknowledgment of the King's words. He understood his role in upholding tradition and preserving the monarchy's integrity, even if it meant grappling with his personal reservations.

Prince Nicolas, with a worried look on his face, found his voice. "Father, Olivia's past should not overshadow the love and support she has shown me. She has proven herself to be a remarkable person, and I believe in the strength of our connection."

Marco, who had been silently observing the conversation, interjected with a calm and thoughtful tone. "Your Majesties, it is crucial to consider the public perception and the impact these reports may have on the monarchy."

Prince Frederick, his voice laced with caution, voiced his concerns. "Father, we cannot ignore the implications of this scandal. The public's perception is vital, and we must consider the impact on our family's legacy."

The King, a wise and composed figure, looked at his sons with a measured gaze. "Frederick, Marco. I understand your apprehension. However, we must not let the past define the present. People change, and it is essential that we evaluate individuals based on who they are today."

Prince Frederick, although still apprehensive, relented, his voice softened with reluctant acceptance. "Nicolas, I may not fully comprehend your decision, but as your brother, I will support you. However, I urge caution and consideration of the potential consequences."

Prince Nicolas's face softened with gratitude; his voice filled with sincerity. "Thank you, Frederick. Your support means a great deal to me. I understand the challenges ahead, but I believe in our love and the strength we possess."

The King nodded in agreement, his eyes shifting between his sons. "Indeed, we must balance our duty with our humanity. Nicolas has found a deep bond with Olivia, and we should respect his choice. Let us approach this situation with open minds and hearts."

Nicolas, his heart filled with determination and a desire to protect Olivia, looked at his father with earnest eyes. "Father, I implore you to intervene and issue a statement to clarify the truth about my relationship with Olivia. We cannot let the tabloids continue to distort our love and tarnish her reputation."

The King, aware of the weight of his son's plea, considered the options before him. He understood Nicolas's concern and the urgency to address the situation. Yet, he also recognized the wisdom in proceeding cautiously.

Marcus, loyal and steadfast, spoke up, his voice resonating with measured wisdom. "Your Majesty, while I understand Prince Nicolas's concern, I believe it is in our best interest not to intervene hastily. The storm will eventually calm itself, and we risk further exacerbating the situation by giving it more attention. Our silence can speak volumes, allowing the truth to prevail over time."

Nicolas's frustration and worry were palpable as he turned to face Marcus. "But Marcus, we cannot allow the false narratives to persist. Olivia's reputation is at stake, and she deserves our support and protection."

Marcus met Nicolas's gaze; his expression unwavering. "Prince Nicolas, I understand your concerns, but we must trust in the resilience of the truth. The more we engage with the tabloids, the more they will have to publish. Let us maintain our dignity and let the storm pass. The people will see through the falsehoods in due course."

The room fell into a contemplative silence as the weight of the decision hung in the air. The King, torn between his son's plea and his trusted advisor's counsel, recognized the significance of the moment.

After a moment of thoughtful deliberation, the King spoke with a tone of resolution. "Nicolas, I understand your desire to protect Olivia, but Marcus raises a valid point. We must exercise caution and allow time to rectify these misconceptions. We will closely monitor the situation and step in, if necessary, but for now, let us trust in the resilience of truth and the unwavering bond between you and Olivia."

Nicolas, though disappointed, respected his father's decision. He understood the delicate balance between personal desires and the greater responsibilities that came with their position. With a determined nod, he vowed to stand by Olivia's side and weather the storm together.

In the days that followed, as the media frenzy persisted, the royal family maintained a composed silence, honoring the King's decision. As the storm raged on, the world watched with anticipation, eager for the truth to prevail and the couple's love to triumph over the superficiality of tabloid speculation.

***

CHAPTER 10:

IN A PAST LIFE

Olivia stood on the bustling set of her TV series in Los Angeles, the air buzzing with the excitement of creativity and camaraderie. As the director called for action, Olivia stepped into the shoes of her character, letting go of her own worries and immersing herself in the world of the story. She embraced the fictional realm as a sanctuary—a place where she could channel her emotions, drawing from her own experiences to infuse her performance with depth and authenticity.

The energetic atmosphere, the hum of conversations and the click of cameras, served as a welcome respite from the storm of her personal life. Here, amidst the artifice of the television world, she could momentarily escape the harsh glare of the spotlight and immerse herself in the sanctuary of her character.

But just as she was beginning to find her footing again, a sudden hush swept through the set. The vibrant energy on the set abruptly dissipated, leaving behind a heavy silence that hung in the air like a foreboding cloud. The news broke like a thunderbolt, reverberating through the corridors and reaching Olivia's ears in an instant.

Olivia's heart skipped a beat as she glanced at her phone, her hands trembling. The headlines blared, vivid and accusatory, exposing the raw wounds of her past for the world to see. Her heart sank as she read the headlines that flashed across her phone screen, revealing the unthinkable—her past had come back to haunt her.

Her personal assistant, Justin, noticed the sudden change in Olivia's demeanor. Concern etched across his face as he hurriedly approached her, attempting to shield her from the onslaught of news that threatened to unravel her newfound stability.

"Olivia, what's happened?" Justin asked, his voice filled with a mix of worry and urgency. "You look pale. Is everything all right?"

Olivia's voice quivered as she tried to steady herself. "Justin, it's... It's my past. It's resurfaced. The headlines... they're dredging up things that I thought were buried. I can't believe it's happening."

Justin's eyes widened in disbelief as he took in the gravity of the situation. He had been Olivia's steadfast ally, navigating the treacherous waters of fame by her side. He knew the sacrifices she had made to distance herself from her past, and the pain she had endured in order to rebuild her life.

Seeking a moment of respite, Olivia and Justin retreated to her private trailer. Her thoughts swirled with a whirlwind of emotions as she contemplated the best course of action. Together, they dove into the sea of headlines, digging deeper to understand the scope of the revelations and the potential consequences they might face.

As they sifted through the articles, Olivia's heart sank further with each passing minute. The media had dredged up intimate details of her past, weaving a narrative that painted her in a distorted light. The salacious headlines fueled a frenzy of speculation and judgment, threatening to overshadow her hard-won success and the love she had found with Nicolas.

Olivia's ex-husband, a man she had hoped to leave behind in the shadows of her former life, had resurfaced, eager to exploit her secrets for personal gain. Images of his smug face accompanied by sensationalized quotes filled the media landscape, igniting a firestorm of public interest. Memories of their failed marriage and the painful moments she had tried to forget resurfaced, threatening to unravel the happiness she had found with Nicolas.

The media frenzy intensified as reporters, hungry for a scandal, dug deeper into Olivia's past, digging up every skeleton they could find. Sensationalized headlines and salacious stories flooded the airwaves, painting a distorted picture of Olivia's life. Photographs of intimate moments from her past relationship were splashed across gossip magazines, as if to strip away her newfound happiness and expose her vulnerabilities to the world.

For Olivia, it was a reminder of the dark shadows she had fought so hard to escape. She had worked tirelessly to rebuild her life, to forge a path in the unforgiving world of showbiz. But now, her past threatened to consume her present, casting a dark cloud over her blossoming relationship with Nicolas.

The public's interest grew insatiable, their hunger for scandal fueling the firestorm. Pundits dissected Olivia's every move beginning from her childhood, speculating on the motives behind her previous marriage and her subsequent divorce. They questioned her character, attempting to paint her as a manipulative seductress who had deceived a prince.

As she absorbed the shocking news, Olivia's hands trembled with a mix of anger and vulnerability. How could he dredge up the past and use it as a weapon against her? The scars of that failed marriage had long since healed, or so she thought.

Her mind raced, contemplating the potential consequences of this public revelation. Would her professional career be jeopardized? Would her personal life be endlessly dissected by the tabloids? The weight of uncertainty pressed down on her, threatening to drown out the sense of security she had fought so hard to regain.

Her phone buzzed incessantly, inundated with messages from concerned friends, family, and her loyal publicist, all urging her to take control of the narrative. Their advice echoed in her mind, each voice contributing a piece to the puzzle of her next move.

Taking a deep breath, Olivia steadied herself and dialed the number of her publicist, Susan. The line rang for what felt like an eternity before Susan's voice finally broke through the silence.

"Olivia, I've been trying to reach you. The situation is getting out of hand. We need to address this head-on," Susan said, her tone a mixture of concern and determination.

Olivia nodded, her voice steady despite the storm of emotions raging within her. "I know, Susan. But I'm afraid I cannot make a statement, not without talking to Nicolas about it first."

Susan's brows furrowed with concern as she listened to Olivia's words. She understood the importance of Olivia's decision to include Nicolas in the process, recognizing the significance of their relationship and the impact it could have on both of their lives. With a supportive nod, Susan replied, "You're right, Olivia. It's important to have a united front. Let's reach out to Nicolas and discuss the best way to handle this together."

Olivia's fingers tapped anxiously against the surface of her phone as she waited for Nicolas to pick up. Her heart yearned for his calming presence, his unwavering support that had become her anchor in times of turmoil. After a few rings, his voice finally filled her ears, and she breathed a sigh of relief.

"Nicolas, it's me," she began, her voice filled with a mixture of urgency and vulnerability. "Something has happened. My ex-husband is trying to exploit our past for personal gain, and the media is running wild with it. I wanted to talk to you before making any official statement."

There was a brief pause on the other end of the line, as if Nicolas was processing the weight of Olivia's words. Finally, he spoke, his voice a steady reassurance in the midst of chaos.

"Olivia, my love, I'm here for you. We will face this together," Nicolas replied, his tone filled with unwavering support. "Let's meet in person and discuss our next steps. I'll fly to Los Angeles as soon as possible."

Relief washed over Olivia, grateful for Nicolas's unwavering commitment to their relationship and his understanding of the gravity of the situation. She knew that with his guidance and strength, they would navigate the storm and emerge stronger than ever.

A few days later, Olivia and Nicolas sat together at her apartment, as they poured over the details of the situation. They discussed the potential repercussions, the best approach to address the media, and the importance of remaining true to themselves amidst the chaos. Their conversation turned to the advice they had received from their respective advisors. The tension in the room was palpable, as they grappled with the conflicting perspectives before them.

Olivia's brow furrowed with concern as she recounted Jack's words about the potential implications of any public statement she might make. She understood the delicate position Nicolas held within the royal family and the scrutiny that would inevitably befall them if their relationship became entangled in the public eye.

Nicolas sighed heavily, his fingers tracing patterns on the surface of the table. He knew the weight of responsibility that came with his title and the complexities of balancing personal desires with his duty to his family and the kingdom. His mind wrestled with the desire to protect Olivia and their love, while also safeguarding the reputation and stability of the royal family.

"I don't want you to bear the brunt of any negative repercussions, my love," Nicolas said, his voice tinged with a mix of frustration and protectiveness. "Jack has a valid point. Any public statement you make will be attached to the royal family, and I cannot bear the thought of you facing unnecessary backlash."

Olivia's heart ached as she listened to Nicolas's words. She knew he was torn between his love for her and his commitment to his role as a prince. She reached out, her hand gently cupping his, a gesture of understanding and support.

"I understand, Nicolas," Olivia replied, her voice filled with a mix of empathy and determination. "We need to find a way to navigate this without jeopardizing either of our positions. We can't let the circumstances define us or force us into silence, but we must also be mindful of the consequences."

Nicolas nodded, appreciating Olivia's unwavering support and her understanding of the intricacies they faced. They delved deeper into their conversation, exploring alternative strategies to address the media storm while protecting their individual interests.

Together, they devised a plan that struck a delicate balance. Instead of issuing a public statement, they decided to focus on their actions speaking louder than words. They would continue to live their lives authentically, unapologetically embracing their love, but with a heightened sense of discretion.

***

In the opulent halls of the royal palace, tension lingered in the air as Prince Nicolas, Prince Frederick, King Edmund, Marcus, and Jack gathered for an urgent meeting. The room, adorned with grand tapestries and gilded furniture, seemed to reflect the weight of the discussion that was about to unfold.

Nicolas, his usually warm demeanor clouded with frustration, stood tall, facing his father and brother. His eyes reflected a mix of determination and conflict, torn between his love for Olivia and his loyalty to his family.

Frederick, the elder brother, wore a stern expression, his gaze fixed upon Nicolas with a mixture of concern and disapproval. He was a man of duty and tradition, struggling to reconcile his own beliefs with the undeniable connection between his brother and Olivia.

King Edmund, the patriarch of the royal family, sat on his throne, his features etched with a mix of weariness and authority. He had witnessed the impact of fame and public scrutiny on his family, and the presence of an actress like Olivia threatened to further destabilize their carefully curated image.

Marcus, the king's trusted aide, stood beside him, his countenance reflecting a blend of loyalty and caution. He had always been a voice of reason, guiding the king and the princes through the trials and tribulations of their roles.

Jack, the personal secretary, stood slightly apart from the rest, clutching a stack of documents in his hands. He had been the bearer of news and information, carefully navigating the intricate web of the royal family's affairs.

Nicolas took a deep breath, breaking the silence that engulfed the room. "Father, Frederick, I understand your concerns. But I cannot deny the love I feel for Olivia. She is the love of my life."

Frederick's stern gaze softened, revealing the complexity of his emotions. "Nicolas, I want nothing but your happiness. But we must consider the consequences of your actions. The monarchy is built on tradition and stability. Olivia's presence threatens to disrupt that."

King Edmund leaned forward, his voice filled with a mixture of authority and concern. "Nicolas, you must understand the weight of your choices. The public's perception of the royal family is delicate, and any misstep could have far-reaching consequences."

Nicolas' eyes searched the faces of his family members, his voice tinged with a touch of desperation. "But what about my own happiness, Father? Can I not pursue love and happiness, even if it defies tradition?"

Marcus, ever the voice of wisdom, stepped forward, his eyes meeting Nicolas'. "Prince Nicolas, I understand your desires. However, we must tread carefully. The media storm surrounding Olivia has brought scrutiny to our doorstep. We must consider the ramifications and protect the integrity of the royal family."

Nicolas sighed; the weight of his conflicting emotions evident in his expression. "I hear your concerns, all of you. But I cannot simply turn my back on the woman I love. We must find a way to bridge this divide and navigate through the storm together."

The room fell into a heavy silence, each member of the royal family grappling with their own thoughts and reservations. They were bound by duty, tradition, and the expectations placed upon them. The rift between Nicolas and his family seemed insurmountable, with no clear resolution in sight.

As the tension lingered, the weight of the decision they faced threatened to fracture their unity. The destiny of not only Nicolas and Olivia's relationship but also the future of the royal family hung precariously in the balance, the outcome uncertain and riddled with complexity.

The room remained still, the echoes of their conversation reverberating against the opulent walls. In that moment, the royal family stood divided, each grappling with their own convictions, and the path forward remained shrouded in uncertainty.

***

Nicolas paced restlessly in his study, his mind weighed down by the conflicting demands of his heart and his duty. He glanced at the portrait of his ancestors that adorned the wall, a constant reminder of the legacy he was born into. The weight of responsibility bore down on him, threatening to drown out the voice of his love for Olivia.

In the quiet moments of solitude, Nicolas found himself reflecting on the conversations with his father, his brother, and the weight of expectation that accompanied his royal bloodline. He understood the necessity of preserving the legacy, the centuries-old traditions that had shaped his family. But the love he felt for Olivia burned fiercely within him, an unyielding force that defied logic and rationale.

At the other end of the world, Olivia's heart ached with the weight of the constant scrutiny and invasion of privacy. The paparazzi seemed to lurk around every corner, capturing her every move, and turning her life into a spectacle for the world to see. Days turned into nights, and nights into days as Nicolas and Olivia found themselves caught in a whirlwind of uncertainty and longing. Separated by distance and the walls of tradition, their hearts ached for each other's touch.

A heartbroken Olivia, sought solace amidst the familiar walls of her mother's house in Los Angeles. Stella and Max, her loyal canine companions, nestled at her feet as she curled up on the couch, lost in a sea of thoughts and emotions. Their presence brought her a sense of comfort and stability, a reminder of the unwavering love that existed beyond the chaos of the outside world.

Evelyn, her mother, greeted Olivia with open arms, her eyes filled with concern and empathy. They shared a special bond, a deep understanding that transcended words. As Olivia sank into the worn couch, Stella and Max nestled beside her, their presence providing a soothing relief to her wounded soul.

She watched her daughter, her heart heavy with the knowledge of the pain Olivia endured. She gently placed a comforting hand on Olivia's shoulder, offering her strength through touch. "My dear, you are strong and resilient. Remember that the opinions of others do not define you. Your true worth lies within."

Olivia gazed at her mother, her eyes brimming with a mix of gratitude and exhaustion. "I know, Mom. It's just... It's overwhelming sometimes. I never expected the level of intrusion and the toll it would take on me. I just want to live my life without constantly being in the spotlight."

Evelyn's voice softened as she spoke, her words filled with maternal love and wisdom. "Sweetheart, fame comes with a price, but you mustn't let it diminish your spirit. Remember who you are and the strength that resides within you. Look around, there is so much love that surrounds you. All you have to do, is stay true to yourself."

Olivia nodded, finding solace in her mother's words. She knew that she had to find a way to rise above the noise, to reclaim her peace and happiness. Stella and

Max, sensing her turmoil, nuzzled against her, their warm presence offering a sense of comfort and grounding.

Days turned into weeks, and Olivia found herself slowly regaining her strength. She immersed herself in moments of stillness, finding solace in the serenity of her mother's house. The laughter and wagging tails of Stella and Max brought a spark of joy back into her life, reminding her of the simple pleasures that mattered most.

Back in Creudor, Nicolas sat in his study, surrounded by the grandeur of his ancestral home. His eyes fell upon a collection of old photographs, capturing fleeting moments frozen in time. His fingers slowly traced the edge of a worn photograph. The image captured his mother, radiant and compassionate, standing against the backdrop of India's vibrant landscapes. It had always been a cherished memory, a glimpse into a part of his mother's life he had never had the chance to experience himself. The desire to walk in her footsteps, to feel a connection with the woman he had longed to know, burned within him.

Yet it was Olivia's absence that weighed heavily on his heart. The physical distance amplifying the ache of their separation. He yearned for her presence, for the warmth of her touch and the sound of her laughter. And in the midst of their trials, he found solace in the promise they had made on their first date—their shared determination to use their fame and influence to make a difference in the world.

With a sense of purpose renewed, Nicolas picked up his phone, his fingers trembling with anticipation. He dialed Olivia's number, his heart racing as he waited for her to answer. After a few rings, her voice finally echoed through the line, a blend of surprise and longing evident in her tone.

"Nicolas," she breathed, her voice filled with a mixture of longing and delight. "How I've missed you."

His voice, laced with determination and vulnerability, responded, "Olivia, my love. Do you remember that we made a promise to each other—to use our fame and influence to make a difference in the world. Let's fulfill that promise together."

A pause filled the air, the weight of their shared dreams and aspirations lingering between them. Olivia's voice, filled with curiosity and hope, broke the silence. "What are you suggesting, Nicolas?"

He took a deep breath, his voice filled with conviction. "I want us to get on a humanitarian visit to India. I have these pictures of my mother there, and I've always wanted to walk in her footsteps. I want to see the world through her eyes, hoping it will bring me closer to her, the mother I never had the chance to know. And I want you by my side, Olivia. Together, we can make a difference and hopefully rediscover us."

Olivia's voice trembled with a mix of emotions. "India... it's a beautiful and complex country. But it's also a place where we can make a real impact."

The anticipation in his voice was palpable. "Olivia, my love, this trip will not only be about our shared purpose. I'm hoping that this journey away from the eyes of the world, can help us in finding our way back to each other. Will you come with me?"

A soft sigh escaped Olivia's lips, followed by a resolute answer. "Of course, Nicolas. I will come with you."

In that moment, their shared vision of a brighter future reignited the flame of their love. The prospect of walking hand in hand, navigating the complexities of India, and channeling their influence to impact lives filled them with a renewed sense of purpose. The challenges they faced only served as stepping stones on their path to personal and shared growth.

As they put their plans into motion, the flame of hope burned brightly within their hearts. With every step they took, Nicolas and Olivia were reminded of their unyielding commitment to each other and their shared mission—to make the world a better place, guided by the love that bound them together.

***

CHAPTER 11:

WINDS OF CHANGE

Nicolas and Olivia sat in a corner of the economy section; their hoodies pulled up to conceal their famous faces. They had intentionally chosen to travel incognito, wanting to experience the journey to India without the weight of their public personas. It was a conscious decision, a way to immerse themselves fully in the experience and connect with the people they were about to meet.

As the plane descended through the clouds, Nicolas and Olivia looked out the window in awe. The vast expanse of India stretched out beneath them, a land of vibrant colors, bustling streets, and breathtaking landscapes. The sight alone ignited a sense of adventure and anticipation within them.

Olivia leaned closer to the window, captivated by the view below. The sprawling landscapes unfolded like a patchwork quilt, with emerald-green fields, majestic mountains, and winding rivers that seemed to whisper tales of centuries past.

Nicolas watched Olivia's face, her eyes sparkling with excitement and curiosity. He could not help but smile, grateful for the opportunity to share this adventure with her. He reached out and gently squeezed her hand, his voice filled with tenderness. "Look at this, Olivia. Can you imagine all the stories waiting to be discovered? The people we'll meet, the lives we'll touch—it's truly humbling."

Olivia turned to him, a mixture of awe and determination in her eyes. "Nicolas, I can't believe we're here. I feel a sense of purpose that I haven't felt in a long time."

He nodded, his voice carrying a sense of eagerness. "That's exactly how I feel, too. This trip isn't just about giving back; it's also about us. Remember when we talked about using our fame and influence to make a difference? Well, here's our chance."

Olivia's eyes sparkled with a mixture of determination and vulnerability. "I remember, Nicolas. And I believe in those promises. Let's make this journey about more than just ourselves. I want to feel connected to something greater than us—to experience the world through their eyes."

Nicolas squeezed her hand tighter, his gaze filled with admiration. "That's why I fell in love with you, Olivia. This journey is about us, but it's also about the lives we'll touch along the way."

As the plane descended further, they prepared themselves mentally for the adventures that awaited them. Their hoodies may have concealed their identities, but their hearts were wide open, ready to embrace the unknown and let the magic of India unfold before them.

They landed in Delhi, greeted by the warm embrace of the Indian sun. Stepping onto the busy streets, they were immediately enveloped by the sights, sounds, and scents of the city.

Nicolas and Olivia hailed a taxi, their excitement palpable as they embarked on their first venture into the vibrant streets of Delhi. The taxi weaved through a symphony of honking horns, rickshaws, and pedestrians, navigating the bustling chaos with practiced ease.

Olivia turned to Nicolas, a radiant smile lighting up her face. "Nicolas, can you believe we're here? It's like stepping into a different world, filled with vibrant energy and captivating beauty."

Nicolas gazed at her, his eyes filled with awe and adoration. "It's truly incredible, Olivia. The sights, the sounds, the scents—it's a sensory overload in the best possible way. I'm grateful to experience this with you."

As evening descended upon the city, they arrived at their hotel—a sanctuary of tranquility amidst the bustling metropolis. The elegant decor and warm hospitality provided a welcome respite from the vibrant chaos outside. They settled into their room; their excitement still palpable.

Olivia glanced out of the window, taking in the view of the city skyline. "Nicolas, this journey is already so much more than I could have imagined. The colors, the culture, the people—it's as if India has awakened something within me, a newfound appreciation for the beauty and diversity of our world."

Nicolas approached her, his voice filled with tenderness. "I feel the same way, Olivia. India has a way of igniting a sense of wonder and awakening the soul. I'm grateful that we can share this experience together, that we can rediscover ourselves and our love amidst the rich tapestry of this country."

As they stood by the window, their reflections merging with the lights of the city below, they felt a renewed sense of purpose and connection. They knew that their journey had only just begun and that the days ahead would bring challenges, growth, and a deeper understanding of themselves and each other.

***

Nicolas and Olivia woke up with a sense of excitement, ready to embark on their first day of exploration in the vibrant city of Delhi. They dressed in comfortable attire, eager to immerse themselves in the cultural tapestry of India.

Their first stop was the bustling streets of Chandni Chowk, a renowned market known for its rich history and delicious street food. As they strolled through the narrow lanes, their senses were overwhelmed by the vibrant colors, enticing aromas, and the cacophony of sounds that filled the air.

They couldn't resist the temptation of the

mouthwatering street food stalls lining the streets. Olivia's eyes lit up as she caught sight of a vendor expertly preparing a plate of spicy chaat. With a mischievous grin, she beckoned Nicolas to join her, and they savored the explosion of flavors, relishing in the authentic taste of Delhi's culinary delights.

Nicolas and Olivia strolled through the bustling Indian market, their senses alive with the vibrant colors and intoxicating scents that filled the air. The sound of eager merchants calling out their wares mingled with the laughter of shoppers, creating a symphony of bustling energy.

As they meandered through the maze-like alleys, their eyes caught glimpses of shimmering textiles, delicate silver ornaments, and intricate pottery. Olivia's eyes sparkled with excitement, her spirit reminiscent of the first day they met in Creudor, where her bargaining skills had impressed Nicolas.

"Do you remember our first encounter?" Olivia asked with a mischievous smile, her eyes twinkling.

Nicolas chuckled, the memory of that fateful day playing vividly in his mind. "How could I forget? You were fiercely haggling for that little trinket, your determination unwavering. I was captivated by your spirit and wit."

They stopped in front of a stall adorned with strings of vibrant beads, their colors dancing in the sunlight. Olivia's gaze fixed upon the beaded bracelets, each one unique in its design and charm. "These remind me of that day," she said, her voice filled with nostalgia.

Nicolas reached out, his fingers grazing the strands of beads. "They're beautiful, just like you," he whispered, his voice carrying a warmth that made Olivia's heart flutter.

They exchanged a knowing glance before turning their attention to the merchant. In a playful exchange of words and laughter, they selected bracelets for each other, carefully considering the colors and patterns that resonated with their souls.

As they continued their exploration of the market, the bracelets adorned their wrists, a symbol of their love and shared experiences. With every step, the gentle jingle of the beads served as a reminder of their journey —a journey that had brought them from the opulent halls of royalty to the vibrant streets of India.

Eager to capture their memories, Nicolas and Olivia stopped at a photo studio known for its vintage aesthetics. As soon as they stepped into the photo studio, they were instantly transported to a world of rich colors and nostalgia. The walls were adorned with old Bollywood movie posters and vintage photographs, while the soft glow of traditional lamps cast a warm, inviting ambiance.

Olivia's eyes widened with excitement as she perused the racks of exquisite sarees, each one more vibrant and captivating than the last. Her fingertips grazed the luxurious fabrics, feeling the smoothness and marveling at the intricate designs.

"I think this one would look stunning on you," Nicolas said, holding up a saree in shades of deep crimson and gold. Its intricate embroidery and shimmering embellishments were a perfect match for Olivia's radiant beauty.

She laughed, her eyes shining with anticipation. "Alright, let's go for it. It's time to embrace our inner Bollywood stars!"

With the saree draped elegantly around Olivia's figure, she twirled in front of the mirror, mesmerized by the way the fabric flowed around her. Nicolas stood by her side, donning a tailored kurta in a complementary shade, his eyes filled with adoration as he took in her breathtaking transformation.

The photographer, a jovial man with a twinkle in his eyes, guided them to a vintage backdrop that resembled an ornate palace. He instructed them on poses and gestures, capturing the essence of their playful love. Olivia and Nicolas shared lighthearted banter, whispering inside jokes and stealing glances that spoke volumes.

"Okay, now strike a pose as if you're dancing under the stars," the photographer suggested.

Nicolas extended his hand toward Olivia, his eyes filled with mirth. "May I have this dance, my queen?"

Olivia playfully placed her hand in his, a mischievous grin playing on her lips. "Only if you can keep up with my incredible dance moves, Prince Charming."

As the camera clicked, freezing the moment in time, their laughter echoed through the studio. They twirled and swayed, their joy radiating from within. The camera captured their vibrant spirits, their love shining through every frame.

After the photo session, they eagerly gathered around a table to view the results. The photographs were a testament to their love, encapsulating the joy, playfulness, and deep connection they shared. Each image told a story, a chapter of their journey, and a reminder of the boundless adventures that lay ahead.

Nicolas looked at Olivia, his eyes filled with awe. "You look breathtaking, my love. These photos are a treasure, capturing the essence of our love and the beauty of this moment."

Olivia blushed, a mixture of excitement and contentment washing over her. "And you, my prince, look so dashing."

As they left the photo studio, the images in their hands and their hearts full of love, Nicolas and Olivia knew that this day would forever be etched in their memories. The photographs would serve as a reminder of their playful spirits, their shared adventures, and the profound love that bound them together.

***

Throughout the day, Nicolas and Olivia found

themselves captivated by the juxtaposition of ancient and modern, tradition and innovation that defined Delhi. From exploring the historic Red Fort and marveling at the intricate architectural beauty of Humayun's Tomb to wandering through the serene gardens of Lodhi Gardens, they embraced every moment with wide-eyed wonder.

As the sun began to set, casting a golden hue over the city, they found themselves in the heart of Delhi at India Gate. Hand in hand, they walked along the majestic monument, surrounded by the buzz of the city and the humbling presence of history. They stood in silence for a moment, taking in the grandeur and reflecting on the significance of this momentous journey.

Olivia turned to Nicolas, her eyes sparkling with joy. "Nicolas, today has been absolutely incredible. Delhi has captured my heart. I can't believe how lucky we are to experience all of this together."

Nicolas smiled, his love for Olivia shining through his eyes. "You've found a new purpose here, haven't you?" he asked softly.

Olivia nodded; her voice filled with conviction. "India has opened my eyes, Nicolas. I've realized that my influence can do beyond the realm of entertainment. I have a responsibility to use my voice for those who are voiceless, to shine a light on the injustices that exist in the world. And together, my love, I believe that we can make a real difference."

Nicolas smiled, his heart swelling with pride. "I've missed this fire in you, Olivia. Seeing you so passionate, so driven—it reminds me of why I fell in love with you. And it fills me with hope for our future."

It was just before nightfall, when Nicolas and Olivia finally returned to their hotel. Their hearts still brimming with the enchantment of their day in Delhi. The anticipation of their last night in the city filled the air, promising a moment of intimacy and connection that would linger in their memories for years to come.

Inside their hotel room, the atmosphere was infused with a delicate fragrance, the room adorned with flickering candles that bathed the space in a warm, romantic glow. Soft music played in the background, filling the room with melodic notes that set the stage for a moment of pure magic.

Nicolas stood near the center of the room, a small smile playing on his lips as he watched Olivia's eyes widen in surprise. He extended his hand towards her, the gesture inviting her to join him. "May I have this dance, my love?"

Olivia's heart fluttered with joy as she took his hand, her eyes shimmering with love and anticipation. "Of course, my love. I would, gladly."

The strains of a familiar melody filled the room, and Nicolas drew Olivia into his arms, their bodies swaying gently to the rhythm of the music. As they moved together, they were transported back to their first dance, the night they first met at the grand gala in Creudor.

The memories flooded their minds, intertwining with the present moment, creating a symphony of emotions that only deepened their connection.

With each step, their movements became a language of their own, expressing the unspoken love and devotion that bound them together. Nicolas held Olivia close, his touch gentle yet possessive, as if to convey that she was his anchor in a world of uncertainties.

Their eyes locked, communicating a thousand words that their lips couldn't utter in that moment. The room seemed to fade away, leaving only the two of them in a world of their own, swaying in perfect harmony.

As the music reached its crescendo, Nicolas pulled Olivia closer, their bodies pressed together in an intimate embrace. Their hearts beat in unison, the rhythm of their love echoing in the silence. They paused for a moment, their foreheads touching, and their breaths mingling in the air. It became an exploration of their souls, an affirmation of their love and commitment. And as the final notes hung in the air, Nicolas leaned in, capturing Olivia's lips in a passionate kiss that spoke volumes of their desire and longing.

Their embrace deepened, their bodies pressed together in an intoxicating fusion of love and raw emotion. Time seemed to stand still as they lost themselves in the intensity of their connection, their lips moving with a hunger that mirrored the depth of their love.

They sank onto the plush couch, still holding each other, their lips locked in a fervent embrace. Time seemed to stretch, their desires and longing intermingling with the soft sighs and whispered words of affection. Their bodies molded together, their souls merging in a symphony of passion and love.

Nicolas reveled in Olivia's taste, her scent intoxicating his senses as he savored the moment. He loved how she surrendered to his every touch, her body responding to his every stroke, her every caress heightening his arousal.

She was his muse, the catalyst that drove him to achieve new heights, the only one who could reach the depths of his soul. And yet, the depth of her love for him continued to amaze him, leaving him in awe of her ability to love him so completely. He was certain that she would be his end and his beginning, a part of him that would forever be linked to his heart. And yet, he realized that he had yet to fully show her the depths of his love.

The heat of their embrace began to escalate, their bodies burning with desire as they writhed against each other in a fervent dance of ecstasy. The air was filled with the sound of their sighs, their breath coming out in ragged gasps. He pulled back from the kiss, gazing into her eyes as he murmured his love. "I love you, Olivia. So very much."

She smiled back, her eyes twinkling with a mixture of joy and love. "And I love you, Nicolas. So much that I can barely breathe."

Her words spurred him on, his desire for her growing

by the second. He lifted her up, and she wrapped her legs around him, gasping at the sensation of his hardness pressing against her. His hands slid up her body, caressing her curves with a passion that bordered on madness. She pushed herself against him, her hips grinding in an aching rhythm that sent sparks of desire throughout his body.

His lips trailed along her neck, leaving a fiery path of desire as he continued to stroke her with a rough, possessive touch. She shivered, her body quivering as she succumbed to his every touch. He captured her lips in a hungry kiss, his tongue tracing along the curve of her lips before plunging inside. His fingers reached up to her breast, finding her engorged bud, rolling it between his fingers. She gasped into the kiss, her body arching into him as she reveled in the intensity of his touch.

She wanted him so much that she could barely stand it. Her body trembled as he explored her, her every nerve ending igniting with desire. Her hands slid down to his pants, undoing the clasp before reaching for his zipper. He watched her, his eyes filled with lust and hunger. She could feel the heat radiating from his body, the intensity of his gaze making her ache with need.

Her fingers wrapped around his length, and he shuddered, a low groan escaping his lips. She teased him, her fingers moving along the length of his shaft, tracing the contours of his flesh. She felt the silky smoothness of his skin, her own desire growing by the second. He leaned back, watching her as she continued to explore him.

Her hands moved up and down, her strokes slowly increasing in speed and pressure as her arousal began to take over. She loved the feel of his thick, pulsing shaft, his hardness and heat filling her with a craving for him that could not be quenched.

He thrust into her hand, his body shuddering at the intensity of her touch. His breathing grew ragged, his body burning with a primal desire that demanded release. She smiled as she watched him, her fingers tracing along the thick veins, the sensation almost enough to send him over the edge. She continued to stroke him, her movements deliberate, her gaze locked on his. She could feel his muscles tensing, his hips bucking into her palm.

His eyes met hers, the intensity of his gaze taking her breath away. "I want you, Olivia. I want to be inside you. Please." He groaned, his voice strained with a mixture of lust and raw emotion. "I want to claim you, to make you mine."

She nodded, her body quaking with need as her own desires reached new heights. "Make me yours then."

He lifted her up, his arms wrapping around her back as he turned, his back pressed against the wall. Her legs wrapped around his hips, and she held onto him for dear life as he kissed her. His mouth moved down to her neck, kissing and nibbling on the soft skin. She shivered in response, her breath coming out in ragged gasps.

He pushed her up against the wall, his shaft nestled between her legs as he moved his lips down to her chest. She gasped as he reached for her breast, his tongue teasing her hardened bud through the fabric.

She wanted him so much that she could barely stand it, her body trembling as he took her nipple in his mouth, his teeth grazing the soft flesh. His fingers fumbled with the buttons of her white cotton shirt, his tongue and teeth continuing to torment her. She reached for him, her hands sliding down to the elastic waistband of his underpants. He helped her, both of them working together to get out of their clothes as quickly as they could.

His hands moved back to her breast; his touch gentle but firm as he caressed her curves. She could feel the heat radiating from his body, his fingers trailing down to her inner thigh, stroking the soft skin. He slid his hands up to her panties, tracing along the edges before moving inside. She gasped, her body arching into his touch as he teased her.

His mouth moved down to her other breast, his teeth tugging gently at her hardened bud, his fingers stroking her folds. She felt a rush of desire surge through her, her hips grinding into his hand, her legs trembling as she began to lose control.

Nicolas knew exactly what she wanted. He loved how she responded to his every touch, her body moving in perfect harmony as she relished the sensations. He continued to stroke her, his fingers rubbing her swollen clit as she shuddered with desire. He loved watching her as she reached the precipice of bliss. She was so beautiful that he could barely breathe.

He held her up with one arm, his fingers sinking deep inside her, his thumb continuing to rub against her clit. She let out a soft moan, her eyes fluttering shut as she succumbed to the raw intensity of his touch.

Her body clenched around his fingers, her juices dripping onto his hand as she came undone in his arms. She clung to him, her legs shaking as the intensity of her orgasm washed over her. His mouth moved back up to her breast, sucking her nipple into his mouth as he continued to thrust his fingers inside her.

She couldn't take it anymore. She wanted him inside her. She needed him to fill her with his thick, pulsing shaft.

She pulled back, her eyes gleaming with lust and desire as she reached for his hardness. He smiled, his eyes smoldering with hunger as she guided him inside her. She gasped out loud, "I am already yours, my love."

His eyes met hers, his gaze full of love and adoration. "And I am yours, Olivia. Now and forever."

His lips crashed into hers as he thrust inside her, her tight sheath stretching around him as he filled her completely. She gasped into the kiss, her body shuddering as he plunged deep into her core. He held her in his arms, their bodies fused together in a primal fusion of love and desire.

She wrapped her arms around him, holding onto him for dear life as he rocked her world with each powerful thrust. She could feel him inside her, the heat radiating from his flesh sending waves of pleasure throughout her body. He continued to plunge into her, his hips moving in an aching rhythm as he drove them both to the brink of madness.

She could feel his thick shaft pulsing inside her, the heat from his body spreading through her like wildfire. She shuddered in his arms, her body shaking with ecstasy as her core clenched around him. She was so close.

He moved inside her, his strokes increasing in speed and power, sending her over the edge with a final thrust. She moaned into the kiss, her hips grinding into his as she succumbed to the sensations of her release. She felt herself melting into him, her mind lost in a haze of pleasure as he continued to fill her with his thick, throbbing shaft.

He held onto her, his lips moving to her neck as he whispered into her ear. "I love you, Olivia. You are my world."

His words sent her over the edge, her body quaking with a second release as he came inside her, filling her with his essence.

She clung to him, her body shuddering as the intensity of the moment swept over her. He held her tight, his body pressed against hers as he carried her to the bed.

She fell back, her body still pulsing with pleasure, with

his shaft still inside her. He rolled onto his back, pulling her into his arms. They lay together in a contented silence, their bodies joined together as one, basking in the bliss of their lovemaking.

Olivia knew that her life would never be the same without Nicolas. He was her destiny, the one she was meant to be with. And now that she had found him, she realized that there was nowhere else in the world she would rather be.

***

CHAPTER 12:

A FRAMED MEMORY

Nicolas and Olivia, dressed in casual attire, stepped out of their hotel, their eyes filled with anticipation and curiosity. The bustling streets of Delhi welcomed them with open arms, the symphony of honking horns and the aroma of street food filling the air. They navigated through the lively crowd, blending in seamlessly, their true identities concealed for now.

Their destination was a small cafe tucked away in a quiet corner of the city, where they were scheduled to meet Rajiv Khanna. The cafe exuded a cozy charm, its walls adorned with colorful paintings and photographs showcasing the resilience and triumphs of young girls who had benefited from the Women's Welfare Organization.

As they entered, a warm smile spread across Rajiv's face. He rose from his seat, his eyes sparkling with enthusiasm. He was a middle-aged man, dressed in a casual white t-shirt and jeans. He had a warm complexion, a testament to the Indian sun that he had spent countless hours under as he tirelessly worked to make a difference. He had a neatly trimmed beard that added a touch of sophistication to his face, framing his strong jawline. His hair, peppered with hints of gray, was slightly tousled, as if he had been caught in the whirlwind of his organization's endeavors.

"Nicolas, Olivia, welcome!" Rajiv greeted them, extending a hand in friendship. "I'm delighted to meet you both. Thank you for taking an interest in our cause."

Nicolas shook Rajiv's hand, a genuine warmth in his smile. "The pleasure is ours, Rajiv. We've heard remarkable things about the work you do, and we're honored to be here."

Olivia, her eyes shining with admiration, added, "Yes, Rajiv. We believe in the power of education and empowerment. We want to learn more about your organization and see how we can contribute."

Rajiv's eyes twinkled with gratitude as he gestured for them to take a seat. They settled into a cozy corner of the cafe; the air filled with a sense of shared purpose.

Over cups of steaming masala chai, Rajiv shared stories of the Women's Welfare Organization and the incredible transformations he had witnessed. He spoke of the challenges faced by young girls in accessing education, the societal barriers they encountered, and the urgent need for change.

As the conversation flowed, Nicolas and Olivia found themselves captivated by Rajiv's words. His passion was contagious, igniting a fire within them to make a meaningful difference.

Olivia could not help but admire the way Rajiv connected with the girls, his unwavering belief in their potential. "Rajiv, you're truly an inspiration. Your dedication and the impact you've made in these girls' lives is remarkable," she said, her voice filled with admiration.

Rajiv humbly shrugged his shoulders. "It's not just me. It's the collective effort of countless individuals who believe in the power of education and empowerment. Every step counts, and together, we can create lasting change."

Nicolas leaned forward; his eyes gleaming with determination. "Rajiv, Olivia and I have a proposition. We want to lend our support to your organization. We have the resources, the platform, and the drive to make a significant impact. Together, we can amplify the message of empowerment and create opportunities for countless young girls."

Rajiv's eyes widened with surprise and delight. "Nicolas, Olivia, your offer is truly generous. With your involvement, we can reach even greater heights and touch more lives. It's an honor to have you by our side."

Olivia's gaze shifted to Nicolas, a mischievous smile playing on her lips. "You know, Nicolas, I think it's time to reveal who we really are. Rajiv, there's something we haven't told you. Nicolas is a prince of Creudor, and back in America, I'm an actress."

Rajiv's eyes widened in astonishment, his surprise giving way to a chuckle. "Well, I must admit, you had me fooled. But you know what? It doesn't change a thing. It only reinforces my belief that anyone, regardless of their background, can make a difference."

Laughter filled the air as they toasted to a newfound

partnership. Nicolas, Olivia, and Rajiv vowed to work together, their shared commitment to empowering the girl child becoming a driving force for change.

As they stepped out of the cafe, the Indian sun bathed the bustling streets of Delhi with its warm glow. Rajiv had graciously offered to show them around and introduce them to the incredible work his organization was doing. The streets of Delhi were alive with vibrant colors, the symphony of car horns and bustling crowds creating a rhythm unique to the city. Nicolas, Olivia, and Rajiv weaved through the labyrinth of narrow lanes and bustling markets, each step uncovering a new layer of Delhi's rich tapestry.

Rajiv, with his deep knowledge and infectious enthusiasm, became their trusted guide. He led them through the ancient maze of Chandni Chowk, where the aroma of street food filled the air and the sound of vendors haggling with customers created a lively symphony of its own.

"Ah, Chandni Chowk," Rajiv exclaimed, his eyes sparkling with nostalgia. "This place is a true reflection of Delhi's spirit. Amidst the chaos, there is beauty, history, and stories waiting to be discovered."

Olivia's eyes widened as she took in the sights and sounds around her. The vibrant colors of the shops, the intricately designed architecture, and the endless stream of people painted a vivid picture of life in Delhi. She could not help but be drawn to the energy that permeated the air.

Nicolas, equally captivated, leaned towards Rajiv. "Tell us more, Rajiv. How does your organization make a difference in the lives of these girls?"

Rajiv's face lit up with pride as he shared the stories of transformation. "We provide educational opportunities, vocational training, and support systems for these girls. We want to break the cycle of poverty and empower them to become agents of change in their communities. It's about giving them the tools and resources to rewrite their own narratives."

As they walked, Rajiv introduced them to some of the girls who had benefited from the organization. Their eyes sparkled with hope and resilience, their dreams and aspirations shining through. Olivia found herself deeply moved by their stories, their determination to overcome adversity serving as a powerful reminder of the strength of the human spirit.

Nicolas, sensing Olivia's emotions, gently squeezed her hand, offering silent support. He turned to Rajiv, a fire in his eyes. "Rajiv, we are even more determined to make a difference now. These girls deserve every opportunity, and we want to ensure they have the support they need to thrive."

Rajiv's face beamed with gratitude; his voice filled with appreciation. "Your support means the world to us. With your platform and passion, we can amplify our message and reach even more girls who need our help."

Their first stop was a local school supported by the Women's Welfare Organization, where girls from disadvantaged backgrounds were provided with quality education and a nurturing environment. The school gate opened to a world of hope and possibility. Nicolas, Olivia, and Rajiv stepped inside, greeted by the lively chatter and laughter of the girls as they immersed themselves in their studies and various activities. The classrooms were filled with vibrant colors, displaying the creative expressions of the young minds.

Nicolas and Olivia's eyes met, mirroring the sense of awe and gratitude that swelled within them. It was a humbling experience to witness the impact of the Women's Welfare Organization firsthand, to see the transformation taking place in the lives of these girls.

Rajiv introduced them to the school's principal, Ms. Meera, a beacon of warmth and resilience. Her petite frame seemed to carry a weight of responsibility, but her vibrant energy and warm smile lit up the room as she greeted Nicolas, Olivia, and Rajiv. With her hair neatly pulled back in a bun, Ms. Meera's eyes sparkled with a combination of wisdom and playfulness. She wore a traditional saree, its colors mirroring the vibrant hues of the classroom walls, adorned with delicate embroidery that spoke of her own attention to detail and love for her culture.

Her dedication to the girls was evident in every word she spoke and every smile she shared. With her guidance, they embarked on a tour of the classrooms, witnessing the eager faces and enthusiastic participation of the students.

In one corner, a group of girls huddled together, engaged in an animated discussion about their dreams and aspirations. Their eyes sparkled with determination as they shared their ambitions of becoming doctors, engineers, and artists. Olivia was captivated by their contagious enthusiasm.

Approaching one of the girls, Olivia crouched down to meet her at eye level. "What is your name?" she asked, her voice filled with genuine interest.

The girl, named Aisha, shyly responded, "I'm Aisha. I want to be a teacher someday so I can help other children like me."

Olivia's heart swelled with pride. "That's a wonderful dream, Aisha. I have no doubt that you'll make a fantastic teacher one day."

Nicolas joined the conversation, his eyes brimming with admiration. "Aisha, you're an inspiration. Keep chasing your dreams, and never forget that you have the power to make a difference."

The girls giggled, their innocence and resilience lighting up the room. They were curious about Nicolas and Olivia, unaware of their true identities. For that moment, they were simply Nicolas and Olivia, two individuals driven by a desire to uplift and empower. Olivia couldn't help but feel a deep connection with the girls, her heart swelling with empathy and a shared sense of empowerment. She listened intently as they shared their aspirations and dreams, their voices filled with an unwavering determination to defy societal norms and break barriers.

Nicolas observed Olivia, her eyes glistening with admiration and compassion. He knew that this experience was stirring something within her—a deep sense of purpose that resonated with their promise to make a difference with their fame and influence.

Rajiv, observing the exchange with a sense of pride, approached them. "This is the magic of education and empowerment. These girls are the future change-makers of our society, and with the right support, they can achieve extraordinary things."

As the day progressed, Nicolas, Olivia, and Rajiv engaged in various activities with the girls. They joined in music and dance sessions, their spirits lifted by the infectious energy and laughter that filled the room. Together, they painted vibrant pictures, each stroke a celebration of creativity and self-expression.

In a moment of spontaneity, Nicolas challenged the girls to a friendly game of football in the school courtyard. Laughter and playful banter filled the air as the girls showcased their skills, their determination shining through every kick and sprint.

Olivia, not one to shy away from a challenge, joined in the fun, her competitive spirit fueling the game. They ran, laughed, and celebrated each goal with wild abandon, the boundaries between prince, actress, and students blurred in the joyous camaraderie.

As the day drew to a close, Nicolas, Olivia, and Rajiv

gathered the girls in a circle, their smiles reflecting the shared bond and sense of empowerment that had formed throughout the day. With a twinkle in his eye, Nicolas addressed the girls.

"Remember, you have the power to shape your own destinies. Education is your key to unlocking a world of opportunities. Dream big, work hard, and never let anyone tell you that you can't achieve what you set your mind to."

Olivia's voice joined his, her words filled with warmth and encouragement. "Believe in yourselves, just as we believe in you. Your dreams matter, and we're here to support you every step of the way."

The girls nodded, their faces beaming with newfound confidence and determination. The room was filled with a sense of possibility, a shared vision of a future where these girls would rise above the challenges and leave their mark on the world.

As the day drew to a close, Olivia, Nicolas and Rajiv found themselves sitting on a rooftop terrace, overlooking the bustling cityscape of Delhi. The warm Indian summer breeze caressed their faces as they reflected on the day's experiences.

Olivia turned to Rajiv; her eyes filled with gratitude. "Rajiv, what you and your organization are doing is truly remarkable. The resilience and strength of these girls are awe-inspiring. We are honored to be a part of this journey and to support your cause in any way we can."

Rajiv smiled; his voice filled with heartfelt appreciation. "Thank you, Olivia and Nicolas. Your presence and support mean the world to us. Together, we can bring about real change and create a brighter future for these girls."

Nicolas reached out and took Olivia's hand, and leaned in to whisper. "Olivia, this is just the beginning. I can see the fire burning within you, the passion and purpose that have awakened in your heart."

Olivia's voice trembled with emotion. "Nicolas, being here, witnessing the incredible resilience and strength of these girls, has given me a renewed sense of purpose. I want to use our platform to amplify their voices, to shine a light on the challenges they face, and to inspire others to join us in making a difference."

As they sat there, bathed in the golden hues of the setting sun, a shared determination and passion filled the air. The rooftop terrace became a sanctuary, a place where dreams intertwined and possibilities stretched out before them.

***

In the weeks that followed, Nicolas and Olivia remained committed to their promise, working closely with Rajiv and the Women's Welfare Organization to raise awareness, funds, and support for their cause. Their shared journey in India had not only reignited the flame of their love but had also opened their hearts to a world of possibilities and a greater sense of purpose.

The last day in India arrived, casting a bittersweet shadow over Nicolas and Olivia. They had experienced a whirlwind of emotions, witnessed the beauty and resilience of the country, and ignited a spark of hope in their hearts. As they stood on the balcony of their hotel, gazing out at the city that had embraced them, a mixture of gratitude and longing swelled within them.

Olivia wrapped her arms around herself, feeling a pang of sadness. "Nicolas, it's hard to believe that our time in India is coming to an end. I will forever carry the stories of the girls we met in my heart."

Nicolas turned to her; his eyes filled with tenderness. "I feel the same way, Olivia. India has opened our eyes to a world of possibilities. This journey has redefined our purpose and strengthened our bond. I will cherish these moments forever."

Their hands found each other, fingers entwined, a symbol of the love and unity they had discovered amidst the chaos of their lives. They knew that leaving India meant returning to a world where their responsibilities and challenges awaited them. But they also carried with them the indomitable spirit of the girls they had met, their dreams fueling their own aspirations.

As they prepared to leave the hotel lobby, Rajiv joined them one last time, his warm smile a comforting presence. Emotions lingered in the air, an assortment of gratitude, joy, and a touch of melancholy. Rajiv held a small, beautifully wrapped gift box in his hands, a token of their time together.

"I wanted to give you something to remember this journey," Rajiv said, a warm smile gracing his face. He extended the box towards Nicolas and Olivia. "Inside, you'll find a special memento, a moment frozen in time."

Curiosity flickered in their eyes as they carefully unwrapped the box. Inside, nestled within layers of tissue paper, was a framed photograph. It captured the essence of their journey, the joy and camaraderie shared between them and the girls.

Nicolas gently lifted the frame, his eyes immediately drawn to the image. It was a picture taken right after the exhilarating football game they had played with the girls, their laughter echoing through the field. The genuine smiles on everyone's faces captured the spirit of their connection and the bonds formed during their time together.

Olivia's breath caught as she leaned in to get a closer look. She could not help but feel overwhelmed with gratitude for the experiences they had shared, the impact they had made, and the love that had blossomed amidst it all.

Rajiv spoke softly, his voice filled with fondness. "This photograph represents the beautiful memories we created together. May it serve as a reminder of the profound impact you have had on the lives of these girls."

Nicolas and Olivia exchanged a knowing glance, their hearts brimming with a deep sense of fulfillment. They understood the power of that moment, the significance of their journey in India, and the lifelong connections they had forged.

"Thank you, Rajiv," Nicolas said, his voice filled with gratitude. "This photograph will hold a special place in our hearts."

Olivia's voice was filled with genuine appreciation. "Rajiv, we are forever grateful for your guidance, your passion, and the opportunity to be a part of this incredible organization."

Rajiv nodded, his eyes shimmering with pride and joy. "It has been an honor to have both of you here. Your commitment to making a difference will continue to inspire us. Remember, this is not the end but the beginning of a lifelong journey."

Olivia embraced Rajiv, gratitude pouring from her heart. "Rajiv, thank you for guiding us on this incredible journey. You have inspired us in ways words cannot express."

Nicolas nodded, a sense of purpose emanating from him. "Rajiv, we will remain connected. We will support your organization from afar and continuing to advocate for the rights and empowerment of girls. This is just the beginning my friend."

As they bid farewell to Rajiv, their hearts heavy with the weight of leaving behind newfound friends and a land that had captured their souls, Nicolas and Olivia stepped into their awaiting car. The bustling streets of Delhi passed by in a blur, the vibrant colors and captivating sights etching themselves into their memories.

As the plane carried them away from India, Olivia glanced out the window, tears glistening in her eyes. She whispered to herself, "India, you have touched me in ways I never thought possible. You have given me a sense of purpose, and I promise to do my part, however small that might be."

Nicolas squeezed her hand, his voice filled with determination. "I promise you, my love. I will do everything in my power to make this dream of ours a reality."

As the plane soared above the clouds, carrying them back to their lives filled with royal duties and the glitz of the entertainment industry, Nicolas and Olivia held onto the profound lessons they had learned in India. They knew that their love had found a deeper purpose —one that extended far beyond their own lives. Their love had been tested, and it had emerged stronger than ever—a force that would drive them to continue making the world a better place, one step at a time.

***

CHAPTER 13:

A ROYAL REUNION

As Nicolas and Olivia stepped foot into the grand palace of Creudor, their presence rippled through the opulent hallways, drawing the attention of the royal family and staff alike. The air was thick with anticipation, and a mixture of curiosity and tension hung in the atmosphere.

Jack, dressed impeccably in a tailored suit, greeted Nicolas and Olivia with a warm smile. "Welcome back to the palace, Your Highness, Miss Grey," he said, his voice exuding a sense of professionalism and genuine friendship. "I must say, it's good to have you both here again."

Nicolas nodded, grateful for Jack's unwavering support. "Thank you, Jack. It feels good to be home," he replied, his voice laced with determination.

Olivia glanced around the ornate corridor, taking in the grandeur of the palace. She couldn't help but feel a tinge of nervousness as she prepared to face the royal family once more. However, the steadfast presence of Nicolas by her side provided her with a sense of reassurance.

As they approached the meeting room, the heavy double doors swung open, revealing the royal family gathered inside. King Edmund sat at the head of the long, polished table, his regal demeanor a testament to his years of leadership. To his left sat Prince Frederick and Princess Sophia, their expressions bland and vacant. Marco, the trusted royal aide, stood at the ready, prepared to offer his counsel.

Olivia took a deep breath, her hand tightening around Nicolas's. She knew that their return to Creudor would not be without its challenges, but she also believed in the power of love to bridge divides. As they approached their seats, her gaze met Sophia's, and a subtle tension passed between them.

"Welcome back, Nicolas, Olivia," King Edmund greeted, his voice carrying both warmth and reservation. "We have much to discuss."

Nicolas, his determination shining through his eyes, as he intertwined his fingers with Olivia's. "Father, we are here to face whatever comes our way, united as a couple."

Prince Frederick, the heir to the throne, eyed them with

a mixture of curiosity and skepticism. He had always been protective of his younger brother, and the recent turmoil had put their bond to the test.

Princess Sophia, a woman of poise and ambition, spoke up with a deceptively sweet smile. "Nicolas, Olivia, I have a proposal. With the wedding approaching, I believe it would be fitting for Olivia to become my official maid of honor."

Olivia's eyes widened in surprise, the implications of Sophia's suggestion sinking in. She glanced at Nicolas, silently seeking his support and guidance.

Nicolas, ever the pillar of strength, placed a reassuring hand on Olivia's shoulder. "I appreciate the offer, Sophia, but I believe that Olivia and I need to navigate this delicate situation together."

"Nicolas, Olivia," King Edmund began, his voice with paternal concern. "The events of the past months have caused turmoil within our family and the kingdom. We must find ways to tackle them head on, now that Freddie's nuptials are mere months away."

Nicolas took a deep breath, his eyes locked with his father's. "Father, I understand the concerns and reservations surrounding our relationship. But I ask for the chance to prove that Olivia and I are committed to each other."

Princess Sophia, her gaze fixed on Olivia, spoke with a subtle undertone. "Indeed, Olivia, as my official maid of honor, you would have the opportunity to demonstrate your loyalty and dedication to the royal family."

Olivia felt the weight of Sophia's words, the ulterior motive simmering beneath her polite request. But she held her composure, her voice steady as she addressed the room. "I appreciate the offer, Princess Sophia, but I believe that actions speak louder than titles. I am here to show my commitment not only to Nicolas but also to the values and principles that this kingdom holds dear."

Marco, who had been observing the discussion silently, stepped forward, his expression contemplative yet supportive. "If I may, Your Highness," he addressed Princess Sophia, "I believe Olivia's involvement as the maid of honor could indeed serve as a unifying gesture, demonstrating the strength of our bonds and the spirit of inclusivity within the royal family."

His unexpected support surprised Olivia, and she met his gaze with gratitude. The acknowledgment from Marco held a significant weight, as his opinions were often grounded in practicality and tradition. To have his endorsement meant a step towards acceptance and reconciliation.

Princess Sophia's eyes sparkled with satisfaction as she listened to Marco's words. "Thank you, Marco, for your perspective," she replied, her voice soft yet filled with conviction. "I believe Olivia's presence as my maid of honor will not only symbolize our unity but also showcase the evolution and open-mindedness of our royal family."

As the discussion progressed, Marco's stance shifted

from cautious neutrality to a growing enthusiasm for the idea. He recognized the potential in using Olivia's involvement to bridge the gap between tradition and progress, while also highlighting the importance of acceptance and embracing change.

Nicolas, sensing the positive shift in the room, turned to Olivia, a smile tugging at the corners of his lips. "It seems we have found allies in unexpected places," he whispered, his voice filled with a mixture of relief and joy.

Olivia nodded, her eyes glistening with hope. "Yes, Nicolas. It's a testament to the power of love and understanding. Together, we can overcome any obstacle and build a future where our love is celebrated."

King Edmund nodded, a glimmer of admiration crossing his features. "Very well, Olivia. We shall give you that chance. But remember, the eyes of the world are upon you."

With Marco's support and Princess Sophia's insistence, the decision was made—Olivia would take on the role of Princess Sophia's maid of honor, a position that held both symbolism and significance. It was a step towards acceptance, unity, and the integration of Olivia into the royal family.

As the discussion turned toward the future, Prince Nicolas spoke with a sense of purpose. "Father, I believe that Olivia and I can make a meaningful impact through a foundation focused on empowering women. It's an opportunity to leverage our influence for positive change."

King Edmund nodded, acknowledging the sincerity in his son's voice. "Empowering women is a noble cause, one that aligns with the values of our kingdom. It could be a legacy we leave behind, a testament to the strength of our family."

Princess Sophia, her eyes narrowed slightly, interjected, "And what role do you envision for Frederick and me in this endeavor?"

Nicolas smiled warmly; his gaze fixed on his brother. "Frederick, you have always been an advocate for progress and equality. Your voice and influence could help amplify our efforts. And Sophia, as someone who is soon to be part of our family, your involvement would boost favorable opinion and garner support from the public."

Prince Frederick's expression softened, his eyes meeting Sophia's as he contemplated the proposal. "It would be an honor to work alongside you, Nicolas, and Olivia, for such a worthy cause. Our wedding can be an occasion to celebrate unity and the power of love."

Sophia's features softened, realizing the significance of the moment. "I see the potential impact we can make together. Count me in."

King Edmund, pleased with the resolution, leaned back in his chair. "It is settled then. We shall collaborate on this foundation, pooling our resources, networks, and influence. Together, we can bring about positive change and uplift the lives of women within and beyond our kingdom."

As the meeting came to a close, the air in the room seemed to lighten. A renewed sense of purpose and unity permeated the atmosphere. The once-mixed reactions had given way to a shared vision, as the royal family prepared to embark on a journey of empowerment, love, and philanthropy.

***

Unbeknownst to Nicolas and Olivia, a storm was brewing within the palace walls. They had returned from their journey in India with renewed determination to face the challenges that awaited them. But little did they know that their love story had ignited a spark of jealousy and vindictiveness within the walls of the palace.

Princess Sophia's envy and resentment toward Olivia had grown into a deep-seated hatred. She couldn't bear the thought of Olivia's presence in Nicolas' life, threatening her own position and the stability of the royal family. Determined to uncover any secrets that could tarnish Olivia's image, Princess Sophia sought the assistance of Marco, knowing his unwavering loyalty to the crown.

In the dimly lit corridors of the palace, away from prying eyes and listening ears, Princess Sophia and Marco met clandestinely. The air was thick with tension as they exchanged covert glances, their shared agenda etched in their expressions.

Princess Sophia leaned in; her voice laced with venom. "Marco, we cannot let Olivia continue to infiltrate our lives. She is a threat, and I am certain there are skeletons in her closet. I need you to dig deeper, find any information that can discredit her. We cannot allow her to tarnish the royal family's name."

Marco, torn between his loyalty to the royal family and his growing admiration for Olivia, reluctantly agreed. "Your Highness, I understand your concerns, and I will spare no effort in uncovering any hidden truths about Olivia Grey. Rest assured; I will leave no stone unturned."

With their secret pact sealed, Princess Sophia and Marco parted ways, each with their own agenda fueling their actions. The palace corridors echoed with whispers and the weight of impending revelations, as they embarked on a mission to expose Olivia's past.

Late into the night, Marco delved into his research, meticulously uncovering every detail about Olivia Grey. He sifted through archives, dug into old news articles, and even reached out to contacts in the entertainment industry, hoping to find a chink in Olivia's armor. As he uncovered more about Olivia's rise to fame and the accomplishments she had achieved, a sense of awe mixed with conflict began to wash over him.

Days turned into weeks, and the deeper Marco dug, the more he realized that Olivia's life was an open book. She had faced her fair share of trials and tribulations, but her resilience and unwavering determination had led her to where she stood today. It became increasingly clear to Marco that Olivia was not the person Princess Sophia believed her to be.

One evening, as Princess Sophia impatiently awaited Marco's findings, he approached her with a heavy heart. "Your Highness, I have searched high and low, but I have found no evidence of any wrongdoing or scandal in Olivia Grey's past. She has dedicated her life to her craft and philanthropic endeavors. She is loved and respected by many."

Princess Sophia's face twisted in frustration. "There must be something, Marco! We cannot allow this woman to disrupt the harmony of our family. Keep searching, deeper and harder. Find me something that will expose her flaws and tear her apart."

Marco hesitated, his conscience battling against his loyalty. "Princess, I understand your concerns, but Olivia's character and integrity shine through. She has brought nothing but joy and inspiration to Prince Nicolas. Perhaps it's time to accept their love and support their efforts to make a difference."

Princess Sophia's eyes narrowed with venomous determination. "No, Marco. I will not accept defeat. I will find a way to expose Olivia for who she truly is. She will not have the satisfaction of stealing Prince Nicolas from our family."

As Marco left the room, a heavy weight settled on his shoulders. He knew he had to make a choice between his loyalty to the royal family and his growing belief in the purity of Olivia's intentions. In his heart, he could not help but wonder if Princess Sophia's relentless pursuit of destruction was rooted more in her own insecurities than any genuine concern for the family's reputation.

Meanwhile, unaware of the brewing storm, Olivia and Nicolas found solace in each other's arms. Through handwritten letters, late-night phone calls, and stolen moments of virtual togetherness, Nicolas and Olivia nourished the flame of their love, growing stronger with each passing day. Distance may have separated them physically, but their connection transcended the limitations of time and space. They found solace in the written words that carried their deepest emotions, pouring their hearts onto the digital canvas, baring their souls to each other.

Their conversations were filled with laughter, tears, and whispered promises of a future that they yearned to share. The miles between them seemed insignificant as their voices intertwined, creating a symphony of love and longing.

Back in Los Angeles, Olivia sought refuge in the familiar rhythm of her dogs Stella and Max by her side. They became witnesses to the countless nights spent gazing at the screen, her heart leaping with joy at the sight of Nicolas's face. They listened intently to the whispers of love that floated through the air, their eyes filled with a knowing understanding.

In the royal palace of Creudor, Prince Nicolas, burdened by his many duties, found solace in the secret moments when he could escape the confines of his responsibilities. He would find a quiet corner, his heart racing as he dialed Olivia's number, eagerly awaiting the sound of her voice. Their conversations were filled with dreams, plans, and the unwavering belief that their love could conquer all obstacles.

With each passing day, they grew more determined to bridge the gap that separated them, to navigate the stormy waters of scrutiny and public opinion. They knew that their love was worth the fight, that the bond they shared was forged in a crucible of authenticity and vulnerability.

And as they gazed at the moonlit skies, separated by hours but united by love, they vowed to cherish their love was destined to triumph over the obstacles that threatened to tear them apart.

***

Olivia was resolute in her decision to shield her love life from prying eyes. That sunny morning, she gracefully maneuvered through the swarm of paparazzi hungry for any glimpse into her personal life. Camera flashes illuminated the scene, capturing the moment as the photographers clamored for her attention, their questions flying at her like a relentless storm. Undeterred, she maintained a serene smile, her composure unwavering.

"Olivia, who are you dating? Is it true that you're involved with Prince Nicolas?" one paparazzo shouted, thrusting a microphone in her direction.

With practiced poise, Olivia deflected the question with a wide smile. "Oh, you know how rumors circulate. I'm focused on my work right now, and I'm grateful for the support of my fans."

The paparazzi persisted, firing off more questions, but Olivia remained steadfast in her resolve to protect her privacy. She had learned the hard way the consequences of having her personal life exposed to the world. This time, however, she had something worth protecting, something she cherished deeply.

As the paparazzi continued their barrage of inquiries, a familiar voice broke through the chaos. "Hey, back off, guys!"

It was Justin, Olivia's longtime friend and loyal confidant. He had always been by her side, offering a sense of grounding amidst the whirlwind of fame. Olivia turned to him, relief washing over her.

"Oh, Justin, thank you," she said, giving him a grateful smile.

"Olivia, how do you handle this every day?" Justin

asked, his voice laced with admiration and disbelief.

Olivia glanced at Justin, a twinkle in her eyes. "I've learned that the best way to deal with them is to ignore their questions and focus on what truly matters. My love life is something I hold dear, and I won't let the paparazzi invade that privacy."

Justin chuckled, shaking his head in amazement. "I can't believe how composed you are. It's like you have a shield of calmness around you."

Olivia shrugged playfully. "Well, I've had some practice. But more importantly, Justin, there's something I need to tell you. Nicolas and I are in love."

Justin's eyes widened, surprise and delight colored his features. "Wait, seriously? When did this happen? How did you two fall in love?"

Olivia smiled; her voice filled with warmth. "It's been a journey, Justin. But it was that night when Nicolas took me to a secret rehab that I truly realized he was the one. He saw me at my lowest, my vulnerability exposed, and he stood by me, offering his unwavering support and love. It was in that moment that I knew he was the person I wanted to share my life with."

Justin gasped out aloud, "Wait, a secret rehab? Olivia, why didn't you tell me about this? I thought we shared everything."

Olivia's smile faded slightly, replaced by a gentle understanding. "Justin, I'm sorry I didn't confide in you sooner. It was a difficult time for me, and I wanted to keep it private until I was ready to share."

Justin's brows furrowed; his voice tinged with worry. "But why did you need to go to rehab? Are you okay? I thought we were open with each other about everything."

Taking a deep breath, Olivia reached out to touch Justin's arm, her eyes filled with sincerity. "Justin, I want you to know that I'm okay now. It wasn't something I planned or expected, but I found myself battling some personal struggles, and I needed professional help to overcome them."

Justin's expression softened, concern mingling with compassion. "Olivia, I'm so sorry you had to go through that. I wish I had been there for you."

Olivia's grip on his arm tightened, her voice filled with reassurance. "Justin, you've always been there for me, and I appreciate your friendship more than words can express. But at that time, I needed professional help. It wasn't a reflection on our friendship or my trust in you."

Justin nodded slowly; his gaze filled with understanding. "I get it, Liv. Sometimes, we all need different forms of help to navigate our struggles. I just wish I could have been there to support you."

A soft smile graced Olivia's lips as she squeezed Justin's arm gently. "You have been there for me, Justin. Your friendship has been a constant source of comfort. And now, with Nicolas in my life, I've found someone who understands me in a way no one else could. He saw me at my lowest and stood by me without judgment or hesitation."

Justin's eyes softened. "I'm glad you found someone who truly supports you, Olivia. You deserve all the happiness in the world."

Olivia nodded, a grateful tear glistening in her eye. "Thank you, Justin. Your understanding means everything to me. I cherish our friendship, and I want you to know that you'll always have a special place in my heart."

The two friends stood there for a moment; their unspoken bond stronger than ever. Olivia felt a weight lifted off her shoulders as she shared this vulnerable part of her journey with Justin. She knew that their friendship had weathered the test of time and would continue to thrive, even with the newfound love in her life.

"Olivia, I'm so happy for you." Justin whispered to her as he held her close. "It's clear that Nicolas cherishes you. You deserve all the love and happiness in the world."

Olivia nodded gratefully, a sense of contentment washing over her. "Thank you, Justin. Your support means a lot to me."

Just then, a particularly persistent paparazzo lunged forward, his voice filled with aggression as he clicked her pictures. "Olivia, tell us about your relationship with Prince Nicolas! Are you planning a wedding?"

Olivia turned towards the paparazzo; her smile unwavering. "I'm sorry, but I don't discuss my personal life with the media. I'm here to focus on my work and the causes that are important to me. Have a wonderful day!" With that, she gracefully walked away, Justin following closely behind.

As they moved further away from the paparazzi's grasp, Justin marveled at Olivia's grace under pressure. "You know, Liv, your newfound attitude is inspiring. The way you handle those relentless questions, it's like you've become a force to be reckoned with."

Olivia chuckled, her eyes sparkling with determination. "I've realized that my happiness and the privacy of my love life are worth protecting. I won't let the paparazzi dictate my narrative. Love is a beautiful thing, and Nicolas and I deserve to cherish it without unnecessary scrutiny."

Justin grinned, his admiration evident. "You're right, Liv. Love should always be celebrated. And I'm here to support you every step of the way."

***

CHAPTER 14:

A GAME OF NERVES

It was a week before the royal wedding of
Prince Frederick and Princess Sophia. Olivia is back in
Creudor to partake in the bridesmaid activities. As she
stepped out of the airport, she was greeted by Jack
Smith, Prince Nicolas' loyal personal secretary. Jack's
warm smile and friendly demeanor instantly put her at
ease.

"Welcome back to Creudor, Miss Grey," Jack said,
extending his hand. "It's a pleasure to have you here."

"Thank you, Jack," Olivia replied, shaking his hand. "It's
good to see you again. I hope I'm not causing any
inconvenience with my arrival."

Jack chuckled, his eyes twinkling. "Not at all. It's an
exciting time for all of us, and having you here as part
of the bridal party adds to the celebration. Prince
Nicolas couldn't be happier."

Olivia's heart fluttered at the mention of Nicolas, and
she couldn't help but feel a mixture of anticipation and
nerves as she thought about the upcoming wedding. She
knew the road ahead wouldn't be easy, especially with
Princess Sophia's animosity towards her, but she was
determined to navigate through the challenges and
prove her worth.

Jack escorted Olivia to a luxurious car waiting outside
the airport. As they drove through the streets of
Creudor, Olivia took in the majestic beauty of the city,

the architecture reflecting the grandeur of the royal heritage. Jack, sat beside her, his gaze focused on the passing scenery. After a few moments of silence, he turned to Olivia, his tone serious yet reassuring.

"Miss Grey, I wanted to take this opportunity to brief you on the details of the upcoming royal wedding. It will be a significant event, not only for Prince Frederick and Princess Sophia but also for you and Prince Nicolas. This will be your first public outing together as a confirmed couple."

Olivia nodded, her heart pounding with anticipation. "I understand, Jack. It's a big step, and I want to make sure everything goes smoothly."

Jack offered her a reassuring smile. "You have nothing to worry about, Miss Grey. The palace staff has been diligently preparing for the event, and security measures have been heightened to ensure everyone's safety. The royal family is aware of the public's curiosity and interest in your relationship, and they have made arrangements to handle the media and public appearances accordingly."

Olivia's brows furrowed, concern flickering in her eyes. "I hope the public's reaction will be positive. I want to support Prince Nicolas and be there for him, but I also want to ensure that my presence doesn't overshadow the significance of the wedding."

Jack nodded understandingly. "That's a valid concern, Olivia. But rest assured, the palace is working closely with the media and other involved parties to strike a balance. The focus will be on Prince Frederick and Princess Sophia, as it should be, but your presence will undoubtedly draw attention as well."

Olivia leaned back against the plush seat, her mind racing with thoughts. "I just want to be there for Nicolas, Jack. I want to support him and stand by his side, no matter what."

Jack's eyes softened, reflecting a depth of understanding. " Miss Grey, I've been with the royal family for many years, and I've seen relationships tested by public pressure. I believe in you and Prince Nicolas."

A sense of gratitude washed over Olivia as she looked at Jack, realizing the unwavering support he had provided throughout her journey. "Thank you, Jack. Your words mean a lot to me."

Jack nodded approvingly. "That's the spirit, Miss Grey. Stay grounded, trust in your love, and let your genuine connection shine through."

Soon, they arrived at Codrington Castle, that sat quite far away from the official Royal palace. It was designated for the stay for the bride and her close family. It was where Olivia would be staying during the course of the wedding festivities.

Olivia stepped out of the car; her eyes widened in awe at the sight of the magnificent estate before her. The sprawling grounds were adorned with lush gardens, blooming flowers, and ancient trees that seemed to whisper stories of generations past. The grandeur of the place mirrored the significance of the upcoming royal wedding.

Jack led Olivia towards the entrance of the estate, their footsteps muffled by the soft grass beneath them. The ornate double doors swung open, revealing a spacious foyer adorned with elegant chandeliers and intricate artwork. A sense of tranquility enveloped the atmosphere, offering a respite from the bustling preparations taking place elsewhere in the kingdom.

As Olivia stepped inside, she was greeted by Princess Sophia, radiating an air of regal grace. "Olivia, welcome to our temporary home," she said, extending a hand in greeting. "I hope you find it comfortable here."

Olivia offered a warm smile, feeling a wave of gratitude towards Princess Sophia for her kindness. "Thank you, Princess Sophia. This place is truly magnificent. I am honored to be a part of your wedding celebration."

Princess Sophia's smile softened, a touch of sincerity shining through. "Please, Olivia, call me Sophia. We will be family soon, and formalities are unnecessary among loved ones."

Olivia nodded appreciatively. "Thank you, Sophia. I appreciate your warmth and kindness. I want you to know that I am here to support you and Prince Frederick in any way I can."

Jack, who had been silently observing the interaction, chimed in with his calm voice. "Miss Grey, we have a schedule prepared for the upcoming days. There will be various events and preparations leading up to the wedding ceremony. I will be by your side, guiding you through the process and ensuring everything goes smoothly."

Olivia's eyes met Jack's, filled with gratitude for his unwavering support. "Thank you, Jack. I appreciate everything you have done and continue to do for me. Your presence brings me comfort and confidence."

Jack smiled warmly. "It is my duty and pleasure, Miss Grey. The royal family holds you in high regard, and we all want to see this wedding be a success."

He then excused himself and left the two women all by themselves. Sophia turned her attention back to Olivia; her expression had gotten cold. She motioned for Olivia to follow her, leading the way through the elegant corridors of the estate.

As Sophia led Olivia through the lavish hallways of the estate, their steps echoing softly against the polished marble floors, Olivia could not help but feel a sense of unease. Sophia's graceful demeanor had shifted, replaced by an undercurrent of tension that made the air feel heavy.

They reached a set of double doors, ornately carved and adorned with delicate patterns. Sophia opened them, revealing a spacious suite that exuded both comfort and luxury. The room was decorated with plush furnishings, vibrant tapestries, and large windows that offered breathtaking views of the surrounding gardens.

Sophia stepped aside, allowing Olivia to enter first. Olivia's gaze wandered across the room, taking in the intricate details, but her attention soon returned to Sophia, who wore a cold and calculating expression.

Sophia's gaze bore into Olivia, her eyes filled with a mixture of jealousy and disdain.

"Olivia," she said with a forced smile, her voice laced with venomous sweetness. "I trust you are settling in well."

Olivia maintained her composure, her eyes meeting Sophia's with a calm resolve. "Thank you, Sophia. The suite is beautiful, and I appreciate your efforts in making my stay comfortable."

Sophia's smile tightened, her tone dripping with bitterness. "It's the least I can do, considering the circumstances."

Olivia felt a knot forming in her stomach, sensing that the conversation was taking an unpleasant turn. "I'm not sure I understand what you mean, Sophia. Is there something you'd like to discuss?"

Olivia sensed a subtle shift in Sophia's demeanor. The warmth that had initially radiated from her seemed to wane, replaced by a calculating expression in her eyes. Sophia gestured towards a seating area, inviting Olivia to join her. Olivia sank into a plush armchair, the nerves settling in as she awaited Sophia's next words.

Sophia leaned forward, her voice taking on a slightly

more assertive tone. "Olivia, I must be honest with you. Being a part of the royal family comes with its own set of responsibilities and expectations. It is not an easy path to navigate."

Olivia's brow furrowed, a mixture of confusion and caution crossing her features. She could sense an undercurrent of manipulation in Sophia's words, but she remained composed. "Sophia, I understand that being in a relationship with Nicolas means accepting the responsibilities and pressures that come with his position."

A flicker of annoyance flashed across Sophia's face, quickly masked by a forced smile. "But Olivia, have you considered the impact your presence might have on Nicolas's duties? The media frenzy, the public scrutiny —it can be overwhelming. Are you prepared to endure it all?"

Olivia's voice remained steady, despite the growing tension in the room. "Sophia, I am well aware of the media attention and the public interest that surrounds us. I am committed to supporting Nicolas in his duties, and I know he will do the same for me."

Sophia's gaze turned sharp; her words laced with a subtle threat. "Olivia, you may think you know Nicolas, but you cannot truly comprehend the weight of his responsibilities. He is the future king's brother, and everything he does is scrutinized. Are you prepared to put yourself in the line of fire, to face the constant judgment and criticism that comes with being a part of this family?"

Olivia's voice remained calm, though a hint of defiance colored her words. "Sophia, I understand that there will be challenges, but I refuse to let fear dictate my decisions. I love Nicolas, and I am willing to face whatever comes our way."

Sophia's eyes narrowed, a flicker of frustration passing over her features. "You may be strong-willed, Olivia, but remember that this world can be ruthless. I have seen many come and go, their dreams shattered by the demands of this life."

Olivia's voice remained steady, her resolve unwavering. "Sophia, I appreciate your concern, but I assure you, my intentions are pure. I love Nicolas, and I am not here to jeopardize his happiness or the stability of the royal family."

Sophia's gaze held a mixture of skepticism and suspicion. She leaned back in her chair, a contemplative expression on her face. "Very well, Olivia. But remember, you will need to prove yourself, not just to me, but to the entire kingdom."

Olivia's heart sank, realizing that Sophia's true intentions were not rooted in genuine concern but rather in a desire to test her resolve. However, she refused to let Sophia's manipulation deter her.

Sophia's sudden shift in demeanor was remarkable as she sprang up from her seat with a radiant smile, effortlessly transforming into the cheerful and composed princess she was expected to be. Olivia couldn't help but feel a pang of unease, wondering if the serious conversation they had just shared had been nothing more than a ploy.

"Come, Olivia," Sophia exclaimed, extending her hand towards her. "Let's not dwell on serious matters any longer. It's time for you to meet the other bridesmaids and immerse yourself in the joyous preparations for the wedding."

Olivia hesitated for a moment, the weight of their conversation still lingering in her mind. Nevertheless, she mustered a smile and rose to her feet, taking Sophia's proffered hand. She followed her down the corridor, each step bringing them closer to the grand hall where the other bridesmaids were gathered.

As they entered the hall, Olivia's eyes widened at the sight before her. The opulent space was adorned with exquisite tapestries and sparkling chandeliers, exuding an air of regality. Standing near a lavish display of flowers were the two women Sophia had mentioned.

Princess Charlotte, Sophia's younger sister, stood tall and graceful. Her fair complexion and cascading golden locks gave her an ethereal beauty, but there was a subtle hint of sadness in her eyes. Olivia could sense a certain tension between Charlotte and Sophia, though the cause eluded her for now.

Beside Charlotte stood Lady Amalia, a woman in her late thirties with a sharp wit and calculating gaze. Her refined features and impeccable manners masked a shrewdness that had earned her a reputation as a cunning spinster. It was clear that Lady Amalia had her own agenda, and Olivia couldn't help but wonder how she fit into the intricate dynamics of the royal family.

Sophia beamed as she made the introductions. "Olivia, I would like you to meet Princess Charlotte, my dear sister, and Lady Amalia, our cousin. They will be your companions throughout the wedding festivities."

Charlotte offered a polite smile, her voice tinged with a touch of melancholy. "It's a pleasure to meet you, Olivia. I've heard so much about you."

Olivia returned the greeting with genuine warmth. "Likewise, Princess Charlotte. I'm honored to be a part of this special occasion."

Lady Amalia, her eyes glinting with a hint of mischief, extended a hand adorned with elegant rings. "A pleasure, Miss Grey. I've been looking forward to meeting you. It seems you've captured the attention of the entire kingdom."

Olivia accepted Lady Amalia's hand with a gracious smile. "Thank you, Lady Amalia. I'm humbled by the warm welcome."

Sophia, ever the charming hostess, guided Olivia to a small seating area where they gathered for a brief respite. Olivia took a seat as she observed the interactions between the cousins, their laughter and banter filling the room. But she could not shake the feeling that something was amiss.

Sophia leaned closer to Olivia, her voice dropping to a hushed tone. "I hope you're enjoying the company, Olivia. These ladies are not only my closest friends but also my confidantes. We've shared secrets and laughter, and I trust them implicitly."

As the bridesmaids joined them, Princess Sophia addressed them with a forced enthusiasm. "Welcome, ladies. We have a lot to prepare for the upcoming festivities. Let's make this a wedding to remember. Olivia, as the maid of honor, I trust you will assist me in ensuring everything runs smoothly."

Olivia nodded graciously, her heart yearning for a genuine connection with Princess Sophia. "Of course, Princess Sophia. I'm here to support you in any way I can."

The other bridesmaids exchanged glances, sensing the tension between Olivia and Princess Sophia. They cautiously observed the interactions, unsure of where their loyalties should lie.

Despite the underlying tension, Olivia made an effort to lighten the atmosphere. "So, ladies, any ideas for the bachelorette party? We should plan something fun and unforgettable for the bride."

Lady Amalia's eyes sparkled with mischief. "I have a few ideas, but first we need to figure out where to hold the party. The queen has made all the necessary preparations for a grand celebration at the royal palace, but Princess Sophia might prefer a different venue."

Princess Sophia shook her head, her brow furrowed in vexation. "No, I don't want a big fuss. We should pick a small venue, so that we can enjoy ourselves in private."

"A smaller venue?" Lady Amalia interjected. "Are you sure? That's not what I would recommend, but it is your decision."

Olivia exchanged concerned glances with Lady Amalia, wondering why the bride and groom would have a bachelorette party at all. For the most part, these events were considered to be the prerogative of the bride.

Charlotte chimed in with a casual tone, her sadness giving way to a subtle hint of amusement. "Why not host it here at the castle? We'll have a ball in honor of the princess, and you can enjoy yourselves to your hearts' content."

"A ball?" Sophia scoffed in disbelief. "How does that even make sense? It's not as if we're preparing for the queen's funeral."

Charlotte's expression softened, and she took a deep breath before responding in a measured tone. "You're right. A ball is inappropriate for a bachelorette party. I just thought..."

Princess Sophia sighed and placed a hand on Charlotte's arm. "No, you're right. I'm sorry, Charlotte. I shouldn't have snapped at you. It's just... I want a quiet night of fun without any pressure. A private party in a cozy room seems more fitting."

Olivia watched the exchange with growing apprehension. She had no idea what was happening, but something told her it was not going to end well.

Lady Amalia turned to Olivia with a coy smile. "I have a good idea of where to hold the bachelorette party. Do you like gardens, Miss Grey? I believe they're the most romantic place to enjoy a glass of wine. There's a lovely gazebo near the garden maze. It's the perfect setting for an evening of fun."

Olivia nodded slowly, feeling a sense of unease in Lady Amalia's eagerness to make the arrangements. She had no idea what Lady Amalia was planning, but she couldn't shake the sense that something was amiss.

Sophia beamed, her radiant smile filling the room. "I love it, Amalia. You're so smart, and you have the best ideas. Thank you for looking after the details of the bachelorette party. Olivia, I'll be counting on you to help me make the preparations."

Olivia forced a smile, feeling a sense of foreboding. "Of course, Princess Sophia. I'll do my best to help you enjoy this special night."

As they began discussing the upcoming events, Olivia couldn't help but feel a sense of intrigue and caution. The dynamics between the three women were complex, and she knew she had to navigate the unspoken currents carefully. She remained determined to maintain her integrity and grace, despite the underlying currents of rivalry and hidden agendas.

Deep down, Olivia understood that she was stepping into a world of political maneuvering and personal ambitions. She would need to tread carefully, not only to protect her relationship with Nicolas but also to ensure her own safety amidst the intricate web of alliances and hidden intentions. She knew little about the history between Princess Charlotte and Princess Sophia, but it was clear there was some sort of disagreement. She had hoped to form a bond with the bride and groom, but now she felt as though she had stumbled into a trap.

***

CHAPTER 15:

TAMING THE WILDFIRE

As Olivia lay in her bed, her thoughts consumed by the events of the day, she could not shake the uneasiness that had settled within her. Her thoughts drifted back to her discussion with Princess Sophia. The princess's behavior was inconsistent, with one moment displaying warmth and sincerity and the next cold indifference. Olivia had to admit that she was feeling more than a little conflicted.

Her gaze shifted to her phone, where the unanswered text to Nicolas still lingered, a testament to the distance that had grown between them in the midst of their separate obligations.

Just as she was about to set her phone aside, a soft knock echoed through the room. Startled, Olivia's heart skipped a beat. She peered towards the door, her mind racing with possibilities. Who could be at this hour of the night?

Olivia rose from the bed and approached the door. As she opened it, her eyes widened in surprise, and a rush of emotions flooded her being. With a trembling hand, Olivia unlocked the door and swung it open

"I'm sorry to bother you, Miss Grey," he said, his voice resonating with an almost seductive timbre. "I just wanted to check in on you and make sure you're doing well.

She blinked, her heart skipping a beat as she looked at Nicolas standing there. He wore simple white shirt and jeans, his attire a stark contrast to the opulence of the palace. In the dim light of the corridor, his features were softened, his tousled hair falling gently across his forehead. She was surprised to see Nicolas, but she could not hide her excitement. She stepped pulled him inside, closing the door behind them, and looked up at him.

Olivia's breath caught in her throat as she beheld him, the sight of him stirring a whirlwind of emotions within her. Without a word, she reached out and pulled him into an embrace, their bodies pressing against each other, seeking solace and reassurance.

Nicolas held her tightly, his arms encircling her with a protective warmth. As they stood there, locked in their embrace, Olivia could feel the steady beat of his heart, a rhythm that mirrored her own. She nestled her head against his chest, finding solace in the familiar rise and fall of his breathing.

After a few moments, Nicolas gently pulled away, his hands resting on Olivia's shoulders as he looked into her eyes with a tender intensity. "Olivia," he whispered, his voice laden with sincerity, "I couldn't bear the thought of us being apart tonight. I had to see you."

A mixture of emotions danced across Olivia's face—gratitude, longing, and a hint of vulnerability. She reached up, cupping his cheek with her hand, her touch gentle and reassuring. "I'm glad you're here, Nicolas. I needed to see you too."

They stood there for a moment, their eyes locked, unspoken words passing between them.

"Sorry my love," Nicolas finally said. "Today was one of those days. The palace is so overwhelming with so many expectations. I tried to make the time to see you, but..."

He trailed off as he shook his head, and Olivia could feel his frustration. "It's alright, Nicolas. I know the pressures you're under. Just remember that I'll always be here to support you."

Nicolas smiled in response, his features softening as he leaned in and pressed a gentle kiss against her cheek. "I'm glad I got to see you. Goodnight, my love."

He gently kissed the top of her head and rested his cheek against her hair. "I should get back to the palace before someone notices that I've gone missing."

Olivia nodded in understanding. "But you could stay with me tonight? And leave early in the morning?"

"That can be quite scandalous." he said with a devilish smirk.

Olivia laughed and pulled Nicolas into an embrace, their lips meeting in a deep passionate kiss. She savored the warmth of his touch, the scent of his cologne, and the feel of his strong arms around her. They stood there, lost in each other, their hands exploring the curves and planes of each other's body.

After several moments, Nicolas finally pulled away, his breathing slightly ragged. He gazed at her for a long moment, his expression intense.

"I don't know what I'd do without you," he murmured, his voice husky with emotion.

"You'll never have to find out," she said, her words resolute.

Nicolas smiled, the intensity of his gaze softening. "I don't deserve you," he murmured as he brushed a strand of hair from her face.

Olivia looked at him, her eyes welling with tears. "You deserve the world," she said, her voice breaking.

Nicolas reached out and wiped away the tear that fell

from Olivia's eye. "Hey," he said softly, his voice thick with emotion. "Are you alright my love?"

He leaned in and kissed her again, the warmth and tenderness of his lips assuaging the ache that had been building inside her.

"I'm okay," she said, her voice wavering as she blinked back her tears. "I'm just so happy to see you."

"Me too," he whispered. He held her for a long moment, his gaze intense as he brushed a stray hair from her face.

Olivia gazed up at him, a myriad of emotions flitting across her face. Her heart was racing, her mind clouded with thoughts. There was a part of her that wanted to tell Nicolas about what happened with Princess Sophia.

Olivia closed her eyes, fighting back the tears that welled in her eyes. She felt as if she were standing on the edge of a precipice. She knew that if she chose to open up to him, there would be no turning back. And yet, she felt a nagging uncertainty. She didn't know what he'd think if she told him. In the end she decided against it.

"Come, sit with me." She said as she took his hand in hers.

She led him to the bed and sat down next to him. They sat there for a long moment; their fingers interlaced as they held hands. Olivia leaned in and kissed Nicolas, savoring the warmth of his lips and the feel of his tongue against her own. They lay back on the bed and continued their passionate embrace.

Olivia closed her eyes, losing herself in the moment as her lips caressed Nicolas's. Her hands wandered across his body, exploring every contour of his physique.

She sighed as she pulled away from their kiss, gazing deeply into Nicolas's eyes. "I love you," she murmured.

Nicolas's gaze softened as he brushed a stray hair from her face. "I love you too."

They sat there, looking into each other's eyes, a silent communication passing between them.

Nicolas leaned in and kissed Olivia again, his tongue dancing with hers in a sensuous kiss. His hands roamed across her body, eliciting a moan from Olivia as she felt the weight of his body upon her.

She reached up and caressed his cheek, her fingers tracing the contours of his face. She could feel his hard muscles pressing against her, his breathing ragged and his lips brushing against hers as he whispered her name.

He leaned in, kissing her passionately as he ran his hand through her hair. Olivia moaned softly as she felt him pushing up her night dress, his fingers brushing against her thigh as they slid under the fabric.

Nicolas moved away from Olivia's lips, his tongue dancing along her skin as he trailed kisses down the length of her body.

He reached up, cupping one of her breasts, his fingers teasing her blossomed bud through the fabric of her night dress as he lowered his head to her stomach.

Olivia closed her eyes, her back arching off the bed as she felt his breath on her skin. She let out a soft moan, her hands gripping the sheets as she felt him slide her dress up, exposing her thighs.

He gently ran his hand along her smooth skin, his fingers trailing along the curve of her thigh as he reached for the hem of her night dress. He pulled it off, leaving her naked and exposed to his gaze.

He knelt between her legs, looking down at her with a possessive gaze. Olivia's skin prickled as she felt his fingers brush against her skin.

"You're so beautiful." he whispered.

She smiled, her eyes brimming with tears as she looked up at him. "Not as beautiful as you," she said with a soft chuckle.

She reached up and ran her hand through his hair, her fingers stroking the length of his body as she caressed his muscles through his clothes. He undressed himself before her, taking his time as she watched, her gaze drinking in the sight of his nude body.

Nicolas lowered himself onto her, his skin pressing against her own as he ran his fingers through her hair. He kissed her gently, his lips tender and loving, his breath mingling with hers as he whispered her name.

"I love you," she murmured as she gazed into his eyes.

Nicolas smiled in response, his expression one of intense tenderness. He kissed her again, his lips trailing along the length of her body as he moved downwards. He ran his tongue across the curve of her breast, teasing her sensitive skin as he continued down to her navel.

In one quick motion, he pulled himself up towards her, his lips pressing against hers as his tongue pushed into her mouth. He spread her legs and positioned himself between them. He leaned forward, pressing his body against her own, his manhood sliding against her wet folds. She gasped softly as he entered her, thrusting in and out as they moved in perfect unison, her moans rising in pitch as she felt herself cresting towards her release.

"My love," Nicolas said in gasps of air. "We have to be quiet."

Olivia nodded, her body still trembling as she struggled to catch her breath. As she felt herself reach her peak, her body trembled and her muscles clenched, her skin covered in a sheen of sweat as she called out his name.

Nicolas's body shuddered as he reached his own release, a low moan escaping his lips as he spilled his seed inside her. They lay together for a long moment, their bodies intertwined as they savored the warmth of each other's skin.

Olivia leaned forward and kissed Nicolas, their tongues brushing against each other as they shared a deep, intimate embrace. "I love you." she murmured; her words filled with emotion.

Nicolas smiled, "I love you too." he whispered, his voice choked with emotion.

He reached out and ran his hand along her hair, his touch gentle and loving.

As their breathing returned to normal, Nicolas stood up and began to dress himself. He looked over at Olivia, a hint of sadness on his face.

"I don't want to leave," he said, his voice thick with emotion.

Olivia nodded, her eyes welling with tears as she gazed up at him. "I don't want you to go." she said, her voice wavering.

Nicolas sat down on the bed and pulled Olivia into a tight embrace. "We'll make this work." he said. "I promise I'll make time to see you soon."

Olivia nodded in response, burying her face in Nicolas's shoulder as her body shook with silent tears.

After a moment, Nicolas leaned in and pressed a soft kiss against Olivia's lips. "Goodbye my love."

Olivia watched as Nicolas left the room, his form silhouetted in the doorway before he disappeared into the hallway. She stood there for a moment, her heart aching in her chest as she felt a wave of emotion crash over her.

She leaned against the wall and slid down to the ground, tears streaming down her face as she succumbed to her grief. She hugged her knees to her chest and buried her head in her lap, her body shaking as she wept.

As Olivia sat on the floor, her sobs echoing through the empty room, she couldn't help but feel overwhelmed by a sense of despair. The weight of the situation, the animosity from Princess Sophia, and the looming uncertainty had taken its toll on her. In that vulnerable moment, the walls seemed to close in around her, suffocating her with a suffocating sense of isolation.

Minutes turned into an eternity as Olivia's tears continued to flow unabated. The silence of the room amplified the sound of her grief, a solitary symphony of sorrow. Each tear that cascaded down her cheeks held a fragment of her pain, a testament to the depth of her emotions. For the first time in a long while, she felt truly alone.

***

The grand dining hall of the palace was abuzz with activity as the morning sunlight filtered through the large windows, casting a warm glow on the opulent surroundings. The aroma of freshly brewed coffee and a spread of delectable pastries filled the air, creating an inviting ambiance. Princess Sophia, accompanied by her closest confidantes, Lady Amalia and Lady Charlotte, took their seats at a long, ornately decorated table. As they sipped their tea and nibbled on delicate pastries, their conversation took a turn towards a familiar topic —their recent guest, Olivia.

Sophia, radiating an air of regal confidence, leaned in conspiratorially, her eyes glinting with mischief. "Ladies, have you noticed how Olivia seems to be finding her place here? It's rather amusing, isn't it?"

Amalia, her expression filled with disdain, raised an eyebrow. "Oh, indeed. She thinks she can simply waltz into our world and claim the spotlight. Little does she know; we have a plan in motion."

Charlotte, her features contorted into a mischievous grin, chimed in, "And what might that be, Amalia?"

Amalia leaned closer, her voice dripping with venomous excitement. "I've managed to gain access to Olivia's bridesmaid dress. A little alteration here and there, and she'll be the talk of the wedding for all the wrong reasons."

Sophia's eyes gleamed with satisfaction as she nodded. "Perfect. This will be a lesson she won't soon forget. We'll see how she handles being the center of attention when it's not the kind she desires."

Amalia, a mischievous glint in her eyes, couldn't help but share a rumor she had heard about Olivia's past. "Did you know," she began, her voice dripping with a tinge of malice, "that Olivia used to work as a waitress before she became an actress? Quite a fall from grace, isn't it?"

Charlotte, known for her sharp wit and sarcastic remarks, chimed in with a chuckle. "Oh, how the mighty have fallen indeed. From serving tables to trying to fit in with the royal crowd. It's almost laughable, isn't it?"

Princess Sophia, her lips curled into a sly smile, relished in the gossip. "It seems Olivia has quite a secret past, doesn't she? How fortunate we are to have discovered this little gem."

Unbeknownst to the three women, Olivia had entered the dining hall, her footsteps muffled by the grandeur of the room. Clad in a simple yet elegant dress, she carried herself with a quiet confidence, seemingly unaffected by the conversations that swirled around her. With every step, she mustered the strength to face the day ahead, aware of the challenges that awaited her.

As she approached the table, Princess Sophia, Amalia, and Charlotte exchanged knowing glances, their smirks fading slightly as they realized Olivia had joined them. Princess Sophia, quick to regain her composure, greeted Olivia with feigned warmth. "Ah, Olivia, join us. We were just discussing some exciting wedding plans."

Sophia summoned Olivia to her side with a subtle wave of her hand. Olivia approached; her steps cautious yet determined. Sophia's lips curled into a cold smile as she observed the layers of makeup expertly applied to conceal the traces of tears.

Olivia took her seat, her poise unyielding as she met their gazes. She could sense the underlying tension, the subtle shift in their attitudes, but she refused to let it deter her. "Olivia, my dear," Sophia began, her voice laced with false concern, "is everything alright? You seem a bit... worn out this morning."

Olivia took a deep breath, her voice steady despite the turmoil within her. "I apologize if I appear fatigued, Princess Sophia. It has been a challenging night, but I assure you, I am prepared to fulfill my duties as a bridesmaid."

Sophia's eyes narrowed, her tone growing colder. "Challenging, you say? Care to elaborate?"

Olivia hesitated for a moment, debating how much she should reveal. But she knew that hiding the truth would only give Sophia more power. With a serene smile, she replied, "I'm glad to be here. Weddings are such joyous occasions, after all."

Amalia and Charlotte exchanged a fleeting glance, their expressions betraying a hint of unease. Their attempts to rattle Olivia seemed to fall flat in the face of her composure. Amalia, determined to assert her dominance, attempted to steer the conversation back to the topic at hand. "Speaking of weddings, Olivia, have you seen your bridesmaid dress yet? It's quite... interesting."

Olivia's brow furrowed slightly, but she maintained her calm demeanor. "Interesting, you say? I'm sure it will be a lovely ensemble, as long as it matches the bride's vision."

Amalia, unable to resist the urge to provoke Olivia further, smirked. "Oh, it will indeed be a sight to behold. But perhaps you're used to less extravagant attire, given your humble beginnings."

The remark hung in the air, heavy with an undercurrent of disdain. Sophia and Charlotte glanced at each other, anticipation brimming in their eyes, awaiting Olivia's reaction.

Olivia took a deep breath, a flicker of emotion passing through her eyes before she regained her composure. She locked eyes with each of them, her voice steady and unwavering. "I'm proud of my past, no matter how humble or challenging it may have been. It has taught me resilience, empathy, and the importance of cherishing every opportunity that comes my way."

The room fell into a stunned silence as Olivia's words resonated with a quiet strength. Princess Sophia, Amalia, and Charlotte exchanged uncomfortable glances, their once-confident smirks fading into uncertainty.

Sophia's facade cracked for a fleeting moment, revealing a flicker of frustration in her eyes. But she quickly regained her composed demeanor. "Very well, Olivia. I trust that you will fulfill your role to the best of your abilities. Let's not allow such trivial matters to overshadow the joyous occasion ahead."

Olivia glanced at Amalia and Charlotte, searching for

any signs of discomfort or unease as she broached the topic of their conversation from the previous day. The room fell into a tense silence, the clinking of silverware against porcelain echoing softly. The remnants of their previous gossip still lingered in the air, casting a tense atmosphere over the breakfast table. Sensing their reluctance, Olivia decided to take a bold approach, determined to turn the tables and rattle Princess Sophia's composure.

"So, ladies, about our conversation yesterday regarding the bachelorette party," Olivia began, her voice laced with subtle mischief. The idea of hosting it in the gazebo within the garden maze sounds intriguing, doesn't it?"

Amalia and Charlotte exchanged uncertain glances; their expressions guarded. It was clear that Olivia's suggestion had caught them off guard. Amalia shifted in her seat, her eyes darting between Olivia and Charlotte, as if searching for the right response.

"Olivia, we appreciate your enthusiasm, but it's Princess Sophia's bachelorette party, and she has her own preferences," Amalia finally spoke, her voice tinged with caution.

Olivia smiled, a mischievous glint in her eyes. "Of course, I understand that. But what if we took it a step further? Instead of separate bachelor and bachelorette parties, why not have a joint celebration? A masquerade party with an adult twist, perhaps?"

Charlotte gasped, her hand flying to her mouth in

astonishment. "Olivia, are you suggesting we push the boundaries like that? It would certainly make a statement."

Olivia nodded, her gaze fixed on Princess Sophia, who had been listening intently to their conversation. "Indeed, Charlotte. It would be a night to remember. And who knows, it could be a unique and unforgettable experience for both Prince Frederick and Princess Sophia."

Princess Sophia's eyes flickered with surprise. The idea seemed to both pique her interest and challenge her sense of control. She leaned back in her chair, a calculating smile gracing her lips.

"You know what, Olivia? I think you may be onto something," Sophia said, her voice dripping with subtle amusement. "An adult masquerade party would certainly make for an unforgettable evening."

Amalia and Charlotte exchanged surprised glances, clearly taken aback by Sophia's unexpected agreement.

Sophia, sensing an opportunity to retreat from the conversation, interjected, "Well, ladies, I have a massage appointment I simply cannot miss. Please excuse me."

Olivia watched as Sophia left, a mixture of satisfaction and curiosity bubbling within her. She had successfully rattled the composed princess, planting a seed of excitement that promised an unconventional celebration. Olivia knew that her suggestion would create a buzz among the guests, and she was eager to witness the reactions and embrace the unexpected twist in the wedding festivities.

Amalia clapped her hands together. "Well, this certainly took an unexpected turn. Olivia, I must say, you have a knack for shaking things up. Let's make this party one for the history books!"

Charlotte nodded in agreement, a glimmer of excitement in her eyes. "I never thought I'd see the day when a royal bachelorette party would be so daring. Count me in, Olivia. Let's make it an event that no one will forget."

Olivia smiled, a sense of satisfaction washing over her. As the three women delved into the details of planning the unconventional joint celebration, the atmosphere in the room shifted from tension to anticipation.

***

CHAPTER 16:

SECOND THOUGHTS

Nicolas and Prince Frederick made their way to Princess Sophia at Codrington Castle, where they had been summoned for an important meeting.

"Freddie, what do you think Princess Sophia wants?" Nicolas asked, a hint of curiosity in his voice.

Frederick sighed, his brows furrowing slightly. "I'm not entirely sure, Nick. Sophia has been insistent on discussing some matters regarding the wedding preparations. She seemed quite determined."

Nicolas nodded, understanding Frederick's unease. The presence of Princess Sophia had always been a cause for caution and vigilance, her intentions often shrouded in mystery.

As they entered the room, they found Princess Sophia standing by the window, her gaze fixed on the sprawling grounds of the palace. She turned to face them, a calculated smile playing on her lips.

"Welcome, gentlemen. Nicolas, Frederick, please have a seat," Princess Sophia said, gesturing to the lush chairs across from her. Together they sat, facing each other across the room.

"Thank you both for joining me today," Sophia began, her voice firm yet laced with a hint of persuasion. "As the wedding approaches, it is crucial that we present a united front, demonstrating our commitment and solidarity to the people of Creudor."

Frederick nodded; his gaze unwavering. "I understand, Sophia. The upcoming wedding is a momentous occasion for our kingdom, and we must ensure that it reflects our shared values and aspirations.

Sophia's gaze shifted to Nicolas, a glimmer of calculation in her eyes. "And what about you, Nicolas? Will you stand by your brother's side, showing the world that you fully support this union?"

Nicolas met her gaze, his expression resolute. "Of course, Sophia. As Frederick's brother and best man, I will honor my responsibilities and support him wholeheartedly."

A sly smile played at Sophia's lips. "Excellent. In that case, I have a proposal. Why don't we have a joint bachelor and bachelorette party? It would be an opportunity for us to come together as one, celebrate our union, and showcase the unity between our families."

Nicolas exchanged a quick glance with Frederick, a silent acknowledgment of the unexpected turn of events. While the idea seemed unconventional, there was a part of him that could not help but be intrigued by Princess Sophia's proposal.

Frederick raised an eyebrow, a flicker of surprise crossing his features. "A joint celebration? That is quite unconventional, Sophia. Are you sure it is appropriate?"

Princess Sophia leaned forward, a glimmer of excitement in her eyes. "I believe it would be a memorable occasion, bringing together both our friends and loved ones. We could create an atmosphere of unity and celebration, solidifying our bond and showcasing the strength of our relationship."

Nicolas studied Princess Sophia's expression, detecting a subtle undercurrent beneath her words. There was more to her proposal than met the eye, and he couldn't shake off the feeling that she had ulterior motives.

"I understand the sentiment behind your suggestion, Sophia," Nicolas spoke up, his voice measured. "But we must ensure that the celebration reflects our personalities and desires. We wouldn't want anyone to feel overshadowed or uncomfortable."

Princess Sophia's smile tightened ever so slightly, but she quickly regained her composure. "Of course, Nicolas. The purpose is to unite our friends and family in a joyous celebration. I assure you; it will be a memorable event for everyone involved."

"I believe you're right, Sophia," Frederick nodded, his gaze shifting between Nicolas and Sophia. "However, I want the bachelor party to retain its essence and reflect my personal preferences as well."

Sophia's smile widened, a flicker of triumph dancing in her eyes. "I appreciate your openness, Frederick. Together, we can create an event that showcases our love and brings joy to all."

As the conversation continued, Nicolas couldn't shake off the unease that gnawed at the back of his mind. He was acutely aware that Princess Sophia's desires went beyond a simple joint celebration. There was a hidden agenda, and he vowed to remain vigilant to protect Frederick and Olivia from any potential harm. Lost in disturbing thoughts, Nicolas excuses himself and walks over to the balcony for some fresh air. And a distance, there she was, the love of his life.

Nicolas stood on the balcony; his gaze fixed on Olivia as she moved gracefully through the sprawling garden. The vibrant colors of the flowers seemed to pale in comparison to her radiance, and he couldn't help but feel a surge of pride and admiration for the woman he loved.

She was completely engrossed in her task, overseeing the preparations for the upcoming masquerade party. Her keen eye for detail and unwavering dedication were evident in every decision she made. The garden was being transformed into a mystical realm, with twinkling lights, elegant decorations, and the promise of an enchanting evening.

As Nicolas watched her, a mix of emotions stirred within him. There was joy in witnessing Olivia's passion come to life, but there was also a sense of longing and uncertainty. Their relationship had faced numerous challenges, and the weight of their responsibilities loomed over them like a dark cloud. But in this moment, as he observed Olivia immersed in work, he could not help but be filled with hope.

He took a deep breath, gathering his thoughts, and made his way toward Olivia. The distance between them seemed to vanish as he approached, the sound of his footsteps blending with the rustling of leaves in the gentle breeze. Olivia turned to him, a hint of surprise in her eyes, followed by a warm smile that reached the depths of her soul.

"Nicolas," she said, her voice soft yet filled with affection. "I didn't expect to see you here."

Nicolas took her hands in his, his touch grounding and reassuring. "I couldn't resist watching you, my love. You have a way of bringing magic into everything you do."

Olivia's cheeks flushed with a mixture of delight and shyness. "You're too kind, Nicolas. But I have to admit, I'm feeling a bit overwhelmed with all the preparations."

He could sense that something was amiss, a hint of distance in her demeanor that tugged at his heart. He reached out to touch her arm gently, hoping to bridge the invisible gap that seemed to have formed between them.

"Olivia, is everything alright?" he asked, his voice filled with genuine concern.

She turned to face him; her eyes filled with a mixture of emotions. There was a flicker of sadness in her gaze, overshadowed by a determination to conceal her true feelings. Her voice, usually warm and vibrant, now held a hint of detachment as she responded, "I'm fine, Nicolas. Just dealing with some last-minute party emergencies."

He studied her face, searching for the truth behind her words. His instincts told him that there was more to her response than met the eye. But he also understood that she had a tendency to put on a brave face, to carry the weight of the world on her shoulders without asking for help. It was one of the qualities he admired most about her, but in this moment, he longed for her to let him in, to share her burdens.

"Olivia," he said softly, his voice tinged with a mixture of longing and concern. "You don't have to carry this alone. We're in this together, remember?"

A brief flicker of vulnerability crossed her features before she quickly masked it. "I know, Nicolas. But I can handle it. It's just a few minor hiccups that need my attention."

Nicolas took a step closer, his gaze unwavering as he locked eyes with her. "You've always been strong, Olivia. I've admired your resilience and determination. But I also want you to know that it's okay to lean on me, to share your burdens. We're partners, and that means supporting each other through thick and thin."

A conflicted expression clouded Olivia's face as she wrestled with her emotions. The weight of her responsibilities seemed to bear down on her, and for a moment, it felt as though she might crumble under their weight. She opened her mouth to speak, but before she could utter a word, a member of the staff rushed over, panic evident in their eyes.

"Miss Grey, we have a decoration emergency," the staff member exclaimed, their voice filled with urgency. "We need your immediate attention."

Olivia's gaze shifted from Nicolas to the staff member,

her expression torn between duty and her desire to confide in Nicolas. She glanced back at him, a silent apology in her eyes, before turning to address the emergency.

Nicolas watched her retreating figure with a heavy heart. He knew that her sense of responsibility and dedication were deeply ingrained within her, yet he could not shake the feeling that there was more beneath the surface.

With a heavy sigh, he remained in the garden, his thoughts consumed by Olivia and the connection that seemed to be slipping through their fingers. As the sounds of the party preparations continued around him, Nicolas found solace in the beauty of the garden. The vibrant flowers, swaying gently in the breeze, seemed to mirror the delicate dance of their relationship. And as he stood there, he vowed to remain steadfast, patiently waiting for the moment when Olivia would be ready to let him in once more, to share the depths of her heart and soul.

***

As the day progressed, Olivia's mind remained preoccupied with the mounting pressure and expectations of the royal circle. Her phone buzzed with a text notification, indicating a message from Nicolas. She glanced at the screen, knowing it was him, but chose to ignore it for the time being. She needed some space to collect her thoughts and regain her composure.

Olivia retreated to her room after the whirlwind of preparations for the masquerade party had settled down. Feeling overwhelmed, she needed a familiar voice to ground her. She sat on the plush couch in her suite, dialing Justin's number on her phone. She needed someone she could trust, someone who would listen without judgment. As the phone rang, her mind swirled with a mixture of excitement and anxiety about the upcoming masquerade party. She hoped that Justin, with his unique perspective and creativity, would have some valuable advice to offer.

After a few rings, Justin's voice came through the line, filled with warmth and familiarity. "Olivia, darling! How's the royal life treating you?"

Olivia leaned against the plush cushions of her bed; her voice tinged with exhaustion. "Hey, Justin. I just needed to talk. Being in this royal circle is tougher than I thought. I feel like I'm constantly under scrutiny, and there's so much pressure to conform."

Justin listened attentively; his concern evident even through the phone. "I can only imagine, Liv. It must be incredibly challenging to navigate such a different world. But remember, you've always been strong and adaptable. You've faced obstacles before and come out on top. You can do this too."

Olivia nodded, her eyes welling up with tears. "I know, Justin. But it's just... It's like I'm constantly on edge, trying to measure up to expectations. And sometimes, I feel like I'm losing myself in the process."

Justin's voice softened, his empathy flowing through the phone. "You're not alone in this, Olivia. Remember who you are, where you came from, and the journey that led you here. You've always stayed true to yourself, and that's what makes you special. Don't let anyone or anything diminish your light."

Olivia took a deep breath, finding solace in Justin's words. "Thank you, Justin. I needed to hear that. Sometimes it's easy to forget who I am amidst all the glamour and protocol."

He chuckled lightly, injecting a touch of playfulness into the conversation. "Well, Liv, if you ever need a reminder, just think about our early days in Los Angeles, struggling to make ends meet, chasing our dreams. You've come so far, and you've achieved incredible things. Don't let anyone dull your sparkle."

Olivia could not help but smile, the memories of their humble beginnings bringing warmth to her heart. "You're right, Justin. I've come too far to let doubts and insecurities cloud my path. I'll keep pushing forward and stay true to myself."

"That's the spirit!" Justin exclaimed cheerfully. "And remember, I'm always just a phone call away. No matter the time zone or distance, I've got your back."

A small smile tugged at Olivia's lips as she felt a wave of comfort wash over her. "Justin, I'm so glad I called. I need your help with something else. I'm hosting an adult-themed masquerade party for the bride and groom, and I want it to be unforgettable. But I'm feeling a bit overwhelmed."

Justin's voice took on a playful tone. "Oh, darling, you've come to the right person. As a proud gay man, I know a thing or two about throwing fabulous parties. Tell me, what's the theme you have in mind?"

Olivia took a deep breath, feeling the weight on her shoulders lighten as she confided in Justin. "I want it to be sophisticated yet playful, something that captures the essence of the bride and groom. I'm thinking of an enchanted evening, with a touch of mystery and sensuality."

Justin let out a soft chuckle. "Oh, I love it! Enchanted and sensual? That's right up my alley. We can create an atmosphere of intrigue and glamour with dim lighting, flickering candles, and a lush color palette. Think deep purples, rich reds, and shimmering gold accents."

Olivia's eyes lit up with excitement as she visualized Justin's suggestions. "Yes, that sounds perfect! And what about the costumes? I want everyone to feel confident and empowered."

Justin's voice brimmed with enthusiasm. "Darling, we'll go all out with the masks and costumes. Encourage your guests to embrace their sensuality and indulge in their fantasies. Feathered masks, elegant gowns, and tailored suits with a hint of allure. Let their imaginations run wild."

Olivia could not help but giggle, feeling a renewed sense of energy coursing through her. "Justin, you have such a fantastic vision! I can already picture it in my mind. Thank you so much for your help."

He responded with genuine warmth. "Of course, my dear. I'm always here to support you. Just remember, the key to a successful party is to let go, have fun, and be unapologetically yourself. It's your night to shine."

Olivia took a moment to absorb Justin's words of wisdom. She felt a surge of confidence and determination, knowing that she had the support of her dear friend. "Thank you, Justin. I needed this boost of encouragement. I'll make this party unforgettable, not just for the bride and groom, but for everyone attending."

They continued to chat, exchanging ideas and details, as Olivia's worries began to fade away. With Justin's guidance, she felt more prepared and excited for the upcoming event. As they hung up the phone, Olivia couldn't help but feel a sense of gratitude for having such a wonderful friend like Justin by her side, even from across the distance.

As Olivia hung up the phone, a renewed sense of determination coursed through her veins.

Olivia's spirits were lifted by her conversation with Justin, she felt a newfound sense of readiness to open the text message from Nicolas. With a curious smile, she unlocked her phone and navigated to the message thread where his text awaited her.

The screen illuminated with Nicolas's name, and Olivia's heart skipped a beat in anticipation. She clicked on the message, revealing his heartfelt words.

'Hey, beautiful, I know you've had a lot on your mind lately, and I want you to know that I'm here for you. Take all the time you need, and when you're ready, I'm just a call or a text away. No matter what you're going through, we're in this together. Sending you all my love.'

The warmth that radiated from his text resonated deeply within her, melting away the lingering doubts and uncertainties that had clouded her mind. Nicolas's message expressed his unwavering love for her, his understanding of her need for space, and his promise to be there whenever she was ready to talk. Olivia's eyes welled up with tears of gratitude and affection as she read his words. It was in moments like these that she realized the depth of their connection and the strength of their bond.

She quickly wiped away the tears, a smile tugging at the corners of her lips. Olivia's fingers danced on the screen as she composed her response, eager to convey her feelings and gratitude to Nicolas. Her message reflected the lightness that had returned to her heart.

'Nicolas, your understanding and support mean the world to me. I cherish our connection and the love we share. Thank you for being patient and giving me the space, I need. Know that I appreciate you more than words can express.'

She paused for a moment, her thoughts swirling with playful banter. Olivia could not resist adding a touch of lightheartedness to her message, knowing it would bring a smile to Nicolas's face. With a mischievous grin, she sent a second message,

'And by the way, I hope you're ready for some serious dance moves at the masquerade party. Prepare to be dazzled!'

With a satisfied nod, Olivia hit the send button, her heart feeling lighter with each passing second. She knew that their playful conversation would help ease any tension and remind them of the joy they found in each other's company. She sprang up from her bed and looked out the window, catching a glimpse of the grand palace bathed in moonlight. The masquerade party was just around the corner, and she was determined to embrace the evening with strength and confidence, ready to face whatever lay ahead.

Nicolas's phone buzzed, signaling a new message. He eagerly unlocked it, his eyes lighting up as he read Olivia's response. Her words washed over him, filling him with a sense of warmth and reassurance. The playful invitation to the masquerade party brought a smile to his face, igniting a sense of anticipation and excitement within him.

He quickly composed a flurry of text replies, his fingers dancing on the screen.

'Olivia, your words touch my heart.'

'I am grateful for your presence in my life, and I'll always be here for you.'

'And as for the dance moves, prepare to be amazed because I've been secretly practicing my own repertoire.'

'The dance floor won't know what hit it!'

With a chuckle, Nicolas hit the send button, imagining the playful banter that awaited them at the masquerade party. He could not wait to see Olivia's dazzling dance moves and create new memories together.

***

CHAPTER 17:

A NIGHT TO REMEMBER

Finally, the invitations for the masquerade party were sent out. The grand evening had arrived, and the excitement in the air was palpable as Olivia, Sophia, Amalia, and Charlotte gathered in Olivia's spacious suite. The room was adorned with luxurious decorations, mirrors, and a lavish dressing area complete with an array of costumes, jewelry, and makeup.

Olivia stood before a full-length mirror, her eyes sparkling with anticipation. She wore an exquisite masquerade gown in vibrant shades of blue and silver, adorned with intricate lace and delicate embroidery. The flowing fabric draped gracefully around her figure, enhancing her natural elegance.

Sophia, dressed in a regal crimson gown, exuded confidence and grace. Her intricate mask added an air of mystery to her already captivating presence. Amalia, in a shimmering emerald green dress, showcased her impeccable fashion sense, while Charlotte's lavender gown highlighted her youthful charm.

As the women gathered around Olivia, their excitement

infectious, they began the playful task of selecting masks and accessories to complete their enigmatic looks. The table was filled with an assortment of ornate masks, ranging from delicate filigree designs to bold and dramatic feathers. They each carefully chose a mask that reflected their personalities and added an element of allure to their appearance.

Amalia playfully twirled a feathered mask in her hand, teasing Charlotte. "Oh, Charlotte, this one would suit you perfectly! Embrace your adventurous side tonight."

Charlotte giggled, her eyes shining with delight. "You think so, Amalia? Alright, let's go for it! I'm ready to embrace the unknown."

Sophia, her elegant fingers gliding over a selection of sparkling accessories, turned to Olivia. "Olivia, my dear, have you chosen your mask yet? I want to see the mysterious side of the famous actress."

Olivia smiled; her eyes gleaming mischievously. "Well, Sophia, I thought I'd go for something a little unexpected. How about this?" She held up a stunning black mask adorned with delicate silver filigree and shimmering crystals.

Sophia's eyes widened in surprise, a playful grin spreading across her face. "Olivia, that's perfect! It adds an air of intrigue and keeps them guessing."

With masks selected, the women moved to the dressing area to begin their transformations. Skilled hair and makeup artists worked their magic, creating intricate hairstyles and glamorous makeup looks that complemented the mystique of their masks. The room buzzed with excitement and laughter as the women shared stories, exchanged playful banter, and savored the moments leading up to the grand event.

As the final touches were applied, Olivia looked around at her friends, feeling a deep sense of camaraderie and gratitude. In their shared moments of preparation, they had formed a bond, transcending any differences or conflicts. The masquerade party became not just an extravagant event but also a celebration of their unity and friendship.

And with their costumes complete, the women stood before the mirror, admiring their transformed appearances. Olivia's heart swelled with appreciation for the strong, confident women standing beside her, ready to face the night's festivities together.

Sophia turned to the group, a mischievous twinkle in her eyes. "Ladies, it's time to unveil our masks and let the enchantment begin. Let's make this a night to remember!"

The women exchanged excited glances, their masks adding an air of mystery and allure to their already captivating beauty. As the women stepped outside the suite, they were greeted by a breathtaking sight. The grand hall had been transformed into a mesmerizing wonderland, with opulent decorations that evoked a sense of enchantment. The walls were adorned with cascading draperies in rich hues of gold and deep purple, intertwined with twinkling fairy lights that cast a warm and magical glow.

A magnificent chandelier, resplendent with crystals, hung from the center of the ceiling, casting a dazzling display of light and shadows onto the dance floor below. Lush floral arrangements in vibrant colors adorned every corner, their sweet fragrance filling the air.

The staff, dressed in elegant attire and adorned with their own masks, moved gracefully among the guests, attending to their needs with impeccable service. Their masks added an element of mystery, their identities hidden, enhancing the allure of the evening.

One by one, the guests began to arrive, each one dressed in elaborate costumes and intricate masks that reflected their individual personalities and fantasies. The room was filled with an eclectic mix of characters - from charming nobles in regal attire to whimsical fairies and mythical creatures brought to life. Laughter and animated conversations filled the air as guests mingled and admired each other's ensembles.

Amalia, her eyes sparkling with mischief, leaned in close to Olivia. "I must say, Olivia, your idea for the masquerade theme was simply brilliant. Look at how everyone is embracing it! It's like stepping into a different world."

Olivia chuckled, the sound carrying with it a sense of joy and contentment. "I'm glad you all loved the idea. It adds an element of mystery and excitement to the night.

Who knows what adventures await us behind these masks?"

Olivia's heart fluttered with anticipation as she weaved through the sea of masked guests, her eyes scanning the crowd in search of Nicolas. The dim lighting, coupled with the allure of the masks, added an extra layer of intrigue to the atmosphere, making it a thrilling challenge to spot her beloved prince among the enchanting throng.

Olivia's heart raced with anticipation as she stood alone in the middle of the dance floor, her eyes scanning the crowd for any sign of Nicolas. The enchanting melody of their special song filled the air, evoking memories of their first dance together at the gala. It was a song that had become a symbol of their love, a connection that transcended time and place.

Suddenly, a familiar voice sounded from behind her, causing Olivia to turn around. There stood Nicolas, his eyes sparkling with delight as he admired her. He wore a dashing black suit, accentuated by a silver mask that complemented his chiseled features. His presence exuded a magnetic charm that drew Olivia closer.

As they locked eyes, a mischievous smile played at the corners of Nicolas's lips. "Well, well, my enchanting princess. I must admit, it took me a moment to find you in this mesmerizing sea of masks. But now that I have, I feel like the luckiest man in the room."

"May I have this dance, my enchanting princess?" he asked, extending his hand towards her.

Olivia's eyes sparkled with delight as she placed her hand in his, her fingers intertwining with his in a perfect fit. "I was hoping you would ask," she replied, her voice filled with warmth.

With a graceful sweep, Olivia placed her delicate hand in Nicolas's, feeling an electric current surge through her veins. Their connection was undeniable, transcending the masks and the glamour of the masquerade. It was a bond forged in the depths of their shared experiences, their unwavering support for one another, and the profound love that had blossomed between them.

They swayed to the rhythm of the music, their bodies moving in perfect harmony as they surrendered themselves to the melody that had become a symbol of their love. The world around them faded away, and in that moment, it was as if they were the only two people in the room.

Nicolas rested his hand gently on the small of Olivia's back, drawing her closer. "Do you remember the first time we danced to this song?" he whispered; his voice laced with nostalgia.

A soft smile graced Olivia's lips as memories flooded her mind. "How could I forget? It was at the gala, and that dance changed everything. It was the beginning of a love story I never imagined possible."

Nicolas twirled Olivia gracefully, their bodies moving effortlessly as if they were floating on air. "That dance was just the beginning, my love. And you, my love, have brought me a happiness I never thought possible. You've opened my heart in ways I never knew existed."

As the song reached its crescendo, Olivia and Nicolas held each other tightly, their bodies swaying as one. Their playful conversation gave way to a quiet understanding, their hearts speaking volumes in the silence between their shared breaths.

As the music faded into the background, Nicolas leaned in closer to Olivia, his voice laced with excitement and a hint of mischief. "Olivia, I have a surprise for you. Follow me," he whispered, gently guiding her hand as they made their way through the bustling crowd.

They walked hand in hand, their footsteps quiet as they ventured deeper into the enchanting garden maze. Olivia's curiosity grew with each turn, the air becoming cooler and filled with the scent of blooming flowers. The maze was a labyrinth of lush greenery, its winding paths creating an enchanting atmosphere.

As they turned a corner, Olivia's eyes widened in awe. Before them stood a beautifully decorated gazebo, adorned with an array of flowers in vibrant hues and twinkling lights that danced in the night. The soft glow of the lights created a magical ambiance, casting a warm glow over the surroundings.

Nicolas beamed with pride, his gaze never leaving Olivia's face. "I wanted to create a quiet and intimate space for us, away from the crowd," he explained, gesturing towards the gazebo. "I decorated it myself, with flowers and twinkly lights, to make it even more special."

Olivia's heart swelled with appreciation as she took in the sight before her. The gazebo stood as a sanctuary amidst the lush greenery, bathed in a gentle radiance. Delicate blooms adorned the pillars, their vibrant colors adding a touch of romance to the atmosphere. The twinkling lights entwined with the foliage cast a soft, ethereal glow, creating an ambiance that felt nothing short of magical.

"It's absolutely beautiful, Nicolas," Olivia murmured, her voice filled with awe. "You truly have a way of turning even the simplest moments into something extraordinary."

Nicolas grinned, his eyes gleaming with adoration. "Only for you, my love. I want to create memories with you that will last a lifetime."

They stepped into the gazebo, its inviting space enveloping them in a sense of serenity. Nicolas wrapped his arms around Olivia, pulling her close as they stood beneath the canopy of flowers and lights. Their playful conversation gave way to a tender silence, the air charged with the unspoken promises of their love.

As the gentle breeze rustled through the garden, Nicolas reached up to his mask, untying the delicate ribbon that held it in place. With a mischievous glint in his eyes, he slowly lowered his mask, revealing his handsome face and warm smile. Olivia's heart skipped a beat at the sight of him, feeling a rush of intimacy and vulnerability in the intimate setting of the gazebo.

Not wanting to be outdone, Olivia playfully raised an eyebrow and mimicked Nicolas's actions, reaching up to untie the ribbon that secured her mask. As the mask slid off her face, her features were unveiled, exposing her radiant beauty and the genuine joy that emanated from within.

Nicolas chuckled softly, his fingers brushing against Olivia's cheek as he admired her unmasked face. "There you are, my love," he whispered, his voice filled with affection. "Even without the mask, you are the most captivating person here."

Olivia blushed, a soft giggle escaping her lips. She couldn't help but feel a sense of liberation as the mask was removed, as if a barrier between them had been lifted, allowing their connection to deepen even further.

"You're not so bad yourself," she teased, her eyes twinkling with playfulness. "Though I must say, I'm quite fond of the mystery your mask provided."

Nicolas raised an eyebrow, a mischievous smirk tugging at his lips. "Oh, is that so? Perhaps I should put it back on and keep you guessing."

Olivia playfully swatted his arm, her laughter echoing in the tranquil space. "No, no, I think I prefer your face just as it is. Besides, now that we're unmasked, we can enjoy this moment without any pretenses."

Nicolas pulled Olivia closer, wrapping his arms around her in a warm embrace. Their masks, once concealing their identities, lay forgotten on a nearby table as they reveled in the authenticity of their connection.

"You're right," he murmured, his voice filled with sincerity. "Being here with you, unmasked and vulnerable, feels like a breath of fresh air. No more hiding, no more pretending. Just us, together."

As the moon cast its ethereal glow upon the garden, bathing the gazebo in a soft luminescence, Nicolas gently took Olivia's hands into his own. His eyes sparkled with a mixture of anticipation and love; his voice filled with a warmth that transcended words.

"Olivia, from the moment I laid eyes on you, my life has been forever changed," Nicolas began, his voice steady yet filled with emotion. "You have brought light, love, and meaning into my world, and I cannot imagine my future without you by my side."

Olivia's heart skipped a beat as she looked into Nicolas's eyes, the depth of his feelings evident in their depths. Her breath caught in her throat, her own emotions swirling within her like a tempestuous storm.

He continued; his voice unwavering but laced with vulnerability. "This ring," Nicolas said, reaching into his pocket, "has been in my family for generations. It belonged to my mother, a symbol of her strength, grace, and enduring love. And now, I want it to be a symbol of the love that we share."

Nicolas revealed the ring, a stunning emerald set amidst an intricate band of shimmering diamonds. The emerald sparkled with an otherworldly beauty, its vibrant green reflecting the promise of a love that knew no bounds.

"Olivia Grey, will you do me the immense honor of becoming my wife? Will you embark on this incredible journey of life and love with me?" he asked, his voice filled with hope and a hint of nervous anticipation.

Olivia's eyes welled up with tears of joy as she looked at the ring, its beauty echoing the depth of her emotions. Her voice trembled with overwhelming love as she spoke, "Nicolas, yes, a thousand times yes!"

With a smile that radiated pure happiness, Nicolas gently slid the ring onto Olivia's finger, the delicate touch of the emerald against her skin sending shivers of delight through her.

In that magical moment, surrounded by the beauty of the garden and the whispers of their love, Nicolas and Olivia embraced, sealing their commitment to one another. The world seemed to fade away as they shared a passionate kiss, their hearts dancing in perfect harmony. As they pulled away, their eyes locked in a gaze filled with love and promise. In that gaze, they found the reassurance that they were embarking on a journey of a lifetime, a journey filled with unending love, joy, and the unwavering support of one another.

***

Nicolas and Olivia stepped out of the gazebo, the soft glow of the twinkling lights illuminating their path as they ventured into the vast garden. The air was crisp and filled with the sweet scent of blooming flowers, creating a romantic ambiance that enveloped them.

As they strolled along the winding paths, Olivia leaned her head against Nicolas's shoulder, her heart brimming with joy. The emerald ring on her finger glistened in the moonlight, a constant reminder of their shared commitment.

Nicolas looked down at Olivia, a gentle smile playing on his lips. He could not believe his luck, he had the woman of his dreams, right there in his arms. They walked in comfortable silence for a while, relishing in the tranquility of the garden and the presence of each other. The moon cast a gentle glow on their path, creating a tapestry of shadows and light as they weaved through the lush surroundings.

Eventually, their conversation turned to the practical matter of sharing their news with their families. They knew that their union would bring immense joy, but they also understood the need for timing and sensitivity, especially with the impending royal wedding.

Olivia paused, a thoughtful expression crossing her face. "Nicolas, I believe it's best if we keep our engagement a secret until after the royal wedding. This day belongs to Frederick and Sophia, and we should respect their moment in the spotlight."

Nicolas nodded; his eyes filled with understanding. "You're right, Olivia. It's essential to give Frederick and Sophia the attention and celebration they deserve. Let's cherish this time in secret, and when the timing is right, we will share our joy with our families and friends."

They continued their leisurely walk, their fingers intertwined, their hearts bursting with excitement and anticipation for the future. The garden seemed to come alive around them, with whispers of nature and the distant sound of music from the masquerade party.

As they reached the end of their romantic stroll, they found themselves at a small, secluded spot in the garden. Olivia turned to face Nicolas, her eyes sparkling with love. But just as when he was about to say something, they were shocked to hear muffled breathing sounds. Intrigued, they followed the source of the noise, their steps careful and their hearts pounding. The moonlight cast a soft glow on the scene ahead, revealing a masked woman in a mesmerizing crimson red gown, locked in a passionate embrace with a mysterious man.

Olivia's eyes widened with realization as she recognized the alluring gown and the graceful silhouette beneath it. It was Princess Sophia, entangled in an intimate moment with a stranger. Sophia's deep red gown clung to her form; her hands entwined in the man's hair as their lips melded together in an ardent kiss. Panic surged within Olivia, knowing the potential consequences if they were to be discovered. She quickly turned away, her mind racing for a solution.

Not realizing the identity of the masked woman, Nicolas moved closer, his curiosity piqued. As he approached the couple, he caught a fleeting glimpse of the woman's face. It was a momentary glimpse, and in the dim moonlight, he failed to recognize Princess Sophia.

Suddenly, Olivia saw an opportunity to divert attention and avoid a scandalous confrontation. With a mischievous sparkle in her eyes, she swiftly turned on her heels and dashed away from Nicolas, her laughter floating in the night air.

"Come and catch me if you can, my prince!" she called out playfully, her voice tinged with a hint of excitement.

Nicolas's eyebrows furrowed in surprise as he watched Olivia flee, her figure disappearing into the darkness of the garden. A mixture of amusement and curiosity danced in his eyes as he gave chase, determined to catch up to the woman who held his heart.

Meanwhile, back in the hidden corner of the garden, Princess Sophia and her mysterious companion were still immersed in their passionate embrace, unaware of the unfolding events. Their affectionate whispers and stolen kisses echoed amidst the rustling leaves and fragrant blossoms.

Olivia, now hidden from view, took a moment to compose herself. Her heart raced with a blend of fear, mischief, and the exhilaration of her impulsive act. She knew she had to maintain the façade and ensure that her actions protected both Sophia's reputation and her own secret engagement with Nicolas.

As she caught her breath, Olivia watched the scene unfold from her concealed vantage point. Nicolas, determined and eager, searched for her amidst the lush greenery. His eyes scanned the area, his footsteps growing closer with each passing second.

Suddenly, Olivia stepped out from her hiding place, a sly smile playing on her lips. She stood before Nicolas, her eyes dancing with a mixture of amusement and adoration. "Caught you," she said, her voice filled with playful triumph.

Nicolas chuckled; his gaze fixed on her radiant beauty. "Ah, but the game isn't over yet, my love. I won't be so easily captured."

With a swift movement, Nicolas lunged forward, gently wrapping his arms around Olivia's waist. She let out a delighted squeal as he pulled her closer, their bodies pressed intimately together. They stood there, their breaths mingling in the cool night air, caught in the embrace of their shared laughter and growing affection.

As their eyes locked, the world around them seemed to fade into the background, leaving only the two of them in this moment of connection and intimacy. Nicolas brushed a strand of hair away from Olivia's face, his touch sending shivers of anticipation through her.

"I never want this moment to end," Olivia whispered.

Nicolas's gaze softened; his voice equally tender. "Nor

do I, my love."

Leaning in, their lips met in a passionate kiss that spoke volumes of their deepening connection. In that moment, surrounded by the fragrance of blooming flowers and the gentle rustling of leaves, they surrendered themselves to the power of their love.

Time seemed to stand still as their kiss lingered, sealing their commitment to each other and igniting a flame of desire that burned brightly within their souls. In that maze of love and devotion, they found solace and strength, reaffirming their bond and vowing to protect it at all costs.

***

Nicolas and Olivia gracefully rejoined the masquerade party, the joy of their love radiating from their intertwined fingers. Olivia discreetly slipped the engagement ring onto her right hand, ensuring it remained concealed for the time being. As they made their way back to the dance floor, their steps synchronized, and they moved as one, their bodies swaying to the rhythm of the music.

They spotted Prince Frederick in the center of the dance floor, his energy infectious as he twirled and spun, his laughter echoing through the grand hall. Nicolas and Olivia exchanged a knowing smile and made their way towards him, ready to join in the merriment.

Frederick's eyes lit up with delight as he saw them approach, and he eagerly pulled them into the dance, spinning Olivia with a flourish and then leading Nicolas in an intricate footwork. The trio danced with a lighthearted abandon, their movements a reflection of their joy and the bonds that connected them.

In the midst of their laughter and graceful twirls, Princess Sophia made her way towards them, her gown flowing with elegance. Olivia's gaze met Sophia's, and a flicker of unease passed between them, a silent acknowledgment of the earlier encounter in the garden. Olivia felt a pang of awkwardness, unsure of how to address the situation.

Sophia's smile remained unaffected, masking any trace of the intimate moment Olivia had stumbled upon. "Well, well, look at the three of you," Sophia said, her voice carrying a teasing undertone. "The stars of the night, dancing together as if you were destined to be."

Nicolas joined in the banter, his eyes twinkling mischievously. "Indeed, it seems we were fated to share the dance floor tonight, my dear future sister-in-law."

Frederick, always the jovial spirit, chimed in, "A dance with family and friends, what more could one ask for?"

Olivia, although still feeling a tinge of discomfort, managed a smile and nodded. "Indeed, it is a night to celebrate love and togetherness."

As the night progressed and the masquerade party continued, the atmosphere grew livelier and the guests indulged in the festive spirit. Among the crowd, Princess Sophia's behavior began to change, her demeanor becoming increasingly unrestrained. A few too many glasses of champagne had rendered her tipsy, her usual composure slipping away.

Olivia observed Sophia from afar, her concern growing with each passing moment. She noticed Sophia's stumbling steps and the unsteady sway of her body as she moved through the throng of partygoers. Feeling a sense of duty and concern for her soon-to-be sister-in-law, Olivia approached Sophia, who was leaning against a grand pillar, a glass of champagne in her hand. The telltale signs of intoxication were evident on Sophia's flushed cheeks and slightly unsteady posture.

Olivia reached out and gently touched her arm. Sophia's gaze flickered towards her; her eyes glazed with the effects of alcohol. Olivia took a deep breath, steeling herself for the confrontation that needed to take place.

"Sophia," Olivia said, her voice tinged with both empathy and firmness, "we need to talk."

Sophia let out a careless laugh, her words slurred. "Talk? About what, dear Olivia? There's nothing to talk about. We're all just having a good time, aren't we?"

Olivia guided Sophia to a quieter corner of the hall, away from the pulsating rhythm of the music and the curious gazes of other guests. It was in this secluded space that Olivia hoped they could have an honest conversation.

As they found a comfortable spot, Olivia observed Sophia's disheveled appearance, her normally impeccable hair now slightly undone, and her mask clutched loosely in her hand. It was a stark contrast to the composed and regal princess Olivia had known.

Olivia's grip on Sophia's arm tightened, her concern transforming into resolve. "I saw you in the garden earlier, Sophia. With that man. Who was he?"

Sophia's eyes widened momentarily, a flicker of panic passing through them before being replaced by a defiant glare. "Ah, so you've been spying on me, have you? Well, let me tell you something, Olivia Grey. You would do well to keep your nose out of my affairs."

Olivia's voice remained steady; her eyes locked with Sophia's. "It's not about spying, Sophia. I saw you and couldn't help but be concerned. I care about you, and I don't want to see you get hurt."

Sophia let out a bitter laugh, swaying slightly. "Hurt? Oh, Olivia, you have no idea what it means to be hurt. You think you can just waltz into our lives and take everything for yourself, don't you? Well, I won't let you ruin everything."

Olivia moved closer; her voice filled with conviction. "Sophia, I'm not trying to take anything away from you. I want nothing more than for us to be happy together. But keeping secrets and hiding things will only lead to more pain. Please, trust me enough to be honest with me."

Sophia's eyes narrowed, her voice dripping with a venomous edge. "You want honesty? Fine. But remember, Olivia, if you ever breathe a word of what you saw to anyone else, I'll make sure your perfect little world comes crashing down."

Olivia swallowed hard, her heart pounding in her chest. She understood the weight of Sophia's threat, and she knew the consequences of revealing the truth could be devastating. But she also recognized the importance of staying true to her values, even in the face of adversity.

"I promise you, Sophia," Olivia said, her voice steady, "I will keep your secret. But know this, keeping secrets will only lead to more pain and destruction. We're family, and we need to support and trust each other."

Sophia's gaze held Olivia's for a moment, a mixture of anger and vulnerability flickering within her eyes. Slowly, she nodded, her resistance momentarily subsiding. "Fine, Olivia. We'll keep each other's secrets. But don't think for a moment that these changes anything between us."

Olivia nodded in understanding, her resolve unwavering. She knew that earning Sophia's trust would take time, and that repairing the cracks in their relationship would require patience and perseverance. As they stood there, the weight of their unspoken words hung in the air, a silent agreement binding them together in their shared secret.

***

As the masquerade party drew to a close, Nicolas found himself guiding a stumbling and inebriated Frederick through the crowd towards the waiting car. The night had taken its toll on his older brother, evident in the unsteady steps and slurred speech. Nicolas's protective instincts kicked in, determined to get Frederick home safely.

With a firm yet gentle grip, Nicolas supported Frederick's weight as they made their way towards the waiting car. The night air was cool and crisp, a welcome contrast to the warm and bustling atmosphere of the party. The car's headlights illuminated their path as they approached, casting long shadows across the pavement.

"Come on, Frederick," Nicolas urged, his voice filled with concern. "Let's get you inside the car. We'll be home soon."

Frederick mumbled unintelligibly; his gaze unfocused as he attempted to steady himself. It was clear that he had indulged in more than his fair share of drinks throughout the evening. Nicolas knew it was not his brother's usual demeanor, but he understood the allure of temporary escape from the pressures of their royal duties.

As they reached the car, Nicolas opened the door and gently guided Frederick into the back seat. He fastened the seatbelt securely, making sure his brother was as comfortable as possible given the circumstances. Frederick's head lolled back against the seat; his eyes half-closed.

Nicolas slipped into the driver's seat and started the engine, the quiet hum of the car breaking the silence of the night. The car began to move, gliding through the empty streets of the city as they headed towards the familiar grandeur of the royal palace.

The journey was filled with a heavy silence, broken only by the occasional sigh or groan from Frederick. Nicolas kept his focus on the road ahead, his mind racing with thoughts of the night's revelations and the implications they held for their intertwined destinies.

As the palace gates came into view, Nicolas turned his gaze towards his brother, "Freddie, I'm so happy for you and Sophia."

Frederick managed a weak nod, his lips forming a half-smile. "Thank you, Nicolas. I don't know what I would do without you."

Nicolas parked the car and turned off the engine, the quiet engulfing them once again. With a deep breath, he turned to face Frederick, their eyes meeting in a shared understanding.

"Let's go inside, Frederick," Nicolas said, his voice gentle yet determined.

They stepped out of the car, Frederick leaning on Nicolas for support as they made their way towards the entrance of the palace. The night had taken an unexpected turn, but their bond as brothers remained unbreakable.

As Nicolas guided the intoxicated Frederick through the palace corridors, they finally reached his room. The grandeur of the space seemed to fade into the background as Nicolas focused on the task at hand - ensuring his brother's well-being.

With a careful touch, Nicolas helped Frederick onto the plush bed, making sure he was comfortable before tucking him in. The room was adorned with elegant furnishings, reflecting the opulence befitting a prince. Soft moonlight streamed through the window, casting a gentle glow on Frederick's weary face.

As Nicolas straightened the covers, he noticed the look of unease etched on Frederick's features. Concern filled his eyes, and he took a seat beside the bed, ready to lend an empathetic ear.

"Freddie, what's troubling you?" Nicolas asked, his voice filled with genuine concern. "You can confide in me, you know. We've always been there for each other, and this is no different."

Frederick's gaze wandered aimlessly for a moment before finally settling on Nicolas. His voice was tinged with vulnerability as he spoke, the weight of his emotions evident in every word.

"Nicolas, I... I don't want to go through with the arranged marriage," Frederick confessed, his voice wavering. "Princess Sophia... I'm in love with her. I have loved her since we both we children, but I don't feel that she feels the same way. It wouldn't be fair to her or to me to enter into a loveless marriage."

Nicolas listened attentively, his heart aching for his brother's inner turmoil. He had always known that the weight of duty and responsibility rested heavily on Frederick's shoulders, and this decision would not come easily for him.

Nicolas reached out and placed a comforting hand on Frederick's shoulder. "You're not alone in this, my brother. Tomorrow we can discuss how we'll approach this situation. But for now, it's time to sleep."

With a final pat on an already fast asleep Frederick's arm, Nicolas rose from his seat and made his way to the door. As he turned to look back at his brother, he could not help but feel a renewed sense of determination. They would face the challenges ahead as a united front, guided by their shared bond and the desire for true happiness.

Closing the door gently behind him, Nicolas walked down the corridor, his mind already swirling with thoughts of the difficult conversations that lay ahead. The night was far from over, and the choices they would make would shape the future not only for Frederick but for the entire kingdom.

***

CHAPTER 18:

MAKINGS OF A SCANDAL

Olivia sat in the cozy comfort of her suite, the soft glow of the bedside lamp casting a warm ambiance. The room exuded a sense of tranquility, allowing her to fully embrace the joy that swelled within her heart. She admired the glistening emerald ring that rested on her left ring finger, each facet reflecting a myriad of emotions.

With a smile playing on her lips, Olivia reached for her phone and dialed her mother's number. As the call connected, anticipation filled her, knowing that she was about to share the incredible news with the person who had always been her pillar of support - her mother, Evelyn.

The screen came to life, revealing Evelyn's smiling face, her eyes shimmering with love and curiosity. "Olivia, my darling, it's so wonderful to see you. Is everything alright?"

Olivia's voice trembled with excitement as she replied, "Mom, I have something amazing to share with you. Nicolas proposed to me, and I said yes! We're engaged!"

Evelyn's eyes widened with delight, and her hands instinctively covered her mouth in joyful surprise. "Oh, Olivia, my dear! I'm overjoyed for you! Congratulations! I couldn't be happier for you, my darling."

Olivia's heart swelled with love as she soaked in her mother's genuine happiness. The connection between them transcended the miles that separated them, and in that moment, they were united in celebration and love.

"But, Mom," Olivia continued, her voice turning softer and more intimate, "we've decided to keep our engagement a secret for now. We want to enjoy this special time together before sharing the news with the world. Can I count on you to keep it to yourself for a little while longer?"

Evelyn nodded, her eyes filled with understanding and a mother's unwavering loyalty. "Of course, my dear. Take all the time you need to savor this precious moment."

A sigh of relief escaped Olivia's lips, grateful for her mother's unwavering support. "Thank you, Mom. I wish you were here with me right now to celebrate in person."

Evelyn's voice softened with tenderness. "I wish I could be there with you too, my darling. But know that I'm always here for you, no matter the distance. We'll celebrate together when the time is right."

Olivia's eyes glistened with tears of happiness; her heart filled with gratitude for the strong bond she shared with her mother. Their conversation continued late into the night, as they reminisced about Olivia's journey and spoke about the exciting future that lay ahead.

As the call came to an end, Olivia felt a renewed sense of love and warmth enveloping her. She slipped into her cozy pajamas, still gazing at the sparkling engagement ring on her finger. With her mother's words echoing in her heart, she knew that their secret would be safe, held within the loving embrace of their special bond.

With a contented sigh, Olivia settled into bed, her thoughts consumed by dreams of the beautiful future that awaited her and Nicolas. Her fingertips lightly grazed her phone screen, as she felt a surge of warmth and love for her fiancé. She knew that despite the physical distance between them, their connection remained strong. With a gentle smile on her lips, she sent him a text, bidding him a sweet goodnight and expressing her love for him.

Before she could set her phone aside, a familiar melody filled the room, indicating an incoming call. It was Nicolas. Olivia's heart skipped a beat, and she eagerly answered the call, bringing the phone to her ear.

"Nicolas," she whispered softly, her voice filled with affection.

"Olivia, my love," Nicolas responded, his voice carrying a mixture of tenderness and longing. "I couldn't resist calling you."

Olivia's voice trembled with happiness as she replied, "I miss you, Nicolas. I wish you were here with me right now."

There was a brief pause, filled with a shared yearning. Then Nicolas spoke, his voice filled with sincerity, "Believe me, my love, I wish the same."

"Olivia, there's something important I need to tell you,"

Nicolas's voice grew serious as he began to share the weighty revelation that his brother, Frederick, had confided in him earlier that night. "Freddie, confessed to me tonight that he doesn't want to proceed with the arranged marriage to Princess Sophia."

Olivia's brows furrowed with surprise, her mind racing to comprehend the significance of Frederick's revelation. "Nicolas, that's unexpected. What could have changed his mind?"

Nicolas sighed softly; his voice tinged with empathy. "He didn't provide me with all the details, but from our conversation, I gathered that he has been feeling trapped and uncertain about his future."

Olivia listened intently, her heart aching for Frederick's inner turmoil. She understood all too well the conflict between societal expectations and personal desires. "Nicolas, it must be a challenging situation for Frederick. To have his life planned out for him, without having a say in matters of the heart."

Olivia took a deep breath, contemplating whether or not to share the truth about the mysterious woman they had encountered in the garden earlier that evening. She realized that honesty was essential in their relationship, and keeping secrets would only create distance between them. She gathered her courage to reveal the truth about the mysterious woman they had stumbled upon in the garden.

"Nicolas, there's something I need to tell you," Olivia started. "At garden maze earlier, remembered when we stumbled upon a scene that caught us both off guard?"

Nicolas's eyebrows furrowed in surprise and curiosity. "I remember that moment. It was unexpected, to say the least. Do you know who she was?"

Olivia took a deep breath, choosing her words carefully. "Yes, I do. The woman in the red gown... It was Princess Sophia."

Nicolas's eyes widened in astonishment, a mixture of disbelief and concern crossing his face. "Princess Sophia? Are you certain, Olivia?"

Olivia nodded, even though Nicolas couldn't see her. "Yes, Nicolas. I recognized her unmistakable red gown, and there was no mistaking the intensity of the moment. I was taken aback and felt a wave of awkwardness after witnessing it."

Nicolas's mind seemed to be racing, trying to process the revelation. "This changes everything," he murmured, his voice tinged with disappointment. "Sophia's actions tonight, combined with Frederick's confession earlier... it's evident that our families are facing deep-seated issues."

Olivia's voice softened with empathy. "Nicolas, I can only imagine the complexities and challenges surrounding their relationship. It's clear that things are not as they seem. Perhaps this revelation sheds light on Sophia's own struggles and desires."

"Nicolas, we need to address this situation directly and

give Frederick and Sophia the opportunity to share their perspectives," Olivia suggested, her voice filled with empathy and concern. "I think it would be best if we meet with them in person to discuss what we witnessed and how it may affect their relationship."

Nicolas agreed, his voice laced with resolve. "You're right, Olivia. Face-to-face communication is essential for understanding each other's feelings and finding a way forward. Let's arrange a meeting with Frederick and Sophia tomorrow. We can create a safe space where everyone can share their thoughts openly."

Olivia felt a sense of relief, knowing that they were taking a proactive approach to address the complexities of the situation. "I'm glad you agree, Nicolas. We should make sure Frederick and Sophia know that we're here to support them, regardless of the outcome."

Nicolas's voice held a gentle reassurance. "Absolutely, Olivia. Our love and care for them should guide our actions. We'll listen to their perspectives and offer our guidance."

The couple continued their conversation, making practical arrangements for the meeting the next day. As their conversation drew to a close, Olivia and Nicolas felt a renewed sense of unity and purpose. They understood the significance of their role as confidants and advocates for their loved ones. They ended the call with a shared understanding that tomorrow's meeting would be a turning point, an opportunity to bring the truth to light.

***

As the soft morning light gently filtered into Olivia's room, she stirred from her sleep, still relishing the warmth of her dreams. With a stretch and a yawn, she gradually became aware of the presence outside her door. Curiosity tinged with a spark of excitement fluttered in her chest, wondering who could be there so early in the morning.

Slipping out of bed, Olivia moved towards the door, her heart skipping a beat as she caught a glimpse of the familiar figure standing on the other side. There, with a gentle smile adorning his face, stood Nicolas, his eyes brimming with affection and a touch of mischief.

"Nicolas," Olivia gasped, her voice a soft whisper tinged with surprise and delight. "What are you doing here so early in the morning?"

Nicolas chuckled softly, his voice a warm caress. "I couldn't resist the urge to surprise you, my love. I wanted us to start the day together, to be by your side."

Olivia's eyes sparkled in the morning light as she invited him inside her room. She quickly brushed her fingers through her tousled hair and wrapped herself in a cozy robe, savoring the intimate moments of their unexpected reunion.

As Olivia moved about the room, her every graceful gesture captivating Nicolas's attention. He couldn't help but be mesmerized by her every movement, from the way she effortlessly brushed her hair to the way she selected her attire for the day.

With each delicate touch, Olivia's fingers caressed the fabric of her dress, her choice reflecting her impeccable sense of style. The sunlight filtering through the window danced upon her skin, enhancing her natural radiance and accentuating her features with a soft glow.

Olivia could not help but steal glances at Nicolas, his mere presence filling the room with an undeniable sense of warmth and comfort. He stood by the window, his silhouette bathed in the soft morning light, a vision of strength and tenderness.

Nicolas was captivated by Olivia's effortless grace, the way she carried herself with a quiet confidence that emanated from within. It was a sight that reminded him of why he fell in love with her in the first place—the way she effortlessly commanded attention, yet remained down-to-earth and genuine. And the way her lips curved into a gentle smile as she concentrated on perfecting every detail of her appearance—it all left him breathless.

He watched as she carefully applied a hint of color to her lips, enhancing their natural beauty, and then expertly blended a touch of blush onto her cheeks, adding a rosy flush that mirrored the blossoming of their love. The sound of her laughter filled the room, echoing like a sweet melody that brought joy to his heart.

Nicolas's gaze never wavered from Olivia, his eyes drinking in the sight of her, awestruck by her natural beauty. He marveled at how effortlessly she carried herself, radiating a quiet confidence that only deepened his admiration and love for her.

As Olivia reached for her favorite necklace, carefully fastening it around her neck, Nicolas approached her with a tender smile. He couldn't contain the overwhelming adoration he felt for her any longer. His voice was filled with warmth and affection as he whispered, "You are the most beautiful person I have ever known, Olivia. Every day, you light up my world with your presence."

Olivia blushed; her cheeks tinged with a rosy hue as she met Nicolas's gaze. Her heart swelled with love, his words wrapping around her like a warm embrace. "And I feel the same way, Nicolas. I can't imagine embarking on this journey with anyone else by my side."

Nicolas led Olivia outside to where a sleek, black convertible awaited them. The sun had reached its zenith, casting a warm and golden glow over the sprawling palace grounds. The convertible's polished exterior gleamed in the sunlight, hinting at the exhilarating adventure that awaited them.

Olivia's eyes widened with excitement as she took in the sight of the convertible. Her heart fluttered with anticipation, knowing that this spontaneous gesture from Nicolas would lead them on a journey they would cherish forever. She couldn't help but feel a surge of gratitude for the man by her side, who always went above and beyond to bring joy into her life.

Together they climbed into the car, the soft leather seats embracing them as they settled in. Nicolas adjusted his sunglasses and flashed Olivia a playful grin before starting the engine. The purr of the powerful motor reverberated through the air, filling them with a sense of freedom and possibility.

As the car glided through the palace gates, a gentle breeze tousled their hair, making Olivia's laughter dance on the wind. Olivia's hand reached out instinctively, the wind playing with her fingertips as they soared through the open space. Nicolas glanced at her; his eyes filled with an affectionate warmth that mirrored the sun's rays.

"This moment feels like a dream, Nicolas," Olivia whispered, her voice filled with a sense of wonder.

Nicolas tightened his grip on the steering wheel, as he silently felt the magic of the moment. The words carried away by the wind, as if whispered to the universe itself. With the wind tousling their hair and the warm sun casting a golden glow upon them, they embarked on a carefree adventure in the convertible. The open road stretched out before them, offering a sense of freedom and exhilaration that mirrored the boundless love they shared.

Their first stop was a cozy café nestled in a quaint corner of the town. The aroma of freshly brewed coffee and the tantalizing scent of freshly baked pastries welcomed them as they entered. They found a cozy table by the window, where they could watch the world go by while savoring their breakfast.

As they savored each bite and engaged in lively conversation with the other customers. Their laughter filled the air, blending harmoniously with the cheerful ambiance of the café. The moments they shared were infused with warmth and tenderness, as they reveled in the joy of simply being together.

After their meal, Nicolas and Olivia strolled through the charming streets, exploring the vibrant array of shops that lined the town. The clicking of cameras caught their attention, and they turned to see the paparazzi capturing their every move.

Instead of shying away from the intrusive lenses, Nicolas and Olivia exchanged a knowing glance. With an unspoken agreement, they decided to embrace the attention, realizing that their love story had the power to inspire and uplift others. They greeted the paparazzi with genuine smiles, waving in acknowledgment of their presence.

The paparazzi, taken aback by the couple's graciousness, quickly shifted their focus from invasive snapshots to capturing the authenticity of a love that defied expectations. The clicking of cameras became a symphony of admiration and respect, as the world watched their love story unfold before their eyes.

As Olivia and Nicolas reveled in the joy of their public outing, the ringing of Nicolas's phone cut through the air, shattering the tranquil atmosphere. His expression turned serious as he retrieved the device from his pocket.

Nicolas's brows furrowed in concern as he answered the call, bringing the phone to his ear. Olivia watched his face as it transitioned from delight to deep concentration, a hint of worry etching lines on his forehead. She instinctively reached out, her hand finding his and offering a reassuring squeeze.

"Freddie? What's going on?" Nicolas's voice carried a sense of urgency, mirroring the gravity of the situation at hand. Olivia's curiosity piqued as she listened intently, her heart beating faster with each passing second.

As Nicolas absorbed the information being relayed to him, Olivia could sense the weight of the news weighing heavily on his shoulders. She knew that the call must have held something significant for Jack to interrupt their cherished moment together.

"I understand, brother. We'll be there as soon as possible," Nicolas replied, his voice steady despite the turmoil brewing within him. He ended the call and turned to Olivia, with a worried expression on his face.

"It's an emergency meeting convened by the King," Nicolas explained, his tone laced with a sense of urgency. "We need to go back to the palace immediately."

Olivia's heart sank at the mention of an emergency meeting. She knew that such gatherings were rare and signaled a momentous event. She tightened her grip on Nicolas's hand, offering him strength and support. "Whatever it is, we'll handle it as a team."

Nicolas nodded, gratitude filling his eyes as he looked at Olivia. "Thank you, my love."

Just as they were about to make their way back to the car, a familiar voice called out from a distance. It was Jack, striding towards them with a cup of coffee in his hand. His face carried a mix of unease and resolve, mirroring the gravity of the situation.

"Prince Nicolas, Miss Grey, I'm glad I caught you both. The King has summoned us for an emergency meeting," Jack announced, his voice carrying a sense of urgency. "It's imperative that we make our way to the palace without delay."

Olivia's eyes widened in worry. "Jack, what could be so urgent?" she wondered aloud.

Jack's expression turned grave as he glanced between Nicolas and Olivia. "I wish I had all the answers, but we'll find out soon enough. The fate of the kingdom may be at stake, and your presence is crucial."

As they hurried back to the car, the once carefree atmosphere was replaced by a sense of purpose and anticipation. The convertible's engine roared to life, its power serving as a reminder of the impending responsibility that awaited them at the palace.

***

The emergency meeting was held in the grand council chamber of the palace, its opulent walls adorned with intricate tapestries depicting the kingdom's rich history. King Edmund sat at the head of the long, polished table. Emanating authority, the King cleared his throat before addressing the room. His voice carried a weight of responsibility and determination as he began, "I have been made aware of a situation that has the potential to cast a shadow on the reputation of our family and our kingdom."

His gaze swept across the room, meeting the eyes of each person present, the weight of his words reverberating in the silence. Marco, with a stack of documents in front of him, held the floor, his features etched with seriousness and resolve.

Marco, the shrewd and insightful royal counselor, cleared his throat, breaking the tense silence that enveloped the room. "Your royal highnesses, esteemed members of the royal family, I bring grave news," he began, his voice measured and solemn.

All eyes turned towards him, anticipation and anxiety filling the air. Marco continued; his tone laden with urgency.

"I received information from my informant in the tabloid industry," Marco began, his voice steady. "There are whispers circulating within the press, suggesting that an incident of a scandalous nature took place during the masquerade party.

Princess Sophia's face paled as the gravity of the situation dawned on her. Frederick glanced at her; concern etched on his features. Olivia's hand instinctively sought Nicolas's, their fingers intertwining for support.

"What kind of scandal?" Princess Sophia asked.

Marco's gaze met hers, his expression serious. "It appears that a member of the royal family was witnessed in an intimate position with one of the servers in the garden," he revealed, his words hanging in the air like a heavy cloak. "The press is on the verge of publishing, and we must act swiftly to control the narrative."

Whispers filled the room as the gravity of the situation sank in. The potential consequences of such a scandal were significant, not only for the individuals involved but also for the reputation of the royal family and the stability of the kingdom.

King Edmund, his gaze firm, addressed his children directly. "Frederick, Nicolas, I need to hear the truth from both of you. Is there any validity to these claims?"

Frederick's jaw tightened as he exchanged a glance with Nicolas, the weight of their shared secret bearing down upon them. But it was Sophia's voice that they heard, "Your Majesty, it's Olivia who spread those rumors. I'm sure of it."

Tension filled the room as Sophia's accusation hung in the air. Olivia's eyes widened in shock, her hand instinctively releasing Nicolas's as she turned to face Sophia, her expression a blend of confusion and hurt. The atmosphere grew heavy with a silence broken only by the faint sound of rapid breathing.

Olivia's voice quivered slightly as she spoke. "Sophia, how could you think that I would betray you in such a way? I would never leak such sensitive information to the press."

Sophia's gaze hardened as she met Olivia's eyes, her tone dripping with disdain. "Oh, please, Olivia. We all know how jealous you've been of me. You've always resented my position and sought to undermine me."

The room seemed to hold its breath as the argument escalated, and the true colors of Princess Sophia began to unveil. Olivia's eyes welled with tears as she fought to maintain her composure.

Frederick, torn between his loyalty to Sophia and his growing realization of her true character, interjected, his voice laced with hesitation. "Sophia, are you certain of these accusations? Olivia has been nothing but supportive and loyal to us."

Sophia turned to Frederick; desperation etched on her face. "Frederick, you can't believe her. She's just trying to tear us apart. You have to protect me, protect us!"

The room erupted into a flurry of hushed whispers and exchanged glances, the tension escalating with each passing moment. King Edmund raised a hand, his voice carrying authority as he attempted to restore order.

"Enough!" King Edmund's voice boomed, silencing the room. His eyes held disappointment as he addressed Sophia. "Princess Sophia, we must focus on the matter at hand. These accusations can be addressed later. Right now, we need to determine the best course of action for the kingdom and its reputation."

Marco, the loyal and astute advisor, interjected, his voice steady and measured. "Your Majesty, we should conduct a thorough investigation to ascertain the truth of these allegations. It is imperative that we gather all the facts before deciding on the appropriate course of action."

The room fell into a thoughtful silence as the weight of the situation settled upon them. The fate of the royal family and the stability of the kingdom hung in the balance, and a sense of duty and determination united them all.

King Edmund nodded, his gaze sweeping across the room. "I agree, Marco. We shall initiate a discreet investigation to uncover the truth behind these allegations. We must act swiftly and decisively to protect the integrity of our family and the monarchy."

In a moment of weakness, Sophia's eyes accidentally darted to Olivia's right hand. Her gaze fixated on the emerald ring; she immediately knew that she had found the bargaining chip.

"And what's this, Olivia? An engagement ring? Have you been hiding this little secret from us all?" Sophia's voice echoed out through the walls.

Gasps filled the room as the attention shifted from the scandal to Olivia and Nicolas. Olivia felt a surge of panic, realizing that their carefully guarded secret had been exposed. The weight of the ring suddenly felt heavy on her finger, as if the entire room had turned their judgmental eyes upon her.

The grand council chamber grew silent as King Edmund's gaze shifted to his son, Nicolas. He leaned forward, his voice filled with a fatherly concern.

"Nicolas, is it true?" King Edmund asked, his voice measured yet gentle. "Are you truly engaged to Olivia Grey?"

Nicolas nodded; his voice steady as he spoke. "Yes, Father, it is true. Olivia and I got engaged last night at the masquerade party."

Olivia's hand instinctively sought Nicolas's, their fingers intertwining for support. She faced the scrutiny of the room, her head held high despite the storm of emotions raging within her.

"I understand that this news may come as a surprise," Olivia began. "But our intention was to share this joyful announcement once Frederick's wedding to Sophia was over, out of respect for their special day."

Princess Sophia, her face contorted with a mixture of anger and betrayal, rose from her seat, her voice shaking with emotion. "How dare you keep this from us? Engaged? And to someone like her?" Her voice dripped with disdain as she gestured towards Olivia.

King Edmund raised a hand, his voice carrying authority as he sought to restore order to the room. "Princess Sophia, we shall address your concerns in due time. Right now, we must focus on resolving the crisis at hand and protecting the reputation of our family and the kingdom."

Marco, ever the perceptive advisor, stepped forward, his voice calm yet firm. "Your Majesty, the revelation of Nicolas and Olivia's engagement presents an opportunity. We can offer the tabloid the exclusive news of their engagement in exchange for their discretion regarding the scandal."

King Edmund considered Marco's words; his brow furrowed with concern. The repercussions of the scandal could have far-reaching consequences, not only for the royal family but for the stability of the kingdom itself. The suggestion offered a glimmer of hope in the midst of the turmoil.

Frederick, torn because of his loyalty to the crown spoke up, his voice filled with urgency. "Father, we cannot allow our personal indiscretions to be exploited for the tabloid's gain. We must protect the reputation of the royal family at all costs."

Nicolas, his grip on Olivia's hand tightening, offered his support. "Father, I believe Frederick is right. By controlling the narrative and strategically managing the situation, we can minimize the damage and maintain our integrity."

Jack, the pragmatic strategist, nodded in agreement. "I

concur, Your Highness. By trading the exclusive engagement reveal, we can mitigate the impact of the scandal and maintain a semblance of control over the narrative."

Olivia, addressed Princess Sophia directly. "Sophia, please understand that Nicolas and I never meant to hurt you. Our love for each other grew unexpectedly, and we were planning to share our news with you and Frederick once the wedding was over. We never wanted to overshadow your special day."

Sophia's face contorted with anger and hurt as she listened to Olivia's words. Her voice trembled with emotion as she turned to Frederick, her plea filled with desperation. "Frederick, you can't allow this. Our love, our future together... Don't let them take it away from us."

King Edmund, his gaze shifting from Sophia to Olivia and Nicolas, weighed the options before him. He recognized the gravity of the situation and the need to protect his family and the kingdom from further harm. With a sigh, he nodded, his voice firm yet weary.

"Very well. We shall proceed with Marco's suggestion. We must initiate a discreet investigation to uncover the truth behind the scandal, and in the meantime, negotiate with the tabloid to control the narrative surrounding the engagement."

The room buzzed with a mixture of relief and uncertainty as plans were set into motion. The focus shifted from the scandal to the strategic handling of the engagement news. Sophia, her victory marred by the impending deal, struggled to maintain her composure.

As the conversation continued, emotions ran high, and the room became a battleground of conflicting loyalties and hidden agendas. The once-unbreakable façade of the royal family began to crack under the weight of betrayal and mistrust.

Olivia, her voice steady despite the turmoil inside her, turned to Sophia. "Sophia, I did not leak anything to the press. I saw you in the garden with a stranger, and I was merely trying to protect you by confronting you privately."

Sophia's eyes narrowed; her voice laced with contempt. "Protect me? You have no right to meddle in my affairs, Olivia. This is my engagement, my future, and I won't let you ruin it."

Frederick, torn between his love for Olivia and his loyalty to his sister, stepped forward, his voice tinged with frustration. "Sophia, we need to focus on resolving this crisis. Accusing Olivia without any evidence only divides us further."

King Edmund, his gaze shifting from Sophia to Olivia, spoke with authority. "Enough. Sophia, Frederick is right. Accusing Olivia without proof only adds more chaos to an already delicate situation. We need unity now more than ever."

Sophia's face flushed with anger as she turned to Frederick, her voice dripping with venom. "Frederick, how can you defend her? You know nothing about her true intentions."

Frederick took a step towards Sophia. "I may not know everything, but I know Olivia. And I believe in her."

Jack, always the voice of reason, interjected, his tone calm yet assertive. "Princess Sophia, it's in everyone's best interest to put our differences aside and find a solution. The kingdom's stability and reputation depend on our united front."

Princess Sophia, realizing the depth of her isolation, sank into her chair, her face a mask of frustration and resentment. The room fell silent, the weight of the situation hanging heavy in the air.

King Edmund broke the silence, his voice carrying a hint of weariness. "We shall investigate the truth behind these allegations. In the meantime, we will proceed with the negotiation with the tabloid to control the narrative. Our focus should be on protecting the dignity of the royal family and the stability of the kingdom."

Marco, seizing the opportunity to guide the discussion, addressed the King. "Your Majesty, I will contact our contacts in the media industry and begin the negotiations immediately. We need to ensure that our terms are met and the truth is revealed on our own terms."

The room fell silent once again, the weight of their choices heavy upon them. The fate of the royal family and the stability of the kingdom hung in the balance.

Each member of the family exchanged glances, their eyes filled with determination and uncertainty. In that moment, the grand council chamber felt more than just a room for decision-making. It became a crucible of emotions, where loyalties were tested, and sacrifices were made for the greater good. The journey to redemption and resolution had only just begun, and the road ahead would challenge their every conviction.

***

The grand council chamber slowly emptied, leaving behind an air of tension and unspoken words. Nicolas and Olivia exchanged a worried glance before hurriedly making their way towards the palace courtyard, where Frederick's fleeing figure could be seen in the distance.

"Freddie!" Nicolas called out; his voice filled with urgency. "Wait, we need to talk!"

Frederick's steps faltered for a moment before he turned to face his brother and Olivia. His eyes bore the weight of conflict and sadness, the turmoil within him mirrored in his haggard expression.

"What is it, Nicolas?" Frederick asked. "I need some time alone to gather my thoughts."

Nicolas closed the distance between them, his voice filled with determination as he confronted his brother. "Freddie, we can't ignore what you told me the other night. You said you didn't want to marry Sophia. You can't just brush it off now."

Frederick's brow furrowed as he searched his memory, his face contorting with confusion. "Nick, I... I must have been drunk or confused. I don't remember saying that. Sophia and I have been betrothed since childhood. It's my duty, my responsibility as the next in line for the throne."

Olivia stepped forward, her voice filled with empathy and concern. "Frederick, I understand the weight of your duty, but you can't sacrifice your own happiness for the sake of the kingdom alone. Love should have a place in your life too."

Frederick's gaze shifted between his brother and Olivia, his eyes reflecting the inner battle he was waging. "I appreciate your concern, but the crown carries immense responsibility. The stability of the kingdom rests on my shoulders. I must prioritize my duty above personal desires."

Nicolas reached out, his hand gently grasping Frederick's shoulder. "Freddie, I understand the burden you carry, but there is more to life than duty alone. You deserve to find happiness, to be with someone who truly makes your heart soar."

Frederick's voice trembled with emotion as he shook his head. "Nick, you don't understand. Our family, our kingdom... they rely on me to uphold the traditions, to maintain stability. I can't let my personal feelings disrupt that."

Olivia's voice softened as she spoke, her eyes filled with compassion. "Frederick, we're not asking you to abandon your responsibilities. But it's important to remember that a leader who is true to their own heart is far more effective. You deserve to find love and happiness within your duty."

Frederick's shoulders sagged, the weight of the world pressing down upon him. His voice was barely above a whisper as he spoke, the conflict within him laid bare. "I wish it were that simple. But for now, duty must come first."

Nicolas exchanged a glance with Olivia, his voice filled with determination. "Freddie, we won't give up on you. We'll be there for you. You're not alone in this."

Frederick looked into the eyes of his brother and Olivia, their unwavering support a glimmer of hope in the midst of his turmoil. With a sigh, he nodded, the sorrow evident in his expression.

"Thank you, both of you," Frederick murmured. "I appreciate your understanding and support."

Just as a moment of silence settled over them, a familiar voice broke through the air, catching their attention. It was Jack, their trusted personal secretary, hastily making his way towards them.

"Excuse me, Your Highnesses," Jack called out, his voice carrying a sense of urgency. "I have some urgent news regarding the upcoming engagement interview with the media."

Nicolas, Olivia, and Frederick turned their attention to Jack. They knew that the interview would be a critical moment, one that would shape the narrative surrounding their engagement and the kingdom's future.

"What is it, Jack?" Nicolas asked, his voice steady but tinged with a hint of concern. "We're listening."

Jack took a moment to catch his breath, then continued, his voice measured and focused. "The engagement interview has been scheduled on two days from now. It will be a joint interview, attended by Prince Nicolas and Miss Grey, as well as Prince Frederick and Princess Sophia."

Olivia's eyes widened, and her grip on Nicolas's hand tightened. The reality of facing the media, alongside Sophia, who had become their adversary, added an extra layer of tension to the situation.

Frederick, though conflicted, nodded in understanding. "I expected as much. The media will be eager to capture every moment of this union."

Nicolas leaned in, his voice a blend of determination and concern. "We must approach this interview with caution. We must present a united front for the sake of the kingdom and our loved ones."

Olivia nodded, her gaze meeting Frederick's for a brief moment before turning back to Nicolas. "You're right, Nicolas. We need to remain composed and focused during the interview. I will do my part and talk with Sophia before we go on."

Jack interjected, his voice reflecting the weight of the responsibility he bore as their trusted advisor. "I've already started working on the interview preparations. We will do some mock interview sessions with all four of you."

Frederick's eyes flickered with gratitude. "Thank you, Jack. Your guidance is invaluable to us."

Jack's gaze shifted between the three of them, his voice filled with sincerity. "It is my duty and privilege to serve you."

As they stood in the courtyard, a sense of unity and purpose enveloped them once again. The impending engagement interview loomed over them, but they were resolved to face it together, standing united against the storm that threatened to overshadow their love and the stability of the kingdom.

***

CHAPTER 19:

QUESTIONS OF THE HOUR

The royal study was transformed into a makeshift interview room, adorned with microphones, cameras, and a large screen that displayed a live feed of the previous interviews of the engaged couples. Marco, with his astute demeanor and keen eye for detail, oversaw the proceedings, ensuring that every aspect of the interview preparation was meticulously addressed.

Nicolas, Olivia, Frederick, and Sophia gathered around a long conference table, their expressions a mixture of anticipation and nerves. They knew that the upcoming interview would be a pivotal moment, one that required them to navigate the delicate balance between honesty, diplomacy, and projecting a united front.

Jack stood at the head of the table, a stack of interview questions in hand, ready to guide them through the rigorous preparation process. His presence instilled a sense of calm and reassurance in the room.

"Let's begin," Jack said, his voice filled with confidence. "The purpose of this intensive preparation is to ensure that you respond to each question with clarity, authenticity, and consideration for the impact of your words. Miss Grey, we'll rely on your experience in the limelight to guide us through this process."

Olivia nodded, her eyes focused and determined. "I understand, Jack. I've faced countless interviews in the past, and I'm accustomed to navigating sensitive topics. I will do my best to lead the way."

Frederick glanced at Olivia, admiration shining in his

eyes. He knew that her poise and grace under pressure would be essential in handling the potential pitfalls that awaited them during the interview.

Sophia, nodded in agreement. "Olivia, I appreciate your expertise in this matter. Together, we can present a united front and ensure that our words reflect our commitment to the kingdom."

Nicolas, aware of the weight Olivia carried, placed a reassuring hand on her shoulder. "Olivia, we'll support you every step of the way. This interview is an opportunity for us to show our dedication to each other and the kingdom."

Marco interjected, his voice steady and authoritative. "Jack, let us begin. Focus on the key points that we want to convey during the interview."

As the room settled into a focused silence, Jack, stepped forward with a stack of prepared questions in his hand. He wore an expression of professionalism mixed with a hint of anticipation. With a nod from Marco, he began the mock interview, his voice steady and measured.

"Thank you all for being here. Let's start with some relationship-based questions to establish the foundation of your bond," Jack announced, his eyes shifting from one person to another.

Olivia and Nicolas sat side by side, their hands intertwined, emanating a sense of unity and support. Frederick and Sophia, though visibly more guarded, sat close together, the weight of their impending nuptials hanging in the air.

"Miss Olivia Grey and Prince Nicolas, you have recently announced your engagement. Can you tell us more about the proposal moment?" Jack inquired; his gaze directed at the couple.

Olivia's eyes softened; her voice filled with warmth as she recalled the memory. "It was a magical night at the masquerade party. We realized that our connection ran deep, and we wanted to embrace a future together."

Nicolas added, his voice filled with sincerity, "Olivia's presence in my life brings me joy and a sense of completeness. From the moment we met, there was an undeniable connection, and I knew that she was the one I wanted to build a life with."

Frederick and Sophia exchanged a glance, their silence brimming under a surface of thin ice, that could break any moment. They knew the significance of their impending interview and the role it played in shaping public opinion.

"Now, Prince Frederick and Princess Sophia, as the soon-to-be-married couple, can you share with us the qualities that drew you to each other?" Jack asked, redirecting his attention to them.

Frederick's gaze softened as he looked at Sophia, his voice reflecting a genuine affection. "Sophia possesses an unwavering determination and a strong sense of duty. She has always supported me in my role as the future king. I am grateful for her loyalty."

Sophia, her composure restored, spoke with measured eloquence. "Frederick's kind heart and sense of compassion have always stood out to me. He embodies the values that our kingdom holds dear, and I am honored to stand beside him as we lead our people into the future."

As the preparation session progressed, Jack guided them through various hypothetical questions, allowing each of them to take turns in responding. Olivia's experience shone through as she artfully dodged uncomfortable inquiries, redirecting the conversation towards the love and unity shared between the couples.

As the intensive preparation continued, the room became a safe space for the engaged couples to express their concerns, fears, and hopes for the upcoming interview. They shared vulnerabilities, encouraged one another, and reaffirmed their collective determination to face the challenges ahead.

Hours turned into minutes, and the preparation session drew to a close. Marco, observing the progress they had made, expressed his confidence in their ability to handle the interview with grace and conviction. "You've all done an exceptional job today," he said, his voice filled with pride.

As the mock interview drew to a close, Olivia couldn't shake the feeling of Sophia's intense gaze upon her. It was as if the princess's eyes were burning holes into her soul. Olivia knew that the real interview, with the eyes of the media upon them, would be an entirely different ordeal. She braced herself for the possibility that Sophia's emotions might get the best of her.

Jack, noticed the tension in Olivia's demeanor. He approached her with a reassuring smile. "Miss Grey, I understand that this process can be overwhelming. Remember, you have the power to control your responses and maintain your composure. Stay focused on conveying the authenticity and grace that you displayed here today."

Olivia nodded appreciatively, grateful for Jack's words of encouragement. She knew that maintaining her composure in the face of Sophia's scrutiny would be challenging, but she was determined not to let it affect her. She reminded herself of the role she played in this delicate dance of public appearances and private struggles.

As the group prepared to leave the room, Marco, addressed them with a note of caution. "Remember, during the real interview, emotions may run high. It is essential to exercise restraint and professionalism at all times. We must project a united front, despite any personal disagreements or tensions that may arise."

Frederick, sensing Olivia's unease, placed a supportive hand on her shoulder. "Olivia, I know this is difficult, but we are in this together. Sophia's emotions may be overwhelming, but we must remain composed and rise above any attempts to provoke or unsettle us."

Sophia, standing a few feet away, overheard Frederick's words and shot him a piercing look. The intensity in her eyes was impossible to ignore, hinting at the storm of emotions that brewed within her. Olivia could feel the weight of Sophia's resentment, fueled by jealousy and a desire for power, directed towards her.

Jack, attentive to the underlying tension, stepped in once again. "Princess Sophia, I understand that emotions may be running high, but it is crucial to maintain decorum during the interview. The public eye will be on all of us, and it is in everyone's best interest to present a united and composed front."

Sophia's gaze lingered on Olivia for a moment longer before she finally averted her eyes, a flicker of defiance crossing her features. "I will do what is necessary for the sake of our family and the kingdom," she replied curtly, her voice laden with unspoken resentment.

With the imminent engagement interview on the horizon, the group knew that the stakes were high. They had to navigate the delicate balance of personal emotions and public appearances, all while managing the underlying tensions that threatened to unravel their carefully constructed facade.

***

The grand interview set was adorned with elegant decorations, exuding an air of sophistication and anticipation. The cameras were set, the lighting perfectly adjusted, and the renowned entertainment reporter, Zion Levins, took his seat in the middle of the two couples. Nicolas and Olivia sat on one side, their hands subtly intertwined, while Frederick and Sophia sat on the other, their faces carefully composed. The atmosphere crackled with a mixture of nerves and tension, knowing that the world's eyes were fixed upon them in this pivotal moment.

Nicolas, dressed in a tailored suit that accentuated his regal demeanor, sat upright with a composed expression, radiating a sense of princely charm. Beside him, Olivia Grey, stunning in a gown that captured the attention of the camera lenses, exuded grace and confidence.

On the other side, Frederick, the epitome of the dutiful royal, sat with a regal bearing, his eyes focused on maintaining a composed facade despite the turmoil within. Sophia, beautiful and poised, wore an elegant dress, yet her eyes held a glint of defiance, a sign that she was prepared to defend her position with all her might.

Zion Levins was popularly known for his probing questions and relentless pursuit of the truth, His sharp, piercing eyes, framed by a pair of stylish glasses, surveyed the room with a calm yet focused demeanor. His salt-and-pepper hair, meticulously styled, added an air of distinguished charm to his appearance. He exchanged a few brief words with his production crew, ensuring that everything was in place for the live broadcast. As the countdown began, the room fell into a silence that was palpable.

Nicolas, feeling the weight of the world upon his shoulders, turned to Olivia, his eyes searching hers for reassurance. Olivia, her heart pounding with both apprehension and resolve, nodded in silent agreement.

On the other side of the room, Frederick exchanged a tense glance with Sophia. He knew the potential for explosive emotions and hidden agendas lay just beneath the surface. "Sophia," he pleaded, "let's remember the importance of presenting a united front. This interview is about more than just us."

Sophia's eyes flickered with a mixture of frustration and uncertainty, but she nodded curtly. "Of course, Frederick. The kingdom comes first. We must show strength and unity."

As the seconds ticked away, the stage was set for the royal engagement interview, a pivotal moment that would shape the future of both couples and the kingdom itself. Zion Levins, a master of his craft, took a deep breath, ready to engage in the battle of words and emotions.

Before the interview officially began, Zion turned to the four of them, his voice calm yet authoritative. "Prince Nicolas, Miss Olivia Grey, Prince Frederick, Princess Sophia, this is an opportunity for each of you to share your stories and affirm your commitment to the kingdom. Remember, honesty and transparency are key."

Nicolas nodded; his gaze steady as he absorbed Zion's words. Olivia took a deep breath, her fingers tightly entwined with Nicolas's. Whereas on the other side, Sophia's expression remained guarded, her voice tinged with a hint of reservation. "The royal family's reputation is of utmost importance. We will address any concerns and assure the public that our commitment to the kingdom remains steadfast."

Frederick, his eyes meeting Sophia's, spoke with determination. "We may face challenges, but we are resolved to navigate them for the greater good. Our duty to the kingdom guides our actions."

Zion Levins, impressed by the composed yet solemn demeanor of the four individuals before him, offered a nod of acknowledgment. "I appreciate your commitment to transparency and the welfare of the kingdom. Let us begin the interview."

The camera began rolling, the live broadcast beaming across the globe, as Zion Levins introduced the royal quartet. His voice carried a blend of gravitas and excitement, captivating the millions of viewers tuning in.

"Ladies and gentlemen, today we have the privilege of sitting down with Prince Nicolas and his fiancée, Miss Olivia Grey, as well as Prince Frederick and Princess Sophia. We will delve into the personal lives of these esteemed individuals and explore their upcoming nuptials."

The interview commenced with a series of introductory questions, setting the stage for the deeper inquiries that would follow. Zion Levins skillfully steered the conversation towards their relationships, probing the dynamics between the two couples.

Nicolas and Olivia exchanged knowing glances, their eyes reflecting the bond they had forged amidst the challenges they faced. Nicolas, the embodiment of composure, took the lead, speaking eloquently about their journey together. He highlighted the strength of their connection, the shared values that bound them, and their commitment to supporting one another.

Olivia, her poise and grace shining through, added depth to Nicolas's words. She spoke candidly about the challenges they had overcome, emphasizing the power of love and trust in navigating the intricacies of royal life. Her words resonated with viewers, conveying a sense of authenticity that touched the hearts of those watching.

As the interview progressed, Zion Levins turned his attention towards Frederick and Sophia. The atmosphere grew more tense, as Sophia's piercing gaze once again focused on Olivia's. The unspoken tension was slowly brimming to the surface, and Olivia could sense it.

"Prince Frederick, Princess Sophia, thank you for joining us today," Zion began, his voice steady but laced with curiosity. "Let's delve into your relationship, shall we?"

Zion Levins, ever the observant interviewer, noted the

tension between Frederick and Sophia. He could sense the tension in the air, the undercurrent of unresolved issues threatening to unravel the facade of their carefully orchestrated public image. As the cameras rolled and the world watched, he seized the opportunity to delve into the heart of their relationship.

"Prince Frederick and Princess Sophia, I sense a certain unease between the two of you," Zion remarked, his voice measured yet probing. "Could you shed some light on the challenges you have faced as a couple?"

Sophia's jaw tightened, her eyes flashing with anger. She cast a quick glance at Frederick, her voice dripping with disdain. "Challenges? You mean Frederick's constant indecisiveness and inability to commit fully to our relationship?"

Frederick's face flushed with anger, his eyes narrowing as he retorted, "Indecisiveness? I have always put the needs of the kingdom above my personal desires, Sophia. You know that."

The tension in the room was palpable, the atmosphere heavy with the weight of their crumbling relationship. The cameras continued to roll, capturing the raw emotions that spilled forth. Olivia exchanged a worried glance with Nicolas, the shock of the situation unfolding before them evident on their faces.

Zion, recognizing the opportunity to capture a powerful moment, prodded further, his voice steady yet insistent. "Are you saying there are irreconcilable differences between the two of you?"

Sophia's voice quivered with pent-up frustration, her words biting. "We have tried to make it work, but it's clear now that our visions for the future are fundamentally at odds."

Zion, sensing the rising turmoil, pressed further, carefully choosing his words. "Prince Frederick, rumors have circulated about an incident during the masquerade party. Can you shed any light on those?"

Frederick's expression hardened, a flicker of pain crossing his features. He glanced at Sophia; his voice filled with hatred. "Zion, it pains me to say this, but I cannot ignore the truth any longer."

Sophia's eyes widened in shock, her face flushing anger. "How dare you, Frederick! It was all a misunderstanding!"

Frederick's voice grew sharper, his frustration evident. "A misunderstanding?"

Unable to contain their emotions any longer, Sophia and Frederick erupted into a heated argument. Their voices clashed, words filled with resentment and hurt, echoing through the studio. The room fell into a stunned silence as the couple's private turmoil was thrust into the spotlight.

Zion, his professional veneer slipping slightly, attempted to regain control of the situation. "Prince Frederick, Princess Sophia, I understand that emotions are running high, but we must maintain decorum. This is a live interview, and millions of people are watching."

But his words went unheeded as Frederick and Sophia unleashed their pent-up frustrations, each hurling accusation at the other. The world watched in shock as their relationship unraveled before their eyes, the illusion of a fairy tale romance shattered.

Olivia, sitting beside Nicolas, felt the intensity of the moment as she observed the confrontation unfold. Her heart ached for both Frederick and Sophia, knowing the pain they were experiencing. She exchanged a glance with Nicolas, silently urging him to intervene.

Nicolas, his voice steady yet filled with concern, interjected, "Frederick, Sophia, let's take a step back. Emotions are running high, and this is not the appropriate platform for such a personal discussion."

But the intensity between Frederick and Sophia refused to wane. Sophia's voice grew louder, her frustration mounting. "You've always doubted me, Frederick. You've let your insecurities cloud your judgment. I would never betray you in such a way."

"Prince Frederick, Princess Sophia," Zion intervened, "It is clear that there are deep-seated issues that need to be addressed privately. Perhaps this is not the appropriate setting to delve into them further."

Frederick glanced at Zion, his eyes holding a look of resignation. "You're right, Zion. This is a matter that needs to be dealt with privately."

Sophia's face contorted with pain. "Fine, Frederick. If that's what you want, then we have nothing more to discuss." With a flick of her hair, she stood up and walked off the set, leaving behind a room filled with stunned silence.

Frederick, his shoulders slumped, sat in stunned silence, his eyes fixed on the empty space Sophia had occupied just moments before. The realization of the irreparable damage to their relationship settled heavily upon him.

Zion Levins, shaken by the unexpected turn of events, glanced at the remaining participants, his voice filled with a mixture of empathy and professionalism. "We will take a short break," he announced, his voice tinged with regret. "Please bear with us as we gather ourselves."

As the cameras panned out, the gravity of the situation hung in the air. The interview had taken an unexpected turn, leaving everyone present reeling from the emotional fallout. The carefully constructed facade had crumbled, revealing the raw vulnerability and turmoil that had been concealed beneath.

The room was heavy with unease as the cameras panned out for a brief advertisement break. Frederick, visibly drained and disheartened, leaned back in his chair, exhausted. He ran a hand through his hair, trying to regain his composure.

Zion Levins, ever the professional, recognized the weight of the moment. He leaned forward, his voice calm yet resolute, breaking the silence that had settled over the room. "Prince Frederick, I understand that emotions are running high, but this interview is crucial.

It is an opportunity to address the rumors and present your side of the story. We can still salvage this, if you're willing."

Frederick's gaze shifted between Zion and Nicolas, his internal battle playing out across his face. His voice wavered as he responded, "I... I just don't think I can, Zion. It's all too much. I need some time to process everything."

Nicolas exchanged a determined glance with Olivia. They both understood the importance of salvaging the interview, not only for the sake of the kingdom but also to maintain control of the narrative surrounding their personal lives.

"Frederick," Nicolas began slowly, choosing his words very carefully. "I understand how difficult this is for you, so you must leave. We can push through and complete the interview, for the sake of the monarchy."

Olivia, her voice steady and reassuring, added, "Frederick, you're not alone in this. We're here for you. We'll support you every step of the way. Let us handle the rest of the interview. We can provide the necessary clarity and address the rumors."

Frederick looked at his brother and Olivia, gratitude. "Thank you, brother. And thank you Olivia, my future sister-in-law."

He excused himself from the interview room, his mind filled with concern for Sophia. He knew he had to find her, to find closure.

Meanwhile, Nicolas and Olivia exchanged a brief glance, their silent communication conveying a shared determination to handle the interview with grace and composure. They had rehearsed countless scenarios, prepared themselves for probing questions, and now it was time to put their training to the test.

The cameras began rolling once again, and Zion Levins shifted his focus back to the remaining participants. He adjusted his position in the chair, his expression a blend of curiosity and professionalism.

"Welcome back, ladies and gentlemen," Zion addressed the viewers, his voice steady and measured. "We are back live, and we appreciate your patience. It seems we have experienced a bit of a disruption, but the show must go on. Let's continue with our interview."

Nicolas, his voice steady and resolute, spoke up first. "Zion, we understand the importance of transparency and addressing the questions that have arisen. While my brother had to step away, Olivia and I are committed to seeing this interview through."

Olivia added, "Yes Zion, we believe in the power of honesty and open communication. It is our responsibility to provide the public with the truth and to uphold the integrity of our positions."

Zion nodded, impressed by their display of maturity and resolve in the face of adversity. "I commend both of you for your commitment to transparency. Let us continue then, and address the questions that have been lingering in the minds of our viewers."

His penetrating gaze fixated on Nicolas and Olivia, knowing that their responses would shape the narrative surrounding the royal family. He adjusted himself in his seat to a more comfortable position, aware that this was a critical moment in the interview.

The tension in the room remained palpable as he skillfully shifted the focus to the royal scandal that had gripped the kingdom. His piercing eyes met Olivia's, his expression hinting at the expectation of a candid response.

"Prince Nicolas, Miss Grey, there have been numerous reports and speculations surrounding the events of the masquerade party. Can you shed some light on the nature of the scandal and clarify the truth for our viewers?"

Nicolas exchanged a fleeting glance with Olivia, a tacit agreement passing between them. They knew the weight of their words and the potential consequences of their actions. With a composed expression, Nicolas took a deep breath and began his carefully crafted response.

"Zion, I want to address the scandal that has been circulating in the media. There have been exaggerated accounts and unfounded rumors surrounding the events of the masquerade party. I want to assure everyone that Olivia and I are committed to the truth and will provide you with an honest account."

Olivia nodded in agreement, her eyes reflecting a mixture of apprehension and resolve. She understood the delicate dance they were about to engage in, where the line between truth and deception became blurred. Suppressing a twinge of guilt, she spoke with practiced sincerity.

"Zion, the truth is that the media's portrayal of the masquerade party has been sensationalized and distorted. Yes, there were moments of excitement and emotions ran high, as they often do in such gatherings. However, the rumors are completely unfounded."

Zion's scrutinizing gaze lingered on their faces, searching for any hint of deception. While he had encountered countless instances of public figures bending the truth, he recognized the magnitude of this particular moment. The future of the monarchy rested on their words.

"But, Prince Nicolas, eyewitnesses claim to have seen an intense encounter between Miss Grey and another guest in the garden. Can you explain the nature of that interaction?"

Nicolas maintained a composed facade, though inwardly he wrestled with the complexity of the situation. He chose his words carefully, mindful of the consequences they held. "Zion, I assure you that what transpired in the garden was a private conversation, driven by personal matters that have since been resolved. It was an emotional moment, but it is important to note that emotions can often be misconstrued."

Olivia, her voice infused with sincerity, added, "Indeed, Zion. The intensity of that moment was a result of personal circumstances that were quickly resolved. I hope that the focus can now shift to the positive and meaningful work that lies ahead for all of us."

"And what about the incident in the garden?" Zion probed, his voice carrying a note of persistence. "There were reports of a heated confrontation between Princess Sophia and Miss Grey. Can you shed some light on what transpired?"

Nicolas exhaled softly, aware that the next words would require finesse. "Zion, emotions can run high in any relationship, and disagreements are not uncommon. However, the incident in the garden has been blown out of proportion. There was a misunderstanding, but it was resolved amicably. Princess Sophia and Olivia have since reconciled and put the matter behind them. Our focus now is on moving forward and preserving the unity of the royal family."

Zion's gaze flickered between Nicolas and Olivia, searching for any cracks in their façade. Despite the unease that simmered beneath the surface, they maintained an air of composure, skillfully concealing the truth that threatened to unravel their carefully constructed narrative.

Olivia, recognizing the need to divert attention from the delicate subject, seized the opportunity to steer the conversation toward a more positive and uplifting topic. With grace and charm, she shifted the focus to their recent humanitarian trip to India, where they had witnessed the plight of underprivileged girls firsthand.

Her voice carried a genuine passion as she spoke about their plans to establish a foundation for the empowerment of girls.

"Zion," Olivia began, her eyes sparkling with enthusiasm, "while there have been discussions about the masquerade incident, we want to emphasize the important work we have been doing to make a positive impact in the lives of young girls. During our recent trip to India, we were deeply moved by the challenges they face. It inspired us to take action."

Nicolas, his voice filled with conviction, joined in. "Absolutely, Zion. We believe that every girl should have access to education, opportunities, and a voice to shape their own destiny. Our foundation aims to provide resources, support, and mentorship to empower these young girls, enabling them to break free from the cycle of poverty and discrimination."

Zion, captivated by the genuine dedication in Olivia and Nicolas's words, leaned forward, his curiosity piqued. "That's truly remarkable. Can you share some details about the foundation and its initiatives?"

Olivia smiled warmly, her passion radiating through her words. "Certainly, Zion. The foundation, which we have named 'EmpowerHer,' aims to create safe spaces for girls to thrive. We will be partnering with local organizations in India to provide educational scholarships, vocational training programs, and mentorship opportunities. Our goal is to empower these girls to pursue their dreams, to cultivate future leaders who will bring positive change to their communities."

Nicolas added, "In addition, we plan to collaborate with existing initiatives that focus on healthcare, hygiene, and menstrual health education, ensuring that no barrier stands in the way of a girl's education and well-being. We believe that investing in the empowerment of girls is not only a moral imperative but also an essential step toward achieving sustainable development."

Zion nodded, visibly impressed by their vision and commitment. "It sounds like an incredible initiative that will undoubtedly make a difference. How do you plan to involve the public in supporting EmpowerHer?"

Olivia's eyes sparkled with determination as she answered, "We understand that true change requires collective effort. Our foundation will actively seek partnerships with corporations, philanthropists, and individuals who share our vision. We will launch fundraising campaigns, awareness drives, and engage in advocacy work to rally support for the cause. Our aim is to create a global movement, where every person can contribute in their own way to uplift and empower girls around the world."

Zion, deeply moved by their passion and the potential impact of EmpowerHer, leaned back in his chair, his earlier skepticism replaced with admiration. "It's evident that you both are deeply committed to this cause. I have no doubt that EmpowerHer will touch countless lives. Thank you for sharing your inspiring vision with us."

As the interview concluded, Nicolas and Olivia felt a

wave of exhaustion wash over them. The weight of the lies they had spun hung in the air, but so did the sense of accomplishment for successfully diverting the public's attention toward their philanthropic efforts. They exchanged a knowing glance, acknowledging the delicate dance they had executed under the scrutiny of the world.

Just as they prepared to leave the interview room, Jack, their trusted secretary, emerged from behind the cameras with a smile of satisfaction on his face. He approached them, his eyes gleaming with excitement.

"Prince Nicolas, Miss Grey, that was remarkable," Jack commended, his voice filled with genuine admiration. "You two are trending worldwide, and the response is overwhelmingly positive. People are inspired by your vision and dedication to the 'EmpowerHer' foundation. But we must act quickly, because we only have a few hours at the most."

Nicolas felt a surge of pride mixed with a hint of urgency. He knew they could not afford to rest on their laurels, not when the momentum was in their favor. "Thank you, Jack. We appreciate your support. But what do you mean we only have a couple of hours?"

Jack's expression turned serious as he leaned in, his voice dropping to a low, urgent tone. "While the interview has created a buzz, it's crucial that we capitalize on this momentum. Social media is already abuzz with discussions about 'EmpowerHer,' and people are eager to know how they can contribute. We need to strike while the iron is hot and launch the foundation as soon as possible."

Olivia nodded, her mind racing with the possibilities. "You're right, Jack. We can't afford to waste any time. We have to seize this moment and turn our vision into a reality."

Jack's eyes gleamed with determination. "Exactly. I've already reached out to a few potential partners and sponsors, but we'll need your input and guidance to kickstart the foundation. We have just a couple of hours to start laying the groundwork, gather the necessary resources, and create a strong online presence."

Nicolas, Olivia, and Jack formed a tight circle, their minds buzzing with ideas and plans. They discussed the immediate steps they needed to take, from registering the foundation to setting up a website and social media platforms. They recognized the importance of transparency and accountability, ensuring that every donation would be utilized effectively to make a lasting impact.

***

CHAPTER 20:

SAILING IN THE AFTERMATH

As days passed following the groundbreaking interview, the narrative surrounding the royal scandal began to shift. The public, captivated by the vision and sincerity of 'EmpowerHer,' started embracing the positive news it brought. Olivia and Nicolas' carefully crafted lies had taken root, replacing the scandalous rumors with a wave of support for their philanthropic endeavors. The air was filled with a renewed sense of hope and admiration for the young couple.

Meanwhile, in the serene ambiance of the castle gardens, Olivia and Nicolas strolled hand in hand, enjoying a moment of respite amidst their demanding schedules. The lush greenery provided a soothing backdrop, and the fragrant blooms perfumed the air as they walked, their footsteps gentle on the cobblestone path.

As they meandered through the gardens, a figure approached from a distance. It was Princess Sophia, her face bearing a mixture of humility and regret. Olivia's heart skipped a beat, unsure of what to expect. She tightened her grip on Nicolas' hand, finding solace in his presence.

Sophia, her usually composed demeanor showing signs of vulnerability, stopped before Olivia and Nicolas, her eyes filled with genuine contrition. "Olivia, Nicolas, may I have a moment?" she asked softly, her voice tinged with regret.

Olivia exchanged a brief glance with Nicolas, silently giving him permission to stay with her during this conversation. Sophia's presence alone no longer instilled fear within her, not after the tumultuous events they had all endured.

With a nod, Nicolas stood steadfastly by Olivia's side, his silent support giving her strength. Sophia took a deep breath, gathering her thoughts before speaking. "I want to apologize sincerely for my behavior during the interview and everything that transpired between us," she began, her voice filled with a newfound humility.

Olivia, her eyes locking with Sophia's, sensed the sincerity in her words. She recognized the weight of the apology and the courage it took for Sophia to confront her own mistakes. The bitterness that once consumed Olivia's heart began to soften, making room for understanding and forgiveness.

"Sophia," Olivia replied, her voice calm yet tinged with a hint of empathy, "we've all made mistakes, myself included. The important thing is that we learn from them and grow. I believe in second chances, and I appreciate your apology."

Sophia's eyes shimmered with gratitude as she absorbed Olivia's words. "Thank you," she whispered, her voice filled with both relief and gratitude. "I was blinded by my own insecurities and allowed them to cloud my judgment. I see now how your intentions were genuine, and I admire the positive impact you are making with EmpowerHer."

Olivia offered a gentle smile, her heart opening to the possibility of reconciliation. "I'm glad you understand, Sophia. Our focus has always been on making a difference, and I hope we can work together in the future to create positive change."

Sophia nodded, a flicker of hope lighting up her features. "I would be honored to collaborate with you and support the foundation," she responded sincerely. "Let us put the past behind us and forge a new path, united in our dedication to empowering others."

Olivia extended her hand, a gesture of acceptance and unity. Sophia, appreciating the gesture, reached out and clasped Olivia's hand, sealing their newfound understanding. With genuine concern in her eyes, Olivia decided to broach the delicate subject of Sophia's engagement to Frederick, aware that the decision held significant weight for both of them.

"Sophia," Olivia began cautiously, "I hope you don't mind me asking, but after everything that has happened, are you still planning to move forward with the upcoming wedding?"

Sophia's expression softened as she considered Olivia's question. A myriad of emotions flickered across her face before she finally spoke, her voice laced with contemplation. "Olivia, I've been giving this a great deal of thought. But before I make a decision, I must talk to

Frederick."

Olivia nodded understandingly; her empathy evident.

Sophia's gaze dropped to the ground momentarily, her voice tinged with sadness. "I confess, there have been doubts in my heart for some time now," she admitted. "Frederick and I were brought together by circumstances and expectations, but I have grown to love him. Alas, I do not know, if he feels the same way about me."

Olivia placed a comforting hand on Sophia's arm, offering her support. "It takes courage to face those doubts and to consider what truly makes you happy," she said gently. "Whatever you decide, know that we will be here to support you."

Sophia's eyes met Olivia's, gratitude and vulnerability mingling in her gaze. "Thank you, Olivia." she replied, her voice filled with sincerity. "I need to find the strength to have an honest conversation with Frederick and reevaluate our future together."

Olivia nodded, her admiration for Sophia growing. "Sometimes the most difficult decisions lead us to the path we were meant to walk," she encouraged.

Sophia took a deep breath, finding a newfound determination within herself. "You're right, Olivia," she affirmed, her voice stronger. "Now that Charlotte and Amalia have returned to Kechaedor, I feel quite alone with my thoughts."

Olivia was filled with a sense of gratitude and forgiveness and a longing to heal the wounds of the past to forge a new bond of friendship.

"Sophia," Olivia began, "I want to ask you something important. Will you be my maid of honor?"

Sophia's eyes widened in surprise, her lips parting slightly. She had not expected such a gesture of trust and inclusion, especially after the tumultuous events that had unfolded between them. Yet, she sensed Olivia's sincerity and the genuine desire for reconciliation.

"Olivia," Sophia responded, her voice laced with a mixture of emotions, "I am honored that you would extend such an invitation to me. I humbly accept this great honor."

In that moment, Olivia and Sophia knew that their connection went beyond a simple reconciliation. As the two women stood side by side, Nicolas observed with a sense of relief and pride. The castle gardens, once witness to secrets and discord, now held the promise of unity and shared commitment.

***

Sophia found herself standing outside the grand entrance of the royal palace, her heart pounding with edginess. It was time for her to face Frederick and have the crucial conversation that would shape the course of their relationship. Taking a deep breath, she stepped inside, the regal atmosphere of the palace enveloping her.

Frederick was waiting for her in one of the palace's elegant drawing rooms, away from prying eyes and curious ears. As Sophia entered, her eyes met his, and she could not help but notice the mixture of emotions in his expression—hope, apprehension, and a touch of vulnerability. The weight of their recent struggles lingered in the air as they stood face to face.

They exchanged a few polite words, their gazes meeting and searching for the truth beneath the surface. It was evident that both of them had changed, their experiences and revelations leaving an indelible mark on their hearts. She knew that this conversation could determine the course of their future.

Taking a seat opposite Frederick, Sophia mustered her courage and spoke softly yet firmly. "Frederick, we need to talk. About us, our engagement, and the future that lies ahead."

Frederick nodded. "I've been doing a lot of soul-searching, Sophia," he confessed. "The recent events have made me question the foundation of our relationship, and I can't ignore the doubts that have surfaced."

Sophia nodded, acknowledging Frederick's words. "I've had my own doubts as well, Frederick."

He nodded, his features softening as he took in her

presence. "Sophia," he replied, his voice filled with a sincerity that hadn't been present during their recent arguments. "I've had some time to reflect on everything, and I've come to realize that perhaps we've been rushing into this engagement without truly knowing one another."

Sophia's heart skipped a beat, hope blossoming within her. It was the very sentiment she had wanted to express. "I feel the same way, Frederick," she admitted, her voice tinged with a touch of nervousness. "We've been so caught up in expectations and obligations that we haven't given ourselves the opportunity to truly understand each other's hopes, dreams, and desires."

Frederick leaned forward; his voice tinged with sincerity. "Sophia, I care for you deeply. I don't want either of us to be trapped in a loveless marriage," he admitted, his vulnerability shining through. "I want you to be happy, even if it means reevaluating our relationship."

Sophia nodded, her eyes brimming with understanding. "I want the same, Frederick. We deserve a love that is genuine and passionate, not one born out of obligation or convenience."

"Sophia, despite our disagreements and misunderstandings, I have always admired your strength and resilience," Frederick confessed, his voice filled with sincerity. "And, if I'm being honest, I've found myself drawn to you in ways I never expected."

Sophia's eyes widened, her heart pounding in her chest.

The revelation caught her off guard, but it also sparked a glimmer of excitement within her. "Frederick, I... I've experienced the same," she confessed, her voice barely above a whisper. "There is something undeniably special between us, but we need time to truly explore and understand it."

They fell into a contemplative silence, their thoughts intertwining as they searched for a way forward. It was in that moment of vulnerability and honesty that a mutual agreement began to take shape.

Sophia's gaze met Frederick's, searching for the sincerity she hoped to find. "So, what are you proposing, Frederick?" she asked, a note of cautious optimism in her voice.

Frederick took a deep breath, his words measured yet filled with a newfound determination. "I propose that we put a pause on our engagement," he suggested, his voice steady.

Sophia considered Frederick's proposal, her mind racing with conflicting thoughts and emotions. "A pause," she repeated softly, the weight of the word hanging in the air.

"Sophia, I don't want to rush you into anything." Frederick stirred uncomfortably in his seat. "I want us to take the time we need, to let our connection grow and evolve naturally," he said, his voice filled with a newfound vulnerability. "I want to get to know you, to understand the depths of your heart, and to build a love that is built on trust and genuine affection."

Sophia's breath caught as she absorbed his words, the weight of his sincerity sinking deep into her soul. "Frederick," she whispered softly, "thank you for understanding and for being patient with me."

Frederick reached out and gently grasped Sophia's hand, his touch offering reassurance and support. "I'm willing to take every risk with you, Sophia."

A flicker of hope danced in Sophia's eyes as she squeezed Frederick's hand, a silent agreement passing between them. "Me too, Frederick."

Taking a leap of faith, Frederick rushed over to Sophia's side. In that moment, the world around them faded into the background as Frederick leaned down, his lips meeting hers in a gentle and tender kiss. It was a moment of connection and promise, an acknowledgment of the journey they were embarking on together.

Sophia looked up at Frederick, her eyes sparkling, "I think it's time that we inform our families about our decision," she whispered.

Frederick nodded, understanding the weight of the moment. "I agree, Sophia. It's important that we communicate our intentions openly and honestly," he replied, his voice filled with a sense of assurance. "I need to inform the royal court as well. They have been eagerly anticipating our union, but they deserve to know the truth."

Sophia took a deep breath, summoning her courage. "I

know my parents will understand," she said, her voice carrying a touch of certainty. "They only want what's best for me, and I believe they will respect our decision to take the time we need."

Frederick reached out, gently squeezing her hand in reassurance. "And the royal court will come to understand too, Sophia," he said, a glint of playfulness in his eyes. "They might grumble a bit, but ultimately they will recognize that our happiness and the strength of our future reign is more important than a rushed wedding."

Sophia could not help but smile at Frederick's playful remark. "You have a way of easing my worries, Frederick," she admitted, her eyes sparkling with affection.

As they shared a lighthearted moment, the weight of their responsibilities seemed momentarily lifted. In that drawing room, surrounded by the echoes of their shared laughter, Sophia and Frederick found solace in each other's presence.

***

Frederick and Nicolas walked with purpose through the grand corridors of the royal palace, their footsteps echoing against the marble floor. As they approached the doors of the King's study, a mixture of nervousness and determination filled their hearts. They were about to have a serious conversation with their father, King

Edmund, about the postponed wedding.

Entering the study, they found their father engrossed in his papers, his silver hair glimmering under the soft glow of the room's golden chandeliers. His piercing blue eyes looked up, and a warm smile greeted his sons. "Frederick, Nicolas, what brings you here today?" he asked, gesturing for them to take a seat.

Frederick cleared his throat, exchanging a quick glance with Nicolas for support. "Father, we have something important to discuss," he began, his voice steady but tinged with a hint of nervousness. "Sophia and I have decided to postpone our wedding."

King Edmund's brows furrowed; curiosity etched across his face. "Postpone the wedding? May I ask why?" he inquired.

Frederick took a deep breath, gathering his thoughts before continuing. "We realized that rushing into the wedding without truly getting to know each other might not be the best foundation for a strong and lasting marriage," he explained earnestly. "Sophia and I both feel that it's crucial to take the time to deepen our connection, to understand each other on a deeper level before making such a significant commitment."

King Edmund leaned back in his chair, his gaze shifting between his sons. "I see," he said, his voice measured as he processed their words. His mind swirled with conflicting thoughts and emotions. On one hand, he wanted to honor his sons' decision to postpone the wedding and support their quest for a deeper connection. On the other hand, he couldn't ignore the weight of public expectations and the significance of the royal wedding for the kingdom.

Frederick and Nicolas exchanged concerned glances, sensing their father's inner conflict. They knew that his duty as a king often clashed with his desires as a father. Sensing the need for guidance, King Edmund summoned for Marco, his trusted advisor and confidant, to join their conversation.

Moments later, Marco entered the room, his composed demeanor and keen intellect immediately commanding attention. He approached the trio with a respectful bow before taking a seat. "Your Majesty, Princes," he acknowledged, his voice carrying a sense of calm and wisdom. "How may I be of service?"

King Edmund leaned forward; his hands clasped together as he addressed his trusted advisor. "Marco, I find myself in a quandary," he began, his voice reflecting his internal struggle. " Frederick has come to me, expressing his desire to postpone the wedding. While I understand and respect their reasoning, there are certain expectations that come with being part of the royal family."

Marco's piercing gaze shifted between the king and his sons, his mind racing with the complexities of the situation. He understood the delicate balance between duty and personal happiness, and he weighed his words carefully before responding. "Your Majesty, the expectations of the public are indeed important," he acknowledged, his tone measured. "However, love and happiness should always be at the forefront of any decision concerning matters of the heart."

King Edmund sighed; the weight of his responsibilities heavy upon his shoulders. "I want both of my sons to find love and happiness in their lives," he admitted, his voice tinged with both sorrow and resolve. "But with the postponement of Frederick's wedding, the public's anticipation will be disappointed."

Marco nodded, understanding the king's concerns. "Your Majesty, may I offer a suggestion?" he proposed, his voice filled with a blend of caution and hope. "Prince Nicolas and Miss Olivia Grey have captured the hearts of the public. Their love story has become a beacon of hope and inspiration. Perhaps, proceeding with their wedding could alleviate the disappointment and maintain the public's support."

Frederick and Nicolas exchanged surprised glances, their minds processing the implications of Marco's suggestion. For Nicolas idea of proceeding with his own wedding in light of the postponement seemed both unexpected and yet strangely fitting.

King Edmund considered Marco's words, his features softening as he saw the potential solution before him. "You make a valid point, Marco," he said, his voice reflecting a newfound clarity. "Nicolas and Olivia's love has touched the hearts of many, and their wedding could serve as a source of joy and unity for our kingdom."

Nicolas took a deep breath, his mind swirling with conflicting thoughts and emotions. While he longed to marry Olivia and make their love official, he could not shake off his concerns about rushing into a decision without considering Olivia's perspective.

"Father, I appreciate your support and understanding," Nicolas began, his voice tinged with apprehension. "But I worry about Olivia's feelings in all of this. We have only just become engaged, and I don't want to pressure her into anything she may not be ready for."

King Edmund nodded; his regal features softened with understanding. He placed a reassuring hand on his son's shoulder. "Nicolas, your concern for Olivia's feelings is admirable," he said, his voice filled with paternal wisdom. "It is important to have open and honest communication with her. Express your thoughts and intentions, and ask for her permission to proceed with the wedding."

Frederick, who had been silently observing the conversation, chimed in with a supportive smile. "Olivia loves you deeply, and I have no doubt she will be thrilled at the idea of marrying you sooner," he said, his voice filled with brotherly reassurance.

Nicolas nodded, feeling a renewed sense of determination. He knew that he needed to have a heart-to-heart conversation with Olivia and address the topic of their wedding. The thought of Olivia's reaction both excited and unnerved him.

Marco, always the voice of reason, interjected with a

gentle reminder. "Prince Nicolas, you must take the time to have an open and honest conversation with Olivia. Share your feelings and concerns, and listen to hers as well."

Nicolas nodded, appreciating Marco's guidance. He understood the importance of approaching Olivia with sincerity and respect. The thought of discussing their wedding plans filled him with a rare feeling in his heart.

With a newfound determination, Nicolas turned to his father. "Thank you, Father," he said, his voice filled with gratitude. "I will speak with Olivia and seek her permission to proceed with the wedding. Our love means everything to me, and I want us to embark on this journey together."

King Edmund smiled warmly at his son, his eyes reflecting a mix of pride and affection. "I have faith in your love and the strength of your relationship, Nicolas," he said, his voice filled with paternal reassurance. "Trust in your bond with Olivia, and may your love guide you through this next chapter of your lives."

Feeling encouraged and supported, Nicolas took a moment to gather his thoughts before setting off to find Olivia. He knew that the conversation ahead would shape their future, and he was determined to approach it with love, understanding, and a genuine desire to honor both their feelings and dreams.

***

Nicolas sat in his study, his fingers hovering over his phone as he composed a text message to Olivia. He had spent hours contemplating the best way to approach the conversation about their wedding plans, wanting it to be a moment of love and anticipation rather than pressure. Finally, he decided to whisk her away on a surprise date night, hoping it would create the perfect ambiance for their heartfelt conversation.

With a deep breath, Nicolas typed out the message, his heart pounding with a mixture of excitement and nervousness.

'My love, get ready for a magical evening. I have a surprise date night planned just for us. Love, Nicolas.'

As soon as he hit send, Nicolas anxiously awaited Olivia's response, his mind swirling with the endless possibilities of their future together. He imagined their love blossoming amidst the enchantment of the evening, setting the stage for a heartfelt conversation that would bring them even closer.

Minutes later, Nicolas's phone chimed with a notification. He glanced down eagerly, a smile spreading across his face as he read Olivia's reply.

'Counting down the minutes. All my love, Olivia.'

Nicolas's heart swelled with affection as he read Olivia's message. Their love had grown and deepened with each passing day, and he cherished the way they could communicate their thoughts and emotions so effortlessly. Tonight, would be another opportunity for them to strengthen their bond and explore the depths of their dreams together.

With a renewed sense of purpose, Nicolas prepared for their date night, carefully selecting the perfect outfit that would make Olivia's heart skip a beat. He wanted this evening to be a celebration of their love, a reminder of the magical connection they shared.

As the sun began to set, casting a warm glow across the castle grounds, Nicolas made his way to Olivia's suite. His heart fluttered with anticipation as he approached the door, taking a moment to compose himself before knocking gently.

The door swung open, revealing Olivia standing there. Dressed in a cardigan and flowy red skirt, she was a vision of elegance and beauty. Her eyes sparkled with excitement, and a radiant smile graced her lips. "Nicolas, you look absolutely dashing," she said, her voice filled with genuine admiration.

He could not help but be captivated by her beauty, his heart swelling with love for the incredible woman standing before him. "And you, my love, are a goddess," he replied, his voice filled with adoration. "Shall we?"

Nicolas led Olivia up the grand staircase of Codrington Castle, hand in hand, their steps echoing through the quiet halls. The castle was filled with a sense of history and grandeur, and Nicolas couldn't help but feel a twinge of nostalgia as he entered his childhood bedroom.

The room was a haven of memories, filled with treasured mementos and reminders of his upbringing. The walls were adorned with paintings and photographs, capturing moments of joy and laughter shared with his family and friends.

As Olivia stepped further into the room, her eyes widened in delight. Before her, Nicolas had built a cozy fort using bed sheets draped over the furniture. The fort was adorned with plush pillows and blankets, creating a comfortable and intimate space for them to relax and unwind. The room was bathed in a soft, warm glow from the starry lights that adorned the walls and ceiling. The air was filled with a gentle fragrance of lavender, creating a calming and romantic ambiance.

Nicolas pulled Olivia closer, his heart brimming with love and affection. "I wanted to recreate a bit of our childhood innocence," he said, a hint of nostalgia in his voice. "To remind ourselves of simpler times and create new memories together."

Olivia's eyes sparkled with joy as she surveyed the cozy fort. She felt a rush of warmth and gratitude for the thoughtful gesture. "Nicolas, this is absolutely beautiful," she whispered, her voice filled with emotion. "You always know how to make me feel special."

They settled down inside the fort, nestled among soft cushions and blankets. The air was filled with a sense of tranquility and closeness. Nicolas wrapped his arm around Olivia, their fingers intertwined, as they gazed up at the shimmering starry lights. The starry lights shimmered above them, casting a dreamlike glow on their faces.

"This is amazing, Nicolas," Olivia said, her voice filled with genuine awe. "You've truly outdone yourself."

Nicolas looked into Olivia's eyes, as he thought that was the perfect moment to open his heart to her. He took a deep breath, his fingers gently tracing circles on her hand, before he began to speak.

"Olivia, today, I had a conversation with my father," Nicolas began, his voice filled with a blend of nervousness and anticipation. "He suggested something that took me by surprise."

Olivia's eyes widened with curiosity and intrigue. "What did he suggest, Nicolas?" she asked, her voice filled with genuine interest.

Nicolas took a moment to gather his thoughts, his gaze never wavering from Olivia's radiant face. "Since Frederick and Sophia aren't proceeding with their wedding, he proposed that you and I could take their place," he revealed, his voice filled with a mixture of hope and uncertainty.

Olivia's eyes widened, a mixture of astonishment and curiosity flashing across her face. She sat up slightly, her hand finding its way to Nicolas' cheek, caressing it gently. "Nicolas, that's... unexpected. What do you think about it?"

Nicolas nodded; his eyes filled with determination. "My father believes it could soften the blow that comes with the public outrage regarding Freddie and Sophia's decision," he explained, his words resonating with conviction.

Olivia's mind raced as she contemplated the magnitude of Nicolas' proposition. She had always envisioned a future with him, but the idea of becoming a princess and marrying the man she loved amidst the grandeur of a royal wedding was something beyond her wildest dreams. But she could not deny the flutter of excitement in her heart.

"Nicolas, marrying you has been my deepest desire since the moment I fell in love with you," Olivia confessed, her voice filled with sincerity. "But, are you sure about this? What about Frederick and Sophia?"

Nicolas reached out to gently cup Olivia's cheek, his touch sending a jolt of warmth through her. "Frederick and Sophia have their own path to navigate, and we must respect their decision," he said, his voice brimming with empathy. "As for us, I want nothing more than to spend the rest of my life with you."

Olivia's eyes shimmered with tears of joy and gratitude. "Nicolas, if you're sure about this, then I am too," she whispered, her voice filled with unwavering conviction. "Let's take this leap of faith together."

They lay there, immersed in each other's presence, feeling the warmth of their love enveloping them. Time seemed to stand still as they shared heartfelt conversations, laughter, and whispered secrets within the fort.

As the night progressed, Nicolas surprised Olivia with a tray of their favorite treats, delicately arranged on a small table beside them. They savored chocolate-covered strawberries, sipped on sparkling champagne, and indulged in the simple pleasure of each other's company. Amidst the cozy fort, surrounded by the magical glow of starry lights, Nicolas and Olivia found solace in their love. They shared dreams, hopes, and aspirations for their future together, strengthening the bond that connected their hearts.

***

CHAPTER 21:

THE WHIRLWIND ENGAGEMENT

****

WEDDING ANNOUNCEMENT OF

PRINCE NICOLAS WEDDING AND MISS OLIVIA GREY

The Creudor Royal Palace is pleased to announce the postponement of the wedding between Prince Frederick and Princess Sophia. In accordance with the wishes of the couple, the wedding will be rescheduled to a later date.

In light of this development, we are delighted to announce that Prince Nicolas, beloved son of His Majesty King Edmund, will be wed to Miss Olivia Grey in a grand royal wedding ceremony on the same previously scheduled date. Their union promises to be a joyous celebration of love and unity, further strengthening the bonds of our kingdom.

The Creudor Royal Palace extends its warmest wishes to Prince Frederick and Princess Sophia. We remain confident that their love will endure, and we wish them every happiness in their future endeavors.

We kindly request the media and the public to respect the privacy of the royal family during this joyous and significant time.

Jack Smith,

Royal Spokesperson

****

The announcement sent shockwaves throughout the kingdom and beyond. The news of the royal wedding between Prince Nicolas and Miss Olivia Grey spread like wildfire, capturing the attention on a global scale. The anticipation for this grand event grew with each passing day, as the kingdom prepared to witness a love story unfold before their very eyes.

Very soon, the media frenzy surrounding the royal couple reached unprecedented heights. News outlets, paparazzi, and fans from all corners of the world clamored for every detail, craving glimpses into the lives of the soon-to-be-wedded pair. Television screens were dominated by news segments dedicated to the upcoming royal wedding. Magazine covers were adorned with the radiant smiles of Olivia and Nicolas, capturing the attention of readers everywhere. Newspapers published extensive features chronicling the love affair that had captivated hearts worldwide.

Social media platforms buzzed with excitement as hashtags related to the wedding trended globally. Fans expressed their well-wishes, sharing their favorite moments from Olivia and Nicolas's love story and eagerly discussing their predictions for the grand affair. Memes, fan art, and heartfelt messages flooded the internet, creating a virtual community united in their support for the royal couple.

In the midst of the media frenzy, Olivia and Nicolas remained steadfast in their commitment to each other. They recognized the significance of their love story and the platform it provided to promote positivity, compassion, and unity. With grace and poise, they navigated the whirlwind of interviews, photo shoots, and public appearances, never forgetting the foundation on which their love was built.

Nicolas found solace in Olivia's presence, their love growing stronger with each passing moment. They leaned on each other for support and encouragement during the busy preparations, finding moments of quiet intimacy amidst the chaos. Olivia's infectious laughter and unwavering support became Nicolas' sanctuary, reminding him of the love and happiness that awaited them.

The royal palace was abuzz with excitement and preparations for the upcoming wedding. Every corridor, hall, and chamber were adorned with flowers, symbolizing the blossoming love between Nicolas and Olivia. The castle was a hive of activity as decorators, event planners, and artisans worked tirelessly to create an enchanting atmosphere befitting such a momentous occasion.

As the days passed, invitations were meticulously

crafted and sent to the royal families, esteemed guests, and diplomats from neighboring countries. The guest list included dignitaries, celebrities, and influential figures, all eager to witness the union of Prince Nicolas and Miss Olivia Grey.

Inside the palace, Nicolas and Olivia were swept up in a whirlwind of wedding preparations. They sat across from the wedding coordinators, poring over the detailed plans for their upcoming nuptials. The room was filled with a buzz of excitement as ideas were exchanged and decisions were made.

Olivia leaned forward; her eyes filled with determination. "We want the ceremony to be intimate and heartfelt. We've always envisioned a simple yet elegant affair that reflects our love and the beauty of the palace."

The wedding coordinator nodded, taking notes diligently. "Understood, Your Highness. We have a variety of stunning venues within the palace grounds that can accommodate your vision. Shall we discuss the main hall? Its grandeur and regal ambiance would be the perfect backdrop for your union."

Nicolas smiled at Olivia; his voice filled with warmth. "Yes, the main hall sounds perfect. It holds a special place in our hearts, and it symbolizes the unity of our kingdom. Let's bring our loved ones together in that majestic space."

Olivia nodded in agreement; her eyes gleaming with excitement. "And when it comes to the wedding party, we've decided to keep it simple. We would like only one best man and one maid of honor. Our closest friends, Frederick and Sophia, will be the perfect choice."

The coordinators noted down their choices, impressed by the couple's clarity of vision. "We will make sure every detail is attended to, from the floral arrangements to the music selection. Your ceremony will be a beautiful and memorable affair."

Nicolas leaned back, a sense of relief washing over him. "Thank you for your understanding. We trust in your expertise to bring our dreams to life. We want this day to be about love, unity, and the joining of two families."

Olivia added, "Indeed, and we want to honor the traditions and customs of our kingdom. It's important to us that this celebration reflects the values we hold dear."

They wanted every detail to be perfect, as this day would not only mark their union but also set the stage for a new era of love and unity within the kingdom.

***

And as the royal wedding drew closer, Marco, the loyal and trusted confidant of the royal family, found himself engrossed in the final preparations. Amidst the flurry of preparations and last-minute arrangements, an email notification from his private detective caught his attention. It was an unexpected message that would shed light on a previously unknown aspect of Olivia Grey's past. With a curious glance, he clicked to open the message, unaware of the revelations it held.

As the words unfolded on the screen, Marco's eyes widened with surprise. The email contained detailed records from a rehabilitation facility in Los Angeles, shedding light on Olivia's past struggles with drug and alcohol use. It chronicled her journey towards recovery and how she had successfully completed the rehab program, emerging as a stronger and resilient individual.

However, one particular detail caught Marco's attention —the name Avila Consilio. A playful smile tugged at his lips as he realized it was an anagram of Nicolas and Olivia, a clever combination of their names. Marco could not help but see it as a symbol, a reminder of their intertwined destiny and the obstacles they had overcome together.

However, Marco swiftly made a decision, one that reflected his unwavering loyalty and dedication to his duties. He resolved not to divulge this newfound knowledge to anyone, not even to Prince Nicolas or Olivia themselves. Their past struggles belonged to them alone, and he understood the importance of privacy and respect.

With a firm choice, Marco chose to keep the revelation to himself. He would never use this knowledge to tarnish Olivia's reputation or jeopardize their love. In a single decisive action, he deleted the email permanently from his inbox, erasing any trace of its existence. As he did so, a sense of relief washed over him, knowing that he had made the right choice. His commitment to the royal family went beyond just their public image; it extended to safeguarding their personal stories and maintaining their trust.

With a tune humming softly on his lips, Marco refocused on his daily tasks, ensuring that the preparations for the upcoming wedding continued seamlessly. He kept Olivia's journey tucked away in the depths of his heart, a silent reminder of the strength and resilience she embodied. Deep down, he knew that Olivia's journey, with all its triumphs and challenges, had shaped her into the remarkable person she was today. And that was what mattered most.

Marco, the silent guardian of their secrets, carried on with his duties, his commitment unwavering. His heart brimmed with unwritten tales and unspoken truths, entrusted to the depths of his loyalty, forever concealed.

***

As the grandeur of the royal wedding approached, the Castle gates swung open to welcome Olivia's parents and her personal assistant Justin. Her close friend Samantha, regrettably could not join them due to a medical emergency.

The towering turrets, meticulously manicured gardens, and the air of regality seemed straight out of a fairy tale. Excitement tinged with a hint of nervousness surged through their veins as they entered the opulent gates of the Creudor Royal Palace. The air buzzed with excitement as the arrival of esteemed guests added an extra layer of anticipation to the already bustling atmosphere.

Olivia, adorned in a flowing gown, stood at the entrance of the Castle, her heart aflutter with a mix of nerves and joy. As she caught sight of her parents stepping out of the elegant carriage, her face lit up with an infectious smile. Nicolas, stood by Olivia's side, extending a warm welcome to her family. His eyes sparkled with genuine happiness, knowing that this reunion was a momentous occasion for Olivia.

Her mother, Evelyn, could not help but admire the transformation her daughter had undergone since her Hollywood days. She beamed with pride, seeing the poised and confident woman Olivia had become.

Richard, Olivia's father, stood tall and composed, his eyes glistening with emotion. He took a moment to absorb the grandeur of the palace, realizing the magnitude of this moment in his daughter's life. The tender father-daughter bond was palpable as they exchanged heartfelt glances, their unspoken connection saying more than words ever could.

Inside the Castle, the guests were led to their luxuriously appointed chambers, where they could settle in and prepare for the upcoming festivities. The rooms were adorned with exquisite decorations, reflecting the opulence befitting the occasion. Every detail had been meticulously planned to ensure the utmost comfort and indulgence for Olivia's loved ones.

As Olivia settled her parents into their chambers, she couldn't help but feel a surge of gratitude for their presence on her special day. She embraced them tightly, their love enveloping her like a warm embrace. "Thank you both for being here," she whispered, her voice filled with emotion.

Evelyn held her daughter at arm's length, a mixture of pride and maternal affection radiating from her eyes. "Oh, Olivia, my darling, look at how far you've come," she said, her voice catching slightly. "You've grown into an extraordinary woman, and today, you're marrying the love of your life. I couldn't be prouder."

Tears welled up in Olivia's eyes as she replied, her voice laced with gratitude, "Mom, I wouldn't be where I am today without your unwavering support and belief in me. You've always encouraged me to chase my dreams, and I'm so grateful for that. Today is as much your celebration as it is mine."

Richard, Olivia's father, stood by their side, his strong presence anchoring the moment. He reached out to grasp Olivia's hand, his voice filled with warmth. "You've grown into an incredible woman, my dear. It fills my heart with joy to see you so happy."

Olivia squeezed her father's hand, her eyes brimming with affection. "Dad, I'm so grateful to have you by my side on my wedding day."

As the family shared this intimate moment, their love and support formed an unbreakable bond. It was a testament to the enduring power of family, the unwavering support that had carried Olivia through the highs and lows of her life.

***

As the evening unfolded, the wedding eve festivities commenced with a touch of enchantment and a hint of nostalgia. The Castle's grand ballroom had been transformed into a magical setting, adorned with cascading floral arrangements, twinkling lights, and a stage fit for a royal celebration. Soft melodies from a string quartet floated through the air, setting a romantic ambiance that resonated with the love and joy permeating the room.

Olivia, radiant in a flowing gown, moved gracefully among the guests, her laughter and warmth infectious. She found herself surrounded by loved ones, each conversation filled with heartfelt well-wishes and shared memories. The air was abuzz with excitement as friends, family, and esteemed guests mingled, savoring the anticipation of the momentous day to come.

Sophia, Olivia's maid of honor, approached her with a twinkle in her eye. They embraced; their bond evident in the way their smiles mirrored each other's. "Olivia, can you believe it? Tomorrow, you'll be marrying the love of your life," Sophia exclaimed, her voice filled with joy.

Olivia's eyes sparkled with anticipation as she replied, "Sophia, it still feels like a dream. But I couldn't be happier. This journey with Nicolas has been nothing short of a fairytale."

Sophia's gaze turned sentimental as she squeezed Olivia's hand. "You deserve all the happiness in the world."

Olivia's heart swelled with gratitude as she looked around the room, catching sight of Nicolas engaging in a lively conversation with his closest friends. She turned back to Sophia and said, her voice laced with emotion, "And I'm so grateful to have you by my side, Sophia. Having you as my maid of honor means the world to me."

Sophia's eyes glistened with tears as she pulled Olivia into another embrace. "Olivia, you're like a sister to me. I'll always be here for you, through thick and thin. Tomorrow is going to be the most magical day, and I'm honored to stand beside you."

As the evening continued, Olivia's parents, Evelyn and Richard, immersed themselves in conversations with the esteemed guests. Richard, Olivia's father, found himself engrossed in conversation with King Edmund, discussing shared interests and the joys of fatherhood.

The King's voice carried a fatherly warmth as he said, "Richard, Olivia is a remarkable woman, and I'm grateful that Nicolas has found his soulmate in her. They are destined for great things, both as a couple and as individuals."

Richard's eyes shone with pride as he replied, "King Edmund, your words mean the world to me. Seeing Olivia find her happiness and knowing that she will have a partner like Nicolas fills my heart with such joy. They truly are meant to be."

And as the enchanting melodies faded into the background, the guests gracefully made their way to the elegantly set tables. The soft glow of candlelight flickered, casting a warm and intimate ambiance over the grand ballroom. Olivia and Nicolas took their seats at the head table, their eyes locked in a silent exchange of love and gratitude.

A hush fell over the room as the first course was served, and the clinking of silverware against delicate porcelain filled the air. Once the guests had savored their culinary delights, a sense of anticipation permeated the room, signaling the beginning of the heartfelt speeches that would weave a tapestry of love and memories.

Sophia, Olivia's maid of honor, stood from her seat, a shimmering smile gracing her face. With a gentle clearing of her throat, she captured the attention of the room. The guests turned their heads toward her, their eyes shining with anticipation.

"Tonight, we gather to celebrate the love between two remarkable individuals," Sophia began, her voice steady yet filled with emotion. "Olivia, my dearest friend, from the moment we met, I knew our connection was something special. We've laughed, cried, and shared countless memories together. You have always been there for me, supporting and encouraging me in every step of our journey."

The room filled with a collective nod of agreement and soft murmurs of affirmation, acknowledging the profound bond between Olivia and Sophia.

Sophia's gaze shifted to Nicolas, her voice brimming with genuine affection. "And Nicolas, you have shown Olivia a love that is unwavering, a love that has helped her grow into the incredible woman she is today. Your presence in her life has brought a newfound radiance and joy that shines through her every smile."

Nicolas smiled warmly, his eyes fixed on Olivia, his love evident in his gaze.

Turning her attention back to Olivia, Sophia continued, her voice laced with nostalgia. "As we stand here tonight, on the eve of your wedding day, I am filled with memories of our adventures, our triumphs, and even our moments of vulnerability. Olivia, you have taught me the true meaning of resilience, strength, and the power of love."

A wave of emotion swept over the room, and guests reached for their napkins to dab at their eyes, touched by the sincerity of Sophia's words.

Sophia raised her glass, a symbol of celebration and unity. "To Olivia and Nicolas, may your love continue to shine brighter with each passing day. May your journey be filled with laughter, support, and unbreakable bonds. Here's to a lifetime of shared dreams, unwavering support, and a love that knows no bounds. Cheers!"

The room erupted in applause, and heartfelt toasts filled the air as guests stood, raising their glasses to honor the union of Olivia and Nicolas. Words of love, encouragement, and well-wishes reverberated throughout the ballroom, each speaker painting a unique and heartfelt portrait of the couple's love story.

Evelyn, Olivia's mother, stood next, her voice carrying a gentle strength that captivated the room. "To my beloved daughter and her Prince Charming, today marks the beginning of a beautiful chapter in your lives. Olivia, you have always possessed a resilient spirit, an unwavering determination to follow your dreams. I have watched you grow, stumble, and rise again, and through it all, your kindness and compassion have remained constant."

Her voice trembled with a mixture of nostalgia and pride as she continued, "Nicolas, from the moment you entered Olivia's life, I could see the light in her eyes burn even brighter. Your love has brought out the best in her, and for that, I am eternally grateful. You have become not just her partner, but a cherished son in our hearts."

Richard, Olivia's father, stood beside Evelyn, his eyes shimmering with paternal affection. "Olivia, my precious daughter, you have always been a source of joy and inspiration. Your tenacity and grace have made us immensely proud. Nicolas, you have shown us what it means to be a true partner, supporting Olivia's dreams with unwavering devotion."

The room resonated with heartfelt applause as the guests acknowledged the love and support that surrounded Olivia and Nicolas.

Amidst the speeches and toasts, Olivia and Nicolas exchanged stolen glances, their hearts overflowing with gratitude for the love and warmth enveloping them. They felt blessed to be surrounded by such incredible friends and family, whose words painted a vivid picture of their journey and the love that had brought them together.

In that moment, as the speeches continued, Olivia and Nicolas held hands, their intertwined fingers representing their commitment to facing the future hand-in-hand. They knew that with the love and support of those gathered around them, their union would be an everlasting testament to the power of love.

And so, the wedding eve festivities continued, punctuated by heartfelt speeches, laughter, and tears of joy. The air was filled with a sense of unity and anticipation, a celebration of love that would carry on into the grandeur of the following day, when Olivia and Nicolas would finally say their vows and begin their journey as husband and wife.

***

CHAPTER 22:

FOREVER AND EVER AFTER

The sun bathed the royal chambers in a soft, golden glow as Olivia sat before her vanity mirror, surrounded by an array of delicate pearls and shimmering jewelry. Her hands trembled with a mixture of excitement and nervousness as she prepared to embark on the most significant journey of her life.

Justin, ever the steadfast pillar of support, stood beside her, adjusting her veil with gentle precision. His eyes reflected both joy and a hint of melancholy, knowing that their paths were about to diverge. Olivia turned to him, their gazes meeting in the reflection of the mirror.

A tender smile curved Olivia's lips as she spoke, her voice filled with affection. "Justin, I can't imagine going through all of this without you by my side. You've been my rock, my confidant, and my constant support. I want you to know how grateful I am for everything you've done."

Justin's eyes shimmered with unshed tears as he clasped Olivia's hands, his voice filled with a mixture of pride and bittersweet acceptance. "Olivia, it has been an honor and a privilege to be a part of your life's journey. Seeing you grow, both personally and professionally, has been a source of immense joy for me. I have cherished every moment spent by your side."

Olivia's voice trembled slightly as she continued, her love for Justin evident in every word. "Justin, you've become more than just my personal assistant. You've become family to me. I can't help but think that this incredible chapter of my life wouldn't be complete without you. Would you consider staying with me here in Creudor?"

Justin's eyes softened with warmth as he gently squeezed Olivia's hands. "Olivia, you know how much I care for you, but Los Angeles is my home. My roots run deep there, and I have responsibilities that I need to attend to. However, distance will never diminish the bond we share. I will always be here for you, no matter the miles that separate us."

Olivia's heart ached at the thought of their impending separation, but she understood and respected Justin's decision. She let out a soft sigh, her voice tinged with sadness. "I understand, Justin. Your loyalty and dedication have never faltered, and I know that Los Angeles is where your heart truly lies. But please know that a piece of my heart will always belong to you."

Tears glistened in both of their eyes as they embraced, cherishing this moment of shared love and understanding. The air was thick with unspoken promises and unbreakable bonds, forged through years of companionship and mutual respect.

As Olivia prepared to step into the grandeur of her wedding ceremony, she carried with her the memories, lessons, and unwavering support that Justin had provided. Their paths may diverge, but their connection would remain unbreakable, a testament to the enduring power of true friendship.

With a gentle squeeze of hands and a lingering glance, Olivia and Justin parted ways, each filled with a sense of gratitude for the role they had played in each other's lives. As Olivia stepped into her bridal gown, she knew that, no matter the distance that would separate them physically, their hearts would forever remain intertwined in a bond that transcended time and place.

Olivia stood in front of the mirror, her heart pounding with excitement and nervous anticipation. Dressed in a resplendent wedding gown adorned with delicate lace and shimmering pearls, she took a deep breath to calm her racing thoughts.

Olivia turned to see her father, standing outside her door, his eyes filled with a mixture of pride and emotion. He looked dapper in his tailored suit, a hint of tears shimmering in his eyes.

"Olivia, my dear," he said, his voice filled with a blend of tenderness and nostalgia. "You look absolutely radiant."

A smile spread across Olivia's face as she walked towards her father. She took his arm, cherishing the bond they shared. "Thank you, Dad," she replied, her voice filled with gratitude. "I couldn't have asked for a more loving and supportive father. Today wouldn't be possible without you."

Richard's gaze softened as he squeezed Olivia's hand gently. "My dear, seeing you so happy and fulfilled is all I could ever wish for. Nicolas is a remarkable man, and I am honored to see you embark on this journey together."

He enveloped Olivia in a warm embrace, his love for his daughter overflowing. "Olivia, my darling, you will always be my little girl. I am filled with joy to witness this momentous day in your life. Remember, love is the greatest gift we can give and receive. Cherish it, nurture it, and let it guide you through the years ahead."

Olivia held onto her father tightly, finding solace in his embrace. "I will, Dad," she whispered.

With tears glistening in their eyes, Olivia and her father made their way towards the grand hall, where the ceremony awaited. The air was filled with anticipation and a sense of magic, as if the universe itself was celebrating their union.

With each step forward, Olivia felt a surge of gratitude for the love that had brought her to this moment. Her heart was filled with hope and a profound sense of purpose, knowing that her love story would forever be intertwined with Nicolas, creating ripples of love and inspiration that would endure for generations to come.

As Olivia and her father reached the entrance of the grand hall, they were met by the sight of Prince Frederick, dressed handsomely in a tailored tuxedo, awaiting them. His eyes sparkled with warmth and a touch of mischief, his smile conveying both joy for Olivia and a shared understanding of their intertwined destinies.

Beside Frederick stood Sophia, resplendent in an elegant gown that accentuated her grace and beauty. Her eyes held a mix of emotions, a blend of pride for Frederick and a bittersweet longing for what could have been. She took Frederick's arm, and together they prepared to walk down the aisle.

As Frederick and Sophia began their journey, the guests in the hall rose, their gazes fixed on the striking couple. The aisle was adorned with fragrant flowers, their delicate petals gently swaying in a soft breeze that seemed to carry the whispers of love and celebration.

As they walked side by side, Frederick turned to Sophia, his voice filled with affection. "Sophia, I am honored to have you by my side on this special day. Your support and presence mean the world to me."

Sophia's eyes shimmered with unshed tears, a mixture of happiness and nostalgia. "Frederick, you've always been my pillar of strength, my confidant," she replied, her voice filled with tenderness. "I may have lost my way for a while, but today, seeing you so happy, I realize that love truly conquers all."

Frederick reached out and gently squeezed Sophia's

hand, his touch conveying both reassurance and forgiveness. "We've all made mistakes, Sophia. It's how we grow and learn from them that matters. Today, let us celebrate the love that surrounds us, and may it guide us towards a future filled with happiness."

Sophia's gaze met Frederick's, and in that moment, a silent understanding passed between them. It was a farewell to what could have been, an acceptance of their separate paths, and a newfound appreciation for the enduring bond they shared as friends and siblings.

As they continued their walk down the aisle, their steps steady and synchronized, they couldn't help but steal glances at Olivia and Nicolas, who stood at the altar, their eyes locked in a tender embrace of love and anticipation. It was a testament to the power of true love, a reminder that even amidst the twists and turns of life, love could find its way and create beauty out of the most unexpected circumstances.

The guests watched with reverence as Frederick and Sophia reached the end of the aisle, their roles as best man and maid of honor fulfilled. They took their respective places, standing alongside Olivia and Nicolas, ready to witness the union of two souls destined to write a new chapter in the annals of love.

***

The opulent hall of the royal palace was transformed into a breathtaking sanctuary of love and enchantment.

The soft glow of countless candles danced upon the walls, casting a warm and ethereal ambiance over the grandeur of the space. Guests, adorned in their finest attire, took their places, eagerly awaiting the arrival of the radiant couple.

As the music swelled and the guests rose to their feet, the hall fell into a hushed silence, all eyes fixed on the entrance of the bride. The massive doors of the hall swung open, revealing Olivia in her resplendent wedding gown. Every eye turned toward her, captivated by her grace and beauty. The intricate lace and delicate beadwork adorned her like a shimmering waterfall, cascading down her figure with an ethereal elegance. Her eyes sparkled with joy, and her smile radiated pure happiness.

Nicolas stood at the altar, his heart pounding in anticipation. Dressed in the regal attire of a prince, he looked every bit the noble and devoted groom. His eyes fixed on Olivia, his beloved, as she walked toward him.

Olivia took her first steps down the aisle, her father gently guiding her with an undeniable sense of paternal love. As they made their way towards Nicolas, their eyes never wavered from each other, their connection growing stronger with each passing moment. It was a moment frozen in time, where the world seemed to fade away, leaving only the two of them in a realm of their own. The room seemed to hold its breath, caught up in the magic of the moment.

As Olivia made her way down the aisle, her steps light

and graceful, her eyes caught sight of her mother, sitting in the front row. A wave of emotions washed over her as she noticed the tears glistening in her mother's eyes. The love between mother and daughter was palpable, a bond that had weathered storms and emerged stronger than ever.

Without hesitation, Olivia veered slightly off her path, drawn toward her mother's silent tears. As she reached her, her heart filled with empathy and tenderness, she gently embraced her, their arms encircling one another in a warm, comforting hug. The soft rustle of fabric mixed with the hushed whispers of love and reassurance that passed between them.

"Mom," Olivia whispered, as she held back her own tears. "Today is a day of joy and celebration."

Her mother, her eyes still brimming with tears, nodded and held Olivia even closer, as if trying to convey the depth of her love without words.

"You are radiant, my dear," her mother finally spoke, her voice a gentle tremor. "I am so proud of the woman you have become. And to see you so happy, marrying the love of your life, fills my heart with overwhelming joy."

Olivia smiled, a tear of her own now glistening in the corner of her eye. She pulled back slightly, taking in her mother's beautiful face, etched with the lines of experience and love. "Thank you, Mom. Your love and support have carried me through the darkest of days. Today, as I walk toward my husband, I will carry your love with me."

With a final, loving embrace, Olivia released her mother, a sense of serenity and purpose guiding her steps once more. She took a deep breath, her spirit renewed, and continued her journey down the aisle toward Nicolas, who stood there, his eyes shimmering with love and anticipation.

As she reached Nicolas, Olivia's eyes met his, and they exchanged a knowing smile. Her father placed her hand in his, a silent affirmation of trust and blessing. The couple stood together, their hands entwined, their souls intertwined in a love that had weathered storms and surpassed all obstacles.

Nicolas leaned in, his voice a soft murmur only for Olivia to hear. "You look so beautiful, my love. I am the luckiest man in the world to have you by my side."

Olivia whispered back quietly, "No my love, I am the lucky one."

The grand hall fell into a hushed silence as the officiant, a distinguished figure in a regal robe, stepped forward, radiating an aura of wisdom and serenity. The soft glow of the candlelight highlighted the gentle lines etched upon their face; evidence of a life spent guiding souls through the sacred union of marriage.

With a voice that commanded attention, yet embraced the couple with warmth, the officiant began the ceremony. Their words carried a timeless wisdom and an understanding of the profound bond about to be forged.

"Dearly beloved, we gather here today to celebrate the union of two souls, Nicolas and Olivia, who have found love and companionship in each other's embrace. We come together in the spirit of joy and unity, to witness and bless this sacred union."

The words resonated throughout the hall, reaching the hearts of all in attendance. The guests leaned forward, captivated by the officiant's eloquence and the significance of the moment. Each word carried the weight of tradition and the promise of a new beginning.

The officiant continued, their voice rich with reverence. "Marriage is a journey of two individuals intertwining their lives, sharing their dreams, and supporting one another through all the seasons of life. It is a covenant of love, trust, and respect. Today, Nicolas and Olivia stand before us, ready to embark on this remarkable journey together."

The couple, standing side by side, their gazes locked in a loving embrace, listened intently as the officiant spoke. Their hands gently clasped, their fingers entwined, their love shining brightly in their eyes.

"Nicolas and Olivia, your love has blossomed against all odds, and today, you affirm your commitment to one another in the presence of your loved ones."

Nicolas spoke first, his voice filled with a mixture of tenderness and unwavering dedication. "Olivia, from the moment I first saw you, I knew that my heart had found its home. Today, in the presence of our loved ones, I pledge my love and fidelity to you. I promise to cherish you, support you, and honor you through every joy and challenge that life presents. With you by my side, I am confident that together we can conquer any obstacle and create a love that lasts a lifetime."

Olivia's voice trembled with emotion as she met Nicolas' gaze, her eyes shimmering with unshed tears of joy. "Nicolas, from the depths of my soul, I vow to love and cherish you for all eternity. You are my anchor, my safe haven, and my truest companion. I promise to stand by your side, to lift you up when you stumble, and to celebrate the triumphs of our shared journey. With you, my heart has found its home, and today I give you all that I am, with a love that knows no bounds."

Their vows, filled with heartfelt promises and unwavering devotion, echoed through the hall, resonating in the hearts of all who bore witness to this momentous occasion. The love that enveloped Nicolas and Olivia seemed to transcend the boundaries of time and space, creating an ethereal atmosphere of pure bliss.

As they exchanged rings, the symbols of their eternal commitment, a profound silence fell over the room, allowing the significance of the moment to sink in. The collective breath of the guests seemed to catch in their throats, and not a dry eye remained as the officiant declared them husband and wife.

With triumphant joy, Nicolas and Olivia sealed their vows with a tender and passionate kiss, their love bursting forth like a beacon of light. The room erupted in applause, joyous cheers, and the cascading melodies of celebration.

The King, Edmund, stood tall at the front, a smile adorning his regal features. The room fell into a hushed silence as he stepped forward, holding a beautifully adorned box in his hands. His voice resonated with pride and affection as he addressed Olivia.

"Today, we gather to celebrate not only the union of two souls but also the joining of families and the beginning of a new era. Olivia, my dear, you have brought light and love into my son's life, and for that, I am eternally grateful."

Olivia stood beside Nicolas, her eyes sparkling with anticipation. Her heart swelled with gratitude and awe as she looked at the King, who had become like a second father to her.

King Edmund extended the box towards Olivia, and as she opened it, her breath caught in her throat. Inside was a delicate tiara, encrusted with shimmering diamonds and precious gemstones. Its design was intricate and exquisite, symbolizing her newfound place within the royal family.

With a gentle smile, King Edmund continued, "Olivia, as a token of my love and acceptance, I bestow upon you this tiara. It is a symbol of your status as Princess Olivia of Creudor, a cherished member of our royal family. Wear it with grace, for it represents not only your beauty but also the strength and dignity you bring to our kingdom."

Tears welled up in Olivia's eyes as she reached out to take the tiara from the King's hands. She looked at Nicolas, her voice trembling with emotion. "I am deeply honored and humbled by this gift, Your Majesty."

Nicolas, standing beside her, beamed with pride, his love for Olivia shining in his eyes. As the applause filled the hall once again, Olivia placed the tiara upon her head, the jewels catching the light and illuminating her radiant smile. She embraced King Edmund and whispered words of gratitude, knowing that she had found not only a life partner in Nicolas but also a family that had embraced her as their own.

In that moment, as Princess Olivia of Creudor, she felt a deep sense of belonging and purpose. She knew that her journey as a member of the royal family had just begun, and she was ready to embrace the responsibilities and joys that came with her newfound title. Hand in hand with Nicolas, she stepped forward, ready to embark on a future filled with love, unity, and the unwavering support of the kingdom she now called home.

***

The wedding after party was a grand affair, a celebration of love, joy, and the union of two souls. The venue, adorned with twinkling lights and vibrant floral arrangements, exuded an atmosphere of enchantment and merriment. Soft melodies of live music filled the air, inviting guests to dance, laugh, and revel in the festivities.

As Olivia and Nicolas entered the exquisitely decorated ballroom, their eyes alight with happiness, they were greeted with thunderous applause and cheers of admiration. The room seemed to glow with an ethereal radiance, mirroring the radiant love that emanated from the newlyweds.

Family and friends mingled, their laughter and animated conversations creating a symphony of joy. The guests, dressed in their finest attire, moved gracefully across the dance floor, their steps perfectly synchronized to the rhythm of the music. The atmosphere buzzed with excitement and the promise of memorable moments.

Nicolas, his heart overflowing with love and gratitude, sought Olivia's hand and led her onto the dance floor. As they swayed together in each other's arms, the world around them seemed to fade into a blur, leaving only the two of them immersed in the magic of the moment.

"This is a dream come true, my wife," Nicolas whispered, his voice filled with adoration, his eyes locked with Olivia's.

Olivia's eyes gleamed with happiness as she gazed lovingly into Nicolas' eyes, "My husband, it feels like the beginning of a beautiful chapter in our lives."

They danced, their movements synchronized and graceful, their connection palpable to all who witnessed their love. As they swirled across the dance floor, the guests watched with awe and admiration, inspired by the depth of their affection and the resilience of their bond.

The sound of laughter filled the air as guests shared stories and memories, reveling in the joyous atmosphere. The room was adorned with tables adorned with delectable delicacies, the aroma of exquisite cuisine tantalizing the senses. Glasses clinked in toasts to the newlyweds, the sweet melodies of happiness resonating with each celebratory cheer.

Among the crowd, Sophia and Frederick, their eyes brimming with happiness, stood hand in hand, their smiles a reflection of the joy that enveloped the room. They, too, had found solace and healing in this celebration of love, their own journey tangled with that of Olivia and Nicolas. Their hands intertwined; their gazes locked in a profound connection that spoke volumes without words.

Sophia's eyes glistened with tears of happiness as she leaned closer to Frederick, whispering, "This is such a beautiful moment, isn't it? To witness the love that has bloomed between Olivia and Nicolas, it fills my heart with hope and gratitude."

"Sophia, seeing them so happy, it warms my heart," Frederick whispered, his voice filled with affection. "And to think that we played a part in this journey, that we have found our own happiness as well, it is a testament to the power of love and forgiveness."

Sophia's gaze softened as she leaned into Frederick's

embrace, their hearts united in gratitude and love. "Indeed, my love. Love has a way of guiding us to unexpected places, and I am forever grateful for the path that has led us here, to this moment of shared joy and renewed hope."

"Can you believe how far we've come, Frederick?" she spoke softly as her grip around his hands tightened. "From the uncertainties and doubts to this moment of pure happiness. I am so grateful to have you by my side."

Frederick equally tightened his grip on Sophia's hand, a genuine smile gracing his lips. "Our time will come, my love. I hope sooner than later."

In a moment of tenderness, Frederick raised her hands to his lips and gently kissed her bare skin. Feeling the warmth of his lips against her hand, Sophia's heart skipped a beat. A tender smile graced her lips as she met his gaze.

"Frederick," she whispered, her voice filled with tenderness, "you have a way of making me feel cherished and loved in the simplest of moments."

Frederick raised Sophia's hand to his lips once more, pressing a gentle kiss on her knuckles. "Sophia, you deserve nothing less than the utmost love and devotion. You've brought light into my life, and I can't imagine a future without you by my side."

Their eyes locked, and for a fleeting moment, the world seemed to fade away, leaving only their love and the promises they had made to each other. In that tender exchange, they found solace and reassurance that their love was real and enduring. As they basked in the magic of the moment, surrounded by the joyful ambiance of the wedding reception, Sophia and Frederick knew that their love had been tested and proven.

The night continued with laughter, heartfelt speeches, and moments of pure bliss. The dance floor remained alive with the rhythmic movements of the guests; their spirits buoyed by the palpable energy of love that filled the air.

As the vibrant festivities of the wedding after party began to wind down, Olivia and Nicolas found themselves drawn to the tranquil beauty of the vast grassy grounds surrounding the venue. Hand in hand, they strolled along a meandering path, the gentle breeze caressing their faces and the soft glow of moonlight guiding their way.

The night sky above them twinkled with a myriad of stars, as if bearing witness to their profound love. As they reached a clearing, they paused, their gazes turning skyward to behold a magnificent display of fireworks illuminating the darkness. Brilliant colors burst forth, painting the heavens with cascades of shimmering lights, creating a breathtaking spectacle.

Olivia leaned her head against Nicolas' shoulder, their entwined fingers a testament to their unbreakable bond. "Nicolas," she murmured, her voice filled with awe and wonder, "look at the sky."

Nicolas, his eyes reflecting the kaleidoscope of colors above, tightened his grip on Olivia's hand, a smile gracing his lips. They stood there, immersed in the awe-inspiring beauty, each explosion of light and color echoing the depth of their emotions. The crackling sounds of fireworks blended harmoniously with the rhythm of their beating hearts, creating a symphony of love and enchantment.

Olivia turned her gaze from the sky to her husband, "Nicolas, I never imagined that a love like ours could exist. It defies every explanation."

Nicolas brushed a strand of hair behind Olivia's ear, his touch gentle and filled with adoration. "My darling, I believe that love has its own way of weaving magic into our lives. It guided us through the darkest of times, giving us the strength to heal, grow, and find solace in each other's arms."

As they stood there, bathed in the kaleidoscope of lights, Olivia and Nicolas shared a silent understanding, a recognition that their love was extraordinary, destined to leave an indelible mark on their hearts and the hearts of those who witnessed their journey.

In that magical moment, as the fireworks soared higher, painting the night sky with their brilliance, Olivia and Nicolas made a silent promise to each other. They vowed to nurture their love, to cherish every moment, and to build a future together filled with adventure, laughter, and unwavering support.

As the final burst of fireworks dissolved into a shower of glittering sparks, Olivia and Nicolas embraced, their hearts filled with gratitude for the love that had brought them to this breathtaking moment. They reveled in the beauty of the night, knowing that their love, like the stars above, would continue to shine brightly, guiding their path through the years to come.

*** THE END***

ABOUT THE AUTHOR

Kathy Winslower is a gifted storyteller with a passion for weaving tales of love, resilience, and triumph. With her captivating narratives and richly drawn characters, she takes readers on unforgettable journeys that explore the depths of human emotions and the power of love to transform lives.

Born with an insatiable curiosity and a love for words, Kathy began her writing journey at a young age, filling countless notebooks with her imaginative stories. As she grew older, her passion for storytelling only deepened, leading her to pursue a career as a novelist.

Drawing inspiration from her own experiences and the world around her, Kathy's writing is characterized by its heartfelt authenticity and emotional depth. She skillfully delves into the complexities of relationships, capturing the raw and tender moments that shape her characters' lives.

When she's not immersed in her writing, Kathy can be found exploring nature, seeking inspiration from the beauty of the world around her. She believes that every moment holds the potential for a story, and it is her mission to capture those moments and share them with her readers.

Ingram Content Group UK Ltd.
Milton Keynes UK
UKHW041942040723
424529UK00004B/67

9 781399 958837